# UNDER THE SOUTHERN LIGHTS

# UNDER THE SOUTHERN LIGHTS

## Lorrae Victoria

Wordalicious PUBLISHING

# AUTHOR'S NOTE

I have always been passionate about the rights of women.

Down through the ages, women were denied their rightful place — being acknowledged as half of the world's population and with the same quantity and quality of brain power as men.

Mao Zedong famously said that 'women hold up half of the sky.'

Traditionally, in Western civilisation, a woman's place was often one of subservience, servitude or sexual slavery. They were treated as chattels, dismissed as being "too emotional" or too "lacking in intelligence" to hold valid opinions or to transact their own business, even being denied the right to maintain an identity in their own right once they signed marriage vows.

In ancient cultures, however, women often held positions of power, with the right to own their own property, to have a say in the affairs of the community, and were often leaders of their tribes. Boudicca is a shining example of ancient female leadership.

Fortunately, conditions have improved vastly for many women in the Western world, with the right to vote, to govern their own bodies, to be acknowledged as equals in science, literature, politics, etc.

In *Under the Southern Lights*, the protagonist is a bright and surprisingly well-educated young woman from an impoverished background in the north of England, who is forced to flee her home after being unjustly accused of a crime. Through her determination and grit, despite setbacks and tragedy, she rises to claim her place, eventually, as a woman of power and substance in her own right, in the male-dominated world of colonial Australia.


*Lorrae Victoria*

*December 2024*

# DEDICATION

To all the women in history who fought for women's rights.

And to my friend Alex who gave me the strength to carry on.

*Harcourt*: unloading in Sydney
Women passing time by quilting on board.
*Sarah Lee:* on the Murray River.
Town of Gulgong.
Photos and sketches taken from paintings and family files.

Sarah's Journey
SARAH'S HOME
MANCHESTER
LONDON
PORTSMOUTH

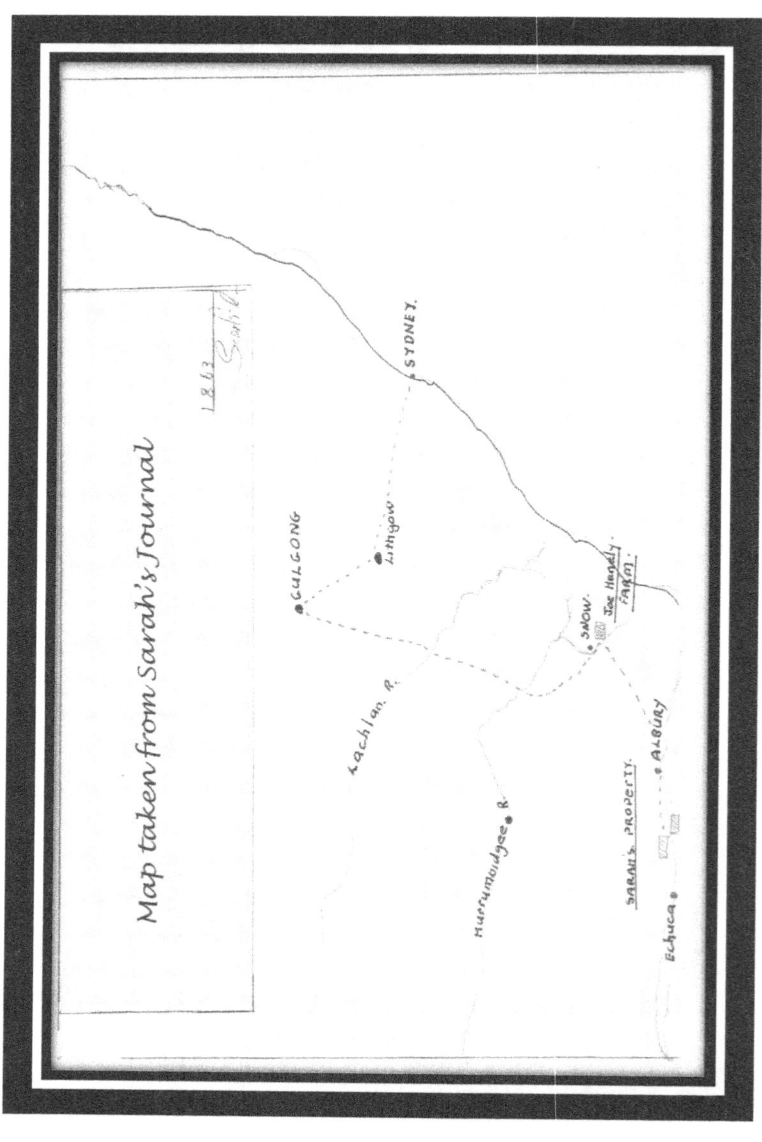


*Sarah's property ran along both sides of the Murray River between Echuca and Albury.*

# Sarah's family tree

Alistair Noonan married May Ravenhall. They produced two children, a son, and daughter, Sarah.

James Lowe & Sarah Noonan (unmarried) produced one child, James Junior.

Tom Brian & Sarah Noonan (married) produced one surviving child, Josephine.

James Junior married Lucy Masters and they produced a daughter, Prudence.

# Part One
## Sarah

# Prologue

**Sydney, summer, 1966**

It was hot, bloody hot. The clouds hung low in the sky, the top of the skyscrapers reflecting the heat down onto the streets below. The anticipation of a storm that never seemed to arrive was enough to drive people and animals alike to near desperation.

Heat shimmered along the foreshore. The people looked like drowning rats, all scurrying to find any type of shade. Pubs were full, men spilling out onto the street. Women sat in hotel lobbies sipping on long cool Pimm's and lemonade. Above, in the heavens, the sparrows were falling out of the sky, dead, in the worst heatwave of the decade.

I seldom came into the city. I didn't like the hustle of the crowds and the smell of perfume mixed with the sour stink of perspiration.

Why was I here in Martin Place trying to find a number 437? The Thursday before, I received a letter marked Private from a firm of solicitors asking me to attend their office.

Dad had assured me that I wasn't in any trouble, but how could he know? He had not received a letter. I had no boyfriend, my love life was up the shit and now a solicitor wanted to add more misery to my current seventeen years of frustration. *Hell, there goes a ladder in my stocking; what else could go wrong?*

Crossing at the lights, I entered the large sandstone building. I asked at the reception desk if they knew of a Mr Barnaby and the receptionist pointed towards the lifts. The marble tiles looked so cool, and I slowly looked around. Since I was the only person in front of the lifts, I carefully removed my shoes; the cold tiles felt like heaven. Then, with a swish of a cold breeze, the lift door slid open. Guiltily, I slipped my shoes back on.

'Going up. Mr Barnaby's office is on the third floor; please come in, Miss.'

The lift attendant slammed the door. My stomach stayed on the ground as my body reached the third floor. After leaving the lift, I walked down a carpeted corridor towards a set of double doors marked 'Solicitor' then I knocked and waited.

'Please enter.'

I introduced myself and waited.

'Ah, Miss Jamieson, we've been expecting you. Did you bring a copy of your birth certificate?' A small older man, at least forty and dressed in a brown suit, shook my hand then pulled out a chair, beckoning me to sit. It was the first time a man ever pulled out a chair for me, let alone in a legal firm.

'You must be wondering why I wrote to you.' He panted, pulled out a hanky and wiped his brow. 'The reason that I couldn't tell you much in the letter was that your claim needed to be validated.' Paul Barnaby explained to me that he had been contacted by a legal firm in London regarding an inheritance and was asked to explore the claim.

'What claim? I didn't make any claim; you must have the wrong person.'

'Is your father Raymond Jamieson from Gundagai, your mother Anne Hayes, late of Penrith?' enquired the solicitor.

'Yes, that's me.' I pulled the certificate out of my purse and slid it across the desk, watching as the solicitor examined it.

'Good. Now we've established that… Your great-grandmother, on your mother's side had two children. We believe Josephine may be a relative of yours, and this is where it becomes interesting. She and her daughter both disappeared during the Great War. I don't have any more information about her.'

Looking around the office, I tried to look intelligent, but I couldn't help wiggling around as my backside stuck to the leather seat.

'So what does all of this have to do with me, Mr Barnaby? I was very close to my grandmother, and she never talked about any relatives. She would have told me about anything to do with her family. She wasn't stuck up and would have loved a bit of gossip. A skeleton in the closet would have tickled her fancy. That's what she would have said. She spoke like that, Mr Barnaby.'

'Margaret… may I call you Margaret?'

'Please call me Maggie.'

The solicitor watched me. By the way he was looking at me, I felt that I was not old enough to be here, let alone deal with an inheritance. Without waiting for my reply, he continued.

'I have received a letter from a firm of solicitors in London. They are trying to contact any living relative of a Sarah Noonan. That was the family name before it was changed to Brian. As your mother has died and your father is not eligible, you seem to be the only living relative.'

I felt like a stunned mullet. Looking down at my wrinkled linen dress, I wondered if maybe I should have bought a new dress for this visit, but consoled myself that at least my gloves were new. Putting on my most sincere voice, I whispered, 'Thank you. Will the inheritance be delivered to me, or is it in cash?'

I wanted to scream. *I'm rich.* I wanted to dance on his desk; I could have kissed his bald head. *Er, maybe not. God, I hope this is not only in my head.* My mind was travelling at a million miles an hour. I would be able to buy clothes and more clothes, lots of makeup and best of all, more shoes, high heels with that shiny stuff on the top. *I must be getting at least a hundred pounds,* I thought.

'I have been authorised to offer you a return trip to London to meet with these people. A ticket will be provided for an adult to accompany you. There is also part of a journal that was found, it may help you in some way to understand more. I know this must seem very daunting. Think about it, and let me know what you decide to do.'

*What's to decide? Money or parcel, what did he say? London, was I hearing correctly? London, where the queen comes from!*

The suburbs flew by as I sat in the railway carriage thinking over my good fortune. That night Dad was holding court, as usual, at the dining table, asking me questions but not waiting for the reply.

'I can't believe it, Dad, I'm going, and you're staying here, all because you don't trust planes!'

Dad was stubborn. 'Take a friend with you, Maggie.' Dad put down his glass of beer. 'You know I don't want to have anything to do with your mother's family, doesn't matter how long ago they died.'

Later that night, I opened the battered, brown cover of the journal and started to read. The hours slid by; I couldn't put it down. Who was this Sarah? I started to feel cold, so reaching down to the bottom of the bed, I pulled the doona up around my neck, leaving only my head and hands out to read. I was being transported back to another time and place. I sat there transfixed, watching her. I tried to touch her, but I couldn't move. It was as though a pane of glass separated us; I read, fascinated as a child listens to a story unfolding…

***Northern England, December 1851***
*Thursday afternoon*
The snow was heavy. Blinding sheets of ice laced the gales that blew in from the north, freezing everything in their path. Sarah had to attend a meeting in the church to finalise the Christmas festivities. Earlier in the day, the committee had decided to postpone the meeting, due to the extreme cold, but the message hadn't reached her.

The wind howled. Large snowdrifts were banked up along the buildings. She sat in the warm hall of her lodging and pulled on her overshoes. Her overcoat reached almost to the ground. Sarah had wanted her mother to cut it short, just below the knee, which she had considered to be far more stylish. How grateful she now felt that her mother had the good sense to leave it long.

Opening the front door, she pulled her scarf closer to her face and stepped out onto the icy path. Clutching the fence, she stepped carefully forward. The ice cracked under her feet as she eased herself along the street, until she reached the steps of the small stone church. It seemed strange that there was no smoke billowing out from the chimney in the vestry. As she walked up the front steps, the girl thought that she could hear sounds through the closed entry. Stopping, she leaned forward and listened, but the noise seemed to have stopped. Her gloves slipped on the frozen door handle, so she lifted one hand and pulled the glove off with her teeth.

Turning the handle, she entered and slipped the glove back into her pocket as she stepped from the side vestibule into the church. The interior was dark. There was no candlelight as she had expected. Had the meeting been cancelled? Steadily and quietly, she made her way up towards the altar and reaching up she found the candle and matches. The match was used so she found another one and struck it.

A flicker of light and her candle was lit. The smell of the candle wax rose and tweaked her nose. Then she froze. There on the carpet behind the low altar lay two people.

At first, she thought it was a young couple in the embrace of intimacy. Shocked, she started backing away from the writhing figures. Suddenly, a young man stood up and faced her, exposing his nakedness. Beside him, another man scrambled up, someone she knew well, whose sermons she listened to every week. She tried to avert her eyes, but the scene burned into Sarah's mind. Reverend Samuel had a loving wife and was the father of the sweetest little girl. It couldn't be. She felt sick. Stumbling backwards, she turned and ran.

Banging the church door behind her, she flew up the gravelled path and along the street. She didn't see old Mr Smith shuffling past her towards his house. Bumping against her, he turned to apologise. 'Oh sorry,' he said as she slipped over on the ice.

He put out a hand and pulled her up, while with the other he brushed the snow from her coat. She pulled away, not answering him. She knew already that no one would believe that the kind and gentle Reverend Samuel could be guilty of such an act. Unfortunately, Sarah didn't notice that her glove had fallen to the ground.

She couldn't have known of the murder that was taking place in the quaint little chapel behind her, or of the cobweb of lies that would ensnare her; or of the carved candlestick dripping with blood which lay beside the murdered boy; and of the preacher, white with fear, trying desperately to scrub the blood from his hands. Sarah ran forward along the twisted street, leaving her orderly life behind forever.

Gathering her possessions, she bundled them into a small bag. Sarah wanted no more of this village life. She recalled how they disapproved of her teaching in their village. Called it favouritism and thought that one of their own should have been given the position. They mistook her kindness to the young men as flirting. No, she would never fit in.

She started to walk home through the woods that divided the two valleys. The sky turned black, and sheets of rain dramatically reduced visibility. But through the downpour, Sarah spied a small wooden hut set on a ridge. She pushed through the wind and rain to the abandoned building just as a bolt of lightning hit the tree under which she had been sheltering. The cottage was cold but dry, and rats scurried away as she struggled to close the door behind her. Gathering some twigs left near the door, Sarah started a small fire in the hearth. Shadows danced against the walls, giving a sense of comfort that the distraught girl embraced as she sat down on a pile of hessian bags strewn over the floor.

Time had no meaning as she sat there remembering the last five years.

Sarah had precious little to show for her eighteen years of life. She had been born on a large estate owned by the Earl of Bradford. Her father, Alistair, was the coach driver and her mother, May, worked in the main house as a cook. As they too had been born on the estate, it was expected that Sarah would also eventually work there. Sarah was a bright child and quickly endeared herself to the ageing earl. Having fathered four sons, his wife had hopes for a daughter, but their prayers weren't answered. His wife had taken a liking to little Sarah, and after the death of his good lady, the earl found comfort in speaking to Sarah and watching her play.

On her thirteenth birthday, she was taken up to the main house to start work in the scullery. Sarah stayed close to her mother, not sure what all the fuss was about as a man dressed in a black suit entered the kitchen.

'Edith, get the girl upstairs, the earl wants to speak to her,' said a rather surprised butler.

'Hurry up, Sarah, change your apron, look lively. No, not that one, the white one with the pocket.'

The cook, Sarah's mother, also wondered why the earl would want to speak to the girl. She had not been there long enough to have caused any disturbance to the running of the household.

'Come in, my girl, I want to have a little talk with you.'

The earl watched Sarah enter the study. It was one of the original rooms in the manor house. The top beams were thought to be from the Tudor period. Dark panelling framed the walls behind the bookshelves. On the far wall, a large fireplace had been built, its mantel carved from oak. Above it, taking pride of place, hung the family crest. Along the end wall, a large window overlooked the garden and in front of it stood a matching carved desk.

Although she had never entered the formal living areas of the house before, she walked proudly. Her back was straight, and her head was held high. She showed no fear. The window had been opened and Sarah could smell the sweet perfume from the roses that climbed up the trellises. Big bright red ones: she remembered seeing them on the day she had her interview when she came to apply for a job. This was necessary as Sarah's mother did not want any talk of favouritism.

'Sit down, Sarah. I've had an idea, and I want to talk to you first, before speaking to your father. Would you like to take lessons, instead of working downstairs?'

Sarah wondered how she could tell the master that the little amount she was to earn would help to educate her brother.

'You will still receive your wages.'

Pure sunshine shone from the girl's face as she curtseyed and left the room. Later that evening in the driver's cottage, Sarah's father exploded in anger when her mother told him of the earl's proposal.

'They are putting the girl above her status. She should work, it's not proper like.' He slammed his fist onto the table with such force that the teapot tipped over. 'Now see what you have made me do.'

'Don't take on so, dear, you know it's not good for you. Besides, I'm sure that the earl knows best.'

Sarah's mother knew that her husband would eventually calm down, and not dare question his employer's judgement. She picked up her sewing box and settled back, knowing that this was a time to remain quiet.

The storm finally blew itself out and the stars shone down, lighting the way through the drifts of snow. Sarah pulled her cloak around her shoulders and gathered up her carpet bag before she headed out into the snow.

'Girl, wait.' Two men appeared from nowhere. Sarah froze; she recognised the taller of the men. He was a policeman from her village.

'Sarah Noonan, you are wanted for questioning.'

Before she had a chance to ask why, she was thrown into a lockup cart and taken into the village lockup. For hours she waited in the cold, damp cell, too frightened to call out. Why was this happening? Women seemed to have no voice. It was nearly dawn when the cell doors were opened, and a man dressed in a black suit entered.

'Sarah, you can leave. Go directly to the manor house, use the back stairs, and speak to no one. Do you understand me, girl?'

'But, sir, I don't understand…'

'For God's sake go, haven't you caused enough trouble for the earl?' The solicitor wondered why the earl bothered to bribe the constable as he watched the bedraggled girl leave. *She did it*, he thought to himself, *better to let the law have her. One less whore to worry about.*

Although the Manor house was only four miles from the hut, it was midmorning before Sarah crept up the back steps of her former employer's main house on the estate. How could she tell the old earl that she left her teaching position because of what she had seen? Breathing in deeply, she entered the servant's kitchen and waited until the butler escorted her to the library.

'Come in Sarah, quickly girl.' The old earl looked concerned as he beckoned for her to sit. 'Sarah, what have you done? Two men from the law have been here enquiring after you. I told them you hadn't come here.'

'Sir, I saw a terrible thing.' She hesitated and before she could spit out the details of the scene that she had witnessed the evening before the elderly earl cut her short.

'Sarah, you have been accused of murder.'

Murder! The words vibrated in her mind. Stumbling backwards, her heel caught on the leg of the settee, and she toppled over onto the small table which held his brandy decanter. He trembled as he helped her up, then turned to replace the glass and added a small drop of brandy that he then handed to her.

'Take this.' She leaned over to accept the crystal goblet. He watched her hand quiver as her small fingers wrapped around the stem. 'I think you had better tell me everything.'

The earl had known Sarah for all her life. Hadn't he paid for her education and helped secure her a paid teaching position in the next valley? When she finished reliving all the shocking events of the night before, they both sat in silence.

'Sarah, they have a witness who saw you leaving the church. And you dropped your glove.' He looked into her large, scared eyes. 'They won't believe your story over the minister's, my dear. Listen closely, girl, as this is what you must do. Go to London. Your father will take you to meet the London coach, and there you will take passage to Australia until this affair has been resolved. I will give you a letter of introduction and money. Sarah, you mustn't go to your parents' cottage, the police will be waiting there for you.'

'What about my mother? Who will tell her?' Her eyes pleaded as she waited for him to answer.

'I'll let her know when you are safely away. Good luck, my dear, and may God go with you.'

# Chapter one

**London, January 1852**

Two days later, the coach entered the outskirts of the city. Sky the colour of distant mountains threw rays of sunlight up and into the coach, causing the weary passengers to rub their already tired and smarting eyes.

Sarah leaned back, her head resting on the soft interior of the coach. The rhythm of the horses lulled her into a sense of timeless loss; her world seemed to be disappearing with every mile that passed. Closing her eyes, thoughts of the last week brought waves of panic and bile up into her throat, cramping her whole body. Would she ever be safe?

Smog and mist covered London, and carts rattled over the cobbled streets. Homeless people mingled aimlessly in the alleys, accustomed to the filth and stench, which was a constant reminder of the poverty in which they lived.

Sarah leaned over and lifted down a woollen travelling cloak from the parcel rack. Deep blue, trimmed with a twisted cord, this cloak was the most beautiful garment she owned. It had been a gift from her employer when she passed her higher studies. The coach stopped, and she stepped down onto the filthy roadway, horse and human excrement littering the gutters. She held her bag close to her. Everything she cherished lay within this little bag.

From the doorway of a nearby house, a shrivelled old crone, whose face was battered and scarred with time, watched her. The stench that rose from her didn't come from the clothes she wore; it came from the evil within. Sarah ran her hands down her skirt, trying to straighten out the crumpled folds. It was useless. The cramped coach had made a mess of the neatly ironed frock. Stretching up, she felt her muscles relax after the cramped eight-hour trip and she turned, looking for a street sign.

'Need some help, love? Alone, are ya?'

Sarah turned in surprise, and seeing the older woman, backed away.

'I'm looking for the shipping office,' whispered Sarah as she approached the old woman.

Millie smiled, her wrinkled lips curling up at the corners. *Fancy manners*, she thought to herself, which only confirmed her summing up of this young girl.

'The office don't open till later, lovey. Why don't you get a cuppa for yourself? I could sell you one, only live over there.' She pointed to an old building, whose architectural splendour had been lost in time and now stood derelict. 'Help you fill in some time, not safe for a lady alone on the street.'

Sarah was not sure about this offer, and she looked around but there was no sign of a tea house.

'Won't get another offer in this neck of the woods,' said Millie. 'Come on, I'm Millie, and I don't bite.' She beckoned to the girl. 'Just over here a bit.'

She followed the woman across the narrow street; they stopped in front of a small narrow terraced house. The century-old building, patched up with rotten timbers, looked derelict, its windows cracked and black with filth. The hall smelled of urine and rot. Millie pushed her into the front room where a lopsided table and a broken chair filled the space.

'Sit down, and I'll nick in and put the kettle on, it won't be long.'

As Sarah looked around the room, her skin crawled, and she wondered why people lived in such squalor; water was cheap and elbow grease cost nothing. Millie returned carrying a small tray containing an assortment of broken crockery. Sipping her tea from the uncracked side of the cup, Sarah felt the warmth spreading throughout her body, and her eyes became heavy. She did not feel the cup slip from her fingers and or hear it smash as it hit the floor.

Struggling to open her eyes, Sarah could hear the shouting of the people in the street below. A coarse dirty rug covered her. She could smell the nauseating stink that rose from the thin mattress under her.

Where was she?

Millie sat watching the girl; she stood up and, leaning forward, said, 'Open your eyes, we ain't got all day,' as she poked at her. A grubby hunched man stood beside Millie.

'I told you that you gave her too much. Is she dead?' he asked.

'Don't be daft, you silly oaf, been at this game too long to make a mistake like that,' replied Millie.

Sarah opened her eyes, and blinked to remove the heavy shadows that were still glazed over them, before she looked around the room. The squalor and stench gave way to the fear she felt, and sighting Millie she asked, 'How did I get here?'

'Fainted, we've been looking after you. Tom here carried you upstairs. Lay back, dearie, rest a bit longer; he'll bring you up a cuppa later.'

Sarah struggled to sit up. 'Thank you, but I must go.' She let her head fall back onto the pillow as she heard a voice say, 'Not so quick, girlie, you owe us.' Millie's face fell into a sarcastic grin, as she stared into the innocent eyes of the lass in front of her.

Sarah looked around for her bag, and sighting it, she replied, 'I can pay you.'

Millie waved her hand dismissively. 'We will talk about that later. By the way, my name is Mrs Shaw to you from now on.'

Sarah leaned back to avoid the stale breath that wafted from Millie's decaying teeth.

'Come on, Tom, out of here, she's not for the likes of you.'

A look of disappointment clouded the imbecile's face. Turning, they left the room, slamming the door behind them.

*Were they really talking about me?* Sarah thought. And what did she mean by 'not for the likes of you'? Struggling to the door, Sarah pulled on the handle, but it didn't open. She banged and yelled but there was no sound, only the cockroaches scattering, leaving more room for the bugs that infested the mattress.

Above the bed a small grimy window faced the street. Sarah climbed up to the window ledge to look out, but it was nailed shut, leaving only a filthy lace curtain, torn and dangling from a nail. Sinking back onto the bed, Sarah prayed this nightmare would end and she would wake up.

The day drew on, and the sun sank behind the buildings that she had seen from the window. The room became colder. She pulled the rug up over her shoulders and waited. By nightfall, Sarah was desperate to empty her bladder. Looking under the bed, she found a small chamber pot pushed to the back behind a mess of dirty rags. Nervously, she watched the door as she weed into the pot. Later as the dark of night filled the room, she heard the steps creak. Cringing, she watched as the door opened. Millie stumbled in, barely able to hold the candle in her hand. She reeked of gin. The door slammed behind her; Sarah could hear the bolt being slid across. Sarah's heart pounded in anticipation as she watched the woman.

'No need for us to be disturbed. When are ya folks going to arrive, ducky?' Millie sensed the fear in the girl. She just needed to make sure that no constable or family member would be nosing around.

'I don't have any folks here, but I told you I can pay for this bed.' Tears trickled down Sarah's face.

'Well, that's what I want to talk to you about. You seem a nice girl, just down on your luck. You owe me ten bob. Pay up and you can be on your way.'

'I don't have ten shillings; anyway, a night's accommodation is only ten pence, this is outrageous.' Sarah voiced her disgust at Millie's prices.

'Well, you do have a problem, don't you? Sit down and shut up. What do we call you, anyway?' asked Millie.

'Miss Sarah Noonan, thank you very much,' said Sarah with determination. Her head jerked back as a hand slapped her face. Her teeth shook and the pain stopped her from taking a breath.

'No smart talk from you, girlie, you will pay mind to old Millie, by God you will! Now let's start again, Sarah. The way to pay me back is quite easy. I have a few gentlemen staying here from time to time and they are in need of a lady's company. You will entertain them up here, do whatever they want and mind your tongue.'

Sarah was young, but she wasn't stupid. She'd seen with her own eyes what gentlemen did to working class lasses.

'No man has ever violated me; I have never even entertained a man at my home. You can't make me,' cried Sarah.

'Then I'll send up Tom. He wants first go at you.' Millie smirked. 'Think about it, wouldn't a fancy man be better? I have a nice chap in mind; do the right thing and there will be a few pennies in it for you.'

With that Millie banged on the door, the bolt slid open, and she disappeared through the opening, slamming the door closed behind her. Sarah stared at the door. Could this really be happening?

A little later, Tom entered without knocking, carrying a wash bowl and a dress. 'Mrs Shaw told me to tell you to wash your face and put on the dress, a man will be dining with you tonight.'

Sarah lay there, and when Millie returned, she had not stirred. 'Tom, get in here and strip this girl.'

'No, I will do it,' screamed Sarah, dashing out of the bed and reaching for the clothes.

'Well, mind you do, and be pleasant like. Do you understand, girl?'

Sarah looked at the dirty dress that had been given to her. After putting it on, she pulled frantically at the bodice. Never had she worn a dress which revealed the swell of her breast. The skirt was made of fine transparent cotton that showed off her drawers underneath. When Millie saw this, she ripped the drawers from Sarah's body.

'What do you think this is, a blinkin' tea party?'

Twenty minutes later, Sarah heard a coach pull up, followed by banging on the front door. After a time, the bedroom door was opened, and a man entered. He was tall, and well groomed. His cloak was made of the finest worsted cloth and by his side he carried a small leather riding whip.

'Remember, she is shy, and as pure as the driven snow. You will have to show her.' And with that, Millie left.

'Come here, girl, I won't eat you. Let me look at you so I can see what I've paid for.' Sarah watched the man as he removed his hat and gloves.

'Please, sir, I can see you are of noble birth, there has been a terrible mistake, and I have to leave here.'

'Not until I have my money's worth, now be a good girl and come here.'

The pleasant smile had now become a sneer, his ring finger twisting the right side of his moustache. Sarah backed away, but her legs hit the bed. The man stepped forward, grabbing her around the wrist. Pulling back, Sarah hit out with her other hand.

'Want to play a bit, do you?' He laughed and pulled her closer to him. He could feel her body through the dress. Her nipples brushed against his chest. He saw the dark patch above the vee of her legs. His arousal pushed against her. 'Play time is over, my sweet.'

As much as Sarah struggled, she could not stop the pain as he pushed his manhood into her, over and over again. She tried to block out what he was saying, yet still felt his mouth tearing at her nipple, biting into her flesh. She closed her eyes and prayed that she would die. Sarah felt the coins as they hit her hands and fell onto the bed. She remembered the Sunday services that she attended with her family. Why had God allowed this to happen to her?

John Lowe had come to London to purchase a new hunting gun, or that was what he had told his father, Lord Lowe. John didn't care a rat's arse about the estate. London meant gambling and women. His father wouldn't stand for any of the servants being pestered by any man in his employment; that included his sons.

Later that evening, Sarah tried to wash the blood from her thighs. She remembered his signet ring: two eagles with a diamond in the shape of a star. This ring had scratched deeply into her flesh; the tear ran down the inside of her thigh, leaving outward scars that would heal, but the inner scars she would bear forever. Hearing his coach leave, she knew it would not be long before Millie entered her room. Sure enough, she arrived, swaying and stinking of gin, and put a tray on the table.

'You did all right, but you will be better tomorrow. Get them to buy my gin from you.'

Staggering out, she swore at Tom, slammed the door and left. Sarah could hear a bell chime and a nightwatchman sing out, 'Two o'clock and all's well.'

Lying there, she relived the horror of the night, the man, and Millie coming back and slamming the door. Then somewhere in the turmoil of her mind, it occurred to her that she hadn't heard the bolt slide shut. Creeping to the door, Sarah turned the handle. It opened and cautiously, she peered onto the landing, her eyes slowly focusing in the dark. Straight ahead of her, a narrow staircase led down to the street below. Gathering up her bag and cloak, Sarah stepped lightly on to the stairs. One foot at a time, her back scraping the wall behind her, she crept down towards the front door.

Gently, she turned the latch and just as Sarah pulled the door open, a screeching voice ripped through the darkness. 'You little cow, get back here, you still owe me!'

Sarah turned around in time to see Millie lunging towards her, and instinctively pushed both of her fists into the old crone's face. The old woman fell backwards, hitting her head on the wall as she went down. Jumping over Millie's crumpled body, Sarah ran out into the street. Not knowing which way to go, she ran blindly forward, not noticing the winding alley or the beggars who watched her.

The pavement was slippery, and yet on and on Sarah ran, stumbling until she could not run any further. Gasping for breath, she stopped and looked around. Ahead were large trees and a hedge that led to a locked gate. Cowering in the shadows, she tried to remember where she had run. She kept looking back; were they following her? A voice in her head kept talking to her, telling her to run to escape. The bell chimes struck again, it must be four o'clock. There must be a church nearby. Hadn't she seen a steeple from the window? Perhaps they would help her?

Following the hedge to the corner of the two streets, Sarah stopped to catch her breath. A cat sneaked past her, disappearing into the shadows. Stepping out onto a wide clean street, she watched a team of four heavy draught horses pulling a brewery dray that demanded centre position in the road. People pushed carts of fruit, trying in vain to avoid the rotting garbage and sewage that ran freely down the narrow gutters.

Sarah leaned against a lamp post. The gas lamp gave off a green-tinged light in the mist that swirled around her body, the cold biting into her bones. She tasted the coppery tang of blood as she bit into her cheek in fear. A livery boy, dressed in a dark red coat trimmed with gold ribbon, walked by, and seeing Sarah he stopped. Lowering the lead and harness he was carrying, he turned and spoke out to her.

'Lady, it isn't safe to be alone at this time. Where are you going?'

Bursting into tears, Sarah asked where the shipping office could be located.

'Don't blubber so, I'll show you. It's only on the other side of the park. Come on, you'll be there in a jiff.'

Sarah thanked the boy when they arrived and sat down on the steps of a large brick building. Above the door hung a sign: Imperial Shipping Line. As the cold penetrated her body, her teeth chattered, and her limbs started to shiver. She wrapped her arms around her body and pulled the cloak closer to her face.

'Please, God, make me forget.'

At six o'clock the office opened. A small clerk with rimmed glasses looked at the girl sitting on the step.

'You are a mite early, but come in.'

Rusty Earl was forty years old, balding and slightly stooped, having bent over the same desk continuously for the shipping company he had worked at for more than twenty years. He had seen them all, the traders, landed gentry and all the in between. A family man with daughters of his own, he watched the lass and sensing her distress, spoke out.

'Where are you heading to, miss? Can I help you?'

'Thank you, sir. I have a paid ticket to New South Wales. That's in Australia.'

The clerk smiled to himself, examining the ticket then stamping it, and then he gave it back to the girl. 'You are lucky, lass. I have booked you on the *Harcourt* and she's leaving tonight on the evening tide.'

Sarah settled on to a bench seat to wait out the time.

'Would you like a cuppa, miss? I was just going to make myself one. You'll have time before the coach leaves for Portsmouth.'

The *Harcourt*, a masterpiece of construction, lay low on the tide. The three-mast frigate bobbed gently against the ropes that held her anchored to the mainland. Once a ship of the line and built in Liverpool, she had been refitted to accommodate human cargo. The ship was spotless, with gleaming paintwork and freshly scrubbed decks. She lay in contrast to many of the shabby vessels anchored nearby. Her mainsail was slowly and painstakingly heaved skyward. The chants of the crew methodically kept the rhythm. Heave ho, heave ho.

James Lowe was tall and heavy set. He stood six foot six inches in his stockinged feet and he had a frame to match his height. A distinguished-looking man, with cheek bones sculpted under his taut brown skin. His piercing brown eyes were set apart, the trimmed beard adding strength to his angular face. Well educated and a product of upper-class England, James was always destined to follow his father, a retired sea captain and lord of the realm into the British Navy.

Leaning over the starboard rail, James watched his first mate supervise the loading of supplies. Checking his own manifest, he counted 40 crew and 62 passengers. They were made up of a mixture of landed gentry, single men, young ladies escorted by their governesses and last on the list were five nuns travelling to join their mother house in New South Wales. The young men mingled and talked about the gold strikes in Victoria, all believing that the streets were paved with it.

At the far end of the gangway, a lone figure lingered at the back of the crowd, blending into the shadows. Wearing a long blue travelling cloak, the hood tightly pulled around her face, she was someone you could easily glance over and quickly forget. James smiled as he watched the young men board; did they really believe the streets were paved with gold? As he turned, a small shadow caught his eye. He stared into the mist that was descending over the port. The girl came closer and started to climb the gangway onto the ship. James watched as she pressed her carpet bag close to her chest.

'Captain, all the passengers are aboard and the last of the machinery is stowed!' yelled Lieutenant Brian Lewis, second-in-command.

It seemed no time before they heard the cry, 'All ashore that's going ashore.'

There was a scramble to the deck and the emigrants lined the rails as their families pushed forward to shout and wave their goodbyes.

'Raise the gangway, cast off the lines, look lively, lads.'

The decks became a hive of activity. Men unlashed the sails while others climbed to the top of the mainsail.

A lanky pimpled faced lad introduced himself to the passengers. 'Ladies, me name is George, I'm your cabin boy for the voyage.'

This was George's second voyage, and as their cabin boy, he was hoping to make a few bob, if the pickings were good.

James looked up at the mainsail. As it unfolded, a breeze sprang up and he reminisced about the dozens of times that he had relived this scene. A sudden lurch brought him back to reality and he sighed. *One hundred and twenty days to Sydney ... God willing.*

two



*15<sup>th</sup> September 1851*

Three months previously, at the same time Sarah received her first teaching position, James Lowe had received an official crown-stamped notification to attend a meeting at Admiralty House. He had risen early and dressed in the attire his manservant, Harold, had laid out the night before. It consisted of a formal uniform with medals attached and white gloves; all the pomp that James disliked so much.

'Harold, do I have to wear all of this?'

'Yes, sir, one must look the part.'

Harold had worked for James since his retirement from the army. A sergeant in the Royal Highlanders, Harold had been engaged by James Lowe Sr. to care for, and hopefully mould his son, Lieutenant James, in the best of British tradition. For fifteen years, he had watched the young James mature into one of the best sea captains in the Royal Navy.

The trees were just starting to blossom, a sweet smell lingered in the air as James quickly strolled through Hyde Park, across Piccadilly and turned right into Whitehall. From before the time of Nelson, all naval strategies had been formulated in these buildings. The flags were flying high as he walked up the stone steps and through the large brass doors of the admiralty building. Entering a formal room, James found that he was alone. On previous occasions, the room had been filled with all the captains of the fleet. The flag room, as it was known, held all the regalia, and past medals, along with historical maps. The sweet smell of cigars lingered in the air and was imbedded in the woodwork.

James walked through into the next state room where, at the far end behind a large oval table, a man half rose. With arms outstretched and in a commanding voice, he said, 'Come on through, my boy, take a seat. Would you like a drink?'

James smiled. He knew the voice of Admiral Reginald Lowe, James's uncle, his father's younger brother.

'No, thank you, sir, a bit early for me, but please go ahead.'

James watched his uncle pour a whisky. He noticed a small tremor in the elder statesman's hand as he sat waiting for his uncle to speak.

'James, what I'm about to tell you is in the strictest confidence, a matter of the highest security. We want to send you to Australia, on an undercover commission. You will have to be very discreet my boy. You will command the frigate *Harcourt*. She is to be decommissioned and put on the Pacific, London to Sydney. Over the following weeks, you will receive the bulk of your orders. To the navy, it will appear that you have decided to take an early retirement, in order to pursue land grants in New South Wales.'

James was stunned. 'Sir, surely there are more experienced people for this than me?'

The admiral rose from his chair and walked over to his nephew, placing his hand on James's shoulder.

'Yes, James, we have many good men, but none that can fill all the necessary requirements. This is of national importance, and I would trust you with my life. The *Harcourt* won't be ready until next year, so why don't you take some time off. Go home and annoy my brother. I will try to join you later; a spot of shooting would do the three of us good.'

'Sir, can't you tell me about this assignment, and why is it so important?'

'Sorry, James, it is not up to me. Lord knows I would tell you if I could.'

James didn't notice the crowds as he crossed back through the park, the whole morning seeming unreal. Why him? Why now? And why in hell couldn't they tell him?

Entering his apartment, he called for Harold. 'Please pack my hunting clothes. We are going back home to Mulberry Park for a spot of shooting.'

Later that day, James broached the subject with his manservant. 'What do you think, Harold? I have been considering applying for a land grant in Australia, I think it is about time we settled down.'

James watched the expression on his manservant's face. Harold was one of the few people James respected; he had always been a mentor and a friend. Harold had a nose for trouble and this news certainly made his nostrils twitch. James smiled. He could only imagine what was going through the older man's head.

The horses slowed to a trot as they approached the gates of Lord Lowe's country estate. A flock of sheep, driven by a shepherd and his collie, crossed in front of the coach. High up on a hill, a distant rider watched as the coach wound its way up the tree-lined avenue towards the main house.

James loved his home and growing up on the land. He would have stayed there but for his older brother, the heir apparent. John and James Lowe had always been rivals. John, the elder by six years had harboured a deep hatred for his little brother.

'Jealousy is a terrible trait,' stated the local vicar, when he was asked for his advice. The vicar had seen for himself the nasty taunts and tricks John had played on his younger brother. Many of the estate workers had confided in him. They also had to deal with John's cruelty to the animals on a daily basis.

The local doctor often stopped off at the vicarage for a chat and a little snort of whisky. 'I'm telling you, he needs a good thrashing, but we both know he'll never get one, don't we, Vicar?'

James had heard his parents discussing the differences between their two boys. His mother had maintained that she treated the children the same. His father was also at a loss to know why John was so cruel. It had been brought to his lordship's attention, when the grounds keeper discovered Master John trying to slash the throat of his brother's pony.

'My dear, I can't ignore it. Today, Hugh needed to tell me of John's latest doings. He needs a good whipping.'

'Please don't hit him, there must be another way,' pleaded his mother.

John was quickly bundled off to boarding school, where the problem only festered unattended.

Mulberry Park had been built during the reign of James Lowe 1st.

Over the years, a new wing and coach house had been added. James's mother had extended the gardens, making them one of the grandest in England. A large man-made lake complete with a waterfall, lay to the back of the main manor. Hundreds of roses had been planted; high dry-stone fences had divided the gardens, giving way to the walks that led to secluded areas. Each small garden had been designed with a theme in mind. The French gardens were a particular favourite of James's mother, which she had filled with lilacs and lavenders. At sunset, the fragrance had drifted through the surrounding buildings, bringing joy to the mistress and hay fever to the lord.

The coach circled the drive, stopping at the steps in front of the formal entrance, where the young footman hurried forward to open the coach door. Harold gathered up his cloak and stepped out. The footman waited and then looked into the empty coach.

'I thought Master James was attending also?' enquired the lad.

'Oh, he is around,' laughed Harold.

Back at the gate house, sitting at a small table, James was drinking a cup of tea with the gamekeeper's wife. The room never seemed to change; white scrubbed table, curtains crisp and clean, and a pot of soup simmering on the wood range. Throughout the entire world, it was this place that gave James a feeling of security.

'Do you remember, Master James, you gave me that tea set one Christmas Eve?' The old woman smiled, her deep blue eyes twinkled with delight. 'This is just like old times, Master James. You always dropped in to see us.'

The gamekeeper and his wife had been born on the estate, and to them it represented their whole world. To James, this old couple were more like grandparents than employees. He remembered how they hid him from his bully of a brother, whose daily fun was to inflict as much pain on James as he could.

Nan Ellis was a robust woman, having worked in the main house as a cook until her retirement. She still dressed in a clean white pinny and mob cap which covered a head of thick white curls, and she ruled her world with complete authority.

'The old master will be pleased to have you home. He is looking a might poorly these days. Another cup of tea, sir?'

John Lowe watched the coach turn into the estate. Anger consumed him at the thought of his brother returning. Thunder roared up the valley as the black clouds rolled in. Striking the horse with his whip, he spurred it into a gallop towards the main house.

'Where in the bloody hell are you, boy?' John Lowe yelled as he dismounted from his tall black stallion. The stable boy ran towards him. John lifted his arm and placed a hard fist into the boy's face. Blood trickled down the lad's cheek as he led away the horse. John wished it could have been his brother instead.

One week later, the footman walked out into the garden, where James was sitting with his mother. James never stopped marvelling at the beauty of these serene gardens his mother had established. The perfume of the roses lingered in James's memory, when as a lad he'd stood many a lonely night duty on deck at sea.

'Sir, a courier is asking for you. I have shown him into the study.'

'Thank you, I won't be long. Have you offered him refreshments?' asked James. The older footman regained his breath before answering and hurried back to the house.

'If that uncle of yours is going to take you away from us so soon, I will have to have stern words with him,' complained his mother.

James bent down and kissed her on the cheek. He loved the smell of the lavender she wore. He chuckled to himself when he imagined his uncle's face going redder, as he faced the 4'10" ball of energy that happened to be his mother. Later that night, in the privacy of his own rooms, James opened his orders. Breaking the seals, he started to read the pages through carefully. James sighed, and after pouring himself a drink, he turned and walked to the window. He looked out over the manicured gardens and towards a line of oak trees whose dark green foliage contrasted against the borders of yellow daffodils. James wondered how long it would be before he returned.

A few days later, early in the morning and as the cocks crowed, all the servants lined up to say goodbye to James. These people were his family. He remembered the men as they had been when he was a child: strong, with a spring in their step. These were his people. Their age didn't mean anything; he had his father's promise they would remain on the estate until they died.

As James walked down the line of people, shaking the men's hands and acknowledging the curtseys of the ladies, John smiled sarcastically. *With a bit of luck, the ship might sink.*

# Chapter three

On the day the *Harcourt* sailed, Sarah didn't turn around to face the wharf or wave goodbye to the crowd that had gathered on the dock. She followed the cabin boy down the stairs, hanging onto the side rail and along the passageway, passing the first-class cabins, and ending up at door Number 18. Sarah looked around the small cabin that had been assigned to her and another passenger.

'Hello, dearie, I guess we are to share,' said a rather large woman with a broad North Country accent. Pushing in through the small doorway, the woman smiled at Sarah and chuckled to herself. 'My word, I'll never be able to get up there onto the top bunk!'

Sarah turned to the pleasant lady with a rather voluptuous figure. Scrubbed clean, with fat rosy cheeks and smelling of lily of the valley, the woman shuffled forward.

'Well, love, this is to be home. It's a bit of a squeeze, don't you think? By the way, my name is Martha Pork.' With that she slapped her derriere and chuckled. 'Good hams on these. I didn't catch your name.' Martha pushed past and sat down on the chair to await a reply.

'My name is Sarah Noonan. It is very nice to make your acquaintance.'

'Well, ducky, what have we got here?' said Martha.

Both the women looked around the cabin. Two closets, a chair, and one very small table. The first closet was for hanging, but as Martha opened the other door she roared with laughter. Behind the door, a small commode and slop bucket had been placed.

'God love me, only one cheek at a time will fit in there,' she roared, tears of laughter streaming down her face.

Sarah instantly liked this motherly figure. She was unlike her own mother, who was a quiet, refined lady, not outgoing like Martha. Martha oozed care and compassion, something Sarah now longed for. Whistles were blowing, and feet were scurrying on deck as the ship lurched forward into the wind.

'Come up on deck, we need to see the old girl off, proper like.'

With that, Martha pushed Sarah towards the door, and up the steps onto a crowded deck. They both stood by the rail, Martha looking down into the sea of faces mingling on the dock. She scrutinized everyone until at last she yelled, 'Look, there is my Charlie down by the gangway. Bye, Charlie, look after everything while I'm away and don't fight with your father,' screamed Martha, waving madly to the crowd below.

Charlie waved back and then became lost in the crush of bodies as the crowd surged forward. People were clustered at every vantage point. The lines were cast off. Slowly, the ship moved into mid-stream. Sarah could feel Martha's eyes on her as they left port. She didn't wave, merely staring out over Portsmouth as the buildings shrank into the dim light, and were no more.

'Come on, lass. Let's see what we have to do to get a cup of tea.'

They both mastered the stairs that took them below. Just as Martha opened the cabin door and started to enter, the ship rolled, tipping her forward. Her petticoats landed above her head, leaving a spectacular view of a large red pair of drawers. The pimply faced cabin boy walked past at just that moment. Turning bright crimson, he backed away, just as Martha bellowed, 'Take a good look, laddie. Save you peeking on the lassies this trip!'

The humdrum of the days soon became very monotonous. They all lived by the bells, mealtime, time on deck and time to reflect on what they had all left behind. The weather had been kind to them, a fair breeze, with only one storm. But what a storm; the ship rolled as the waves lashed the decks. Many of the passengers were seasick and with Sarah's help, Martha assisted the doctor. The children were the worst affected, but as the storm abated, they quickly recovered.

'I told you, Sarah, the little ones would be just fine,' chuckled Martha.

A turn in the weather had brought Sarah back to reality. The days were becoming warmer as the cold and damp of London were left behind. Sitting on deck, enjoying the breeze with Martha, she watched the sailors up in the crow's nest. They pointed out a pod of dolphins and the children on board clambered to the rail to see them. The dolphins leapt out of the water, as if to show her that her life was about to improve. She felt free too. Walking over to the rail, she looked out to sea, and the breeze tossed her hair about her face, sending fingers of curls out above her head.

As Sarah reflected on her past, she thought perhaps her father might have been right. What good was her understanding of the arts, or being able to speak French and read Latin, when it had taken her away from everything she had held dear? She had lost her family and the security of a home. Now she was being swept up in a world she knew nothing about, and Martha became her constant shipboard companion.

Martha had observed the lass for nearly a month, and she'd seen the pain in those beautiful deep violet eyes, even though Sarah tried to hide it. Martha's pain was different, her heart was torn between the pain of leaving her family, and the joy of seeing her eldest daughter, who had married and emigrated to Australia. On the news of the arrival of Martha's first grandchild, her husband had suggested she might like to take a trip to visit with them. So for a month Martha sang praises about what a kind gentle man her husband was, except when he came home drunk.

Martha remembered Sarah telling her that she had only one summer dress; a plain calico working garment that her mother had sewn for her to start work. Martha took pity on her and cut down a couple of her own dresses to fit the girl. She fitted Sarah in a new style that showed off the girl's figure. As they walked the deck, Martha noticed the heads turning to look at Sarah.

Not only the lads noticed when she strolled by. James wondered to himself why an intelligent, educated girl was travelling second class and unescorted.

Later in the fifth week, they put into a small Portuguese port to take on fresh water and supplies. The air was saturated with the aromatic smells of tropical fruit, and the blossoms of the frangipani trees that lined the streets. James allowed the passengers to go ashore. He realised the main reason for quarrelling among the passengers was boredom.

Martha, with Sarah in tow, walked through the streets and market. After purchasing a cold drink, they sat under the large eaves of a European-styled house. These brick buildings were in contrast to the adobe buildings of the native people. Sarah was fascinated with the population. The children were clean and happy, not like the dirty urchins she remembered in London. The brightly coloured clothes that loosely swathed the women brought a sigh of envy from the tightly corseted European women.

Armed with their small purchases, Martha and Sarah ambled back to the *Harcourt*. Each one had bought a length of brightly coloured cloth, small bags made with exquisite bead work, and undergarments embroidered with small eyelet holes woven with lace. Sarah felt guilty when she handed over only a few shillings for such lovely hand work.

'Martha, I don't really need these, plain clothes would be more serviceable.'

Martha turned to face Sarah. 'Don't be silly, girl. When will you have the opportunity to purchase such lovely things again? Put them in your hope chest, who knows... with the way the lads are nosing around, any could pop the question, even that pimply lad.'

They both started to laugh, and streams of tears rolled down their faces. Holding their parcels, they tried to wipe their faces before they came on board.


'Is the count correct, Lieutenant?' James was becoming increasingly impressed with the ability of his second-in-charge.

James had been instructed to give over his sealed orders to his second-in-command one week out of Sydney. The young lieutenant would be promoted to captain and sail the *Harcourt* home, back to England.

'Yes, sir, the fresh supplies and water have been stowed. The last of the passengers have just arrived back.'

Looking over towards the deck, James noticed that Sarah and Martha were the culprits. As the gangway was lifted, he walked quickly over to the ladies. Clasping his hands behind his back, and clearing his throat, he said, 'Miss Noonan, when you take shore leave please be back at the appointed time. The tide waits for no man, or in this instance, woman.' Bowing, he turned towards the wheelhouse.

'He's got his eye on you, my girl. Sticks out like the nose on his face.'

'Don't be ridiculous Martha, he doesn't notice me in any other way, except perhaps as a passenger,' replied Sarah.

The weather was becoming warmer. Occasionally, the African coast became visible. Large sharks followed the ship, eating the scraps thrown overboard. Sarah shuddered as she remembered the stories of slave ships that sailed these waters, and how they would throw the sick slaves into the sea.

As the days became hotter, many of the women dressed without their stays. The nights were becoming intolerable for the passengers and crew alike. Without a breeze, the *Harcourt* became stationary, and the seas were as still as glass. When working above the deck, the crew were given permission to remove their shirts, but James had given orders that the men were not to flaunt their bodies in front of the ladies.

Rounding the Cape of Good Hope, the seas picked up. Large black clouds started rolling overhead. As thunder rocked the ship, the heavens opened. Torrents of rain washed over the decks and breathed life into the parched souls below. The sun finally shone. The ladies sat on deck and Martha chattered while Sarah listened to her.

'What are you going to do in Sydney, Sarah? You know, love, you can always stay with me. My Lisa has plenty of room. The more the merrier we always say. I'm not prying, but Sydney is a wild place when you're alone.'

'Martha, I've been offered a position as governess to a family, well placed within Sydney society. Fifty pounds a year and all found.' Looking into her carpet bag, Sarah withdrew a page of the London Daily newspaper, and handed it to Martha to read.

'Don't read the best, dear. Could you read it to me please?' muttered Martha.

Sarah opened the paper and started to read, 'Wanted, courageous young women, well educated, of high moral standard to instruct children in Australia. City and country positions available. Please send a letter of reference from a minister, education and work experiences. No French persons need apply. Send application to Rev J Fox, c/o Box 135, Sydney, NSW.'

'Just keep my address handy like, just in case things don't work out,' Martha said.

# Chapter four

'Land ahoy,' were the words all on board awaited. The coast of Western Australia slowly came into view. The passengers on the *Harcourt* scrambled to take up the best positions to view their promised land. Champagne flowed at the captain's table that night as James entertained the entire passenger list.

'Come on, Sarah, stop fussing or we'll miss the drinks.' Martha refused to accept any of Sarah's reasons for not attending the party. 'Put on the new dress I made for you, the pink looks lovely.'

'I really think the bodice is too revealing,' stammered Sarah.

'Rubbish, girl, don't be ashamed of what God gave you. Hurry on, love, move yourself.'

James watched Sarah with interest. She moved with the grace of a gentle woman, and her manners were impeccable. So why was she travelling alone? Perhaps a fiancé was waiting in Sydney, but she didn't wear any bands. The mystery intrigued him. He invited her to the captain's table, but she refused, stating a headache and left the crowd early for the sanctuary of her cabin. Her air of mystique left James pondering her future.

After berthing at the small settlement of Fremantle, some of the passengers left to start their new lives in the west. James stood at the gangway and shook hands with all of them. Sarah decided to go ashore before they started on the last stage of their trip from Fremantle to Sydney via the port of Melbourne. Government officers checked the manifest and waved on the passengers.

'Please remember we sail with the night tide.' James smiled at Sarah as she brushed past him.

'Sir, I need only to be told something once,' said Sarah in a very haughty voice.

The trip across the Australian Bight was uneventful. The passengers were not aware of these treacherous seas or of the ships that were lost due to rocks and confusion about the lighthouses that were placed along this part of the coast. The crew held their captain in admiration as he guided the *Harcourt* safely to Victoria. They pulled in close to the town of Melbourne to disembark passengers, but none of the remaining folk were allowed ashore.

'Sorry, but we just do not have time,' said Lieutenant Lewis, who by this time had become the darling of all the young unmarried girls and perhaps some of the older women too. He was a little flirtatious, but always the gentleman. One week out of Sydney, James gave Brian Lewis his orders.

'Congratulations, Captain Lewis.'

Rounding the heads, the *Harcourt* sailed into Sydney Harbour. A strange, but pleasant smell lingered in the air. The crew told Sarah that it came from a native tree that they called the gum. Indeed, this harbour, with its pockets of smaller bays was one of the most beautiful visions she had studied. Sarah was the last to leave the ship. Martha's family were all waiting. Her daughter, a younger version of Martha threw her arms around Sarah.

'Mama has told you the truth, you be very welcome to join with us, Sarah.'

After thanking them for their kindness, she gave a final hug to Martha and watched as her friend left the wharf area. Waving the family goodbye, she settled down to wait for the Reverend Fox. After a couple of hours, Sarah walked up to a building that stood at the end of the wharf, overhanging the water. Above the door a sign read, 'Booking Office'. Entering, she enquired if any messages had been left for her. A younger man looked back into his record book.

'Did you say Fox? Why, that old codger was run out of town months ago, miss. Best you get along, we will be closing soon.'

James had watched the girl as she walked back from the office and could not help noticing the look of panic on her face.

'Is there anything I can do for you, Miss Noonan?'

Swallowing her pride, Sarah nodded and asked if she could possibly share his coach, which was waiting.

'I insist I pay towards the cost, Captain,' Sarah said in a soft voice.

'No, the cost has been dealt with, besides I have just retired, so just plain James Lowe will do nicely.'

They were about to leave, when a man jumped up onto the running boards and Brian Lewis's cheeky face looked in.

'By the way, Mr Lowe, can a captain hitch a ride into Sydney Town?'

As the stagecoach moved off, James struck up a conversation with the fourth passenger on board. The man in the fringed tailored jacket, trimmed with a North American headband was Mr Cobb, who had just arrived on a frigate out of San Francisco. James listened with interest as the tall American told him of his plans to establish a fast transport system in Australia.

'Mr Lowe….'

'Please, call me James.'

'Well, James, I saw the need when I was out here last year. Yes siree, the way these folk get around can certainly be improved. I went back home to get the government to invest in this land of gold.'

This pricked James's interest, and he listened more intently. *So, the United States are the new players,* he thought. The web was certainly expanding.

'Miss, where do you want to be dropped off?' yelled the driver.

'Captain Lewis, could you recommend lodgings?'

'He could but I don't think you would approve,' replied James Lowe.

'That's a bit harsh, James.' Brian knew exactly what his friend meant.

'Where are you staying, Brian?' asked James.

'The Rustic Arms is not a proper hotel for ladies, lots of fights,' and winking at James he continued, 'quite a lot of naughty ladies also. I think The Kings Way would be more in keeping.'

'The Kings Way, thank you, driver, for Miss Noonan.'

Sarah was the first to leave the coach. She said her goodbyes and entered the lobby of a small but clean establishment. Booking in, she was shown to her room. The room was small but at last she was alone. A side table and a night candle, a well-worn, but comfortable chair had been placed near the window. Placing her bag on the bed, Sarah slumped into the chair. Sitting there, she contemplated the position she now faced. The situation of being jobless and homeless seemed overwhelming.

'Sorry to disturb you, miss; but a Mister, er … Captain Lewis is downstairs and wishes your company for dinner,' whispered a boy at her door.

Sarah stared at the young boy. His red hair and freckles were accompanied by the largest green eyes she had ever seen.

'Me ma said I should get rid of him if you didn't want to see the swell.'

The boy hopped from one foot to another awaiting Sarah's reply.

'Please tell your mother I will be down directly. And ask her if she would be so kind as to ask the captain to wait.'

Looking in the mirror, Sarah noticed the change in her appearance. She looked much older than the girl who had left her country village four months earlier. Her innocence had gone.

Later that night, returning to her room after a pleasant dinner with the captain, Sarah truly relaxed for the first time since starting out on her voyage. She had found the cramped quarters of the ship stifling. With a sigh, she pulled on her nightgown and sat on the chair in front of the small fire. Holding her hands out to warm, she glanced around the sparingly furnished room. So many dreadful things had befallen her over the last four months. But for tonight, this was home.

James Lowe's coach slowed to a stop. He stared at the low rambling home in front of him. William Masters had completed school with James and although their lives had gone in two different directions, they had always kept in touch.

A man came to the door to greet him.

'Welcome to Australia, James. I've been informed that you are to be a member of the landed gentry.' He took William's hand and the two men embraced. As James looked up, he caught a brief reflection of William's face in the mirror above the fireplace. The eyes of his friend had become hard, and for an instant he thought he saw a smirk. He must be mistaken. William was the only boy at school who stood up to James's bully of a brother. At the end of six years, he had reckoned up as many hidings as James.

'I'd like you to meet my wife, Penelope, and our newest member of the family, Lucy,' William said.

A woman holding a squirming infant stepped forward. 'We are

delighted to have you staying with us, James. Your room is ready, and we will not take no for an answer.'

Penelope was not a classical beauty. Rather plump and small in height, she barely reached John's shoulder. Lifting the infant, she placed it into James's arms and stepped back. Smiling with pride, she said, 'Say hello to your goddaughter-to-be, James.'

James looked at Penelope and remembered the rich beauties who once had thrown themselves at William. He wondered why his friend had decided on this plain Sydney girl. Was it her charm, or maybe the fact that her father had been governor of New South Wales? He had helped William become a rich and important man in the colony.

'Penny, I've not even asked him yet,' laughed William.

James smiled and quickly handed back the child. He would rather handle a slippery snake than a baby. After dinner, the two men relaxed in the study, smoking and sipping on their port. The smell of lavender and beeswax drifted from the parlour into the study.

'Close the door, James. Let's enjoy the smell of our cigars without all that polish ruining the moment.'

'You sound exactly like my father, William.'

'Where do you think I learned it from? When we were hiding in your house, mostly under his desk, eating the pies we nicked from your kitchen. James, I wanted you to know that I have been advised of your travel plans by the High Admiralty attaché. If I can be of any help to you, you have only to ask.'

'I didn't realise you were so well informed, William. It seems you know what I'm up against. Tell me, what do you know about an American named Cobb?'

'I met him last year, interesting fellow, talked about investments in this country. Why are you asking about him?'

'He told me today the American government is funding his company. Makes you wonder why they would throw their weight behind him. Interesting?'

James stood and walked over to the French windows. Peering out onto a verandah, he realised he needed a confidant and decided to be open and frank with his friend.

'I was asked, or rather ordered, to take on this assignment. I knew nothing at all about the loss of gold bullion. All I have been able to establish is that some kind of Russian syndicate based in Shanghai is paying the fares for Chinese to take up the digging leases.'

'But, James, I don't understand how this could possibly be of great consequence to the Crown; what do they have to gain? Maybe a little gold, but is it really worth all this effort?'

'That's what I'm here to find out.'

The following morning, Sarah walked up to the top of York Street. By ten o'clock, the sun was already burning. She barely noticed the crowd gathering to read the daily bulletins that were posted on the community notice board for those to read.

GOLD STRIKE AT MUDGEE!
Claims to be registered: Land Leases available to Free Pastoral Workers only.

Men mingled, swapping stories, mostly of their bad luck. Children ran in the streets, while toddlers clung to their mothers. The women's simple skirts were made of cotton gingham. Sarah noted a similar style to the women in Africa. Hanging on to her purse, she stepped off the kerb and on to the cobbled street. Holding up her skirt and dodging the horses and drays, she headed up Elizabeth Street towards the more established part of town. The small waterside pubs gave way to larger sandstone buildings. Here the people dressed smarter, they strolled along, moving with purpose; the men in their walking-out clothes, the women in the very latest and most expensive gowns and bonnets, kid gloves matching their buttoned-up boots.

The delicious aroma of fresh-baked bread wafted on the air, and she breathed in the welcome and homely fragrance of the small bakery. Her stomach rumbled. Gathering her skirt in her hands, her only thought was of how to obtain work. Walking into the vestibule of St Mary's church, she waited until a member of the clergy approached her. Sarah had never entered a Catholic church before. Looking around, she saw paintings of the crucifixion on the walls, and wondered why candles were lit, especially when the sun was still shining.

A priest hurried towards her, and taking her by the arm, he led her towards a row of seats on the eastern wall.

'Father, I'm not of your faith, but I really don't know where to go.'

'Child, we are all God's children. Can I assist you in some way?'

As Sarah started to tell her story, it was as though the gateway to despair had flooded open. She started in Yorkshire with the story of an earl's cousin, who made her life unbearable, and of the advertisement in the paper promising a job and security in Australia. Sarah didn't tell the priest of the crime she had been accused of or the hell she had gone through in London.

'Well, my child, I do receive requests for teachers from time to time, but in the meantime, maybe the good sisters could do with your assistance. They are always in need of teachers.'

Sarah's first day was not what she'd expected. She was asked to teach the older girls. Mother Superior had explained to her in what order the class was to sit. The paying students had proper desks, up closer to the black board. They were issued with slates and reading books. The poorer children sat to the back on wooden crates donated by the fish mongers. They shared any broken slates left.

Sarah took a particular liking to a little girl named Janey. The child came from the dock area and always wore the same dirty pinny. She had red hair, a freckled face, and a smile that lit up the room. Sarah thought that she was a child of exceptional resilience. One lunch time, as she was marking the children's work, a hand appeared from below the desk. Just as it was about to grab the apple, Sarah spoke. 'I wish I could find someone to eat my apple, I would be so grateful.' A firm friendship was established between teacher and pupil.

The weeks went by before Sarah felt confident enough to send a letter to her mother.

*My dearest Mother,*

*How I wish I could have said good-bye. I know you have been told about my untimely departure. I am safe, have work, and a few shillings put aside. My dream, Mother, is to be able to send home a little money so you can have a house of your own, a safe place for me to return to someday.*

*Know you are always in my heart, Sarah.*

For three months, Sarah worked at the school, receiving board and meals, too proud to accept help from Martha and her family. On her days off, she walked down to the harbour. Gardens had been planted along the foreshore, and on Sunday, families strolled out together; children often flew kites while their parents chatted to friends. The upper gentry's children were paraded around in their Sunday best under the watchful eye of their nannies.

In the harbour, three large ships were unloading passengers and trade goods. Sarah loved hearing the different accents of the people, and to smell the exotic dried foods being unloaded from the Orient. Chinese coolies, dressed in their traditional clothes, pulled carts loaded up with food. Young women sat on the top, while the men trotted beside them.

Chinatown was growing, a smaller version of the large community in San Francisco. Washing was strung across the alleyways of this shanty town. Shops selling foods and herbal medicines lined the streets. Ladies clad in dark coloured cottons sat at the doors selling their own wares. Children, chickens, in fact all manner of animals, added to the crescendo.

On returning to the convent, Sarah reflected on all the marvels of this new town. She felt a little envious of the families but quickly thanked God for what He had provided.

Brian Lewis had left on his return journey, promising to visit with her when he returned in the following summer. In the months previous, they had become good friends.

'Come on, Sarah, why are you really here? If you are in trouble in England, maybe I can help you. God only knows where you could be sent.'

'I will be fine here. The Sisters will have me until a position becomes available, and I've a little money left.'

'Sarah, I think you know how I feel about you. Please, will you sail back home with me? I don't ask, nor do I demand anything from you.'

Sarah took Brian's hands in hers. She couldn't find the words not to hurt him. But she felt deep down in her stomach, that to return to London would spell disaster for them both.

'No, your place is on the high seas, mine is here.'

# Chapter five



*Sydney, 1853*

A young novice popped her head into the classroom.

'Sarah, Father Michael wants to speak with you. I'd go now, before Mother Misery returns; she is not in the best of moods this morning. I did overhear Father mention about a position for you, but she didn't seem pleased at all.'

Sarah smiled; misery was the name the novices had given to their Mother Superior.

'Thanks, I'll go now.' She smiled as she watched the young girl disappear along the corridor.

'Come in, Sarah,'

The girl walked over to the desk and, with her hands folded in front of her, she waited for the priest to speak.

'I've received a letter from a community in the country, a small settlement of farmers who require a teacher. The children range in age from five to thirteen. The name of the place is Gulgong. You would have to travel by coach to Mudgee, where you would be met and taken the rest of the way by horse and dray. The position includes a small dwelling, and a yearly salary of forty pounds. So, what do you think?'

'Oh, thank you, Father, I love working with the sisters, but I do need to support myself. When can I start?'

'There's a mail coach that has started a run to Mudgee. I believe it leaves on Sunday. I could send word then and maybe you could leave the following week.'

Martha was very sceptical. 'What do you want, gallivanting out in the wilderness? I'm sure your mother would not approve, Sarah, if she was here.'

'Please, Martha, don't make it harder for me to say goodbye to all of you.'

The sun was still rising over the coast as Sarah said her goodbyes to Martha.

'Throw up the bag,' cried out the driver to the young stable hand loading the coach. The coach driver was a tall man about forty years old, skin like leather and arms as strong as the bullocks he'd once driven.

'We're leaving in ten minutes, folks.'

The driver checked his fob watch and walked around the horses pulling on the harness. The team was new, good sound horses. They should be, he had brought them with him down from the high country, mountain horses every last one of them. The driver smiled every time he remembered the solicitor explaining to him, as he handed over his bank draft, that he was now the partner 'Co', of the newly formed Cobb and Co. The horses started off at a trot. Sarah's head snapped back onto the head guard. Opposite her sat a small middle-aged lady. She had a pointed chin and eyes that were set very close together. On her head was perched the biggest bonnet Sarah had ever seen. Leaning forward, the lady struck up a conversation.

'My name is Maude Jones. Isn't it marvellous; a real coach to travel on.'

'How do you do, I'm Sarah Noonan. This is the first time I have ever travelled in Australia.'

'Well, let me tell you, Miss Noonan…'

'Please call me Sarah.'

'Sarah it is then. Until now, to travel in this country took at least one week to Gulgong. We slept rough, and it meant one of our men folk had to take time off to accompany us. We now have some independence and best of all we stop at night and sleep in real beds. Where are you heading?'

'To Gulgong. I'm going to teach there.'

'Good, I'm travelling all the way up there myself. My husband is a property owner. We've a bush block along the creek. You will be teaching my Sally, so I hope you believe in discipline.'

Sarah wasn't sure if she liked this woman, but maybe she was judging her too quickly. On the second day they climbed over the mountains, the valleys giving off a blue tinge, which the coach driver explained was caused by the eucalypts of that region.

The small township of Lithgow was bustling with prospectors; pubs were covered by large tents, with trestles running along the middle. Hawkers sold their wares under makeshift conditions.

The driver walked the horses back into their traces. He would hand over the reins to another, now the worst of the mountain tracks were behind them. The country changed, deep valleys gave way to open plains. Sarah was fascinated by the mobs of kangaroos. They crossed many low running creeks with sandy beaches. The local Aborigines watched as they went by. Sarah noted the children's large brown eyes, full of wonder and hoped some of them would attend her class.

'I hope I have some children like these attend my school.'

'Certainly not.' Mrs Jones took on an air of superiority. 'We don't have darkies in our schools.'

The sun was setting when they finally left the coach. Mr Jones was waiting to pick up his wife and one passenger. Barry Jones was a pleasant-looking man, tall with a willowy frame, not the type of man Sarah had pictured married to her travelling companion.

'Miss Noonan?' An outstretched hand met hers. 'Welcome, I see you have met my wife, I'm on the school board at Gulgong, so we will be seeing a lot of each other.' Walking back to his wife, he bent over and gave her a peck on the cheek. 'Maude, I'll load up the dray now, but I think we had better stay here tonight, and get an early start in the morning.'

It was still dark when they left the horse exchange and headed inland. Maude Jones chattered all the time. After a few hours, Sarah's head was spinning from the gabble about shopping, eating only in the best restaurants, and meeting only the best people.

'Maude, for Christ's sake, give it a break, you're driving both of us mad with all of your chatter.'

Barry smiled over at Sarah as peace was restored. There was a gloom that hung in the air, and it was not the clouds. After a time, Maude couldn't keep the silence. And turning to Sarah, she snapped, 'Only one more mile and we can leave you off.'

Barry pulled up the dray in a cloud of dust and reaching up, lifted Sarah down. Before them stood a small cottage with a verandah attached.

'For God's sake, Maude, come on down and make this lady welcome.'

Barry opened the gate and carried Sarah's carpet bag into a small living room. Placing it on the hearth, he walked to the windows and pushed them open.

'It's not much, but it is clean, the privy is out the back and there are supplies in the larder. By the way, here are the keys to the hall and your cottage.'

'When does the privy get emptied?' enquired Sarah.

'They don't here, love,' chuckled Barry. 'We all have what we call long drops.'

Sarah had two days to settle in and explore her new world. At the front of her cottage, a small garden had been established with one rose and flowers that Sarah had never seen before. A small tree, covered with yellow blossoms pushed up to the side of the chimney.

The small cottage was lined with wooden planks, with mud pressed between the cracks to seal out the draught. In the bedroom stood a four-poster iron bed, a small wardrobe and a dressing table, that had been made up from broken odds and ends. A glass bottle had been placed on the table with a single rose in it. As she bent forward to smell the perfume, Sarah caught a reflection in her mirror of a small dark boy peeping over the windowsill edge.

Turning, she walked to the window, but the boy was gone. Sarah looked down past the privy, through a wooden fence to where large gum trees lined the river's edge. Smoke billowed up from the other side of the river. Two hundred yards south, on the far end of a sandbar, a family of Aborigines had made camp. That night after supper, Sarah sat on a crate on the front verandah, looking up at the stars. The sounds were different, somewhat scary but what would you expect in such a strange land. Later that night, she climbed into bed and, curling up into a ball, thanked God for all his blessings.

Next morning, Sarah threw open the door to greet the morning and started her daily walk. She was surprised to find a dish made from bark on her step. In it were small figs and a wildflower.

The small township consisted of the church and hall, a grocer, blacksmith, and a few pubs. The main street was either a dust bowl, or awash with mud. It was not strange to see kangaroos bounding down the street, or rows of horses with rabbit traps slung over their saddles tied up around the locals' drinking hole.

Sarah watched as a man strolled into the township. A broad-leaf straw hat shaded a tanned, weather-beaten face. The cotton shirt was opened at the throat and around his neck was tied a loosely knotted handkerchief. His trousers were tied at the waist with a piece of rope. Over his shoulder was slung a piece of calico tied on to a stick in which he carried all his earthly possessions.

'Any jobs goin?' he asked. The men near the pub shook their heads and the man walked on.

Sarah decided to explore the bush between her cottage and the river. As she strolled through the long grass, a screech from the white cockatoos made her stop and look up at the sky. Hundreds of birds had taken to the air, blotting out the sun, and as she stood there watching, a little voice called out, 'Missy, you no go long grass, snake get you.'

Startled, she swung around and stared at a very small man trotting towards her. His long plait swung in the breeze, a coolie hat balanced on his head. He was pushing a wheelbarrow loaded up with shovels and men's pants.

'You buy shovel, Missy, kill snakes, hit bad men.'

'Maybe I do need one, Mr…'

'You call me Charley, Charley Wong.'

'Yes, Mr Wong, I will take one.'

Sarah entered her house, to take two shillings out of her purse to pay for her newly acquired shovel.

Later that morning, she examined the church hall, where she was to start school the following day. All the desks and chairs were arranged in neat lines, facing a large blackboard. Overhead, blowflies buzzed in the heat of the day. A bell had been placed on a post near the flagpole.

As she was locking the door, a sulky pulled up, and a woman with sweet features and a dainty figure climbed down. She was dressed in a brown serge skirt and a Sunday best white cotton blouse.

A straw bonnet was tied firmly to her head. She raised her arm and waved to Sarah.

'Hold up, I've been trying to catch up with you. I'm Marge Bow. I live on the other side of the river.' Panting for breath, she climbed down from the gig. 'Would you like to come to dinner tonight?'

Sarah was delighted to have female company and quickly accepted the invitation. 'I'd love to come. How do I get there?

'My husband will pick you up, say about 5 p.m.?'

To speak to a younger woman would be quite a treat for her. As Sarah walked back towards her cottage, Charley Wong waved and crossed over the road to speak to her.

'Here, Missy.' He pushed a billy can into her hands. 'Milk for you, from Mister Tom.'

He then shuffled away before Sarah could thank him or ask him who Tom was.

Mr Bow arrived at the arranged time. He chatted to Sarah as they travelled along the river's edge and crossed between two sandbars. As they rounded a bend, the track ran near the Aborigines' camp. The black children ran beside the dray, laughing and pointing to the white lady. Sarah asked Mr Bow if they could stop for a moment. He watched Sarah as she started to talk to the children.

'Thank you for the lovely flowers that were left for me.' She watched their faces. One small boy lifted his hand up, and smiled, with the most perfect white teeth she had ever seen.

'I hope you'll visit me sometime soon, thank you again.'

As they pulled up at the Bow's homestead, Sarah suddenly longed for the food and people she had left behind. She thought of her own childhood and the mother who was always there in the doorway, with open arms and a loving smile that took away her hurt.

The Bows had two children, a boy of six and a girl of four, both a mirror image of their parents. They were timid kids, but as the supper drew to a close they became more talkative. Billy was to be in her class.

John Bow was a woodcutter. He supplied the planks for the cottages and timbers to shore up the mines. Marge, like most country wives kept house, milked the cow, and generally made the house a home for her family.

'We are so happy that you took this position, Sarah. The school board had been advertising for some months now. It is very hard to get a teacher to leave the cities. I don't blame them. Without John, I wouldn't be here either.'

Sarah liked this couple. The cottage was very clean and homely, smelling of fresh bread and lye soap, and she could feel the love that the family had for one another.

Fresh flowers had been placed on a carved mantle above the fireplace. A shotgun balanced higher up the wall out of reach of the kids. After the children had been settled into bed, the adults settled back to enjoy their coffee, which Sarah realised, was a treat for them all. Black tea was usually the order of the day.

## six

Later that night, as she sat on the side of her bed, Sarah thought of James Lowe, and wondered where his life was heading. Next morning at nine sharp she rang the school bell. Only two kids arrived, but as the day wore on more children appeared, and by lunchtime her class had reached ten. They were a mixture of kids, some wore shoes, but the majority were bare-footed. The thing they all had in common was their dislike for their previous teacher.

'He hit us, miss, and my dad hit him. He said that we were little heathens,' shouted Tommy.

'What are heathens?' asked a small girl with a clean pinny and long plaits tied with a blue ribbon that matched her dress.

'Heathens are people who do not believe in God. None of you are heathens,' laughed Sarah.

At the close of school and after the last of the children had left, Sarah walked down by the river and along the bank. As she drew level with the camp on the opposite bank, she sat and watched the old people preparing meals and the children running around the fires. By using a rope attached to a large gum, they swung over the water. Some let go, landing in the deeper running current.

The weeks went by, but not one of the Aboriginal children attended school. Sarah often received small gifts from them, though. She left a picture book by a tree and found in its place a tanned rabbit skin. The first school meeting was scheduled for Saturday. Sarah dressed carefully, choosing a dark blue serge dress with a lace collar. She pulled her hair back into a chignon. The School Council supplied a lunch to formally welcome Sarah. The president was a local landowner, with two beefy boys who, in Sarah's opinion, were kindhearted, but not very smart.

'Miss Noonan, we are so pleased that you have started here with our little school. A wagon is due from Mudgee on the first of the month. I've ordered school supplies for you, and basic food will also be on this run. By the way, we are killing a sheep on Saturday so I will drop off some fresh meat too.'

The crowd of people milling around were all introduced to Sarah. Many invited her to their homes.

Leaning against a horse-hitching rail, a tall man dressed in clean, serviceable clothes watched the young woman. His arms bulged with muscles. His large hands were calloused from hard work, and he stood proud. Tom Brian attracted women like bees to honey and the pleasure he found in them was always given freely. He watched her; it was not often a pretty woman like Sarah moved into their area. He studied her figure, from the swell of her breasts, down through the small waist, along the curve of her hips and up to the fullness of her red lips. This woman had hair the colour of the brass that he worked over his forge, and eyes that sparkled like amethysts.

Tom Brian had moved up to the Hill End district, lured there by the promise of gold. A blacksmith by trade, Tom had set up his forge when the rivers of gold eluded him.

'Good evening. I'm Sarah.'

Tom turned and looked down into the deepest violet blue eyes he had ever seen. 'I'm Tom Brian, and the pleasure is mine,' he said, smiling down at her.

Sarah blushed, something she hadn't done since she had been a girl. 'I think I have to thank you for the milk, Mr Brian.'

'Couples that share their morning tea together should be on first name basis, don't you think, Sarah?'

With cheeks the colour of peaches, Sarah turned and hurried over to a group of ladies standing in the corner. *We will certainly meet again,* he thought and, laughing to himself, strolled over to the men who were smoking and discussing the fall in wool prices.

In the following weeks, the school days ran to a routine, that is, until the mail service delivered an official sealed letter addressed to Sarah. Charley Wong delivered it to the school.

'Missy, come quick, very bad news, maybe?'

Sarah trembled as she tore away the seal and unfolded the letter.

She started to read.

*Dear Miss Noonan,*
*We, at the Governor's office, would like to invite you to the New Year's celebration. It is to be held at Government House. Your travel and accommodation will be arranged. Please let us know if you are able to attend.*
*Your servant,*
*William Masters*

'It's all right, Charley, this is good news.'

The old Chinaman watched her, and when she smiled, he must have decided that all was well. Picking up his bucket, he started off down the road, turning to wave goodbye.

'I couldn't possibly go to Sydney. I don't have anything to wear for such an occasion. Besides, Marge, all the ladies will be dressed to the nines.'

'You showed me a length of lovely silk you bought in Africa. We'll make you a dress.'

Sarah had spent a whole pound on this piece of extravagance, which had taken a chunk out of her small savings.

Marge turned out her sewing box to reach the patterns and magazines she had collected. Two other mothers, all experienced seamstresses, offered to help. Five days later, Sarah had her last fitting two hours before she climbed on to the supply wagon, next to the driver.

Three days later, the coach stopped at Parramatta. As Sarah stepped down from the coach, a smiling face greeted her. James Lowe stepped forward and took her arm, leading her to his carriage.

'James, I didn't expect you to meet me.'

'It's good to see you too,' James replied.

'Of course I'm pleased to see you again.' Sarah blushed as her eyes met James's smile.

'The Masterses are friends of mine. I'm staying there with you, Sarah. William asked me to pick you up.'

'Thank you, I hope it has not been an imposition.'

'No, Miss Noonan.'

Sarah noticed a twinkle in his eyes. Deep down, James knew that only in the colony would he be able to accompany a working-class woman even though her employment was respectable. He smiled to himself as he imagined what his family, especially his brother, would think.

James looked very handsome in his civilian clothes. Gone were the medals and sword, to be replaced with a well-cut long jacket over fitted breeches. He took her hand and guided her up the steps. She could smell his masculinity as her face came close to him.

In the carriage, Sarah told him all about her school, her little cottage, and the camp down by the river. James listened with interest and thought how this girl had blossomed in the months since he had last seen her.

Within an hour, the coach had pulled up in front of the Masters' residence. The front door flew open, and Penelope hurried down the stairs. The footman opened the coach door and helped Sarah down onto the gravel.

James made the formal introductions. But before he could finish, Penelope threw her arms around Sarah and linked their arms, leading her into the foyer.

'Sarah, I have heard so much about you from James, I feel I know you already.'

'Mrs Masters, thank you for inviting me to this celebration. I have to admit, I was a bit surprised to receive the invitation.'

'Well, to tell you the truth…' She leaned forward so that James couldn't hear. '…it was all James's idea. He thought it would be a good way for you to meet people. And besides, dear, all the people I suggested he partner he showed no interest in at all. When William enquired about you, a real spark shone in James's eyes.' Sarah blushed; she seemed to blush a lot lately.

'Come on, I'll have your case put in the room that overlooks the gardens.'

Together they climbed the steps, and arm in arm Penelope led Sarah into a room that had been painted pale lemon with cream lace-swathed curtains. A four-poster bed dominated the room. A rich yellow silk counterpane, neatly folded, lay at the foot of it. On the side table, a bunch of cream roses added to the beautiful décor. Sarah was spellbound; she had never seen such a lovely room, let alone stayed in one.

'Oh, Penelope, this is so lovely. Thank you.'

Both women lifted out Sarah's evening gown.

'Oh, this is gorgeous; I will have the maid iron it for you. Will you need help with your hair? My, I do ramble on, but I'm so thrilled to have another woman staying here. Get some rest now and I'll send the maid to you when dinner is ready. By the way, we dress informally for meals.'

Penelope closed the door behind her, leaving Sarah to absorb all their latest conversation.

The candlelight bounced off the mirrors, sending ripples of shadows down the stairs and along the hall. James and William stood at the bottom of the stairs waiting for the two women. They looked debonair in black dress suits. James wore his navy regalia and the medals shone in the dimmed light. Both men turned as Penelope started down the curved staircase. She was dressed in lavender brocade with deep frills, which accentuated her plumpness. William walked forward to meet his wife. As he leaned over to whisper something to her, a movement on the landing above caught all their attention. The vision there took James's breath away.

Sarah was dressed in a white pearl-lustre silk gown. The dress was not of a popular style, but it had been cut on a Grecian line. It seemed to fold over Sarah's slender body. Her hair had been piled up high on her head, with a few ringlets pushed around to the side. As she started down the stairs, James walked forward, extending his hand to take Sarah's gloved arm. Heat rose through her as James's eyes followed the outline of her body.

'Miss Noonan, you are a vision of beauty, and it is my honour to be your escort. May I present you with this small gift?' James could feel his passion rise as his eyes followed the outline of her body.

Sarah wasn't sure whether to accept. She looked over to Penelope, who smiled and nodded. When she opened the lacquer box, it revealed a gold chain on which a single pearl hung. James took the chain and fastened it around her neck. As Sarah lifted her face, a tear glistened on her cheek, and she felt her skin tingle as his hands brushed her neck.

Government House was abuzz with the talk of all the dignitaries. Music played throughout the rooms. In the main ballroom, the guests were being presented to the governor. The door opened and a voice announced, 'Captain Lowe and Miss Noonan.'

There was a hush and only the murmur of whispers could be heard as the couple approached the dais.

James spoke. 'Your Excellency, I would like to introduce Miss Noonan to you. She is quite new to the colony and a teacher.'

Sarah curtseyed and stepped forward. 'Thank you for inviting me, sir.'

The room quietened as they all listened to her speak. James could hear the small talk from the men at the back of the room. Where did James meet such a beautiful woman? William leaned forward and with a mischievous smile said, 'He imported her.'

'Miss, with James's permission, may I have this dance?'

James turned and shook the outstretched hand of an old friend. 'Perhaps I had better introduce you. This is Captain Poplavich, an old friend and great chess player. Although he cheats, and…'

A thick-set man, tall and dressed in black breeches with a red dress coat, took Sarah's hand, and smiled, saying, 'I am Bradic and you are lovely, my dear. James and I met at the Naval Office in London. I taught him all he knows about sailing.'

James laughed and slapped his friend on the back.

Sarah's dance card quickly filled. All the men were intrigued by her. James felt a little left out, as every time he looked for her she was twirling past in the arms of another man. As the last dance was announced, a pair of strong hands pulled Sarah onto the dance floor. Guiding her into his arms, James looked down into her eyes. *Oh God, you are lovely.* As they waltzed, he could feel the movement of her body under the dress she wore. His sexual desire was hard to control. Unlike any of the women he had known before, his need for *this* woman gripped every fibre of his body.

Sarah could sense his urgency. The room became lost to her, the people didn't exist. Her feelings of desire sent ripples deep within her soul. The chandeliers threw their soft light across the room, reflecting the rays off the polished floor. James twirled her around the room, faster and faster as the other dancers became a blur, lost in her fantasy. The smell of the daphne floated on the air through the open French windows, stirring her senses and lulling her into a hypnotic state. Then the music stopped, and she was clinging to a man who had stirred her heart.

The carriage swayed as the horses trotted along the streets. Sarah tried to stay awake to converse with James, but finally sleep overtook her. She dreamed of the music, and the gaiety. Then through the mist of her dreams, she was back in London. A tall figure in a cloak was laughing, the ring on his finger shining as he pulled her backwards onto the bed. She started to scream, the coach lurched, and her eyes flew open as the coach pulled up.

'Are we home, James?'

As she looked out of the coach window, she felt his embrace. He lowered his head and kissed her, effectively sealing any protest she might have had. Sarah arched her back and as James started to apologise, her mouth found his. Time seemed to stand still. She was aware of the coach driving away and of being lifted up and held tenderly in a strong embrace.

James carried her up the stairs and through to his bedroom. There he unlaced her bodice, allowing the skirt to fall free. As he touched her skin, her whole body vibrated with awareness and anticipation. The smell of his body aroused all her senses, and his touch lifted her to new heights. She held his head to her naked breast, her own hands moving down the smooth rippling muscles of his back. His tongue softly plucked at her rose-coloured nipples. She arched her back, waiting as he entered her gently. The slow rhythm of their movement quickly increased, turning into a frenzy of passion. She was aware of a woman murmuring somewhere in the distance and later that night, with their bodies intertwined, neither of them noticed the beads of sweat rolling off them.

He was single minded. He was captivated. He was in love. Later that night as Sarah slept, James sat up smoking. Had he gone too far with this young woman?

Sarah stirred in her sleep when the door of the bedroom closed. Instinctively, she tried to snuggle deeper into her lover's embrace, only to find him gone. Her eyes opened, trying to find him as she remembered all that had happened the night before.

Sarah had never felt such love as she had for this man. For the first time in her life, Sarah felt cherished, and was now able to block out the trauma caused by the man who had taken her virginity so cruelly that night in London.

# Chapter seven



***Sydney Cove***

James was quickly accepted into society. Balls, horse races, and gambling took up a lot of his time. The young ladies chased after him, their mothers extending invitations to lure him into their web.

With William's help, he applied for a large land grant south along the river, which divided the state of Victoria from the home colony of New South Wales. William was very helpful, insisting that he accompany James to all his meetings. An annoying thought kept lingering in James's mind. Why the devil was William so nosy?

Harold, James's manservant, had settled into their routine. He had plenty of time on his hands to explore Sydney and had taken up company with a gentle lady who owned a millinery shop. Myrtle had come out to the colony as a governess and later opened a small shop. With a keen eye for fashion and a hand that was used to sewing, her creations were eagerly bought by the ladies of the colony. Harold found it easy to deliver messages for James without being detected. No one thought twice about a servant wandering through Chinatown looking for a particular address.

James had made contact with a Chinese banker, a Mr Lo Lee. One particular day, as he had been walking down the back alleys of the dock area, James became aware that he was being tailed. At first it was only a sense of being followed, but too many years of training had taught him to trust in his gut feeling.

He reached the entrance to the bank. Two thick red doors with brass inlays blocked his way. He knocked twice. Turning, he caught a glimpse of a person drifting into the shadows and he stared, willing the individual to show their face. His focus was broken when the doors were opened by servants, who bowed and escorted James into an office, the likes of which he had never seen before.

The walls were covered with rich silk paintings. Large oriental rugs covered the polished wooden floorboards, and at the far end of the room stood an exquisitely carved desk. By an open window stood a short man dressed in traditional silk garb. He watched James as he entered the room. Mr Lo Lee walked forward with an outstretched hand, and in a clear Oxford diction spoke.

'How may I help you, Captain? Please, be seated,' he offered, pointing to a sofa opposite the desk.

'Sir, these are my letters of introduction. I have been told that in the past, you have conducted business with my government.'

James waited for a reply. The man read all the pages carefully, then retied the sealed envelope, and sat back in his chair. 'So, Captain, the mighty lion needs the dragon again.'

'Sir, the lion pays very well for your help. If you can't, or don't wish to help, I'll thank you for your hospitality and be gone.'

'Not so fast, sir, I didn't say I wouldn't help, but I'll need time, many of my people's lives are at risk. The Russians can be ruthless.'

James wondered what cat and mouse game he was involved in. He was pondering this question as he stared out the window of his returning coach. The lights on the gates loomed ahead of them as the horses swung around the large drive.

'Sarah, we have been invited to a soiree on Saturday at the Poplavich residence. It should be very agreeable. The men are sure to come later,' said Penelope.

Sarah walked over to the door. She wore a simple morning gown of apple green jaconet. Her crinoline was wide with a bustle at the back falling into folds that were trimmed with velvet ribbon. The sleeves were tight and the neckline high, which accentuated her pointed bust line.

'What do we do there, Pen?' enquired Sarah.

'There will be a recital, and afterwards a high tea. The men join us after their card game. Oh, Sarah, I wish you would reconsider your decision to go back to teaching. Any blind fool can see James is smitten with you.'

Sarah blushed. 'I know you saw us the other night, but James hasn't asked me to stay. At night we are one, but during the day I don't exist.'

'Grow up, my dear. Men don't want to get married; they have to be tricked into it.' Penelope's smile changed, and a look of cunning crept over her face. 'Don't think for one moment William would have married me without Daddy's money and position.'

Sarah was flabbergasted. Was this really how women in society acted? She looked again at the mild and meek façade of little Penelope and wondered what really lived beneath that mop of blonde curls.

Saturday was a mild, sunny day. The afternoon was full of excitement as the servants bustled around preparing the women's attire. Sarah decided to wear her recently purchased crimson silk dress with a low neckline.

'Pen, are you sure this is not too audacious for the occasion?'

'No, Sarah, the gown is lovely. You will look stunning in it. If James is not careful, someone else will sweep you off your feet.


The Russian captain's home was richly appointed. Imported carpets from the Orient and paintings from Europe made the décor quite beautiful. The women were met in the foyer and escorted to the banquet room. A string quartet played as the ladies mingled with the new arrivals in the colony.

'Do you sing, or play an instrument?' a soft voice asked, catching Sarah by surprise.

'I play rather badly, and I can't keep a tune.' Sarah laughed as she turned to see who was talking to her.

A woman of about Sarah's own age smiled at her. 'I'm Karla, the captain is my father, and he's told me all about you. Did you know that James and Father are great friends?'

Karla reached out for Sarah's hand. This pretty young woman was dressed in a modest voile evening dress, cut more for a thirteen-year-old than a woman in her first year out in society.

'I think that you are so brave travelling all by yourself. Mama won't even let me go shopping unescorted.'

Sarah liked this young girl; this could have been her, in another world, another time.

'Maybe we could go shopping together? I still have some gifts to purchase before returning to Gulgong,' she said.

'That would be lovely. Tell me, Sarah, do you really live alone among the darkies?'

'Well, we don't call them darkies, Karla,' Sarah gently chastised.

'Oh, Sarah, I did not mean any disrespect,' stammered the rather embarrassed young woman. 'I just thought that Aborigine is a rather long name.'

A large woman walked over to the piano, and clasping her hands to her bosom, started to sing. As she hit the higher notes, her bodice strained at every stitch. Glowing bright red, her cheeks puffed out, like the gulls that flew high over the cliffs during Sarah's childhood. People quickly found their seats and listened in silence to the repertoire that had been prepared for them.

Towards the end of the evening, a buffet was served, food Sarah had only dreamed about. The double doors were opened, and the men joined the ladies. Sarah felt a hand on her shoulder. Swinging around, she was surprised to see William standing there. He moved closer, touching her body with his shoulders. Even in this crowded room, his close presence with her would cause nothing but a scandal.

'William, have you seen James? I promised to eat with him.'

'He's still talking business. Wouldn't you rather eat with me?' William slipped his hand around her waist. She could feel his fingers rubbing the fabric. Jumping back and pushing his hand away, Sarah whispered to him, so as to not arouse any gossip.

'Please go and find your wife, she will be waiting for you.' She could smell the rum on his breath and see the lust in his eyes.

When he turned and walked off, Sarah felt a cold shiver pass through her. She wanted to leave the party. She wanted James. Supper was almost finished when James finally walked towards her. He looked every bit the gentleman, dressed in tight-fitting pants and a long evening coat. Gold cuff links engraved with the naval cross adorned his sleeves.

'Sorry I'm late, Sarah. My meeting with Bradic took longer than I thought.'

'I really would like to return home.' Sarah waited for his reply.

'Is there something wrong? Are you feeling ill?'

'Please, can't we just go?'

'I would like an answer to my question, Sarah.'

'I have women's trouble.'

James went to get her wrap and his coat. As she had known, no more would be said on this delicate matter.

Over the next week, Sarah completed her shopping. She bought new readers, slates, and crayons for her pupils, and took Karla on a shopping spree in Chinatown. They both enjoyed the silk shops, and drinking tea out of dainty fine china cups. Karla giggled as she opened a biscuit to find a small heart in the middle. Sarah explained to her that it represented good luck.

'Could we get our fortunes told? Mama won't let me.'

'Karla, if your parents have said no, then no it is.'

The month passed with Sarah and James enjoying each other's bodies on a number of occasions. Their lovemaking brought a reckless feeling of guilt and pleasure to their relationship. She waited for James to declare his intentions towards her. Sarah was sitting in the library, reading one of Jane Austen's romances, when James stormed in. She had let him know the day before that she was planning to return to her school.

'Sarah, I know you expect more than I can offer you now.' He sighed and took her in his arms. 'Please don't ask me to explain. Things are far too dangerous to have you involved. But I do love you very much.'

Sarah could feel her chest caving in. It was becoming hard to breathe, her eyes pooled with mist, and her only word to him was, 'Why?'

'Oh God, Sarah, please don't look at me like that. I have to leave now. I'll try to be back in two weeks.'

Turning, she walked away. He started to follow her, but stopped and dropped his arms to his sides, sighed, and watched her depart. James left early the following morning for parts unknown.

Sarah watched as Penelope flitted around the drawing room, rearranging the flowers for a dinner she and William were hosting that night. She smiled as she glanced over the placement cards, clearly quite proud of the way she had arranged them.

'Stop moping, Sarah. Two weeks will go quickly enough, and in the meantime, there are more fish in the sea.'

Penelope looked quite pretty in the dress Sarah had designed for her. The frills were gone, and replacing them were stripes running lengthways, adding height to her figure. The pale blue seersucker complemented her eyes.

'There is something I wish to speak to you about. I have had the most enjoyable time with you, but it's time for me to return to my school. I would like to leave on the coach tomorrow.'

A look of astonishment appeared on her hostess's face. 'Really, Sarah, I thought all of that was finished with. William told me that he is able to get you a position in a refined school for young ladies. So why would you go back to the riffraff?'

'I have a contract to fill.'

She couldn't tell her friend how she really felt—alone and let down by the man she loved. No, solitude was what she needed now.


In was nearly dusk, the sun was setting over the mountains in the west as James pushed his horse on. The horse he rode was only fifteen hands, small in comparison with the warm blood breeds in England. But this horse came from the mountains, fleet of foot and as fast as the wind.

Mr Lo Lee had told him of a large gold shipment that was to be smuggled out of the small coastal township of La Perouse. The sea mist swirled up and over the sand dunes as James steadied his mount to start the steep descent onto the sandbar below. He cantered along the beach, watching the sea. The stillness was deafening. He dismounted, tethered his horse and stretched out to wait. *This could well be a long night.*

The moon was full, and but for the fog that had begun to roll in, his vision was perfect. He closed his eyes for only a moment as fatigue overtook him. Suddenly, he woke to the muffled sound of voices. A long boat was being heaved ashore. High up on the cliffs, a lantern swung from side to side, and a man from the boat replied. At the far end of the sand dunes, higher up on packed ground, two wagons slowed to a stop. James could not hear what the men were saying, but he heard their Chinese accents.

The light on the cliffs was coming closer; he could now see a tall man, mounted on a large-framed horse, leading another saddled mount. James cautiously approached the boat. He knew the animal, he had raced against it, but why was it here? If only he could get closer to see who the rider was. One by one, the heavy crates were carried out into the sea and loaded onto the boat. By this time, a second boat had pulled in and a well-dressed man came ashore. Thrusting his hand out, he handed a parcel to the mounted rider.

'Good to see you again,' he said in a thick Russian accent.

The riders left, their horses slowly climbing up onto the track.

James could not hear the reply. He mounted his own horse and followed at a distance. The two riders were heading for Sydney. James entered the town at dawn, seeing the horses tethered at the back of a small tavern near the dock. Entering by a side door, James moved from room to room, listening for any voices he might know. He was about to leave, when suddenly from a room above the staircase, he heard, 'I warned you, Polick, that this was the last shipment I would be involved with. They have sent an investigator, and it is far too close for my liking.'

James staggered backwards, the realisation of what he heard sucking the air from his lungs. William owned the horse he had followed, and now it was William's voice coming from behind the closed door.

'Sir. Don't think you can walk away now. The Russians have paid you a lot of money for your help, and you will repay your debt.'

James crept forward, finding the door ajar. He peered through the crack and watched William sink down onto a chair, his head in his hands.

'I will give it back.'

'What will you give back? The money lost in gambling to the Chinese, or the money you spend in the whore house each week? Don't you think we have made it our business to know all about you? Your family would disown you if we made all of this public knowledge. Your father-in-law will chase you out of the colony to wait a rope in Mother England. No, you will carry on stamping the land grants to the Chinese miners, they in turn sign them over to us, and we sponsor them out to Australia. They keep all their gold, and we help them get it back to Shanghai without paying any taxes.'

The door opened wider, and James backed into the scullery as William rushed down the stairs and onto the street. James managed to slip out unnoticed. Later that morning, he burst through the door into Mr Lo Lee's private apartment. The old man turned around to face him.

'I've been waiting for you, James.'

'Why didn't you warn me?' He shouted the words, more to ease his own pain than to make a statement.

'Would you have listened to me? I don't think so. Often the

hardest secrets have to be found out by one's own hand.' The old Chinese statesman observed the hurt that lined James's face.

'Sit down, listen to me. This man, William, is like your brother, but you do not know him. He owes large sums of money all over Chinatown. I have his promissory note for two thousand pounds. Gambling, women. If it was not for his wife's father, I would have dealt with him myself. But who wants to upset the governor?'

James raised his head slowly and looked at the Chinaman, asking, 'Mr Lo Lee, is Bradic Poplavich involved too?'

'I don't think so. It would be unwise for the Russian captain to have anything to do with this. They are using him like a puppet, all pulling the strings. Let it go, James. Go back to England, re-join your ship; these people only bring death.'

# Chapter eight

Later that night, back at the Rustic Arms, James sat alone in the corner, a half-empty bottle of whisky on the table in front of him. There was only one decision he could make. He would have to confront William.

James rose early the next morning. He walked to the stable and was confronted by a small lad, eager to saddle his horse.

'I took good care of him, Mister. Got nice eyes, ain't he?'

James smiled at the boy. 'A good job deserves a reward,' he said and tossed a silver coin to him.

The boy scooped it up. 'Thanks, I'll look after him anytime. My name is Harry, I live in the loft. Just ask for me.'

James didn't notice the countryside as he let his mount have its head. Carts, people and drays being pulled by teams of bullocks passed him. He stopped at Ruse Hill to allow the horse to rest, and settled himself at the counter of the small pub, waiting for the barmaid to take his order. A pretty girl made her way over to him. Her curly blonde hair was pulled up under a mop cap, and over her plain woollen dress she wore a clean linen apron. James couldn't help but think that she looked out of place behind the bar.

'What do you want, ducky? We have beef and lamb. Better have the lamb, the beef is a week old.'

'Thanks, the lamb it is then and a pint of your best too.'

An hour later, he was on the road again. How would he approach William? And there was Sarah to consider? The horse quickened its pace as it got closer to its home. James could now see the homestead through the trees that lined the avenue.

It was raining, and the wind howled through the elms as he

turned into the row of stables to the left of the main building and dismounted. A stable boy led his horse away and James walked slowly towards the house. The door opened as he approached, Penelope looking out curiously at him.

'James, I thought it was William. You didn't pass him, did you? Oh, I'm forgetting my manners, welcome back.'

James brushed the mud from his breeches before walking in and embracing her. 'No, I haven't seen him. Is Sarah around?'

Penelope took James's arm and led him into the study. 'Didn't she tell you, dear? She has returned to that godforsaken place. I expect she was a little miffed with you for not telling her where you were going.'

'I couldn't tell her; it was a business meeting. She was not involved.'

'I know, I tried to tell her that men do not involve ladies in that type of thing, but she said something about a contract. Rubbish if you ask me. I told her William could get her better employment anyway. Mark my word, she will be back, but that's enough about that, come and have some refreshments...'

James blocked out the chatter of his hostess. All he could think about was what his revelation would do to William's family. And then there was Sarah. Why hadn't he made his declaration of love to her and his plan to make her his wife? The sound of the maid entering the room returned his thoughts to the present moment.

'Like I was saying, all that business only gives me a headache. William doesn't worry me with it.'

The evening dragged on. They had dinner together and later played a hand of cards.

'Excuse me, I think I'll go for a stroll. Don't wait up for me,' he said, and leaning forward he kissed her cheek and said goodnight.

James stood by the stockyards, his mind reliving the past few days. Earlier in the week, he had been asked to attend the Lands Office in Martin Place. There he had met with George Curlewis, a crown solicitor, who had granted him a lease in perpetuity. The land title was for three thousand acres along the Murray River, stretching below the town of Albury to the punt crossing further downstream at the junction of the Broken River.

James had made provision in his will, that on his untimely death, the land along with a small annuity would be transferred to a Miss

Sarah Noonan. He knew that his brother would not acknowledge Sarah until they were legally married. Why could she not have waited until he returned? Oh well, he would put it all right when he went up to fetch her back.

William was not home yet. 'Blast him, where in the hell is he?'

Lying in a ditch, his face covered by water, William lay dead. A shot through the back of the head had spilled his brains out onto the bank. A murder of crows gathered to feast on the corpse.

A horse galloped into the holding yard, the reins wrapped around its leg. James tried to calm the beast and as he steadily placed his hand on the bridle, he saw the dried blood.

'Boy, help me,' he shouted to a lad working in the stable. 'Quickly, go and get all the men.'

The men searched the road and banks for several hours. The crows lifted into the air as the horses approached them.

'There, boss, over there in the water,' yelled Billy, the tracker.

James leapt off his horse and waded into the water. As he turned the body over, cold terror engulfed him. They pulled William to the bank and covered him with the spare blanket.

'Go for the law, Billy, and tell them to come quick. We will meet them at the homestead. Ride straight there.'

Penelope was inconsolable. The housekeeper put her to bed and her father was sent for.

'Who will take care of the poor mite? And what about the babe, who is to look after it?' wailed the housekeeper. 'I can't possibly look after it and do all my chores, it's all too much.'

'I'll see that extra is added to your wages, Mrs Murphy.'

James's face was stony. The woman re-thought the situation and spoke more quietly. 'That won't be necessary, sir. It is such a shock to us all, but the maids and I will manage for now.'

William had been laid out in the parlour. The doctor had finished examining him and later entered the study to talk to James.

'This is a sorry business, Mr Lowe. My God, the son-in-law of the governor being killed this way. Has the constable been sent for?'

'Yes, he has.' James poured out two stiff drinks.

'Here, take this, Doctor.' After handing over the glass, James slumped back into a chair. His body was exhausted, but his mind would not stop. Thoughts plagued him. Who and why?

'You had better wash up, and eat something before you collapse. I have another patient, but I will wait with Mrs Masters until someone arrives.'

'Please get me as soon as anyone arrives, Doctor.'

### Parramatta, Sydney

William was laid to rest in the church yard at Parramatta. James worked with Penelope's father to arrange for a manager and his family to move onto the property to run it.

'Pen, I really do think your father is right. You would be far better off living in Sydney. Try to start your life again, if not for you, then for your baby. Did I tell you I received a letter from Sarah? She has resigned but will have to wait on until her replacement arrives. She seemed a bit mysterious, the way her letter read.'

'James, you will lose her if you don't make your true feelings known.'

'Don't you think I know that?'

'Well, what is your concern? Do you want to go back to sea?'

James could see the annoyance in the young widow's face. He realised she wanted Sarah back, close to her, to be her confidant and friend. James hated to see the woman still so distressed, but deep down he realised it was a blessing. William had taken the shame and guilt to his grave, and James would never have to tell any of the sordid stories. Harold, James's manservant, was waiting for him, as he strolled into the main bar of the Cock and Crown.

'It's so good to see you, sir.'

James's eyes lit up as he spotted Harold sitting at a back table. 'Thank God you're here, Harold.'

James needed his friend, the one person in this godforsaken country he could trust. Slapping him on the back, James turned to the bartender. 'Two of your finest, thanks, mate.'

Harold watched the younger man. Sometimes a boy still lurked in the dashing sea captain, whom he had guided and loved, since James was placed into his care as a young man.

'I heard about William, James. God works in mysterious ways, doesn't he? Can we finally go home now, sir?'

'I wish we could, but there is more I need to find out. I didn't tell you, Sarah is coming to Sydney to stay. Harold, I am hoping we might all go home together.'

'Oh, sir, that would be grand news. Your mother would welcome a daughter.'

'But not my brother.' James frowned, as he thought of the unpleasant reception they would receive from his pompous, overbearing older brother.

'Please don't let that worry you; we will both be there to protect her.'

James had never felt more gratitude than he did for his friend at that moment.


Life returned to normal. Penelope returned to her parents in Sydney, and James returned to playing the rich, 'retired' sea captain.

He was lying in bed waiting for Harold to return from the early markets, when a soft knock at the door made him stir. As he opened it, a small boy, dressed in coolie garb of plain cotton, handed him a sealed envelope.

'Please wait, I may need to reply.'

As James read the beautifully embossed invitation, a look of seething anger crept onto his face. His once-gleaming eyes became as hard as steel.

'How dare the bastards,' he muttered to himself before turning to face the lad. 'Thank your master; I will come at the required time.' The boy bowed to James and left.

*So the plot thickens*, thought James as he dressed quickly to leave. On the stairway, he passed Harold, coming in from his early stroll to the market with their breakfast supplies.

'Give me a moment, I will come with you.'

'No, I'll be safe.'

'Then at least take a pistol with you.'

As soon as he entered the kitchen, Harold dumped the produce on a table and, placing a small derringer in his waistcoat, hurried after James. By the time he had reached Chinatown, James had disappeared. Harold stopped to ask the shop keepers if they had spotted him. The Chinese stall keepers, who usually had a conversation with Harold as he bought the daily provisions, suddenly couldn't understand English, and crept back into the shadows of their stalls. Windows shut, and children were pulled off the streets as he went by.

Fear suddenly engulfed Harold. He started to run. Every alley turned into a dead end. He shoved past the carts; chickens flew out of his way and piles of oranges fell into the gutters as he pushed forward. He didn't even smell the usual stench as he ran on.

Later that evening, Harold returned to the residence. James was not back. All night he walked the floor. *What to do, what to do?* At daybreak, Harold bashed on the doors of the governor's residence.

'Out of my way, I must see the governor.' Harold pushed past the butler and barged straight into the living quarters of the family.

'What in the hell is all that noise about?' A tall, distinguished man dressed in a morning robe entered the living room. 'Harold, what on earth's wrong.'

The governor had met Harold at the burial of his son-in-law, William.

'Sir, Master James has not returned home from a meeting early yesterday morning. This is not like him not to let me know. I fear the worst.'

'Sit down and tell me all about it. You know, Harold, he might be just visiting a young lady. We are both men of the world…'

Just then Penelope burst into the room. Her night coat flew open, revealing a pretty lawn nightgown underneath. Masses of curls toppled down onto her face, and with a flick of her hand she pushed them aside.

'What's wrong, Harold, where is James?'

'Calm yourself, Penelope, as I was just saying to Harold, a lady might have delayed him.'

'Rubbish, Father, he has eyes only for Sarah.'

A hush settled over the three of them. Harold sat back into the large leather chair. His mind raced. Should he tell William's secret? James had instructed him to never mention it, whatever happened in the future. The governor sensed Harold's hesitation to speak.

'Penelope dear, perhaps you could inform the cook that there will be one more for breakfast. Harold and I will be in the study until then, please see that we are not disturbed.' He drew Harold into his study.

'Please close the door behind you and sit over here, by my desk. I know it's early, but I have the feeling I'm going to need a drink.' He pulled a bottle out of the bottom of his desk and poured two brandies, replacing the bottle in the locked drawer. 'I don't use the decanter much, as my dear wife thinks drink interferes with my health.'

Harold stood to take the glass. His hand trembled and his legs shook. Despair was written all over his face.

'What is it that you are not telling me, Harold?'

The governor had always been able to sum up situations; good or bad.

'Sir, there are terrible things afoot.'

'Come on, man, out with it.'

'Well, it started in England…'

By the time Harold had finished the whole sordid story, Sir Charles Fitzroy, Governor of New South Wales, sat there white faced, rage seething from him. 'Does my daughter know any of this?'

'No, I was instructed to take it to my grave. But now I fear for Master James. Please excuse me for telling you, but I have nowhere else to go.'

'You did the right thing, man.'

Later that morning, the military guard was called out. The town of Sydney was searched. The dwellings on the waterfront were turned inside out. Ships in the harbour were boarded.

There was no sign of James.


'Mr Lo Lee, thank you for coming. You are now aware of our concern for the welfare of Mr Lowe? Can you tell us anything that might help locate him?'

The elderly Chinaman stood quietly waiting. His appearance, as always, was immaculate. Dressed in western clothes, he stood out within his own community. The game had started, and the dragon's face was as serene as usual.

'My people tell me that he is missing. But why do you ask *me* about his disappearance? Surely, your own people would know better than I.'

The governor ignored the innuendo, saying, 'Would you like tea or coffee, Mr Lee?'

'Tea would be most enjoyable.'

The two men sat, each playing out their next move.

'Mr Lee, I have been aware for some time of your people's

involvement in the smuggling of gold out of Australia. Until now, I have chosen to turn a blind eye.' After handing the cup and saucer to his guest, he stood, and with his hands crossed at his back, walked over to the window and looked out over the harbour.

'How lucky we are, to enjoy all that this country has to offer.'

The Chinaman's face changed, the smile became a look of hatred, and his eyes stared at the white man.

'I am sure you are aware that with the death of my son-in-law, many things will change. The power that you exercise now could change at any time, Mr Lee.'

'Thank you, Your Excellency; you are as gracious as ever.' With that, Mr Lee stood, bowed and left the room.

'I want him followed.' Sir Charles Fitzroy spoke to the sergeant of the guard waiting in the next room. He felt that this might be their only chance of tracking down the whereabouts of James.

# Chapter nine



James was unaware of the clammy bodies as he pushed through the crowded alleys. Every child in Chinatown seemed to be in his way. He could smell the highly spiced aromas, and his eyes smarted as the peppers burnt into them. The note he had read warned him not to be followed, to stand by the tavern and wait. Someone would meet him and guide him the rest of the way.

To where? And why the urgency? The note stated that many of his questions would be answered. His mind pondered these questions as he waited outside the small tavern close to the dock area. James felt a tug on his sleeve and looking around he noticed a small girl dressed in Chinese trousers and long coat. She smiled at him, and stepped forward.

'You come, sir, follow me. Come quick.'

With that she turned and disappeared into the crowd. James struggled to keep up as she weaved in and out of the crowd. They left the main shopping area and continued down the back alleys. As he turned the next corner, he saw her waiting by an open door.

'In here, quick.'

The heavy wooden door lined with metal banged shut behind him. He followed her down a dark corridor. At the end was a smaller, more elaborately carved double door. The girl spoke quietly into a grille; a voice replied in Chinese and the doors opened. Before him sat one of the most beautiful women he had ever gazed upon. Her eyes were a perfect almond shape. The small body was exquisitely draped in silk, her long black hair shone as though a thousand lights glistened through it. The small girl bowed and waited to be dismissed.

'Leave us, girl, and close the door behind you. Come forward, Mr Lowe. I'm sure you must have a lot of questions. But first let me introduce myself. I am Sue Lo Lee, daughter of your illustrious friend.'

The woman spoke in English. He watched the way her hands moved in perfect unison as she stretched them towards him.

'How do you do, Miss Lee, but why all this mystery?'

'First of all, my father could not come, he is being watched. So I am here to help you.'

'Why do I need help? And in God's name, who is trying to hurt me?'

'Mr Lowe, my father has been told of a threat against your life. This is most serious. It would be in your best interest to stay here for now.'

'You must know who made this threat.' James was becoming angry and frustrated. Why would they think he needed to be watched like a child? 'I can look after myself. I will not stay here like a rabbit curled up in a burrow.'

Beads of sweat trickled down his forehead; pure frustration welled up inside him, burning his gut.

'My father is not sure of all the facts… please stay…'

The words disappeared as James re-entered the street. He walked back towards the boarding house where he was staying with Harold. Just as he was entering the main street, a carriage pulled up beside him.

'James, I've been looking for you, I've had word from Sarah.' The carriage door opened, and Penelope's hand beckoned him to enter. 'Quickly, I've something to show you.'

James swung up into the coach. 'What is it, Pen? Is anything amiss?

'You had better see it yourself, we won't be long, we're nearly there.'

The horses and driver pushed through the bustling street. At the end of Market Street, they changed direction and slowly headed out of town. The scenery was familiar to James, but it was not until the sand dunes came into sight, that the memory of that night flashed in front of him—when he lay there, observing the strange ship and the loading of the gold bullion.

'What is going on, Pen? For God's sake just tell me!'

'All I know is that a farmhand came to see me. He told me that Sarah was sailing back to England, and that she wanted you to meet her onboard the *Oriental Princess* today.'

Just then they reached the crest of the sand dunes, and they both could see the tall ship lying at anchor in the harbour.

'James, would you mind if I come aboard too?'

Penelope's voice was sincere. He knew how much she missed Sarah. They both walked towards the small lifeboat waiting to take them aboard. James lifted Pen up into his arms and carried her out into the surf, placing her into the boat. The sea was rough, and the waves lashed the larger vessel as the men hauled the woman aboard. Close behind her, James fought the wind as he pulled himself up the rope ladder on to the deck.

'Sir, step this way.'

A short, dirty-looking crewman ushered them to the hatch that led below. Only one small lamp was lit, casting shadows along a narrow galley way. James felt a bit hesitant. 'Shouldn't we be staying above deck, mate?'

'Don't argue, James, just follow the man. He knows what he is doing,' said Penelope, pushing him forward.

They went down the stairway and along the narrow, dimly lit passage, through a row of boxes that had been stored there obviously in a hurry, and over a few that had already fallen over. James cursed to himself as he felt for the pistol that wasn't there. A door opened into a small cabin. There was a table, two chairs, and a tray on which had been placed a decanter of spirits, and a jug of what appeared to be brandy.

'The lady said to help yourself, sir.'

With that, the little man backed out of the tiny cabin and left them alone. Pen leaned forward and lifted the decanter to pour James a drink.

'Don't bother, I don't want one.'

'James, where are your manners? I am having one.' With that she continued to pour their drinks.

'Where in the hell is she?' he murmured in a low voice as he glanced over to Penelope.

'Patience. They must have gone to inform her that we've arrived.'

Penelope watched as James lifted the drink to his mouth, but hesitated and replaced it on the table. A minute later he picked up the glass and drank the brandy.

'Did you like Daddy's best brandy?'

Penelope's voice was fading, the room started to move, spinning faster and faster. Daddy's brandy? What in the hell was this? He tried to get up; his legs and arms wouldn't move.

Penelope sat and watched him. 'I really am so sorry. But I could not let you find out about *my* money. My husband was so silly. Did you know he was going to go to my father and tell him everything, all about the gold we had shipped to England? I had to have him killed. You understand, don't you? You won't suffer; and I will look after Sarah.'

James's mind didn't have time to grasp what she was saying. The light disappeared and then there was emptiness. The poison she had placed in the brandy had done its diabolical work.

Three days later, James's body washed ashore. Children fishing with their father made the grisly discovery.


'No, don't send word to Sarah, I will go myself.' That seemed the least Harold could do for his master. Walking down the steps of a small solicitor's office in Pitt Street, Harold carried with him the details of James's will.

For three days, Harold stared out the window of the coach. The dust and flies and the constant chattering could not interrupt his thoughts. How was he to tell the girl this news, which would break her heart?

Sarah watched from the school room as a dray came into town. She hardly recognised the tall English gentleman sitting up beside the driver. Harold carried the results of a dust storm they had run into twenty miles out. After asking directions from the driver, he walked over to the small hall where she taught.

She had already dismissed her students for the day, and was cleaning up when Harold walked in. Throwing her arms around him, and looking over his shoulder, she asked, 'Where is James, is he still coming?'

Letting her go, Harold took a step back. 'My dear, you must prepare yourself. I have grave news to tell you.' The silence was deafening. 'James is dead.'

The room went black as Sarah slipped towards the ground.

Scooping her into his arms, Harold held her tenderly. He watched the blood drain from her face. Harold would remember forever the blood-curdling scream that came from Sarah. Later that evening after her sobbing stopped, he was able to go into more depth.

'How did it happen?'

'We don't really know.'

Harold wondered if he should tell her the truth, and decided that for her sake and protection, she had better know everything. They sat down in her small living room, and he made her a cup of tea with a dash of brandy.

'I've told you all I know. I think the people who murdered James might believe that you and I have information about what James was investigating.'

'That's preposterous, James never confided in me at all, Harold.'

'Unfortunately, dear, they don't know that.'

That night, as they sat around the table, Harold produced an envelope and handed it to the distressed woman.

'James added a codicil to his will, and you have been mentioned in it.' Sarah slowly opened the envelope and withdrew the documents inside. As she started to read, tears welled up in her eyes and blinded her.

'I can't read this. Please help me.'

Harold cleared his throat and started to read, 'I, James Lowe, make the following changes to my last Will and Testament. I bequeath the following to a Miss Sarah Noonan; Two Thousand Pounds to be given to her over a period of two years; and the land title in Australia; and all my salary owing to me.'

Sarah blinked. 'Why did he do this for me?'

'He loved you very much, my dear, and he was coming to get you; to marry you.' Sarah stared at him, and the sadness in those beautiful eyes reached deep into his soul. 'Try to get some sleep now and we will talk about it in the morning.'

Harold watched Sarah close her bedroom door behind her and then settled back in an armchair to reflect over the last few weeks. He thought back over the questions that had been put to the Chinese, and the sorrow that had filled the face of the Russian Captain, Bradic Poplavich, when he had been told. What devil had done this to his young master? This thought tormented him day and night.

A loud banging on the front door woke Harold. A cheeky smile from a small Aboriginal lad greeted him.

'Where's the missus? Aunty wants to see her.'

'I will tell Miss Noonan when she gets up. What is your name?'

'Sam, mister, they call me Sam.'

'Well, Sam, thank your aunty.'

'She ain't me real aunty, all the oldies are Aunty.'

Harold didn't get the point of the conversation, but he would ask Sarah later. After breakfast they sat down to go over the will.

'Harold, what am I going to do with the land grant?'

'I have been enquiring on your behalf with the land council, if you can sell it. Unfortunately, you can't dispose of it, or even trade it. So I think the best thing is to sign it back. Sarah, you have two thousand pounds that would buy you a house and keep you in comfort. We will all be there to help you, my dear.'

Grasping Harold's hands, she held them tightly and sighing, said, 'I need time to think, to consider what would be the best thing for both of us.'

The whole district heard of Sarah's plight. People from far and near came to give their condolences. The ladies supplied an endless array of cooked dishes for her larder. Her pupils picked a large bunch of wildflowers, tying it up with one of Jenny Murphy's best hair ribbons, much to the annoyance of Jenny's mother.

Harold stayed with her for a week. He didn't push the girl for any answers. He knew that they would come in their own time. Harold had been made executor of all James's legal affairs. Word had been sent to his parents in England on the fastest clipper leaving Sydney. The land he owned in England, along with his inheritance, would revert to his older brother. Harold had made it very clear, that the codicil had been legally witnessed, should James's greedy brother decide he wanted it all. He would do everything in his power to protect this girl, the love of his master's life.

On his return to Sydney, he contacted the Guard, to see if they had made any progress in their investigations into James's death.

'I wish that I could be more helpful, Harold, but all our leads have turned up blanks. The Medical General believes James was poisoned, causing paralysis; maybe some oriental substance could have been used? But we can't link it to anyone.'

Harold thanked the officer and walked out of the large sandstone building. He strolled across the newly planted gardens down to the waterfront. Sitting on the harbour foreshore and watching the boats sail in, Harold reconstructed their life together. As a hardened soldier, he had faced death many times, burying many of his company on the plains of India. But this was James, his friend and the closest thing he would have to a son. Why hadn't he listened and taken a pistol that day? Why hadn't James waited for him?

A man blocked his view. He looked into the face of Mr Lo Lee.

'Mr Harold, sir. May I have some of your most valuable time?'

'Of course, Mr Lo Lee, here, sit beside me.'

For a while neither of the men spoke. The air was still, enhancing the smell of sea salt, as the waves licked up onto the rocks. The seagulls scavenging near their legs looked for morsels thrown down by passers-by.

'I cared for the boy, too, Mr Harold. I warned him not to trust anyone. I had the ways to protect him, but he would not listen. The last thing I can do for him is to give you this information.'

Harold appraised this oriental lord. He was obviously wealthy and controlled all the Chinese merchants.

'I know what you must be thinking, but you are wrong. The gold you are seeking has already been divided, half to China and the other half left on a fast clipper to your country.'

Harold thought before he replied, 'Mr Lee, I can understand you telling me about the thief going to England, but why, for God's sake are you telling me about your own country?'

'Have you heard of the rebels in my country, known as the Righteous and Harmonious Fists or better known by the Westerners as the Boxers?'

'Only vaguely, aren't they a group of religious fanatics?'

'The gold is to support their cause, to overthrow our Empress of the Ch'ing Dynasty. The Russians are fools; they are of no importance now. The person we need to stop is much smarter than that.'

They both sat in silence, each with his thoughts. Quietly, the Chinaman left, leaving Harold to absorb what he had been told.

# Chapter ten

The waves washed over the deck. The storm had been blowing for more than three days. The bow of the ship creaked as its master fought to gain control over the elements.

Penelope had not left her cabin in a week. Why had she let her father persuade her to return to England? At the time it seemed a way of escaping her mundane life, controlled and under the watchful and snooping eye of her parents. A servant was accompanying her to care for her little girl, barely out of arms.

Penelope loved her little daughter, Lucy. She was the only decent thing William had given her, besides the gold. She sat at a small desk in the cabin thinking of Sarah. When she returned, maybe she would have Sarah live with her, be like a sister. *Yes*, she thought, *Sarah was far better off without James.* She laughed to herself in a high shrill tone, which sent shivers down the spine of the young servant, who was trying to calm the fretful child in the next room.

Amy had been employed by Penelope's mother, when it had become apparent that her daughter was not managing. The death of James had seemed the last straw for her daughter, and she worried about Penelope's sanity. Both parents hoped that the sea trip, along with the care from London's specialists, would help their child get over her grief.

Amy was very capable. She came from a family of free settlers who had taken up a small land grant near Windsor. When the opportunity for her to travel to England was presented to her father, he was against it, as his memories of the old country were different from those of his daughter. But with the constant nagging of his wife, he finally gave in.

Amy loved her little charge and waited on her hand and foot. When the weather was fine, she took the baby up on deck for an airing. She smiled with pride as the crew remarked on the child's beauty.

'She's a little cutie, miss. Is her mother poorly? She never comes up on deck or attends meals.'

The captain smiled at the antics of the child. 'Please give Mrs Masters my regards.'

'I shall relay your message to her and thank you.' Amy strolled past the captain. How could she tell him, that she too, was quite nervous when around her mistress and tried to stay away from her as much as possible?

The captain was very concerned about all his passengers, especially the young widow. He had been given reports by other passengers about her odd behaviour. But trusted that her father, the governor, knew what was best for the girl.

The storm was now raging. Water overflowed the hatches and ran down the stairs. Amy wrapped the child in double blankets and held her securely in her arms. As she started to sing to the fretful child, the ship lurched forward, and then rolled to starboard. A voice from above shouted, 'Man the lifeboats, leave all your possessions and dress in warm coats. Quickly, we don't have much time, the ship is breaking up.'

Terrified passengers scrambled to climb the stairs. Amy called out to Penelope, 'Mrs Masters, we must hurry.'

'Take the child up now. I will follow soon.'

Amy held the child close to her breast and stepped back, just missing the door as Penelope slammed it shut. Turning, Amy ran to the stairs and with all her might, pulled herself and the baby up the rail and pushed past the mass of people trying to reach the small boats.

Penelope hurried and tied small calico bags filled with gold coins to her waist. She placed jewellery into the lining of her overcoat that she intended to exchange for more bullion.

'Hurry, Mrs Masters, we need to launch the boats,' yelled a deck hand from above.

By the time she had mastered the stairs, all the boats had been lowered into the sea. She could see Amy and her baby in the first boat, which was pulling away from the stricken ship.

'Madam, jump now, the men will try to catch you,' screamed the captain.

Penelope hesitated; she felt hands pushing her over the rail. Spray from the sea hit her face first as she plunged into the deep foaming cold water. The men on the lifeboat waited for her to resurface. They plunged their arms down into the water trying to reach her.

Down, down she sank; she struggled to no avail. The light faded as the water entered her lungs and fingers of seaweed wrapped around her. The struggling stopped, and she sank gently to the sea floor.

The following day, the storm stopped. Warm winds helped to dry out the people who had survived. Amy tried to comfort the child and finally, in a state of sheer exhaustion, the baby fell asleep. A clipper heading to China out of Sydney picked up the survivors. Out of ninety-four passengers, only twenty-one plus a baby arrived in Shanghai. Amy went to see British trade officials, and with their help continued on to London with Lucy.

The skies were grey when the ship docked in Portsmouth. Amy had been given money and an address to go to, and had been instructed to wait there until she was contacted. After taking the coach up to London, Amy booked into a well-run boarding house and settled down to wait.

The owners were two old maids, genteel in their upbringing. They offered an establishment for single ladies of suitable refinement. The first week was very pleasant; Amy had borrowed a perambulator and strolled through the city gardens, admiring the flowers and the large expanse of grass. On the night of the fifth day, a telegram arrived for her. She was to take the child to Manchester, where she would be met on the eve of Sunday.

Amy was still in a state of shock and wondered what would await them in Manchester. It was a long trip for both Amy and Lucy, as the poor child was restless and would not settle. Other passengers held the child to give Amy a rest. They passed by neat little farms and villages as the train rattled on. Oh, how different they were from the vast dry plains of Australia.

The air was thick with smoke as she stepped down onto the

platform. At the other end of the station, standing to the back of the crowd, an elderly couple stared into the faces of the passing passengers. Suddenly, the woman stood up and walked towards Amy.

'Miss, are you a Miss Amy?' The older woman looked longingly towards the young girl.

'Yes, madam.'

With that, the plump, gentle-faced lady threw her arm around the girl. 'Come. George, they have arrived.'

With that the man struggled to his feet and shuffled towards his wife. Mrs Masters took the sleeping child into her arms, and gently kissed her grandchild.

'Amy, we have arranged for you to work in the main house, if that is your wish and you can stay with us.'

It was only a short trip by coach to the Lowe's estate. On the way there, Mrs Masters told Amy how William and James had been great friends, and how Lord Lowe had sponsored the education of her son. The footman lowered the steps and helped them down.

The manager's cottage was painted white, with green ivy climbing up the front walls. There was a cottage garden with a circular path laid down in stone, leading to the front door. Over to the side, a large stone barn blocked out the sun and looked quite menacing to the young girl.

'Welcome to our home, Amy. It is now your home, dear. Yours and little Lucy's.'

Amy settled Lucy into her cot and walked into the small kitchen.

'Sit down, dear, tea is ready. Come along, George, don't keep the lass waiting.'

As they were sitting in front of a small fire, Amy produced the documents given to her regarding their future. George read them carefully and turned to his wife. 'Well, dear, it seems that Penelope's parents are giving up their post in Australia at the end of the year. They have asked if the child could stay with us until they arrive back in London and they have also asked Amy to stay on and help you with the child's care.'

'Mr and Mrs Masters, I love your granddaughter, and it would break my heart to leave her.'

'Well then, dear, it's settled.'

Amy soon came to respect the older couple. They treated her like a daughter. Mr Masters was well respected by the farm hands and villagers alike. He only supervised the workers now, seeing that the estate ran properly. Mrs Masters worked on the church committees, taking hampers to the sick and elderly. When the weather was fine, they pushed the pram into the village. The locals loved to see the baby and her doting grandparents.

'She certainly has her father's eyes and look at those lovely curls,' exclaimed the local gentry.

Indeed, Lucy was a beautiful child, with a disposition to match.

Lucy looked up at Amy with all the love that a baby has for its mother. The governor had been delayed in Australia, so Amy settled into a routine of work and playing with Lucy.

# Chapter eleven

***Sydney***

Sarah's head drooped and her eyes closed as the coach moved closer towards Sydney. The memories of Harold's visit and the confirmation that old Munu had given her as they sat on the dried-up riverbank, made the decision she had to make somewhat easier. Sarah opened her eyes and looked out. The countryside was becoming more familiar. She dropped her hand down to her stomach to feel the small life that was growing inside her, that precious life that had been entrusted to her alone. Closing her eyes again, she recalled the words of Munu.

'Listen to old Munu, Missy. You are junta, baby come when the cold winds blow. You have no man, you stay here, and we look after you.'

Pregnant! That was all Sarah heard. Three days before, Sarah had visited the camp on the river and spoke to Munu, an aunty and elder of the local tribe and keeper of the women's business, about her sickness and fainting spells. Sarah had realised her monthly flow had stopped, but surely that was due to shock.

Munu embraced the young woman. Her understanding of English was not that good, but she knew that not having a fella would make the girl ostracised in the white community. This girl had no mum, no aunty. The white women would treat her as they treated the black gins. No respect: no, better she come with them. They both sat under the shade of a large eucalypt. Everywhere was still, the ants filed past carrying the last of the bread she had thrown out to the birds. The flies were troublesome. An occasional splash could be heard as a fish jumped out of the stagnant pond that had once been the mighty Lachlan River.

'Munu, I have to go to Sydney, but I will be back in two weeks to say goodbye.'

Munu knew that it was not goodbye, that Sarah would come back.

'We are on time, miss, Sydney in thirty minutes,' the driver called to his passenger. The rest of the folk had departed at Parramatta, a small farming settlement that now had a police garrison due to the number of people passing over the mountains in their search for gold. Small Chinese market gardens had sprung up along the route. Sarah watched the women labouring in the fields, their babies tied to their backs. This only strengthened her own belief; that her child was going to be looked up to in society, no matter what it cost her.

'Come in, my dear, you must be exhausted after such a long trip.' Governor Fitzroy had not been surprised to receive a note asking for an appointment. 'Please sit, I've rung for tea. Or would you prefer coffee?'

Sarah looked around the spacious, well-appointed room with its leather lounges and fine drapes. A large bookshelf occupied the entire northern wall. It reminded her of the earl's study back in her home estate. Over the fireplace hung the coat of arms for New South Wales, mounted on a piece of polished mallee root. There was a rustle of taffeta and as Sarah turned her head, a pretty but dignified woman entered the room.

'Sarah, do you remember my wife, Lady Fitzroy?' Sir Charles Fitzroy felt that a woman's presence would put the young lady at ease. He knew that Sarah would be looking for answers he couldn't give.

Gliding forward, Lady Fitzroy embraced Sarah. She oozed refinement. Her greying hair was swept up in the latest style. She was in mourning and would remain in black for one year. This made Sarah aware of her own gown, a dove grey. Perhaps she should have worn black?

'Come, my dear, we know of your terrible loss. How can we help you?' the older woman enquired.

'Sir, Madam, I certainly have a terrible problem, or God's blessing. I find that I'm with child, James's baby. He died before I knew myself.'

'Sarah, I would advise you to marry as soon as possible. There are many suitable men looking for a wife in the colony. I can introduce you to one or two.'

Lady Fitzroy gasped, and looked sternly towards her husband. 'Oh, Sarah, this is wonderful news. You are welcome to stay with us. My husband and I have to remain here for seven more months.'

Sir Charles Fitzroy watched his wife. He knew her burning desire to love, and her need to mother this child. The death of Penelope had left her numb, and for the first time in weeks, he saw a spark of life return to his wife's eyes. The older woman placed her arms around Sarah's shoulders and for a minute a calmness filled the room, allowing only the sweet perfume of the freshly cut lilacs to linger in the air.

'Have you discovered who killed James?'

The governor breathed deeply and looked into Sarah's pleading eyes, replying, 'No, dear, but we do believe that foreign agents were involved. We have to be very careful, and step forward with extreme delicacy. But be assured, we will never give up.

'Sir Charles, I have given this a lot of thought, and I've decided to accept James's land grant. I need your help to have the grant put into my name, to be made legal.'

'Sarah, what do you know about farming? You wouldn't survive, and legally a woman unmarried can't be given the title.'

'But if my child is a boy, can't he be given the grant?' Sarah shifted in her seat, clearly agitated. 'Can't you see that if I marry, then my child can't receive his rightful inheritance?'

He saw the desperation in her eyes and glanced over to his wife who was holding a lace handkerchief to her face.

'Sarah, your child isn't here, and we don't know of what sex it is, besides, this is foolish talk. Buy a cottage here if you don't want to return to England. I'm of the understanding that you will have an income, and I believe you have friends to help you. This would be far more prudent.' The man stood and walked over to his wife for moral support.

'Sir, I really have given this a lot of thought. Please, put the grant into your name for now. Later, if I have a boy, it will go to him. If I have a daughter, I will marry. Whatever happens, the land will be my child's.'

Lady Fitzroy was horrified. 'Child, this is grief speaking. You must be sensible and listen to my husband. He is only thinking of what is best for you both. Please come to dinner tomorrow and we can speak further on this.'

'Thank you for your kind invitation, but I have made up my mind. If you can't help me, I'll understand my only choice will be to marry in haste.' Sarah curtseyed and prepared to leave.

'Remember, seven tomorrow evening.'

Lady Fitzroy's heart was breaking for Sarah. What if it had been her Penelope? The governor studied the young lady; he admired her determination and could see how she had won the heart of the dashing sea captain.

The next day, Sarah dressed with particular care, paying attention to the finer points, dressing in her best black dress with a subdued bonnet that matched her kid gloves. This was her only chance to impress the governor, and to convince him to sign the legal paper that would give some security to her child.

She pressed the doorbell and waited. Through the glass in the carved front doors, she could see a figure coming closer. She could see he was well built and tall. Her heart seemed to stop as she drew in a deep breath and waited for the door to open. There stood a young butler; a few seconds seemed like an eternity. Her mind knew James was dead, so why couldn't her heart accept it also?

'Please come in, they're waiting for you in the study, miss.'

Sarah nodded her thanks and followed him down the hall through the sitting room, with its Persian rugs and silk drapes, into the study. The governor bent forward and kissed the girl on her cheek.

'Sarah, I've looked into the legalities of those documents.' With that he turned them over on his desk. 'There is one fault in your plan. Do you realise that the land must be farmed?'

He could see by her facial expression that this had come as a complete surprise. She quickly regained control and sat upright in her chair. He smiled to himself. How could he not admire such a woman?

'Look, Sarah, this is what I have decided to do. I'll take on the guardianship of the lease, provided you can farm this land.'

The older couple had decided this would be the appropriate action to take. They knew the girl would find it almost impossible and decide not to go on further with all this foolishness. Sarah exhaled with relief. She had no idea how she was to accomplish this, but she was determined to find out.

'Oh, to hell with all this business. I'm starving, how about you? Come, ladies, let's eat.'

Sir Charles Fitzroy, with a lady on each arm, led them back into the dining room. The ambience of the formal room was quite surreal for the younger woman. Never in all her dreams had she, Sarah Noonan, expected to dine at Government House. The table was set with silver and fine china ware. Roses adorned the centre piece. The food was delicious — veal and a chocolate charlotte. How she wished her parents could see her now, and how she longed to talk to her mother.

'Are you sure we can't talk you out of this decision?' were the final words Sarah heard as she walked down the path to her awaiting carriage.

Wandering down the city's main thoroughfare, Sarah hardly noticed the people as they hustled past her, all going about their own business. The shop owners opened up their premises and swept the flagged walkways, chatting to the passersby.

A stiff breeze was blowing down from the distant mountains, engulfing Sydney town in a perfumed smell of the rich, sweet gum leaves that covered the mountains. This gave their appearance a distinct misty blue colour. Quickly, she crossed over George Street and headed north towards the shoreline. Park bench seats had recently been placed in the newly developed botanical gardens. Sarah stared out over the harbour. *I must be mad,* she thought, *to endanger myself and my child. But if I don't, what can I give? How do I show my child the love its father would have had for his offspring?*

Sarah had learned from an early age that land represented power, prestige, and a higher standing in society. It had always been a difficult road for her, but this would be her greatest challenge. She made a mental list of all the things she needed to do before returning to the bush. After walking into the First Colonial Bank in Macquarie Street, she was ushered into the manager's office.

'Miss Noonan, you are here to finalise the paperwork regarding your inheritance. Mr Dean, the manager, has asked me to assist you.' The young man blushed, and with a low voice said, 'Beg your pardon, I'm Mr Lucas, his assistant.'

'Thank you, Mr Lucas. This is the bank draft I need to cash immediately.' She handed him a neat but concise list. After reading the list, he pondered a moment, as if not sure what he was to do.

'Miss, don't you have a gentleman to take care of your needs? To advise you on financial matters?'

Sarah just looked at this well-meaning fool. 'No, I don't. I would have thought that was perfectly obvious. Mr Lucas, please let's get on with it. I'm booked on tomorrow's coach and I've a lot of shopping still to do.'

Walking out of the bank, she hurried up George Street, and then a large mercantile store came into view.

'May I help you?' enquired a young sales assistant.

Sarah noticed the girl's lovely rosy cheeks, the look of youth, and thought it was a pity that someone so young needed to dress in black, the chosen colour of the sales assistants. Surely a man's doing.

'I need soft wool to knit and fine woollen material, suitable for baby clothes. And, oh yes, cotton lawn and five yards of that soft towelling over there.' Sarah pointed to the display in the front window. 'I'll need cotton, needles, and a length of that satin ribbon, thank you.'

The girl wrapped up the goods and wished Sarah a good day. Next was the ladies apparel, where she bought two strong cotton dresses, checking that there was enough seam allowance to let out to accommodate for her advancing pregnancy.

The strong smell of coffee made Sarah suddenly remember how hungry she felt. And the feeling of nausea, which had plagued her, suddenly vanished. The quaint tearoom that she entered was clean and neat. Small tables were covered with checked tablecloths, and dainty cakes and scones were piled up on display in the glass cabinet. She was ravenous and had some of each.

While sitting back and sipping her coffee, Sarah picked up the newspaper. The heading in bold print stated, 'Chisholm on war path again.' Sarah had heard of the woman who was campaigning for the rights of women in the colonies. Suddenly a wave of fatigue swept over her, and she decided to take a cab ride to her next port of call: Chinatown.

# Chapter twelve

**Chinatown, Sydney**

Elaborate shopfronts were built to hide the maze of lanes leading to opium dens, brothels, and places where young girls, often as young as eight, were spirited into Sydney to meet the demand of the brothel owners or to fill the role of wives to the men who had left their number one wife in China.

'Look, miss, you really shouldn't venture on foot alone in this heathen area.' The cab driver had daughters of his own and shuddered as he thought of one of his girls walking into this den of iniquity.

'Thank you, I'll be careful.' Sarah handed him the fare and stepped down into a sea of people.

'Look, missy, we have lovely silk, lovely ivory necklaces, or maybe you need a girl, she work very cheap.'

The old Chinaman smiled at her, his teeth rotted out — the opium god had claimed another soul. He pushed the items into Sarah's hands. The smell of fresh fruit helped disguise the odour of unwashed bodies thronging towards the passers-by. Children, boys and girls alike, swung their pigtails as they ran by. The barrowmen pushed their wares onto the corners, hoping to catch the folk as they were leaving the congested streets.

Sarah fumbled with the piece of paper containing the address of a Mr Lo Lee. She was pleased that she had sent her purchases back to her lodgings; it would have been difficult hanging on to them in this bustle. Stopping at a set of heavy wooden doors, she again checked the folded paper that she clutched in her gloved hands. Taking a deep breath, she knocked once. Before she could knock again, the door opened.

'I realise that I don't have an appointment, but could I see a Mr Lo Lee? It is of the utmost importance.'

A small slip of a girl bowed and asked the English woman into the hall. 'Please wait, missy.' She turned and shuffled down the darkened hall and out of sight, returning five minutes later. 'Please follow me.'

Sarah walked through the elaborately carved doors and was amazed by the rich ambiance of the inner room.

'Sit, missy. Mr Lee won't be long.'

Sarah sat on a silk brocade chair opposite a desk. She crossed her hands over her lap and looked around the room. The beautifully carved desk complemented the drapes and wall hangings, which were woven with scenes of China in peacock blue, and trimmed with gold thread.

The girl hadn't noticed the slight movement of a picture hanging on the opposite wall, or the eyes that watched her. Lee observed her for a few minutes, following her every movement. So this was James's lady. He could see why James had been infatuated with her. But what had led her to him?

Sarah looked up. She hadn't heard the door open. A man entered, dressed in an English suit, rather than the traditional Chinese garb she had expected.

'Miss…'

'I'm Miss Noonan, Mr Lee. Thank you for seeing me at such short notice.'

Mr Lee smiled, and taking both of her hands in his, said in a soft deep voice, 'How can I help you?'

'My friend James Lowe passed away recently and in his possession I found a letter addressed to you. I thought it may be important.' Sarah lowered her eyes and blinked away the tears before this man could see them. 'And also there might be a clue in it, as how and why he died? Mr Lee, I know that this is unconventional, but I really don't know where else to turn. The military don't have any answers, or at least they are not telling me any, so you are my last hope.'

Once she started to talk, the words just spilled out. The Chinaman became concerned for her. If she was going around inquiring about James, she could be in danger herself.

'I have been waiting for James's lady to call. It is a great honour to meet you. But first, let's have tea.'

He hit a small gong on his desk and the maid entered. After a brief conversation she left, only to re-enter the room carrying a tray containing the finest and most exquisite china cups Sarah had ever seen. They both settled back to enjoy the sweet-scented lemon tea.

'James also left a letter for you, to be given in the event of an untimely passing. I was instructed to hold it for some time, but I now consider this to be the time. But first, I must talk to you about a most serious and dangerous situation. I don't know how much you know about James?'

'Only that he was a retired sea captain and had decided to take up a large land grant here.'

'Miss Noonan—'

'Please, call me Sarah.' At this point in time, it seemed ridiculous to keep up with formalities. All Sarah wanted was answers.

'If that's what you want, my dear, but let me advise you, as a father myself, formalities are there to protect us.'

He watched her glance upwards, and as their eyes met, he could feel the loss deep within her soul. Yes, this was a woman worthy of James. In a slow voice, he started to convey his story. 'James was a fine captain, a hero decorated for valour, but he was not retired. His government sent him here to uncover a fraud of the highest magnitude, including treason to the Crown. I know he had discovered a person who was involved but not the mastermind, or what country was implicated.'

'This can't be true! Surely, he would have told me?'

'No, Sarah, your lack of knowledge was your protection. My concern is that these murderers might think you have knowledge about them, and your life might be in danger also.'

Unknowingly, Sarah's hands folded over her waist; a natural motherly instinct to protect her young. The gesture didn't go unnoticed by Lo Lee.

'Mr Lee, I don't know what you are talking about.'

Sensing the girl's fear, he continued, 'Go back to England, go to your family, for in family you are protected.'

There was silence, then the young woman started to speak. 'I can't return to England. What am I to do?'

'Sarah, I could hide you until the culprits are caught, but it will be difficult.'

*Fan Wey*, or white persons, could be very difficult to understand. He noticed the colour draining out of her face.

'More tea I think? And maybe a little brandy?'

They talked well into the night. Sarah told him of her plans and finally he also agreed that no one would look for her on a remote bush property. He handed her the letter and watched as she placed it carefully into her purse.

'Sarah, I have arranged for my coach to take you home. Are you sure you want to go back to your lodgings? Wait here until your transport is ready to leave in the morning; my servant will collect your belongings.' This was the least he could do for James.

'Thank you for everything, but I must go. Can I write to you?'

'I will wait for your letters. Take care of yourself and James's heir.'

Back at her lodgings she opened James's letter.

*My darling Sarah,*

*If you are reading this, then I'm already dead. I'm so sorry that I had to lie, but, darling, it was to protect you. I have taken care of you in my will, something I couldn't do in real life. Harold will, I'm sure, help you. Please go on with your life. You were made to love and be loved. Don't let my death stop you from finding it. Always in my heart.*

*James.*

She held the letter to her breast, as though James's arms were holding her tightly and comforting her. Her mood lightened; she was sure now what she must do. *Life seems to go on,* she thought.

The coach left on time. Sitting opposite Sarah was a minister of the cloth. A pleasant-looking young man, who seemed horrified to learn that she was travelling unescorted. He talked about his new parish and all the things he hoped to achieve. She smiled and thought to herself, *the pathway to hell was paved with good intentions.*

'Yes, Miss Noonan, as I was saying…'

Sarah closed her eyes, and the memories of the last week filled her mind. She thought of the letter that she had written to her mother, letting her know of James's death. She asked her for advice, especially on the situation that had driven her away from England. Had the culprits been caught? She agonised over the fact that it would be eight months before she could hope to get a reply.

'Katoomba in ten minutes,' yelled down the driver as he steadied the team for the last winding miles down into the changeover station. One hour to eat and freshen up, before the long descending track led into Lithgow. A woman in her mid-thirties joined the coach just before it departed.

'Come on, love, let me climb aboard. I'll give you sixpence and a good fuck…'

'Molly, shut your mouth. We have a lady aboard,' yelled the driver.

Molly smiled and poked her head in the coach door. 'Sorry, miss.'

Before Sarah stood a woman, dressed in a rather undersized garment. The low cut of the bodice revealed a bit too much cleavage. Her cheeks had been painted bright pink; that did nothing to improve her tangled red hair. The minister started to say something, only to be cut off by Sarah.

'I don't mind if she travels with us, driver. It would be quite pleasant to have another woman on the journey.' Sarah certainly knew what it was like to be down on one's luck.

'Ta, miss, yer a lady and that's no mistake.'

'Enough of that nonsense!' said the driver. 'Climb up here next to me, Molly, and for God's sake, don't mention this to anyone, or it will be my job, yes it will, by George.'

Lithgow was a growing township that supplied the landholders of the district and the miners alike. A number of brothels had been established to cater for the women who chose to sell their wares and the men who wanted to buy. One hour before they reached Lithgow, the coach came to a stop, and a voice could be heard arguing with the driver.

'I'm telling you I need a pee, or I'll wet me britches. I won't be long.'

'Well, you won't want to be, Molly, or I'll leave you here.'

The minister, who hadn't lifted his head out of his Bible since Molly came aboard, looked over towards Sarah. 'She shouldn't have been allowed to travel with us. She is full of the devil. Don't you agree, Miss Noonan?'

Sarah ignored him and climbed down the stairs, stepping onto the dusty track to stretch. 'Driver, when Miss Molly returns, please have her seated in the coach. I'll pay the extra fare.'

She turned to face the preacher. 'As you said, she is in need of God's help. This is your chance.'

The last hour brought more laughter to Sarah than she had experienced in all the month before. Molly, as Sarah found out, had come to Australia to work as a servant for a rich shipping family. The son had other things in mind, and when she complained, she was fired without a reference or even given what monies were owing to her.

'So what could I do, miss? I sold the only thing I owned. And got good money for it, might I say, twenty pence a pop.'

The minister bashed his head as he tried to stand, proclaiming the need to cleanse the wicked. Sarah couldn't contain her laughter. The tears of sweet pleasure rolled down her cheek.

'Lithgow ten minutes,' yelled the driver over the sound of the horse's hooves.

'Goodbye, and good luck.' Sarah waved to Molly as she left the coach and hurried towards a large wooden building that stood alone at the far end of town.

At nightfall the next day, Sarah saw the lights of Gulgong. When the dray came into view, Charley Wong was pushing his cart along the street delivering milk.

'Welcome home, Missy.' He waved with both hands, and a cheeky smile showed up his missing front tooth.

The dray pulled up beside the blacksmith's yard. Tom downed tools and walked over to help Sarah alight and unload the weekly supplies. 'It's good to see you back, Sarah. Those little rascals have been running amok while you've been in Sydney.'

He smiled up at her as she took his hand. He held it for a minute before lifting her down. As she leaned forward, she slipped on the worn tread of the step, landing against his chest. The curls from beneath her bonnet swept across his face.

'Steady up, Miss Noonan, people here will talk,' he said with a twinkle in his eye.

'That they will, Tom, soon enough.'

Suddenly, the humour left his face and he became immensely

serious. 'Sarah, when you have rested, I need to talk to you.'

'Can you come over in the morning? I'm too exhausted tonight.'

Sarah awoke to banging on the front door. She looked at the clock: 10:00 a.m. She had not in all her life slept in so late.

'Am I too early? I can come back later if you like. I'll go now.'

'No, wait up, I won't be a moment. Come in and put the water on.' Sarah pulled on a skirt and blouse, rammed her feet into her shoes and tried to tidy her hair all at the same time. She heard the back door bang and realised Tom had gone to the wood pile.

A few minutes later she heard the *crack* of logs being split. Sarah hurried to open the back door just in time to see Tom returning to the cottage with an armful of timber and small kindling perched on the top.

'I'll have this stove blazing in no time at all. I've got some fresh bread and milk, and I met Mrs Lewis at the store. She handed me a basket of provisions. I guess she must have heard that you arrived last night.'

It wasn't long before the kettle was boiling. Sarah washed the cups to remove any traces of dust. She could see someone had been in. The floor had been swept and fresh flowers had been arranged on the windowsill.

'I'll make the tea, if you will cut the bread. I'm not very good at that.'

Sarah smiled. *What man is?*

Watching him, it made her wonder what this was really about.

'Did you enjoy the city?' he asked, trying to keep up the "I've just popped in" approach.

'Come on, what's this all about? You're not the tea and cake type.' She was becoming sick of the charade.

Tom looked uncomfortable. He had come there with a purpose, and he couldn't avoid the question. 'Munu came to see me a few days ago. The tribe have left to go walkabout to their winter camp, and she was worried about you being here alone.' He waited for her to reply, and when she remained silent, he continued, 'Your secret is safe with me.'

The air became electric.

'I didn't even have a chance to tell James about the baby, Tom.'

'I know, but I've been thinking and it's not because of the baby. I know I'm not the best catch, but I work hard, have my own business and a bob in the bank. I would love and care for you both. Nobody need know that the baby is not mine. There, well, you have it all now.'

Sarah started to speak, but the words wouldn't come out.

'Take your time, I know this must be a shock and all, but, Sarah, it would be an honour if you were to become my wife. I want you so much.'

He sat still, not touching her, not invading her private space. Just waited. After what seemed a lifetime of waiting, Sarah walked over to him. And taking his hand in hers, she started to speak to him.

'Tom, the honour you have given me is more than I have ever received from anyone. No one has ever really cared what became of me. But I care for you, Tom, too much to marry you. There are things in my past life that need to be settled before I could marry anyone. Don't worry about us; we are going to be farmers.'

At first Tom thought that the comment was supposed to be a joke, to lessen her refusal of his offer of marriage. But the sincerity in her eyes portrayed a different story.

'And how, my dear, are you going to manage this?' he asked with an amused smile.

Sarah explained all about the land grant, and how she had to prove that she was capable of running a large farm, and how James must have wanted her to at least try.

'Sarah girl, have you any idea at all what this entails? The bloody land is at least five hundred miles away, through some very harsh country. You will need stock and someone to drive them, supplies and a place to live when you get there. That is, *if* you get there. There are droughts and bush fires the likes of which you couldn't imagine. And to top it off, you are pregnant.'

'Tom, please don't say that I can't. I have to try.'

The look of desperation on her face only showed the need for his approval. He remembered his last crossing of the desert between the Murray and the hill lands. Forty-five days without rain. Cookey, his old mate, was buried out there. They were returning from a drive to Wagga Wagga, a native settlement on the banks of the Murrumbidgee River, with a herd of horses, fifty of the best that they were intending to sell to the army. Water was scarce, but they still continued. At Jerilderie, the natives told them to turn back, but

Cookey wanted to push on. After all, he knew the country, and Tom was fresh out here. They lost half the team. The constant heat and little water brought on a fatal heart attack. Cookey now lay under the dry sand of that endless plain.

'Sarah, if I can't talk you out of this stupid idea, then I guess I'll have to come too.'

'I can't ask you to leave your business.'

A look of amazement crossed her face, and everything became real; she heard the kettle boiling over, the water running across the hotplate and dripping on to the floor.

'I will pay you, if you will be my foreman?'

Pay or no pay, he knew he was going. By the end of the week, the whole district knew and all but a few thought she was stark mad. And some even thought it was a result of grief.

# Chapter thirteen

Tom left the next day without a word to anyone. Early, before sunrise, he saddled up a sure-footed mare and headed out after the Wiradjuri tribe. Every year, small camps of Aborigines headed south, to meet up for the winter months on the vast Jerilderie plains, where they would celebrate with the Wareroo and Yorta Yorta people. At these gatherings, stories of the dreamtime were danced and told to the young people. For more than forty thousand years these traditions had kept their culture alive.

Tom pushed forward, stopping only to rest his horse. He needed to find these stockmen before they reached the Murrumbidgee River. He tracked them for five days before seeing the smoke from their fires. They were camped down in the gully beside a billabong.

Reining in his horse, he let the mare have her head as she started down the side of the steep gully. The natural rock formation and tall vegetation made this a great camp site. A flock of pink and grey galahs rose into the cloudless blue sky, as the man and horse came closer. The kids were the first to notice him as he entered their camp. Munu was walking among the tall reeds that encased the shallows of the river, gathering the young shoots that could be woven into baskets. Suddenly, she saw the dust rising from the horse's hooves. Grabbing her dilly bag, she scrambled up the bank and hurried back through the grass and reed shelters to where the man was dismounting.

'What's wrong, Tom? Why you come walkabout?'

Tom knew that Munu was an aunty and an elder in her tribe. She carried the laws and all the secrets of the women's business. He trusted her word and needed her support. Deep within his heart,

Tom knew that if Sarah was to have any chance of succeeding, she would need the Aboriginal men to work as stockmen for her because there were no better cattlemen or trackers in the country. Tom gave the reins to a boy he had seen hanging around Sarah's cottage.

'Give her a drink, son, but only a little mind or she will get a big bellyache.'

The kids were swimming and diving off the ledges into the water.

'Good to see you, Munu. We need to talk, Missy is in a bit of trouble.'

They walked over to where a group of men stood. Squatting by the campfire, Tom told the elders of Sarah's plans. The older men shook their heads and talked loudly in their own dialect. Munu didn't interrupt—this was men's business. After the ruckus had quietened down, the women talked, and Munu stood up to address them. For an hour, a heated conversation took place. Tom had no idea if Sarah's plan was going to be accepted or not. Finally, Munu walked over to him and sat down on the bough of a dead eucalypt that overhung the water. She held up her hand, showing four fingers to him.

'This many men come to work, but want to take all their family long way, and I can also look out for Missy.' The Aborigines were heading in that direction anyhow.

'Me come with ya, Aunty,' yelled a mischievous lad.

It took three weeks to organise the journey south. Charley Wong threw in his milk and vegie run to sign on as a cook. He arranged the large dray wagon with dried goods and medical supplies. Sarah was to drive a smaller dray, which contained her personal goods and sleeping quarters.

'The stock is going to be your biggest problem. I've been talking with the graziers around here. They can sell you some stock, but we will have to collect more around Gundagai.'

'But that will take us at least a month out of our way.' She was pacing around the camp, frustrated by her own restlessness. She wanted to start the journey. 'Why can't we buy cattle in the Riverina?'

'There's been a drought in the south and only the breeding stock was kept. No farmer will sell his breeders.'

*This girl really has no idea what is ahead of her.* Sighing, he tried to explain. 'There are still a large number of cattle in the high country, and maybe you can purchase yours from these graziers.'

She realised she needed him, his strength and knowledge. She realised that eventually she would have to bow down to his leadership.

Her boots had not fitted her that morning and her ankles were swollen. Sarah realised that it was too early in her pregnancy to be experiencing such symptoms. Was this an insight into what was to come? *Well, I will just have to make the most of it.*

Sarah had done the rounds of all her pupils and their families to say goodbye. The new school master would turn up in three weeks. He was a young man and by all accounts very capable. He hailed from Sydney, and was very interested in the local Aboriginal community. Sarah had left him a complete record about all her pupils and a detailed account of the Aboriginal camp and the people who would remain. On the last day that Sarah taught her class, the children brought in their home-made gifts. The parents arrived just after lunch and by nightfall the little hall was alive with the sound of music and the smell of lamb roasting in the camp ovens. Sarah cried as she lifted the beautiful quilt given to her by the mothers of her pupils. Each section was taken from pieces of cloth precious to these women.

When the last of the buggies left, a sad longing swept over Sarah. She wanted to call out, to run down the street not letting them go.

Next morning, Sarah settled back to write three letters. One was to her mother, one to Harold, and the last to Mr Lo Lee in Sydney. With her mother's letter she enclosed a copy of James's last will and testament. She had agonised over the story that she was forced to tell her mother, especially of the child that she might never be able to take back to England. *Please God, let Mum understand.*

That night, Sarah finished packing up all her belongings. Into the first crate she packed the lovely cup and saucer given to her by Martha, her friend on the long voyage out protected by her linen. Her precious books, her clothes, and household possessions filled the last two. The baby goods she had purchased in Sydney were carefully wrapped in an oil cloth to protect them.

'I want to load up now, Sarah, so we can leave before dawn.' Tom looked at her baskets and asked, 'Are you sure you need all these?

We have three rivers to cross, and God knows what else.'

As she started to apologise for her belongings, he looked into her eyes and saw the sadness they reflected. How could he have been so tactless? He could have bitten off his tongue. This was everything in the world that she possessed.

They travelled west for five days before they came to their first river crossing.

'We'll make camp here tonight and cross in the morning.' Tom was becoming more experienced in giving orders. On the first day out, he had given a direct order to Charley. The Chinaman flatly refused to listen to him, screaming, 'You no boss; Missy boss.' And with that he swung a meat cleaver above his head in defiance. 'I chop you into many pieces.'

Sarah, who was just waking up from a disturbed sleep, quickly summed up the situation, and climbed down from her dray, laying down the law to Charley, who continued to shout in Chinese. But he put down the cleaver and with some persuasion started breakfast.

They decided to take Sarah's dray across first. Tom took the reins and with the brake on, he slowly guided the horses down the bank. He had decided to put the older team on, hoping that their experience would lead the younger horses across.

Tom waved to the stockmen who had tied ropes to their saddles and attached the ends to the dray then fanned out on both sides. As the water crept up over the steps, the flow increased in speed. Sarah couldn't contain the panic she felt. Bile rose in her throat, and she wanted to close her eyes but then a hand gripped her arm. She looked up at Tom. *Thank God for him,* she thought as he winked at her.

'Not much longer now, love, and you'll be standing on the other side.' He felt her panic and wanted to reassure her.

The water ran off the side guards, there was a jerk forward, and then the horses stood still on the bank as the men unhooked the team. Tom swam the horses back to the other bank.

'Charley, pull back on the reins and allow the horses time to get a footing, and stop your panicking. You're frightening the horses.'

The whites of Charley's eyes stood out as he nervously sang out, 'You right now, boss, Charley plenty scared.'

The back wheels sank into the mud. Tom waved to one of the stockmen who swam over to take a closer look.

'No good, boss, she's stuck.'

Tom stripped off his shirt, turned and swam back to where he had left his horse. 'Charley, we'll have to unpack Sarah's goods, and take her dray in and unload half on to it.'

Sarah sat on the bank and watched attentively. Tom's body was browned by the sun, lean and strong. She knew that she should avert her eyes, but her need was as strong as ever. She wished they were alone and could be naked together in this land.

Finally, after everything was unloaded and the dray was moving, they were all safe on the opposite side. While the men attended to the horses, Sarah walked along the riverbank and around a corner. There before her, a small sandbar led out into the river. Looking back to where the men were, she quickly decided to wash herself in the clear water. Tom had told them all, that the next fifty miles would be very dry. She had removed her dress and was just about to step out of her petticoat when she noticed something unnerving. There, sunbaking on a partly submerged log, lay a brown snake. Raising its head and with its forked tongue flicking the air, it started to move towards her.

A *crack* echoed through the air. The snake flew up and landed higher up the bank.

'Sarah, please don't leave the camp unless you tell someone, and keep away from snakes.'

Tom wound up his stock whip and turned to leave. Sarah's hands flew up to her breasts.

'You needn't look so smug, Tom Brian.'

'Don't bother to thank me.' He paused, and in a lighter voice said, 'Oh, don't worry about the hands, you have nothing to be ashamed about.'

He could still hear her yelling the words that a bullocky would use as he entered camp.

'Boss, Missy pretty cranky.'

Charley was tending to the fire. On a table made up of a length of board that was carried under the wagon, sat an iron camp oven. A damper was ready to be set into the hot ashes and the last of their beef would be cooked on a grill over the flames.

Sarah wandered back, her hair dripping wet. She had on her dress, but carried her wet petticoat. The stockmen were anxious to reach the billabong, where their families would be waiting for them. At night, Sarah sat by the fire sewing. She had decided to alter a dress; her breasts were expanding, and the buttons and seams were stretched.

Charley and the stockmen didn't miss anything. They knew the signs of pregnancy. Tom had picked up a few words, enough to know that they thought he was the father.

'Wonder why they don't get hitched,' said a stockman to Charley when he went to refill his teacup.

Charley yelled at the bloke, 'Mind you bloody business, no talk about Missy.'

From that day on, the stockmen gave Charley a wide berth.

'How much longer to the men's camp, Tom?' Sarah asked.

They had travelled over the dry plain for three days. The horses were restless having travelled on a short ration of water. Tom watched them as they tossed their heads and pulled forward in their harnesses.

'We'll soon be there, a few more hours only.' Two of the stockmen had gone ahead to notify the camp. Late in the afternoon, they made camp above the river. Munu scrambled up the slope to see Sarah. Munu stared at the white woman and thought that these white people were such a funny colour. It was difficult to tell if they were sick or not.

'You not worry, Munu and Aunty look after you.'

With that, another woman came forward and smiled.

'She not speak English, but understand all you say, good worker, her name is Inu.'

Sarah smiled at the women; it would be great to have female company, even if only one of them could speak to her. The children rushed up to her. At the back of the crowd, a boy hung back. She recognised him as the lad who placed the wildflowers on the windowsill.

They stayed there by the creek bed for a week, resting the horses and gathering supplies to add to the dry goods they brought from Gulgong. Tom shot a kangaroo, and the women collected honey from the eucalypts on the other side of the billabong. The men speared fish and Charley smoked them. Sarah was concerned for the welfare of the women and children who had decided to accompany their men. The seven of them that left Gulgong had now reached fourteen with two joining them on the way. Three hundred miles to Gundagai and to where she hoped they might be able to purchase stock.

The kids took it in turns to ride up on the dray, but the women walked, not accepting a lift. The routine was the same every day: Charley left before dawn and had their camp set up when they arrived. The worst of the heat was over; the autumn days were warm and the nights clear. Sarah lay in her wagon and looked up at the heavens. The stars were so bright that they looked as though she could reach up and touch them. That day she had felt her baby move. Munu laughed as she placed her hand on Sarah's belly. They travelled south, keeping the mountains on their left. The game was plentiful; with the women collecting berries and roots, and with Tom's keen eye and rifle, they ate well.

Ever since their argument at the river, Tom had addressed Sarah in a more business-like manner. Both were stubborn, neither of them would back down.

Charley watched them for weeks, and one evening after supper while Sarah was sewing and Tom was smoking on the other side of the fire, he started a monologue with himself speaking out aloud. 'Missy and Boss both stupid, both need quick smack, both act like stupid children.'

Sarah smiled and stood up and walked over to Tom. 'Do you think he is right?'

'Maybe, you are a little childish.' He shuffled from one foot to another, half expecting her to hit him. Suddenly, they could feel many pairs of eyes watching them.

'Don't tempt me.' She now smiled. 'Why don't you join me for a cup of tea?'

'The pleasure would be mine.'

Sarah watched him as he approached her. He radiated manly appeal, from his suntanned complexion and broad shoulders, down to his slim hips. It was hard for her to take her mind off him.

The mornings were starting to become cool. Patches of mist rose from the lowlands and by the second week, the little caravan turned towards the hills. The stockmen took the lead, finding flat tracks of land that the horses could manage. Sarah marvelled at the beauty of the valley. The galahs had given way to beautiful, coloured parrots, the likes of which she had only seen in a picture book in the earl's library, which now seemed like an eternity ago. The dust had settled, and the smell of the eucalypts and wattles scented the air.

The sun sparkled down through the mist that covered the valley below, and the air was still and crisp the higher they climbed. With only one broken axle that had caused a few days' delay, the trip was uneventful.

The stockmen placed their ropes on the drays, and similar to the river crossing and with the brakes on, they started the slow descent into the mail stop of Gundagai. Tom made Sarah walk with the women behind the drays, when the sheer drops made the trip dangerous. Like a troop of battle-worn soldiers, they marched into the tiny settlement.

Gundagai was the main settlement for the high plains. Supplies and mail were unloaded there, and it had become a gathering place for whites and Aborigines alike. The stockmen and their families made camp on the outskirts. Sarah and Charley pulled their drays up next to the stockyards, near the pub and supply depot.

'You go in, Sarah, and see if we can get a feed while I tend to the horses.'

Tom was glad that the settlement had a blacksmith shop; he had shod the team before they left and had tended to them when they lost their shoes over the rough ground. But here he would be able to reshoe them for the long trip ahead.

# Chapter Fourteen

The settlement of Gundagai consisted of a changeover station, smithy's shop, a hall, and small store. It had been built on the high side of the Murrumbidgee River out of flood reach. Tom knew that they had to cross here before the rains started in the high plains and before the winter snows began.

As they sat in the small dining area eating their beef stew, followed by scones and blackberry conserve doused with lashings of fresh cream, Tom started to ask the locals about purchasing cattle. A small man dressed in a worn plaid shirt and canvas pants walked over and entered the conversation.

'Joe Henely was saying he had a few to sell, mate, and so was that drover, you know Bill, the one down from the high country. He's got a mob out there on the flats; they're not a bad lot and he said he was strapped for cash. How many are you looking for?'

Tom shook hands and introduced himself, 'Three hundred, mate.'

The crowd became quiet. The stranger whistled. 'That's a lot of stock; you must have a large holding.'

Tom was careful not to let the men know that Sarah held the purse strings as he realised that the mob would go up in price.

Word was sent out to Joe Henely, and while they waited for a reply, they decided to ride out to inspect the mob of cattle grazing on the flats. They followed the smoke into the camp and found a middle-aged man rubbing down his horse. A large, brimmed hat hung to the left, over a rugged well-tanned face that sported a long beard.

'What can I be doing for you folks?' he asked with a smile that would have gladdened any heart.

'We are looking to buy some stock and was told you might have some to sell,' replied Tom as he dismounted from his horse.

'Could have.' Bill watched the strangers as they settled into his camp. 'Pull up a log and have a cup of tea.'

Bill Mathews observed the woman as she slowly climbed down from her mount. After pouring her a cup of tea from a blackened billy that hung over the fire, he asked, 'How many head are you after?'

'I'm trying to buy about three hundred, if the price is right.'

Bill gave a startled laugh, and then asked, 'How are you paying, bank note or gold?'

'Either, depending on the price,' answered Tom.

'Well I've got one hundred head and fifty due here in a week. You can have the bloody lot if the price is right. To tell you the truth, I'll be glad to see the back of them. I've had this caper babysitting the mob; want to try me hand at prospecting. I've heard they've struck it big, down Bendigo way.'

'Bill, how would you like to sign on with us? Well, at least as far as the river? We are going to need another good drover. That's if we have struck a deal?'

Bill spat into his hand. Then taking Tom's hand, he shook it to seal the bargain.


Joe Henely strode into the changeover station looking for the folk who wanted to buy cattle. He was in his mid-fifties, tall and wiry. He had come out from Scotland thirty years before and had staked his run high up in the alpine country. His wife had died soon after he'd established his property. Many of the local people remembered her and the hardship she'd had to endure living high up in the snow line. She had died in childbirth before the doctor could reach her.

A crew of shearers on their way to the Mallee country joked and told the newcomers that Joe Henely still had the first crown he ever earned. They believed it was his tightness with money that stopped him from remarrying again. Little did they know the guilt he still carried and the loneliness he lived with day after day. All that they saw was a very rich man, who ruled his kingdom with an iron fist.

Joe had a meal with Sarah and Tom and later that evening invited them up to see his stock and stay a couple of days. Tom hired a sulky from the smithy and after leaving Charley Wong to take care of the two drays, they headed out of town and started the climb up onto the next plateau.

The scenery was spectacular; the higher peaks were covered with snow from the first falls. The mountain grasses were still plentiful, and the perfume of the wildflowers blended with the sharpness of the crisp mountain air. Large herds of cattle grazed the slopes. Raising their heads to watch the strangers as they drove by, calves frolicking around the herd returned to the safety of their mothers.

Tom and Sarah took their time as they followed the track to the summit. The track gave way on either side to steep gorges, mountain streams bubbling below. Tom rested the horses, and Sarah sat and breathed in the majesty of the mountains, overcome by the serenity she felt at that moment in this beautiful place with Tom.

As they climbed over the last ridge, the homestead came into view. Sarah had expected to see a small bark house, similar to those she had seen around Gundagai. As they rounded the last bend and the farm came into view, Sarah was astounded to see a large homestead surrounded by other smaller houses and barns.

They pulled up in front of the arched garden gate, greeted by Joe who waved and walked out to meet them. While Tom attended to the horses, Joe helped Sarah down and escorted her inside. The lounge room that smelled of beeswax and turpentine was very well appointed, with a large round table holding centre place. To the side of a window that looked over the mountain range, stood a highly polished piano. Two upholstered lounges stood at right angles to an open fire. On the end wall, taking pride of place, stood a beautifully carved dresser displaying a bone china dinner set and crystal glassware.

A girl entered the room and asked Sarah to follow her. The guest bedroom was clean, and the canopied bed gave way to pure luxury. After she had freshened up, Sarah changed from her travelling outfit into a day dress of blue pinstripe cotton, edged with a lace collar and leg-of-mutton sleeves. Sarah had made the dress with the help of the ladies in Gulgong and wondered if it was suitable for this occasion. Turning slowly to check the back of her dress in a mirror, Sarah smiled, and with an air of confidence, joined the men in the lounge room.

'I'd be expecting you would enjoy a cup of tea, Miss Noonan,' asked Joe in a broad Scots accent.

Sarah thanked him. She noticed that Tom had also changed into a white shirt and tan pants; he had shaved and indeed looked a fine figure of a man.

'Tom has been telling me that you are taking up land on the Murray flats, Miss Noonan.'

'Please, Mr Henely, call me Sarah, we are too far from Sydney for such formalities.' She smiled at him as he placed a cup and saucer in her hand. 'Yes, that's the reason for me being here, to purchase stock. I believe that the drought has wiped out many head of cattle further south.'

'A scone, Sarah?' Joe was playing the perfect host. He found it quite amusing to think that such a beautiful young woman would take on such a demanding challenge. He had noticed there was no ring on her finger, but that was not uncommon for young widows. The folds of the dress still hid her pregnancy to the eye of the unobservant. But Joe was a very observant man; he had noticed the slight bulge in her stomach when he helped her down from the sulky.

'We are hoping to be able to buy another one hundred head.' Sarah looked over to Tom for support and confirmation of her grand plan.

'Indeed, Sarah is investing a lot into her property. As we have not seen it yet, I suggested that three hundred head would be plenty to start with.'

Tom eyed off the tall, well-built Scotsman. He had noticed the way he'd looked at Sarah and felt a sudden flash of jealousy.

'The Riverina hasn't had much rain for three years now. Those lads down there overstocked their runs, lost all their feed and were forced to sell. In fact, I bought some breeders myself last year.'

Sarah sat still, listening intently to Joe.

'That area you're heading into will probably support three hundred, but no more. I tell you what, tomorrow we can ride out and inspect my herds.'

Sarah stood, and after wishing the men goodnight, retired to her room. She was starting to feel uncomfortable, and the thought of a proper bed beckoned her.

'Will ya take a wee dram with me, Tom?' Joe poured two whiskies and handed one to Tom. 'This is a strange situation, a single woman making such a hard journey. Did she lose her husband, poor wee lass?'

Tom knew how to play the game; he paused and then replied, 'I'm an employee of Miss Noonan. These questions are best answered by her.'

Joe appreciated loyalty. This younger man had certainly gone up a notch in his expectations.

'I might be able to let her have some young heifers, about sixty are pastured in the next valley.'

*As long as that is all you want to sell her,* Tom thought.

Later that evening after the house became quiet, the stillness of the mountains cocooned Sarah in thought. The doubts of her decision became very real. *What am I doing? Why am I trying to play at a man's game? Why haven't I taken the easy way out?* But once Sarah stretched out into a comfortable position, her body sank into the down mattress and the dream world overtook her.

The sky was a vivid blue and a mist rose up from the valley floor, not a cloud or a breeze stirred as the riders set out at a slow pace. Joe had Sarah mounted on a gentle mare. He kept his own gelding close to the mare, ready to grab the horse if it spooked. Joe had insisted that she wear a heavy coat that he had lent her. The air was crisp, and the sunlight showed up the particles of dust that danced in the light and were not visible in the plains below.

The trees were becoming more stunted. Along the tree branches, Bogong moths clung to the bark, the females plump and ready to deposit their eggs. Moss covered the rocks; the unfolding country reminded Sarah of pictures she had seen of Scotland. The cattle were black, not what Sarah had expected.

'They are called Angus, a hearty breed from back home, see' — Joe pointed to his herd grazing contentedly in front of them — 'they're shorter in the leg, and much better for our conditions. I brought them out here twenty years ago. And they have not let me down, lass.'

'Would they be suitable for the river conditions?' Tom asked. He liked the look of these small compact cows. 'Are they good mothers, Joe?'

'Aye, just look at how many cattle I've got now, over seven hundred breeders with calf at foot.'

Both Sarah and Tom couldn't deny that Joe and his cattle had prospered. The ride back to the homestead was indeed pleasant. The sun was warm but as the travellers rode behind the rocky outcrops a cold chill bit into Sarah. All along the men talked about interbreeding and assured Sarah that, with proper management, her stock would improve also.

The night turned cold. Sarah had changed for dinner, and after arranging her hair she looked into her carpet bag to take out a shawl.

*Damn*, she thought, *I've left it back in the dray.*

With a last look in the mirror, she straightened her skirt and, feeling satisfied with her appearance, strolled into the dining room to join the men.

'Aren't you cold?' enquired Joe.

'I left my shawl back down with the drays, but I'll be just fine. You have a lovely fire ablaze.'

She smiled and took her seat at the other end of the table. Joe excused himself, and returned a little later carrying a shawl.

'Here, Sarah, I would like you to have this one. It is new. My wife ordered it just before she died.'

Sarah bent forward and allowed Joe to place the beautiful cream cashmere wrap around her shoulders.

'What type of wool is it?' She felt the lightness and soft texture of the garment. 'Where did it come from, Joe? It feels as light as a cloud.' She started to take off the shawl. 'It is lovely, but I couldn't accept it.'

Joe's hand stopped her. 'Please, I would like you to have it, a gift to wish you luck.'

There was a moment before Joe removed his hand from her shoulder. Feeling self-conscious to a man's touch, Sarah spoke softly. 'Then thank you, I will cherish it.' They finished dinner and retired to the drawing room.

'Do you play, Sarah?' Joe walked over to her, and placing his drink down on the table, sat down in a chair close to the piano stool.

'I did once, but I'm a bit rusty now.' With that she started to play. The music flowed, first classical then a few modern ballads. Joe started to sing. He had a deep rich baritone voice; he sang, and Sarah played, and Tom sat in a corner wishing he could compete in some way.

# Chapter fifteen

A bargain was struck, and seventy cows were purchased. Joe accompanied his men on the drive down to Gundagai.

'I want you to take the mare, a sweeter nature you will never find. The men have already taken her down with the cattle.'

Joe's dominance was starting to annoy her. Sarah wasn't some girl needing to be led to water like the cattle. She needed his knowledge though, so she remained quiet. Back at the stockyards, Bill Mathews had rounded up all his cattle, a scrub mob compared to the pure-bred Angus. Sarah looked at the cattle as they milled around in the yards; they were hers now, with all the trouble that entailed.

At daybreak they all started out, and as usual Charley had left an hour earlier so that he could set up camp at their next site. The black families had moved on days before, leaving their husbands to assist with the droving. Bill Mathews proved to be invaluable to Tom, who had struck up quite a friendship with the drover.

The first day ran smoothly; all the men were old hands at driving stock and the horses were a sturdy mountain breed and knew their job as well as their riders. They made the first camp site in plenty of time to settle the herd and after dinner they sat around discussing what route they would take.

'Crossing the Murrumbidgee will be difficult,' Bill said to Tom.

'We could cross the river by the large sandbars. Do you think the drays can make it across, Bill?'

'It could be tricky but if it comes to it, we will have to float them on the barges further downstream, but that's another thirty miles out of our way.'

Sarah looked concerned and Tom smiled at her. 'Let's not worry about it until tomorrow. A good night's sleep often fixes many things. So with that I will wish you goodnight.'

But worry he did, and the dark sky was turning a lighter shade of blue before he finally dozed off.

The stockmen slowly pushed the first lot of cattle into the river. They tried to turn back, but once the first head got a footing on the far bank, the rest followed. It took over two hours to swim the whole herd through the fast-flowing river. That left the two drays and their teams to go. Tom swam his horse over and returned to tell them the worst of the news. The water was too deep to support the drays.

Tom, Billy, and two of the stockmen who stayed behind came up with a plan. They would try to make a raft out of the gums that lined the river.

'Why don't we go down to the barges? Wouldn't it be easier?' Sarah suggested.

The men shot looks at each other, but Sarah held her ground. Had they forgotten that she was the boss? Tom tried to patch up things between Sarah and the boys.

'You are right, Sarah, but it will take us one week to cross with the barge and return to the stock. And they will have to be moved regularly as there's not much feed about. Look at the trees over there.' He pointed to a stand of trees on the far bank. 'See the black marks. There was a fire about a year ago that destroyed all the feed on the plains and it's still recovering.'

Sarah realised what he was saying was common sense.

'Well let's have a go, but it's on your head, Tom Brian, if we all end up floating down stream, or even worse, drowning.'

With her nose in the air, Sarah flounced away from the group of men, who were sitting around the billy waiting for their orders. One of the men was heard to say, 'She spat the sugar tit.' They spent the day cutting down strong young trees and tying them together to form a large, bulky raft.

'Boys, start cutting away the bank over there.' Tom pointed over to a small beach. 'We will have to push this into the water in the shallows. And for God's sake tie the lines securely to those old gums further back from the bank.'

The sound of the axes shattered the peace; the cockatoos screeched their warning to their flocks. Mobs of kangaroos bounded away as the men went about their tasks. Then it started to rain. For two days it teemed down, causing their ramp to collapse. But on the third morning under a blue sky, they made an attempt to launch the dray. With a pulley and rope attached, the stockmen guided the raft out into the river. When the flow pulled it gently downstream, Tom shouted to the men who controlled the ropes, as their horses sank into the mud. Finally, the raft hit the beach on the other side.

'Back the team into the water, and get that bloody harness attached, before they spook.' Tom swung around and noticed one of the stockmen lifting his whip to hit the horses. 'You hit them again and I'll hit you, you bastard.'

By day's end, both the drays were across, and Tom's temper had settled down to only a small roar. Charley prepared a great meal for all of them; a roll of roast beef, a Chinese version of a Yorkshire pudding, and a currant damper, but the Aboriginal folk ate alone, always preferring their traditional foods.

'Tom.' Billy called him over away from Sarah. 'You had better watch the stockmen; you upset one of them and the whole bloody lot are likely to go walkabout.'

Tom walked away mumbling to himself; a temperamental woman and stockmen was enough to drive a fellow mad.


The next two weeks were uneventful; up at dawn, Charley left, and they pushed on slowly, ever mindful that many of the cattle were heavy in calf. Sarah was growing also; by now all the men knew she was well pregnant, but they knew better than to comment on it. Sarah stayed ahead of the herd with her smaller dray, and Tom or Billy relieved her from driving whenever they could.

Two months to the day, they hit the Murray River. The heat made the water shimmer. Sarah marvelled at the majestic waterway, with its sandy white beaches and large river gums that hung over the water. Koalas looked down from the treetops onto the small gathering below. The Aboriginal families were reunited and that brought calm to the whole group. A local tribe, the Wareroo, made them welcome, trading fish and local berries for cloth and blankets. They rested there, on the banks of the Murray River. Sarah was becoming very uncomfortable. The bouts of nausea had returned so she spoke to Munu about it.

On dusk, Munu returned with a mixture of bark and leaves for

Sarah to make into a tea. Later that night after they had all eaten and the others had settled for the night, Sarah lay looking into the sky. It reminded her of a velvet ribbon covered with thousands of diamonds, twinkling as far as she could see. She thought back to the folk in London. Never would they see such a majestic sight as this.

The brew helped her, and the nausea eased. After a week, Tom informed them that they were to break camp. The next morning, they headed west along the river.

'How much longer before we arrive?'

Sarah was becoming anxious. Her impending motherhood was having an extra tug on her emotions.

'With a bit of luck, we will reach your land in ten days.'

Tom had not stepped over the line of familiarity after their spat on the banks of the Lachlan River.

'Do you think that there might be a cabin there, or anything?

'I wouldn't count on it. But after we build a stockyard, we can start to put something together for you.' Tom watched her and thought how much better it would have been if she had stayed in Sydney. No white woman was sturdy enough for this type of life. Yes, the black women had their babies in the bush, but not Sarah.

Sarah had never seen white beaches on a river before. Some gently stretched out into the water. Charley had placed a folding wooden chair in the shallows so she could sit and let the water flow over her body. That night, Tom shot a kangaroo so they would have fresh meat for a day or so. Charley had cut off a back haunch of the roo and was cooking it in a large camp oven, which he had buried deep down under the coals. They had a few potatoes left and with the tubers the Aborigines had given them, it seemed like Christmas.

Munu was watching the white girl; she was not supple like the girls of her tribe. She was having trouble completing her daily chores; and couldn't climb up into the dray without help. Had the girl mixed up her time? Maybe the baby would come earlier? *Yes*, Munu thought, *I will have to watch her closer now.*

Tom had estimated the timing of their travels with uncanny accuracy and true to his word they reached the union of the Broken River on the ninth day. This was the beginning of her land, and her dreams.

By the end of the first week, a stockyard had been built and the beginning of the perimeter boundary fencing was under way. Tom drove the men nearly to exhaustion; but not as hard as he drove himself. The nights were cold with a mist that rose off the river and backwaters. Tom was very aware that a permanent residence was his next priority. Sarah was now waddling around the camp, always getting in the way of the men as they went about their jobs.

'Sarah, keep away from the stock. If you don't care about yourself, think about the child.' Tom looked at her, his frustration was causing him to yell at the men. He had used all types of rational argument on this stubborn woman. 'Tomorrow we'll make a start on your house. Have you decided where you want it?'

'Over there.' She pointed to a large gum well back from the water on the highest ridge.

'Sarah, it can't be too near that tree…'

'Why ever not? That's where I want it.' She wouldn't let him finish, a habit that she used a lot now.

*Oh God, not another argument with this cantankerous woman,* he thought.

'Well, Sarah, that site is not safe.' He could feel his temper rising. 'These trees drop heavy branches in the summer, and one will bloody well go through the roof.'

There was a standoff. Sarah knew he was right, but she didn't want to admit it.

'So what is it to be, Miss Noonan, in the clearing or sleep in the dray?

Sarah's eyes closed to a squint as she thought of a reply. 'The clearing it is then but don't expect me to like it.'

Soon enough, one large room was nearly completed, only the roof needed to be finished. Bark was stripped from trees and moulded to fit between the rafters. Mud was pushed into the holes and flattened out to give a draught-free room. The floor was earthen, beaten down into a smooth finish. Sarah was anxious to move in. The chimney also needed to be completed. She maintained she could manage without it. Hadn't she managed with the camp ovens for over four months?

'Please, Missy, you don't lift the bags, I carry.' Charley worried about her, and thought to himself, *Mr Tom fights too much with her. Next time I cut his head off.*

Sitting on her little chair, Sarah surveyed her domain. The bed, which Tom had made for her, sat in one end of the room. A pretty patchwork quilt—a present from the ladies of Gulgong—hung over the straw mattress. A table and rough dresser had been pushed up against the far wall.

Sarah was busy unpacking the crockery that had luckily survived the river crossings, when the pain in her lower back started. *I shouldn't have lifted that last box in, Charley was right*, she thought as she stretched up, trying to relieve the pain. The pain came and went all day. The next day, Tom called for Munu to come up to their camp.

'I think it is her time!' said a much-relieved Tom when he saw the Aboriginal women walking up to the cabin.

Munu took a look at the white girl and knew it was time to get her to the dry sandy riverbed. Half lifting, half walking, the two women struggled to get Sarah to the bank. Any Aboriginal woman would have known what to do, but this white girl had no idea.

'Missy, you must keep walking; not time to push yet.' Munu and Inu held her up as they walked around in the sand.

'I can't walk anymore,' cried Sarah.

All the men had stopped work. Tom was pacing around the camp. A loud scream pierced the stillness of the forest; the cockatoos screeched, and their flocks rose on the wind. Tom ran to where Sarah lay.

'Go away, Mr Tom, this is women's work.'

Munu dug out a hole in the soft sand and lined it with dry grass. Beside her sat a hollowed-out section of a branch that she had prepared in advance. The other women in their camp had lined it with a soft koala fur. The coolamon was ready.

Sarah was gently lowered over the hole. Tom sat on the porch, holding his head in his hands, trying to blot out her screams. Then suddenly there was silence, everything was still. Sarah didn't feel the baby slip out from between her legs; she had slipped into a peaceful unconsciousness.

When she awoke, she was back in her bed. Nestled beside her in the carved wooden cot, lay a small bundle wrapped in a cotton sheet. Charley and Tom sat on either side of the bed. As Sarah's eyelids opened, Tom looked up and smiled at her.

'He's a little beauty, Sarah. Munu says he's perfect.'

Sarah looked down into two tiny, surprisingly familiar eyes.

*James, you have a son,* she thought and reached down and placed a finger into the palm of her baby son's hand. Two little eyes looked up at her.

'This is your land, my son, and no one will take it away from you.'

# Chapter sixteen

Sarah's son thrived. He was called James after his father. At two months old, he had gained weight and was the darling of the stockmen and the Aborigines alike. The two aunties continued to monitor his progress. Every day they carried him down to their camp, which was set up around the bend on the river and opposite a deep sandbar, giving Sarah a little time to herself. But when his hunger pains started and his lusty cries could be heard around the camp, they would then return him to his mother.

Sarah enjoyed nursing, feeling him nuzzle into her engorged breasts and watching as beads of milk trickled down his chin. At the end of every day, Tom would look in on Sarah and the baby. James was exercising his lungs as Tom tied his horse to the verandah post. Hearing the footsteps on the wooden planks, Sarah smiled to herself. She was sure that it was the baby who attracted him.

'Come in, Tom, I'm at the stove.'

Tom walked over to the cradle and bent over the baby, taking in a deep breath. 'Sarah, what stinks?'

'It's the goanna oil. Munu applied it to protect James from the evil spirits or something, and to keep away mosquitoes.'

In the two months since his birth, Sarah had stayed close to the cabin. The days were hot, and she often carried him down to the river, to wash him in the pool which she had scooped out of the sandbar. The water was warm, heated by the sun. James Junior was as brown as a little berry and Sarah loved to sit under her large gum tree and watch him sleep in the shade of its large canopy. She would listen to the cicadas and watch the white cockatoos feeding on the gum nuts. She used this time writing to her mother, Harold, and Mr

Lee and completing the daily entry into her diary.

*My dearest Harold,*
*James's son has arrived.*
*Harold, you will love the baby, he is a picture of health with James's eyes. The trip was long but the reward I hope will be worth it. Tom is pushing the men. I have tried to slow him down, for their sake, but to no avail. I have just written to Mama to inform her that she is a grandmother. Maybe in time she will forgive me? I am looking forward to seeing you in the near future.*
*Your loving friend,*
*Sarah.*

The screeching of a cockatoo made her look up. In the distance, Sarah spotted a cloud of dust. As she watched, a horseman approached. Tom appeared from the barn and walked out to greet the stranger, who had dismounted. Taking the reins of his horse from the newcomer, he led him into their stockyards. The horse had lathered up a good sweat; white salt foam had crusted on its chest and flanks.

'Take the horse and give him a good rub down, not much water, mind, or he will get colic.'

Tom handed the horse over to a stockman and walked back towards the stranger. Tom had watched the man step down off his stirrup and dust the dirt from his clothes. He had a large build, with a black beard and piercing black eyes that were set a little too closely together. Along his jaw, a scar could be seen edging out from under his beard. He looked over and past Tom, to where Sarah was sitting with her baby.

'What can we do for you, mate?'

Tom smiled at the stranger. Edging closer to the flat seat that had been chopped from a dead stump, Tom eyed off his rifle that he had placed there earlier. The stranger seemed to sense Tom's caution and turned to talk to him.

'I'm looking for an English woman, a friend of a late sea captain. I was told she might be heading this way.' The accent was heavy, German or maybe Russian; whatever it was, Tom didn't like him. A gut feeling told Tom this man was big trouble.

'Can't say I recall any travellers fitting your description.' Looking over to Sarah, he smiled and asked her also. She murmured back to

Tom some unintelligible comment and he replied, 'My wife hasn't noticed any strangers either.'

The stranger looked around the camp. Charley watched from behind the dray, his meat cleaver tightly gripped in his hand.

'Well, I will be gone then. I want to make the port of Echuca by tomorrow.'

The stranger untied his horse and swung up into the saddle. Tom observed the ease with which he mounted, and he knew instantly that this man was a military officer. Normally, a meal would have been offered to any traveller, but Tom's instinct told him to get rid of this fellow.

Sarah had been listening to the conversation and quickly lifted the baby up, ready in case she needed to flee. Tom looked down at her and took a deep breath, spitting out the words he needed to say.

'What's this about?' He could feel the woman's fear. 'You have a child to think of. I can't protect you if I don't know the facts.'

Charley, who had watched this scene being played out, leaned back and let the cleaver slip down onto the chopping board. He also had realised that this strange man was some sort of a threat.

Tom's eyes never left Sarah. This woman he loved looked so small and vulnerable, standing there holding her child. He watched her trembling.

'Please, Sarah.'

Following her back to the cabin, they entered the small room, and he closed the door with a loud bang in a gesture of protection.

'If I tell you about this nightmare that haunts me day and night, it will put you in danger also.'

'Tell me from the beginning; and don't leave out anything.'

It was past midnight by the time Tom left the cabin. Usually, he slept in a small wattle and daub barn that the men had not long finished, but tonight he laid his swag under the dray near Sarah's cabin. As he rolled a smoke and lay there watching the stars, he wondered what the best course of action would be. Reaching over, his fingers felt the cold metal of his rifle that lay close to his side. A sense of serenity overtook his fears as he listened to the rippling of the river, the splash of a fish jumping, and then the silence of the bush.

In the following weeks, supplies started to run low. Charley was running out of all dry goods. Meat was always plentiful thanks to Tom, and the Aboriginals kept them in fish that they caught in their traps.

'Tom, you had better drive to Echuca. Leave Charley with me, we will be fine. I would go too, but I think the babe is a mite small for such a long trip.'

'I'm not happy about leaving you here, Sarah, even with Charley.'

'You could be back in four days, and I have a small list of things I need also.' She waited for an argument and was surprised when Tom shrugged and nodded. Early next morning, before sunrise, Tom left. Perhaps he wouldn't have felt so confident had he been aware of a man sitting astride his horse on the other side of the river, watching as he left.

Vladimir Sokolov had arrived in the colonies six months previously. An ex-major in the army of the Russian Empire, now a mercenary, he had been assigned to trace a shipment of missing bullion that had disappeared on route from Sydney to China. He had listened to the stories of an English captain who had been murdered, and after a large amount of bribery had loosened the tongue of a servant employed in a Chinese Emporium owned by the Lee family. The loose-lipped servant spoke about a white woman, a friend of the murdered sea captain, who was travelling south to take up a land grant.

On obtaining this information, he quietly took the servant girl into a dark alley way and while whispering into her ear, he cut her throat, leaving the body to be discovered by the merchants. Sokolov had previously corresponded with William Masters before his untimely death, apparently shot on a road by bandits. Fury had made his blood boil when he had been informed that the wife was also dead, having been lost at sea in a storm.

On leaving the settler's homestead, he had ridden into Echuca and after making many enquiries to no avail, had decided to travel back to where he had last seen the couple. Maybe it was the look of fear on the girl's face or the way the man stretched out towards his rifle when he had asked about the white woman from Sydney. Or was it the educated tone that he had picked up from her that evening?

He had camped on the south side of the river, a cold camp with no fire to give away his presence. This was no hardship; hadn't he spent many a night in blizzards with no heating in his own country? There he waited and watched. He saw the woman with a baby stroll to the river but always the man was nearby.

Sarah waved farewell to Tom from her verandah, watching until he was out of sight. She pulled the woollen shawl tightly around her shoulders as a shiver ran down her spine. Staring into the bush, she had a sudden feeling of a person lurking nearby. She scanned the area and cast a sideways glance before turning and walking back inside. Tom had fastened a bolt to the inside of the slat door the day before. He had made her promise to keep it bolted when Charley or the boys weren't working near the cabin.

The water was warm as Sokolov started to cross over. He had tightened the halter on his mount, so that it couldn't whinny to the rest of the working bermuda of horses. Climbing up the muddy bank, he staggered and stepped onto a small twig. Stopping, he listened; there wasn't a sound. Creeping on, he could now see the outline of the cabin. *This will be easy*, he thought to himself, this woman, with a little persuasion would tell him all she knew. Reaching for his belt, he slid out a curved military dagger and ran his fingers over its handle, smiling as he recalled how many people had kissed its blade in the past.

His gun was loaded; he would only use it as a last measure. He didn't want to rouse the workers. Pushing along the side of the building, he turned, listened, and started to approach the door.

There was a heavy breath and a grinding; the air was electric; his body slid down onto the ground. Steam rose from the blood as it seeped into the earth. Finally, the gurgling stopped and Sokolov's body lay still.

Peering over the corpse, a small man lifted back his cleaver and muttered into the stillness of the dawn. 'No one hurts my Missy.'

Later that night, dark shadows moved towards the corpse, and all evidence of death was erased.

The sun's rays were hot and there was stillness in the air. Sarah walked along the river's edge, watching out for any sign of the approaching dray. Charley was watching over the baby as he slept in the small red gum crib Tom had made for him. She studied the wildflowers and marvelled at the beauty of the flowering gums. High in the trees, she could observe the small furry creatures the Aboriginals called koalas. On a large branch that overhung the track, a goanna lay sunning itself.

Sarah saw the aunties lift a throwing stick and before she could blink, the creature lay at her feet.

'Good tucker, Missy,' yelled a cheeky lad as he swung the lizard over his shoulder and tramped back to their camp.

Sarah continued to write in her diary, a legacy for her son. She wanted to record everything about his father in it. She wrote in depth about Harold, the Lo Lee family and their journey to take up their land grant. If anything was to happen to her, she wanted her child to know how much he was loved and wanted. Sitting under her tree writing, Sarah heard a sound and looked up, seeing Munu walking towards her. A tall slender girl walked behind.

'Missy, this girl, good worker.' She pushed the lass forward. 'She work for you. She work hard or else.'

After much arguing, Sarah gave up and accepted the inevitable and Lilly started work. And much to Sarah's delight, she proved to be an intelligent girl wanting to learn and be a little mother to James Junior.

True to his word, Tom drove into the stock lane and pulled up in front of the cabin four days after he left. Looking around, he sighed. Everything seemed to be in order.

'Tom, you're back,' Sarah said, throwing her arms around him as she trembled with excitement. 'I've… I meant *we* really missed you.'

He smiled; *why can't she let her guard down and let me in?* 'Sarah, I've got some mail for you and there's a crate. It was forwarded to Albury, and they sent it on to Echuca. Lucky I went when I did, the postmaster was going to return it to Sydney.'

He handed the letters to her along with the goods she had requested.

'Charley and the boys will unload the supplies; I want to have a talk with him anyway. By the way, here is a small present for the babe.' Tom seemed to blush as he handed it to her. Sarah opened the parcel to find a cake of lavender soap wrapped in a linen handkerchief for her, and a beautifully carved wooden rattle for the baby. She thanked him and carefully balled up the string, placing it inside the folded brown paper.

She sat at the table and looked at the envelopes that had been handed to her. The first had the seal of Sir Charles Fitzroy, the governor of New South Wales. She turned it over and broke the seal.

*My Dear Sarah*

*How are you, and how is that baby of yours? You do realise that my wife has still not forgiven me for letting you travel south. She didn't fully understand the prejudices of our women here and what they might have subjected you to. After much consideration, I think you made the best decision, especially as now you have a son. We arrived back in London after a pleasant voyage and have been reunited with our little granddaughter, a true joy to us both. Sarah, I've been to visit your mother and father and have told them about James and his love for you. I have also deposited into an account of mine the money you wanted her to have. This way your father will not have right over it. We spoke of her buying a house for you and her.*

*Sarah, I feel it is too early for you to return home; perhaps in two more years. If you need anything, please let me know. I know that there is nothing I can do to right the wrong that has been done to you both.*

*I will always remain your faithful servant.*

*Charles Fitzroy.*

Sarah folded the letter and placed it into the small ivory-inlaid box that she kept on the dresser. She made herself a cup of tea before opening the next letter. The envelope was closed with a dragon seal. Looking at it, Sarah nervously tore it open. The penmanship was the finest Sarah had ever seen. A sweet perfume rose from the pages, a mixture of musk and poppies. She started to read it and quickly learned that a Russian agent was looking for her. Mr Lee had tried to lay down false leads but was now very concerned for her safety, after the body of a servant was found murdered. He wished her safety and much prosperity and had sent her a china dinner set, similar to the pattern on the cup she had drunk out of in his office. The porcelain was so translucent you could see the outline of your hand through the cup.

The last letter was from her mother. It spoke about Sir Charles Fitzroy and the blessing that had been given to them both by James. With Sir Charles's help she would secure a house for them both in the next year. The old earl sent his kindest regards and also advised her to stay away for a time longer.

She looked out the window, mulling over all she had read. *No, she thought, This is my home now.*

Tom asked Charley and the boys if they had seen the stranger again. Charley smiled and just shrugged.

'Perhaps I should keep a man here at all times, Charley?'

'No! Mr Tom, you no worry anymore, he not come back.'

Tom could feel the brittle tension and decided against pushing the questions further.

On the first of every month, Charley went to Echuca for supplies. On his third trip he returned home with an extra bonus. Tied behind his wagon, on a long lead, struggled a small jersey cow with a calf trotting close to its mother. On top of the supplies, in a wooden crate that had been roped down, sat ten mottled chooks. With the cow bellowing and the chooks making a hell of a racket, the circus rolled to a stop in front of the homestead. Charley sat up straight, waiting for Sarah to comment.

'Charley, this is perfect! Fresh milk and butter and now eggs, this is the best surprise I've had.'

She clapped her hands and moved over to pat the cow. They all loved to see Sarah smile like a child. Life had been very hard for such a young woman.

Over the next twelve months, the homestead was extended and the first of their stock was ready to be driven into Echuca to be sold. Tom had purchased a dozen good brood mares from a clearing sale that had been held further north into the dry land.

'Sarah, I've heard that the army are giving contracts for the right type of horses. They have always preferred the mountain breed type. In my opinion that was a stupid move. Why take cold mountain stock to India? Captain Lea realises the mistake they made and now needs our hot-blooded stock.' He watched her. He knew the way she thought.

'Could we meet a contract?' She frowned as she considered his proposal.

'Not with our stock alone, but every farmer around here has a few good horses he could sell. Think of it, this could be a big money maker for us all.'

His enthusiasm filled her heart with a deep longing for this man.

If things were different… but they weren't, no — she had a child, and it was her duty to protect his rights.

The vegetable gardens were in full production, and they all celebrated a successful year, both with the cattle and their new enterprise: horse breeding.

# Chapter seventeen

Sarah was becoming a good stockperson; she appreciated good breeding and could now handle the purchase of stock as well as any man. Tom often joked that he soon wouldn't be needed. Although he laughed about it, he realised that there was a grain of truth in what he said.

'Tom, if you want to leave and start your own farm, you know that you have quite a tidy amount invested for you from the last two sales.' Sarah had insisted that he take a percentage of the profits for his work and time.

'For the last time, Sarah, I don't want to leave.' He looked at her, dressed in a riding skirt and open-topped blouse. The rounded top of her breasts plunged to a deep cleavage which added to her maturing beauty.

'Sarah, you know that I love you and only wish to marry you. I don't need or want your holding. If you want me to go, just ask me.'

She reached out for him, but he stepped back, turned, and strolled over to the yards where the men were branding the yearlings. Over the next few weeks, a polite demeanour existed between them.

Standing on the top rail of the stockyards, the stockmen watched as a rider approached.

'They're coming, Missy, maybe only two miles out.'

Sarah raced out of the homestead to see what all the commotion was. Wiping the dust and sweat from his eyes, Jacky, her head drover, wheeled his horse up sharp and jumped down from the saddle.

'The cattle are here,' he cried.

Sarah had bought fifty more head of cattle from Joe Henely in the high country. His stock had proven to be of sound type and had adapted very well to the river conditions.

'Jacky, open the stockyard gates and ask Tom to join me. Will you saddle my mare? I want to ride out and see them.' Sarah re-entered the house and after asking Lilly to watch over her sleeping son, donned a riding skirt and walked over to the barn to get her mount.

'Missy, Tom is already out with the stock. He saw the dust and rode over there. Do you want me to go with you?' Jacky knew that Tom would be angry if he let her ride out alone.

'No, Jacky, you stay here and help the men get ready. Push out the yearlings into the summer paddock. I'll be fine.' With that, she mounted her horse and cantered out into the haze on the plain.

In the distance, a dust cloud swirled around, and she could hear the bellowing of the cows. The drovers had driven them overland and in the last weeks the condition had proved to be very dry. As the herd got closer to the river, they could smell the water. The leaders pushed forward, wanting to break and stampede through the red gums and down into the river.

Sarah could now make out Tom. He and his horse worked at the front of the herd to steady them down. Behind and to the left she could see two heavy drays. As she inspected the cattle as they got closer, she noticed the tall man driving the largest of the drays. He waved at her and as his face came into view she smiled a warm greeting to Joe Henely.

'It's good to lay eyes on you again, lass,' he yelled out.

She dismounted and ran over to where Joe was climbing down from the dray. She shook his hand and was surprised when he pulled her to him and kissed her on the cheek.

'Sarah lass, hadn't we decided not to stand on formalities?'

They both laughed and walked arm in arm over to the shade of a clump of wattle.

Tom's blood boiled as he sat on his horse observing their greeting. He had no claim on this woman, but he didn't need any challengers either. He walked over to where the two were standing and leaned down to shake Joe's hand.

'How was the trip, Joe? I've been told it's pretty dry out there. I'm surprised you didn't take the longer route along the river.'

The note of sarcasm was not lost on Sarah as she watched the two men.

'You are right, Tom; it is very dry, a bad drought, but I was anxious to get here.' He didn't say any more, but Tom grasped his meaning. The three of them walked back over to the stockyards. Sarah climbed up onto the first rail to get a better look.

'They are in extremely good condition, Joe, especially with what they have been through.'

Sarah watched the stock as they settled into the holding yard.

'Leave them in there for a few days to settle down, lass.'

Tom stood back against the rail. He listened to what was being said and knew that he didn't need this man to give advice on how he ran this property.

'I've brought you a few bits and pieces of furniture that I had stored; I thought you might be able to make use of them.' Joe walked to the back of the dray and pulled back the canvas cover. 'Can you give me a hand over here?'

Joe beckoned to a drover who was walking past. The two men lifted the furniture down and carried it inside. A beautiful carved sideboard, mirror, and a leather three-seater couch now adorned her living room. Like a child opening its presents, Sarah's hands went to her face as she giggled with delight.

'Come on in, Joe, you also, Tom, and let's have tea.'

'Later, Sarah, I have things to do.' With that, Tom stormed over to the barn. All of this was watched by Charley, who smiled to himself and thought, *More fun and games for little Missy.*

Joe looked around as he entered the homestead and removed his hat before he walked over to the cot and looked down on the sleeping child. 'You have a bonny lad, Sarah, a boy to be proud of.'

Joe stayed for a week. He inspected Sarah's herd and spent hours advising her on a line of breeding. He was impressed by Tom's contract with the army and agreed that it would give her a substantial extra income. Joe enjoyed the child and spent time every day playing with him. Sarah and he fished and picnicked on the white sands of the Murray. She laughed at his jokes and listened intently to the stories he told of the high country.

After dinner on the night before Joe and his drovers were to leave for home, Sarah strolled down by her tree to look out over the river.

She watched the mist roll in. It seemed to reflect the sombreness that showed the true feelings of the water. She heard the footsteps behind her but didn't turn.

'Sarah, I've wanted to talk to you in private.' Joe lowered his arms so that they now circled her waist. They both stared out onto the water. 'Lass, you have a great manager here in Tom, a man who could run your property as well as I could.'

The sound of Joe's statement brought her back to reality. Turning around, she looked up into his eyes. She remained silent, waiting for his next statement.

'You are a beautiful, intelligent woman. I travelled over that drought-stricken plain to see you. Sarah, my dear, I realise you haven't known me over a long time, but you have visited my home and I hope that we have become good friends. Love comes in many ways and sometimes it comes over years.'

She watched Joe struggling to find the words and a feeling of sympathy welled up inside her.

'I realise I'm older than you, but I've grown to care a great deal for you.' He ran his hand down her face, gently pushing back a strand of hair that had fallen over her eye. 'I am a wealthy man, but I have no one to care for, no heir. If you would accept my marriage proposal you would want for nothing, and the little boy would become my heir. I realise that I'm not a romantic fellow, but...' He looked deeply into her eyes. 'Sarah, would you do me the honour of becoming my wife?'

She felt the words reverberating in her mind; this man was offering her and her baby everything.

'Joe, I don't know what to say. This offer is beyond my expectations. Yes, we are very good friends and what you offer my child...' Tears ran down her face.

'Hush, dear, I didn't mean to upset you.' He wiped her tears away and as he held her close, he could feel her shaking.

'Please, I need some time, Joe.'

The scared look on her face, the mist that was covering her deep violet eyes, only made him want to love and protect her even more.

'Sarah lass, take your time. In fact, I was going to invite you and the lad home for Christmas. It will be much cooler and with none of these bloody flies.'

Sarah had never heard him swear and she burst into laughter as he slapped at the black swarm buzzing around his face.

'Thank you, Joe. Can I leave it until Christmas?'

'Of course, we'll speak no more of it at present.'

Arm in arm they walked back to the house and to a small tantrum being thrown by Master James who had wanted to accompany his mother on her walk. All of which had been observed by the tall head stockman sitting on the verandah of his newly built manager's cabin.

With Joe and his stockman gone, life returned to normal for the people on Sarah's patch of earth. She often wandered down to the river to sit under her tree and write in her journal, a legacy to leave to her son. It was nearly the end of spring when a visiting minister spoke to Sarah about baptising her son.

'Bring him into the fold, embrace the flock,' the pastor suggested.

So, on the second Sunday in October, the little party of Tom, Charley, Lilly, and Billy Mathews, who had decided to stay on a little longer before he went gold prospecting, Sarah and James Junior, all set off for Echuca. Sarah made herself a Sunday dress: a gown of blue silk tied to the back with a short bustle. A hat lined with the same silk completed the ensemble. Little James was dressed in his first complete suit. The child was not amused when his mother tied his little cravat, and he whinged the whole way into Echuca.

The minister, a portly man of the cloth, took a sour approach when a Chinaman, dressed in his best garb and carrying an unholy book, entered the church with the official party.

All of this faded into obscurity when the minister tried to pour the holy water onto the child.

A heap of banshees could not have yelled louder. Struggling, James Junior managed to slip from his mother's arms and took off up the aisle, only to be caught by Uncle Tom who marched him right back to where the minister stood, looking like the devil had invaded his church.

After they left the church, not quite sure if the deed had been completed, they all proceeded to the Wharf Hotel for lunch. Sarah had decided to stay in town for an extra day and after a discussion with Tom, Charley, and Lilly, the small party headed home with James Junior.

Tom stayed in town to bring her back the following day. Sarah hadn't told them why she wanted to stay in town, and they all knew better than to intrude into her privacy. She booked Tom into the hotel where she was to stay. He had wanted to doss down at the stables but with her insistence, he gave in gracefully.

'Tom, I've booked a table for seven tonight. I do hope you can join me?'

'Thank you, Miss Noonan, but I'd planned to eat with the drovers from Albury. They have worked their way down from Gundagai.'

Tom had taken a step back from Sarah after he saw her walking out with Joe Henely. He knew the man was keen on Sarah and that he could offer her all the material things he couldn't.

'Tom, have I done something to offend you? Suddenly I'm Miss Noonan again?' Sarah asked.

He looked into those pretty violet eyes and wondered why women could be so bloody thick at times.

'All right, Sarah, it would be my pleasure to escort you to dinner tonight.'

After dinner, they strolled out onto the wharf and down to the paddle steamers, where bales of wool were being loaded onto their decks. Sarah had never seen so many paddle-wheeled boats. They stopped by an open cart that was selling cups of tea and slices of damper smothered with lashings of golden syrup. The landing buzzed with activity. Large pulleys lowered the bales down from the road above as people pushed the bales into place on the ships.

Along the other side of the riverbank, stacks of river red gum logs had been lined up, ready to be loaded onto the boats. The mail and dry food supplies, special orders from the women isolated on their lonely runs, were also being loaded. The small communities down river relied heavily on the boats for their supplies.

Sarah loved this time of night. The mist rose over the water, the night birds and the mopoke could be heard singing out their long laments. The occasional splash as a fish jumped sent ripples out over the water. She loved it all, the bustling activities, the smells and the constant echo of the moving water. Tom noticed Sarah shiver.

'You're cold, here, take my coat.'

With that, he removed his jacket and placed it around the shoulders of the woman he loved. They strolled back to the hotel. *What is wrong with me?* she thought. Wasn't this the romantic dream of all young ladies, to walk with a handsome man? If only life could be so simple. Turning back, they strolled up to their hotel, past the Mercantile Store, and kept to the boarded walkway to avoid the heaped-up manure lying in the street.

The lights reflected from the mirrors that lined the foyer as they entered. Couples, arm in arm, smiled as they passed each other. Romance seemed to grip the air as Sarah did her best to ignore her handsome escort.

'Would you like a coffee or perhaps a wine?' Tom wasn't really certain what genteel women drank in company.

'A coffee would be lovely, Tom.'

Sarah didn't seem to be in any hurry to go up to bed. He sat watching her sip the cup of steaming coffee. He was also aware of the heads that turned as she entered the room. *God, she's beautiful.*

'What time do you want to leave tomorrow?'

'I'll try to be ready by one. I've a couple of appointments and some shopping.'

One o'clock wasn't too late; without any problems, they would be home by dusk. The track had been improved over the last two years and the time between the property and Echuca had been cut down to five hours, excluding heavy storms and fallen trees.

The next morning, Sarah rose early. She wanted to take a walk before people were up and about their business. She needed to clear her head before her appointment with the newly appointed bank manager. After which she was to see a doctor; nothing to worry about, she was sure but the bleeding she was suffering had not ceased, and that persistent little cough was quite annoying.

'Please come in, Miss Noonan,'

George Marks was a born charmer. Women fell under his spell. Born and educated in Ireland of English parentage, George, like many middle-class lads, had sailed to the new colony to make his fortune. From washing decks to bank manager, George still marvelled at the opportunities available to men in this land.

Eyes locked on to George's, Sarah blushed and moved forward to where he was pulling out a chair for her. She noticed his well-manicured hands and wondered if he had ever done a hard day's work in his life.

'This is a pleasure. How may I help you?'

The tall, fair man studied the young woman. She was dressed in a half crinoline cream gown, the skirt pulled back into a bustle. Cream kid gloves covered her hands and a straw bonnet trimmed with matching stripes sat cocked to the right side of her head. He wondered why this attractive woman was here unescorted.

'Sir, I would like to open an account and then transfer money from Sydney.' Sarah handed him a letter of introduction.

On reading the documents, George Marks sat up straight in his seat and took on a more professional demeanour. He handed the documents back to Sarah and politely asked what type of accounts she wished to open. It took an hour to settle her affairs.

The sun warmed her as she wandered down the street towards the newly built emporium that sat up high on the opposite side to the wharf. This was the first time Sarah had felt like a woman in a very long time. A sales assistant hurried across to her and together they spent her money. James Junior did very well, so did Lilly, and Charley was remembered when Sarah saw a set of knives and knew he would appreciate them.

At midday, she walked into the office of a local doctor and spoke to a young girl sitting near the front door. The practice was conducted in the front of a small house, the residence attached to the back. It was located near the lane that ran from the wharf through to the main street.

'Come on in, Miss Noonan.' A middle-aged man opened a door leading into his office. The bald-headed doctor was stooped, but once he smiled his slight disability was lost in the personification of friendliness.

'How may I help you, my dear?'

*My, this woman could take one's breath away*, he thought, as she sat down opposite him.

Sarah explained her woman's trouble and after an examination, a course of treatment was discussed. Dr Allan Little sat back in his chair, listening to his patient. As she spoke, he noticed a small cough of hers and the guttural sound it made.

'Tell me, Miss Noonan, how long have you had that chest infection?'

'It comes and goes.' Sarah thought for a minute. 'Probably for twelve months or so.'

He listened to her chest and asked her to cough up some phlegm. After examining it, he turned back to face Sarah.

'My dear, I think you may have a mild case of tuberculosis.'

The words reverberated in her ears. 'How could I have caught it here?'

'You probably had it before you came to the colony. We don't know what triggers it. Did any of your family or workmen have any symptoms that I've spoken about?'

'Oh my God!' Sarah's hands flew to her mouth as she felt the panic grip her body. 'Doctor, what about my son?'

'Is he sick?'

'No, he's the picture of health.' She sat there wringing her hands, her hanky twirling around in her fingers.

'Sarah, your contagious period is long over, and if nobody else is displaying any signs then they will all be fine. But we must talk about you now. Remember, plenty of rest, milk, cream, and eggs, and no stress.'

'Thank you, Doctor.' She shook his hand and with the previous hour still a haze in her mind, she walked back to the hotel to meet Tom.

Leaning back onto the verandah rail, Tom watched her figure as she crossed over the road and walked towards him. 'Finished all your chores?'

He couldn't quite make out what she was saying. Was she talking to him or to herself?

'Do you want me to get the rig?' he asked, waiting for her reply. Suddenly, Sarah looked up and stared across as if she were seeing him for the first time.

'Yes, Tom, let's go home.'

# Chapter eighteen

**_Murray River, Echuca_**

The bullock teams stood loaded at the wharf. They waited patiently to be unloaded, stamping their feet as swarms of flies covered them. The heat reflecting off the water below gave little relief to animals and people alike. Sarah looked back as they made their way around the beasts and headed out of town. The day was warm, and Tom had suggested that Sarah use her parasol to protect her from the heat. Small market gardens edged the road. The fresh vegetables were a welcome treat to the prospectors and shopkeepers alike. The smell of eucalyptus and sweat lingered in the air.

Having picked up her mail, Sarah looked at the envelopes and at the postmarks. Two were accounts and as she flicked through them a return address marked Gulgong caught her eye.

'Excuse me Tom, I want to read this letter.'

Tom glanced over at her. She had removed her gloves and was opening the seal. After reading it to herself, she started to read it aloud.

_Dear Sarah,_

_How are you and little James and not forgetting Tom and Charley? All the kids miss you still, although the present school master is well liked and respected._

_Sarah, you will never guess what has happened here. They struck a rich vein of gold not fifty yards further down from Tom's lease. The place is alive with people. Chinese and a few Americans have arrived with all the rest. Pubs are popping up everywhere. Jim has bought into one, The Wool Pack; he says it will make us more money than the gold. But truly, Sarah, I don't_ *think it is any place to raise children.*

*Has Tom proposed yet? We all knew he was sweet on you. Girl, you are too young to be alone. Grab that man before someone else does.*

*Love, Sally, Jim, and the kids.*

When Sarah came to the marriage advice, she muttered something to Tom, as to imply that the rest was women's business.

'Tom, do you want to go back?' She watched his facial expression carefully and waited for him to answer.

He breathed out slowly and looking at her, spoke in a soft poetic manner, 'I made my decision before I left.' Then smiled, stating, 'Besides, there is plenty of gold in Bendigo, if that's what I wanted.'

The air suddenly became sexually charged and an uncomfortable barrier loomed up between them.

The trip home was uneventful. The team shied once as a large snake lay basking in the sun across the track. Tom was too good a horseman to ever lose control of the team. The sun was setting as the familiar bend in the river with its huge gums sweeping low onto the sandy bar came into view. Munu waved as they circled their camp and as she expected, curled up in Munu's arms, wriggled a mischievous little white boy.

That night, Sarah sat on her verandah in a newly acquired rocking chair. Charley had seen it in Echuca lying on a pile of rubbish, or that's what he told her, and she knew better than to ask any questions.

'Charley, have you got the time to have a cup of tea with me?' She patted a bench beside herself, before entering her living room to fetch another cup. 'Aren't the stars bright tonight? I feel as though I could touch them. The heavens here are so bright compared with the cloud-covered sky of England.'

After pouring the tea, she handed the cup to her friend and noticed that he looked a little uncomfortable sitting there.

'Charley, I miss the nights on the drove, when we sat and talked. Here we all seem to be too busy.' She watched him relax, and start to sip the tea. Still, the Chinaman hadn't spoken. Taking the initiative, she started to talk. 'Charley, what made you stay in Australia? I know that your people usually go back to China. But you stayed?'

Charley snorted and blew the smoke from his cigarette out in rings that floated off into the breeze. 'Missy, much trouble in China, many people killed. All my family dead, because they wouldn't betray our empress. My wife and children die because I not join the Boxers. I stay here, much better now because I have Missy and little James.'

Sarah's hand trembled as she replaced her cup. Leaning forward, she took the old man's hand in hers and gently said to him, 'Charley, we are all family now.'

On the first week in December, Sarah and her son left on a stage for Albury. There they were to stay a few days before the coach left for Gundagai, where Joe was to meet them.

Albury was a colourful town. Stockmen and drovers made up most of its population. The Murray was wide and deep, with barges tied up to the landing. A bridge was in the process of being built, which would join the two states.

Not all Victorians were eager to have such free access to the state, making an easy road for all the drifters that wandered the land in search of anything that was not nailed down.

Sarah loved walking with her son along the newly laid out parks that bordered the river. In the afternoon after James had rested, they walked up a steep hill to a lookout. Sarah carried him most of the way and was starting to wonder why she had taken on such a task. But when she put the child down and looked out at the view, she found that it was breathtaking.

In the far distance, she could see the Snowy Mountains and to the west she looked back towards her own land and to where Tom was waiting for her. James was starting to become restless, so with him firmly planted on her hip, she started back down to the hotel.

That night, James Junior fell asleep as she was dressing for dinner. Sarah stood by the tall mirror, not sure what to do with the child, when a maid offered to listen out for him while she dined downstairs. Sarah smiled and thought how nice it was to have a few moments to pamper oneself. She loved her son more than life itself but occasionally it was lovely to dress up and pretend. Sarah had chosen an apricot taffeta dress with a trim of heavy ochre-coloured lace, and to complete the dress she wore the cashmere shawl draped over her shoulders. Around her neck hung the gold chain with the pearl drop, the one James had given her the night of the ball. She placed a cover over her sleeping child, and with a quick last look in the mirror Sarah closed the door and headed down the stairs towards the lounge.

There, standing by the bar at the end of the public lounge room, stood a familiar figure. Joe Henely was a straight-cut man, he stood with one foot raised on the brass rail and as he was lifting a drink to his lips, he noticed Sarah standing in the doorway.

'Are ya surprised, my dear?' He watched her walk to his side before waiting for her to reply.

'I can't believe it, Joe. Weren't we supposed to meet at Gundagai?'

'I had some business to conduct, so I decided to wait for you. We can travel back together.'

The excuse sounded a bit boyish, but the truth was he couldn't wait even two extra days to see her.

'Sarah, you look lovely. I hope you are hungry.'

'How did you know I would come down to eat?'

She watched him burst into laughter.

'I sent up a maid to investigate. She told me she was going to watch over the wee lad.'

Sarah knew Joe was fifty-three but standing there he looked quite dashing in his well-cut breeches and tweed jacket.

'Come on, lass, let's eat.'


The trip up to Joe's property was picturesque. The mountain lorikeets screeched from their high branches and rose into the sky in a kaleidoscope of colour as they passed underneath: red, blue, and yellow, a living rainbow against the blue sky.

Sarah didn't know in which direction to look. The mountains were silhouetted against a sky so blue she felt she could touch it. Never in England had she seen anything so beautiful. Joe had taken young James from the dray and sat him against the pommel of his saddle, in front of him. The child loved it all; hanging on to the bridle and a 'Giddy up' could be heard by his mother as they went by.

It was about midday when the homestead came into view. Sarah dismounted from the dray and walked alone to the verandah, where she waited for Joe and her son.

'We've got a good rider in the making here, Sarah. What he needs is a wee pony.' After lifting the child down, Joe handed the reins over to a stockman and walked through the gate, past a bed of roses and up the steps onto the porch.

The homestead was one storey with a broad verandah running around three sides of it. Grapevines covered the walkways leading to the kitchen and meat rooms, giving shade to the house in the blistering heat. The windows ran down to the floor; the doorway was wide and inviting and opened onto a spacious cool tiled hall.

'Rest a while, and I'll have the girl watch young James. Dinner shouldn't be long. Sarah, perhaps you would like to wash up? You know where your room is.'

'Thanks, Joe, I think I will.' Sarah made her way down the hall to the familiar bedroom she had used before. The men had placed her carpet bag on the foot of the bed.

'The cook has informed me that dinner will be in an hour, so take your time.'

She could hear footsteps growing fainter as Joe left the house and walked over to the barn to inspect a new foal that he had been telling her about on the way up, half Arab and half thoroughbred.

She remembered what Tom had said about the horse breeding during Joe's last visit. It had started an argument, Tom insisting the horse would be far too highly strung for stock work.

They ate lunch on the verandah overlooking the valley and out towards the distant snow-covered peaks. Sarah loved the white cane furniture with its brightly covered cushions that occupied the sunroom. It was a touch of femininity in a man's world.

'Sarah, I've invited a few neighbours over on Saturday to meet you. They are a nice lot of folk. I think you will like them.'

Saturday dawned bright and sunny, and true to Joe's word, the temperature was much cooler. Sarah rode out with Joe to inspect the cattle and they stopped at a drover's hut for morning tea. She enjoyed his company especially as he hadn't pushed her for an answer to his proposal.

'We don't have to hurry back, lass, let's sit a while and talk.' Joe moved closer to her and threw the dregs from his mug onto the fire, then sat looking down at her, waiting for the conversation to start.

Sarah knew what was coming. She had seen how good he was with James, and the kindness he showed her. Her mother said love would come after marriage, but would it?

'Joe, I realise you need an answer. You've waited so patiently, never pushing. The truth is, dear, I don't love you the way I should.

You've offered me the world and I don't know what to say to you.'

Her mind was in turmoil; she didn't know what the right thing to do for herself was but more importantly what was right for her son.

'Sarah, I don't expect you to love me the way you loved the boy's father. But I do love you. Think! A good life for you and the boy. I would not be a demanding husband and you could still have control of your own place.'

Sarah thought to herself, *Control of my* own *place*, her son's place, suddenly the answer was very clear, but how to tell him…

'Please, Joe, don't be angry with me, but at the moment I don't wish to be married.' There, she had said it. She waited for him to speak.

'It's all right, dear, I'm a patient man, and I can wait.'

A look of relief came over her face. *Why is everything so dammed hard?* she thought.

'Come on, Sarah, I'll race you back to the homestead.'

Christmas was wonderful. Sarah met the neighbours and loved talking with the women. She realised how lonely she had become for women's talk. The longing to see her family was overwhelming.

Joe drove her back to Albury, and as the coach pulled away, she wondered if she had done the right thing. Joe watched the coach until it moved out of sight. *She will be back*, he thought as he mounted his horse, and turned its head for home.


'Welcome back, Miss Noonan. I hope you had a good trip.'

Tom and Charley had driven to Echuca to meet the coach. Tom didn't know what to expect from Sarah. On seeing the child, his face softened, and he bent down to scoop James up into his arms.

'It's great to be back here, Tom, and yes, I did have a lovely time. How is everyone?'

Tom's face hadn't broken a smile. 'Very happy to have our mistress back, or is she?'

'Is she what?' Sarah could have hit him. How dare he make her feel guilty for having a life!

'We thought that perhaps you were coming back with a new master.'

Tom stepped back. Just in time or he would have collected her bag as she swung it at him.

'Tom Brian, if, or whom I marry, is my decision and I'll thank you to keep your thoughts to yourself.'

Charley watched the pantomime as it unfolded. His Missy was back, and Master Tom was in strife. Tom's facial expression mellowed.

'Sorry, Sarah, I guess I must have missed you and the kid.' His eyes sparkled as he suddenly realised she was not to wed Joe. 'Do you need to do any shopping?'

'Stop trying to weasel back into my good books, Tom Brian.' She broke into a smile and replied, 'Now, boys, let's go home.

On James Junior's third birthday, a small pony had been delivered from Joe along with the mail from Echuca. She flicked through the usual mail, stopping to look more closely at an embossed envelope. There on the back, a seal of a noble family was stamped across the flap. Sarah sat at her desk and broke the seal, then started to read.

*Dear Miss Noonan,*

*It is with great delight that my husband and I have just learned about you and the birth of our grandson. James's death both shocked and saddened us.*

*Harold arrived in June and told us all about you and the love that James felt. It breaks my heart to realise that he never knew about his son and heir. Harold told us about James's will and the courage that you have shown in the colony. After much discussion with my husband and our solicitor, it gives me pleasure to tell you that the baby will legally be James's heir. He will be entitled to James's share of his inheritance.*

*My husband has, with your permission, already enrolled him at Eton and later on at Oxford. All the Lowe men attended there. We hope that you might be able to visit, or better still come and live with us. A trust fund has been set up for the child and if you should care to live here, a living allowance would be paid to you. Harold is returning to New South Wales and will bring back this letter. God keep you both safe.*

*Maria Lowe, James's mother.*

Sarah sat staring at the letter, then she read it again, trying to take in everything—allowance and inheritance; it all seemed surreal. But there were years before James needed to attend school in England and in the meantime there was a party to attend and a farm to run.

The neighbour's children, along with the kids from the

stockmen's camp had been invited. Rusty, the little pony, was a great hit with all the kids and Sarah alike.

Sarah now had neighbours with children, and she was very friendly with them all. Across the river, a family of Irish immigrants had taken up a small holding near Tom's. Sarah and Tom had a small punt built so that Tom could access his property, so every Saturday she would go across the river, laden with fresh eggs, butter, and milk. The parents were proud, but with Sarah explaining that they were doing her a kindness by taking her overproduction of these foods, she was able to help them out. The wife was small and quite pretty. Before eight children, Sarah felt that she would have been beautiful. Eight pregnancies in nine years had taken a toll on her, coupled with a drunken husband, and her lot was one of hard work.

Joe had looked far and wide for a suitable mount for James Junior. If Joe had learned anything over the last few years, it was that the way to Sarah's heart was through her child. He visited her often, much to the annoyance of Tom who was always civil but never joined them for dinner, although he was always asked.

'Why don't you ask her again, Tom? Your own property holding has grown and you are certainly rich enough.'

Lieutenant Paul Adams, adjutant to the army supply officer and horse buyer, had become good friends with Tom. Over the years, Tom had confided in Paul and talked often of his feelings for Sarah and her rejection of him.

'Tom, you do a splendid job managing her large property and starting your own. She would be buggered without you, and she knows that.'

The lieutenant was a nice man, friendly, stiff upper lip and all that. But in spite of their difference in upbringing, Tom had found a real mate.

'The trouble is that Sarah would not admit she needs me. You should have seen her, Paul, when she told me she was going to be a farmer. She was so determined to go; I knew that I had to come along, to protect her from herself.'

They both sat drinking. Tom looked forward to the buying visits that occurred twice a year. He had made Sarah and himself a lot of money, and with his share of their investments, he had been able to buy one thousand acres on the Victorian side of the river.

'Paul, she is so stubborn. Beautiful, but stubborn.'

Tom sat there rolling another cigarette. Both the men knew the anguish that women could cause men.

'Maybe you should forget her. There's many a fine lass around, Tom, and you are reasonably good looking. Not as handsome as me, but fair enough.' Paul ducked as a boot came flying his way. 'Come on, mate, ride into Echuca with me, it will be five months before I'm back.' Paul grabbed his friend's shoulder.

'Yes, maybe I will, Paul. Maybe I *do* need a change of scenery.'

The whips cracked as the bullock team rolled into the inland port. More and more people were streaming into Echuca, expanding the town along the river. Clouds of smoke billowed down the street and over the buildings from the charcoal burners on the far side of the river, often making it hard to breathe.

A wood carver had set up shop alongside a potter and with local artefacts and practical goods now on sale, the women of the area no longer needed to transport all their goods from Melbourne.

Tom strolled up from the river and entered the new shops. He appreciated fine workmanship and the quality of what he saw was some of the finest.

The wood turner looked up as the tall stockman entered. 'Can I help you, mate?'

'Thanks.' Tom strolled around the workshop and walked back to where the older man bent over the steam-driven lathe. 'I like that table and cabinet, how much?'

'For you, twenty pounds, and I'll throw in a couple of chairs.'

'Fifteen quid and four chairs and we have a deal.' Tom smiled as the man stretched out his hand to seal the bargain. 'And by the way, I want one of those fancy beds and wardrobe. I can pay you now, but I can't pick them up until I finish my house.'

'Have you finished spending your money yet?' Paul had been waiting on the dock and spotted Tom ambling towards him. 'I could die of thirst waiting for you.'

'Paul, you told me to start to make a life for myself and now I have.'

# Chapter Nineteen

Rain! Sarah stood on the verandah and looked up to the sky. The black clouds hovering over the river plains now bucketed down the rain. The humidity had finally lifted, and a clear sweet smell lingered in the forest. Droplets of water dripped down from the eucalypt foliage, refreshing her senses. In the six years she had owned her property, she had never experienced such a big wet.

The elders of the Aboriginal camp had warned her of the water that was to come. Joe had written to Sarah telling her of the heavy snowfalls in the mountains, all of which would end up in the Murray.

'Tom, have all the stock been moved to the northern paddocks?'

She looked across to the bunk house and could see the stockmen coming and going, their horses as drenched as the men themselves.

'Even the bloody chooks are safe. Charley had already moved the milkers yesterday. He took the dray out to stay with them, two are close to calving.'

Tom was drenched, the water running off his felt hat was nothing compared to the squishing in his boots.

What about your stock on the other side of the river, will they be safe?'

Sarah realised that Tom should really have stayed on his own property, not be there with her. Tom had built his house on a high ridge overlooking the river flats.

'Sarah, my place is fine; it's yours I'm worried about. Don't let James escape again. The little bugger wants to see the river rising.'

Tom had previously carried back a most indignant five-year-old from the Aboriginal camp where he had hidden, hoping his mother would forget about him.

'Keep the shovel handy.' Tom handed a long-handled shovel over to her. 'The snakes are also looking for high ground and please, don't go to the river unescorted; in fact, don't go at all.'

Tom knew where young James got his streak of defiance from. Sarah was far worse than any child.

'The water won't reach here, will it?'

Sarah had already put all her treasures up high. Her journal and letters were safely tucked high up in the rafters along with a baby possum that must have been separated from its parents.

Higher and higher up the bank, the water rose. Great gums were now toppling into the river as the banks were being eroded away, causing blockages in the river flow that needed to be cleared away. Sarah hung on to James. Was this the Armageddon that had been preached to all the sinners? The land shook under her feet as a gum crashed down beside her.

'Tie the ropes to the lower branches and get those drag lines fastened to the horses,' yelled Tom, whose voice could barely be heard above the roar of the water.

'That's the most we can do, boss, it's too dangerous to try again, the bank won't last.' The stockmen knew their jobs. Tom had confidence in their good judgement which they had proved over and over again throughout the years. There was nothing more anyone could do but watch and wait.

The men had placed hurricane lamps in the trees and long poles were rammed into the banks as markers; still they waited. With an almighty roar on the third day, the banks collapsed, and the river broke through, spilling out onto the flats, engulfing all before it. The water was level with the verandah boards on Sarah's house when Tom waded over to her steps.

'Sarah, it won't be safe here for you. Those stumps'—he pointed to the far end of her cabin—'are moving. Get ready; I'm bringing back the horses so that James and you can be led out. You can only take a few things, love. The men will put the furniture up.'

'Tom, can't we use the drays?' Sarah was saddened to leave all the lovely things that had been given to her by Joe and the pieces that she had bought herself, all memories of her life here.

'No, the ground is too soft now for the metal wheels. Even the horses are bogging down.'

James tugged on his mother's skirt. 'Mummy, I need to go down to the river to get my pony. Can I go now? And I need to do a wee.'

Before Sarah could reply, Tom yelled back, 'No, James. Sarah, for God's sake, please, watch over the boy.' Then rethinking the conversation, he said, 'Yes, James, do a wee.'

She packed some of their clothes. It hurt her to think that all that lovely furniture would probably be ruined but that could be replaced. After wrapping her inlaid Chinese puzzle box, containing some letters and James's pearl drop, in her bedspread—a present from the women of Gulgong—she placed a chair on the table and climbed up to reach the rafters. There she hoped the parcel would be safe. Sarah took her child's hand and led him to the door to wait for Tom. Suddenly remembering the baby possum and climbing back up, she placed an apple on the beam near it and speaking in a soft tone said, 'Good luck, little one, you're on your own now.'

As she was closing the door, she turned and ran back inside. A few minutes later, she returned with a little bundle wrapped in a towel.

'I couldn't leave her, Tom, she has nobody.'

Tom was lost for words and shook his head, lifting Sarah, complete with possum, up into the saddle. Looking back at James, he smiled. 'Son, I think your mother is a little mad.'

Tom led them out and along the track to where the Aborigines had made their new camp.

'Sarah, please stay here!' Tom turned to Lilly, who was heavily pregnant, and spoke, 'Please keep an eye on them. I'll be back before dusk.'

He mounted his horse and rode out towards the northern boundary.


It took a week for the water to recede. All the stock survived, which was more than could be said for the homestead. Sarah looked in disbelief at the pile of timbers that had once been her home. Reaching into the mud, she located her rather dirty parcel.

Tom watched her cry and knew he had to say something comforting. 'Sarah, stop that snivelling.' He wanted to comfort her. 'We can build again but not so close to the water.' He groaned to himself as he thought of the words that had escaped his lips. They weren't exactly what he had meant. She turned to face him; her lips trembling as she tried to stop crying. 'Oh, Sarah, I'm sorry. I always put my foot in it, don't I?' Putting his hands on her shoulders, he pulled her closer to him. 'Stay with me. No, bugger it! Marry me.'

She thanked him again but only agreed to stay with him until her home was rebuilt. Why did he make it so difficult? Didn't he realise how much she wanted him, how much she wanted to feel his body pressed into hers? It would be so easy to go to his bed but then what about James's inheritance? The question never left her. What of her son's security?

Out of the disaster, something great had occurred for them all. The water level was now higher, and the steamboats were able to reach further up the river. The men had built a jetty and once a fortnight they all waited on the bank, listening for the blast of the horn as the boat rounded the bend and headed over to Sarah's side of the river, just missing the sandbars that were always moving. James Junior knew every captain that sailed past. Often they would take him aboard and deposit him upstream on a neighbour's property, where Sarah would have to fetch him back. The older Aboriginal children swam out to the boats, much to the annoyance of the crew.

'I'm telling you, these kids will be killed. Can't you talk to the parents? I've more to do than avoid kids, these sandbars are enough.'

Sarah listened but knew that the parents couldn't control the kids either. The Aborigines controlled their children with love, and the kids ran free and wild, and the parents seldom handed out any physical punishment, ignoring the preacher's words. *Spare the rod and spoil the child.'*

Life was returning to normal. Tom liked his house guests and was not in any hurry to see them depart.

'Tom, Joe is sending down half a dozen men to help with the build.' She had written to him telling him of her disaster. And he had acted immediately. 'That's kind of him, don't you think?' she said as she folded the letter and replaced it back into its envelope.

Tom smiled and muttered something about kindness, but really wished Joe would mind his own bloody business.

The new house was larger than the old one, two extra bedrooms had been added. They had picked out a location on a small rise that looked down to the river and over to where she could see Tom's property. Yes, the new place was beautiful with its sweeping verandahs, but she missed the little cabin, her first home, her piece of Australia.

Sarah, Charley, and Lilly — complete with her baby son, Jack — spent most of their time in the veggie garden. Neighbours had brought over herbs and seedlings to start it off. Tom had insisted that all the scrub be cleared back from her house. 'As a safeguard,' he had said to her, when she had tried to stop the men. Only three large gums were left in the home paddock.

Charley had just returned from Echuca. Sarah walked down to the dray to collect the mail and a local paper that had been started up, when an excited Charley waved and yelled out to her. 'Look, Missy, presents from Mr Joe.'

Sarah untied the hessian bags and was thrilled to find rose cuttings and a lavender bush, a little worse for wear after the long trip. Tom took one look, sniggered and stated that the man must be crazy but wished secretly he had thought of that.

The roses grew and the cuttings taken from the lavender lined the gardens. At night, the perfume of the lavender, mingled with the star jasmine that grew up the verandah posts, was sensual and bewitching. A small lawn had been planted, a little remembrance of her childhood home.

James was a good pupil. Sarah had started to educate him and any of the Aboriginal children who wanted to learn. He hurried through his lessons and then scampered off to the river with the other kids. The Aboriginals had taught James to swim, and he now swam like a fish, jumping from ropes into the river, much to the horror of his mother.

It was stinking hot. Small birds fell from the heavens, dead. All the grass had turned a shade of brown, withered up and died. The stockmen had taken Sarah's herd out on the stock route looking for feed, leaving only a nucleus of breeders behind.

The river was low again; the boats had stopped coming and at places the sandbars stretched from bank to bank. Small billabongs were drying up, leaving the fish to die in the mud banks. Sarah struggled with little water to keep her garden alive. But once a week she gave her roses a cup of their liquid gold.

A horse galloped into the holding yards, in a lather of sweat. It dropped its head into a water trough as its rider headed up to the homestead.

'Miss, there's a fire broken out not two miles away. The boss says to get James and go to the native's camp, stay close to the water.'

Sarah waved back her acknowledgment and turned to run back to the house. Just then the smell of smoke drifted towards her. High up in the sky, swirls of black smoke gathered like storm clouds. Cockatoos screeched and rose in their hundreds. Mobs of kangaroos bounded away through the cleared paddocks toward the plains.

Sarah searched the horizon. The sun had turned blood red and flames could be seen leaping across the treetops, growing in strength as they came ever closer.

'James, where are you? Quickly now, we need to go to Munu.' Grabbing her box and journal from the bedroom chest and keeping a close eye on James, they ran down to where Munu was waiting for them. Digging out a hole, Sarah buried her treasures in the sand just above the water line.

The fire was roaring by now and the air was thick with smoke. Sarah couldn't see, the smoke irritated her eyes. Their lungs burned as they breathed in the intense heat. Above her the gums burst into flames; the roar of the fire was deafening as Sarah pulled James towards the water.

'Missy, hurry!'

Munu pushed her and the boy into a hole in the bank down under the water line. The trees were exploding above them, dropping their burning branches into the river. The old Aboriginal lady had lived through many fires and knew what to do. She gave them a hollow reed to suck on and as the fire engulfed the air above them, she pushed their heads under the water.

Sarah didn't know how long they stayed there. She could feel her son and the older woman beside her, but suddenly her mind was taking her to a place long ago. Her mama and she were picnicking on a stream near her home. She could hear her mother telling her not to go near the water, but she wanted to paddle her feet in the cool clear liquid. The water swirled around and around, her mother's face faded... Then she was lifted up. Strong arms were holding her, carrying her across the river to safety. She struggled, was that her screaming? Where was her child? What were they saying? She couldn't make out the muffled voices. Then the peace that only unconsciousness can bring engulfed her.

When she woke, she was lying in Tom's bed, and he was sitting watching her, a look of concern covering his face.

'Tom, where's James?' Her throat was so painful she had difficulty saying the words.

'He's safe. Sleep now and we can talk later.'

He held her hand as she drifted off again. She had been lucky. Only her hands had been burnt and with the salve that the Aboriginal women had covered her in, not even a scar would remain. Tom watched over her. He wondered at her spirit and untiring fortitude. If she had died in the fire, his utter sadness would have destroyed him. What would he have done? *How could I keep going*, he thought. And how could he love someone again? This event had made it clearer than ever to Tom just how much he was in love with Sarah.

On the second day, Sarah got up and wanted to know what damage had been done by the fire and if all the camp dwellers were safe.

'The homestead was spared, we had cleared enough area around it, but we lost the barns and some of the stock.'

She sat on Tom's verandah looking over to the scorched earth that was hers. Tom crouched down beside her, a long piece of grass poking out the side of his mouth, his large-brimmed felt hat firmly on his head. Sarah had rested easy after seeing her child. She would never be aware of the large, calloused hands that had attended to her every need.

'Munu saved your lives, and yes, they are all safe. They've lived with the elements for thousands of years and know the signs and how to survive.'

'What about the mares, Tom, and the foals?' It seemed ghostly quiet there, not a sound; not even a bird flew above the blackened forest.

'We lost James's pony. He couldn't keep up with the others, and they trampled him. James knows. He took it like a man.'

The words raced out of her mouth. 'Tom, he isn't a man, he's only a child.'

'Sarah, here they have to grow up early.'

On his ninth birthday, James Junior wrote to his grandparents to thank them for his present. He told them that he could swim and shoot, and that Uncle Tom was showing him how to use a stock whip and how his Latin was progressing nicely. His grandmother wrote often to Sarah, enquiring about the lad and always asking after her also. Her latest letter seemed sad; she told Sarah that her husband was not well and desperately wanted to see the boy before he died. Over the years, her ladyship had played that card often but this time the story seemed to have depth. The old lady had played every card in the pack to have Sarah and James return to England — such as education and money — but this was desperation.

Sarah wrote to Harold who had returned to England to retire. She enquired as to the lord's health and if it would be safe for her to return. His reply arrived while she was holidaying in Sydney and attending to the final transfer of paperwork for her property. Now her property was in her child's name with her as guardian. Sarah trusted Harold in the same way that James had. Sitting in her familiar tea shop, she started to read the letter.

*Dear Sarah,*

*How are you both? Still avoiding that wedding ring of Tom's? Sarah, you were right, James's grandfather is ailing, and if the boy is to see him alive you will need to act with great haste. I've spoken with Sir Charles Fitzroy and he now assures me that you would be quite safe again in England. The court decided a man was responsible for the murder, the father of the lad involved, he was finally released, mental problems. Sir Charles also says your mother is enjoying good health and loves the house he bought for her with your money.*

*While I was there I saw the Masters's little girl. She appears to be a sweet child, must take after her grandparents. Sir Charles has bought a place in Scotland. I really don't know why anyone would want to live in that harsh climate. I heard from Tom, he informed me that your farm is a great success. My dear, I know that my James would be so proud of you. Let me know if I can help in any way. By the way, I ran into that woman you sailed out here with, she said that you owe her a letter.*

*All of my love, Harold.*

It took two months for Sarah to finalise her business and book a passage to England. Tom tried to talk her out of it but when Sarah's mind was made up, nothing could change it. James Junior had protested; he used charm and when that didn't work, he threw a temper tantrum. Even Joe Henely, who had now given up his pursuit of Sarah, joined Tom in trying to stop her going.

'You must be mad, Sarah. Taking that child on such a long sea voyage is irresponsible.' Joe had returned with her to the farm after meeting her in Gundagai at the changeover station. Later at Sarah's homestead, the three of them talked over the problems that may occur with such a long sea trip.

'James has a right to meet his grandfather, my James's father.'

Tom looked at her and the old feelings of anger and sadness engulfed him. He wondered if she would ever forget this man, who according to his reckoning, had only been in her life for months, not years. For nine years he had danced to her tune. Yes, he had tried other women; many wanting to be mistress of both Tom and his large homestead but none of them had shone as brightly as Sarah.

'Sarah girl, you can't expect Tom to run this place as well as his own, while you gallivant off to England.'

Joe lit a smoke and waited for her to reply.

'Well, Joe, I haven't asked him yet,' she stammered.

Tom sat back, pleased that someone was speaking up for him.

'Don't you think you are asking a bit too much this time, Sarah?' Joe put it to her; someone had to.

She stood and backed away from the men, rustling her skirt as she went. It reminded Tom of a chook leaving the nest. Tom wanted to go after her but decided that time fixes most things.

'Thanks, Joe, but I guess I've drawn the lucky straw. She has decided to go, and Hell or high water won't stop her now. I'll look after this bloody place for her, but I swear to God, this is the last time.'

# Chapter twenty

The morning was clear, as crisp as a summer apple. Seagulls circled the ship, waiting to consume any food that might have been thrown overboard. A northerly breeze had sprung up rocking the *Dove*, a three-mast schooner, in its swell. The ship strained on the ropes that held her firmly tied to the wharf. How different the air was here, not that vile stench that polluted the air in London.

When they heard 'All Ashore' the words struck a chord of sadness into the hearts of Tom and Joe alike.

They both had journeyed down to Melbourne with Sarah and James Junior and had spent a week at the Grand Duchess, a luxurious hotel, a treat from Joe. Right up until that very moment, the two still hoped Sarah would change her mind about returning to England.

Mr Lo Lee was the only one who supported her decision. He had written a letter of introduction to some very influential Chinese in England, just in case she needed to return quickly to the colonies. Sarah understood what he had meant and realised that James must have confided in him about her past before he died, and the dangers that might be still waiting for her in England.

The week with both the men had been lovely but very tiring. They used every excuse they knew to pull at her heartstrings, to keep her there. James was becoming extremely naughty towards the end of the week, which made Sarah regret their stay, thinking that it would have been easier all round if they had travelled down to Melbourne alone.

Both men walked up on deck to say their final goodbyes. Joe kissed Sarah and started down the gangway, leaving Tom alone with her.

'Tom, you know all the bank details, use the money if need be and please make sure Charley is comfortable.' The old Chinaman was supposed to have been in retirement, tucked away in a little cabin that Sarah had built for him on her property. He still liked to potter and had a knack of getting under Tom's skin.

'Sarah, we have been over all of this a hundred times. Relax and enjoy the voyage and come back soon.'

He watched her search for a hanky, twisting it in her fingers, the way she did when she was about to cry. He knew every one of her little idiosyncrasies and he wished that she would forget England and leave the ship with him.

'Sorry, sir, you will need to leave the ship now.'

A smartly dressed cabin boy stood by the rail helping the visitors to leave. Sarah had noticed the change in the crew's dress. Gone were the plain dark colours that the boys had worn, and now standing in front of her was a lad, dressed in a blue top and white bell-bottom pants.

'Sarah, I have to go now. Write often and tell me how James is doing and please take care of yourself. Be careful. You have all the addresses that you can go to, if need be.  Love, if you need more money then go to the Colonial Bank. I've arranged an overdraft on my bank if need be.'

'Thanks, Tom, but I don't think that will be necessary.'

She stood there staring at him, her arms by her sides. He pulled her to him and placed his lips over hers, kissing her with such tenderness. She looked into his eyes and saw tears rolling down his cheeks, then without another word he turned his back on her and walked down the gangway. Sarah tugged at her travelling cloak. She wanted to encase herself from the world. To hide, as only a small child hides from despair.

Slowly, the *Dove* pulled away from the moorings. James Junior held his mother's hand and beside them was a governess who had agreed to assist with the care of the lad on the long voyage. They waved to the men until the ship's main sail was hoisted, and the wind carried it out into the bay. Sarah leaned over to speak to the tall middle-aged woman holding James's hand.

'Would you like to have tea with us? That wind is a bit fresh, and I think that we will be much more comfortable in my cabin.'

'That would be very agreeable, Mrs Noonan.'

Mary Hudson hadn't been able to bring herself to call Sarah by her first name or by Miss Noonan either. She was a spinster who had escorted a young lady back to Australia after attending a school in England and was very pleased to be offered a return passage for assisting Sarah with the child. She appeared to be very straight-laced. Her clothes were ten years out of date. She still wore the high laced-up stays that minimised the figure to give a very flat-bosomed look.

Sarah saw a caring, lonely woman and she knew only too well what that was like.

'I'll be there in ten minutes, madam.'

Mary checked her watch; a large gold fob piece that she had informed Sarah had belonged to her father, a retired clergyman. The cabin boy opened the door to her stateroom. She looked around at the splendour money could buy. She had adjoining rooms for James and herself, and Mary was just across the hall. Off her bedroom was the sitting room, furnished with a leather suite and a small round table on which a vase of roses sat. Sarah opened the card next to them and read the small clear print.

*Sarah,*
*Have a safe trip and return to me.*
*Your loving friend,*
*Tom.*

She placed the envelope into her handbag just as there was a tap on the door.

'Come in.'

Standing there was a middle-aged gentleman dressed in the latest cut of European fashion. A heavy gold fob watch hung from his waist coat and a gold-tipped walking stick was balanced under his arm.

'Madam, it has been brought to my attention that you are travelling alone, so I'm here to offer you any assistance that you might need throughout this voyage.'

It took Sarah only a minute to sum up this dandy, who had poked his foot into the doorway.

'Thank you, sir, but I'm not a damsel in distress and if you don't remove your foot, then I will be forced to close this door on it.'

He started to stammer a reply, but it was lost as the door banged back onto its lock.

James Junior quickly found his sea legs. The crew had heard the scuttle bug that he was the lad of Captain James Lowe. A few of the sailors had sailed under the command of Captain Lowe and he had won their loyalty and respect. In turn they had spoken to Sarah about him. James Junior had been told all about his father and sat quietly to listen to the sailors retell stories of his father's sea adventures. Sarah tried not to listen, as it stirred up the hurt of the past. She had mixed feelings. Sarah clung to the hurt. *It should hurt,* she thought but deep down she knew that time was making her forget.

The first month was plain sailing. It was not until the coast of Africa came into view that the weather changed. Gales raged and all the passengers had to remain below deck. Mary was violently sick, and Sarah nursed her through the worst of it. At one time, the seas were so rough that Sarah wondered at her own sanity for starting out on this journey with a child.

Sitting in her lounge, she thought back over the last sea trip she had made, and the different circumstances that were taking her back to England. Sarah's mind drifted back to her first trip to Gulgong. A young woman going into the bush to find work; but instead finding a kind old Chinaman and Tom, the man she was leaving. This was the man whom she loved, and she knew loved her. She had never doubted it throughout the years. Tom, who had saved her life; Tom, who had been there when James was born and who had made her a very rich woman through his hard work. Her mind wandered on to the high country and to Joe who took her rejection but still remained her true friend.

She remembered the nights that they walked down by the river, her river, and how she had tried to count the stars on the dark blue ribbon that floated in the clear heavens. She thought of the look on James's face when Joe delivered his first pony to him. Sarah thought back when she told old Munu that they were going across the sea and how the old black woman cried.

'My God, please. Am I doing the right thing?' she cried into her hands.

The ship unloaded cargo in Cape Town. Sarah, Mary, and James went ashore and as the ship was to stay there for three days, they booked into a hotel overnight. The building was Dutch colonial, high walled and coated in white lime wash. Heavy wooden furniture filled the sitting rooms and copies of the Old Masters hung on the walls. All of this seemed out of place in the heart of the African continent.

They strolled through the busy markets where cartloads of local fruit and vegetables were laid out on the pavement. The spicy smell of the sidewalk stalls made their mouths water. James's eyes were everywhere. Juices from the tropical fruit he was eating ran down his chin; it was a child's paradise. Women suckled their babies opened breasted as they sold their wares in the stalls. And everywhere in this heat there was the constant buzzing of flies.

'Mummy, why don't you dress like those ladies? It would be much cooler for you.'

*Oh, the innocence of children, why can't it last?* Sarah thought as she made her way over to the other stalls, where jugglers amused the passers-by with their antics and shifty hawkers unloaded rare artefacts of unknown sources. Beside them, colourful rolls of material and clusters of brightly dyed feathers were all for sale.

'Mummy, Mummy, look! Please can I have a monkey?' James had spotted the poor little creature that had been tied to the front of a hand cart. 'Mummy, he won't eat much, and I'll pick up the poo, truly I will.'

'James, it would get very sick if we took it on the ship, and we wouldn't have the right type of food for it.' Sarah looked at her son and wondered if he would accept her words. 'And besides, it is very cold in England, and he would shiver.'

'Couldn't you knit him a coat, Mummy?' Those big familiar eyes were trying their hardest as they looked up into her face.

'No, James, it would be cruel.'

Sarah knew her son and she knew that he could not stand any type of cruelty to animals. So this battle she won.

James was satisfied with a bag of lollies and a wooden shield and spear. She also bought a tribal mask to complete the set. They stopped for tea at a very British teahouse set in the midst of the Dutch trade area. The owners had originally worked for the East India Trade Company but when they left India they had decided on Africa, instead of the cold and fogs of London. Sarah also bought lengths of material and tins of dried herbs that she thought her mother would like. Before leaving the colony, Sarah had two lovely gold chains made for her child's grandmothers. A slightly larger one for her late

James's mother and a small one for her mother, whom she knew would think that it was a waste of money.

One week out of Cape Town, James developed a fever and a mild rash. The child's thrashing in his bunk worried Sarah.

'Doctor Marshall, I can't get his temperature down, I'm using tepid water sponges, with a drop of vinegar in it, but nothing seems to work.'

Sarah had consulted the ship's elderly doctor and was pleased when he arrived at her stateroom.

'He has a mild case of measles. We will need to keep him isolated for two more weeks. The worst is over, he'll be fine.' The doctor bent over the child and spoke softly into his ear. 'When your father was a lad and working on a ship of the line, he developed a fever, and I looked after him also. I don't think your mother knows that.'

He winked at the lad, turned, and after handing Sarah a draught, left the room.

Mary fussed over the boy, and it was not long before he was driving Sarah insane wanting to go up on deck. Sarah ate mainly in her suite with James although she was in constant demand by the socialites to dine with them.

'Come, Mrs Noonan,' as most people knew her, 'It's not good for a young widow to stay so much by herself.'

A want-to-be, as Tom called them, by the name of Mrs Polly Simpson-Jones knocked on Sarah's door. 'You have been invited to sit at the captain's table. Oh, what a privilege.'

As she twittered around the room, Sarah realised that this woman had made a grave error by thinking Sarah must have come from the upper niches of British society. Little did she realise how wrong she was.

'Mrs Simpson-Jones, I have already accepted the captain's kind invitation, so maybe I will see you there but for now you must excuse me, I have a child to see to.'

Sarah smiled as she held open the door, waiting for this social climber to leave. Later that evening after Sarah dressed, she asked Mary for her opinion on what she had chosen.

'Mrs Noonan, you look lovely.'

Mary took a step back to be able to take in the complete picture of beauty and good taste.

'Mary, it is not too late for you to come, I will wait.'

'No, madam, I would rather stay here with Master James, but you go and enjoy yourself.'

Sarah had chosen a burgundy velvet gown in the empress style: simple but well cut with a plunging neckline. She had been informed by a dressmaker in Melbourne that the crinoline was outdated, and a more fitted style was in vogue now. She had put on her single pearl necklace and carried the cashmere stole that Joe had given her the first time she had visited his property. Sarah answered a knock on the door.

'Madam, I've been sent to escort you to the dining room.'

Standing at the door was the second-in-command, a young lieutenant dressed in his formal uniform, a reminder of what Brian Lewis, James's second-in-command on the *Harcourt*, had looked like many years before.

On the arm of the young naval officer and under the watch of men and women alike, Sarah entered the room. Her presence was breathtaking; the captain walked out to meet her and helped her to her seat. The dinner was served and as they relaxed afterwards, a tall American introduced himself to her.

'Madam, do you remember me? I rode with you and Captain Lowe into Sydney, I'm Jim Cobb.' He flashed a smile that shone deep into her heart.

'Yes, Mr Cobb, I most certainly do. And let me thank you for the coach service that you started. I've used it many times. Where are you headed for, Mr Cobb?'

Jim Cobb had turned his dream of a coach line throughout the bush into reality. He was good looking in a rugged way. His chiselled jaw line gave a look of determination to a somewhat boyish smile.

'Please, call me Jim.' He leaned over to take her hand in his. 'I'm heading to London then home to California for a spell, but I'll be back in the fall.

By this time, Mrs Simpson-Jones had nearly fallen as she pushed between the side pillars, where she tried to listen in on the conversations between Sarah and Jim Cobb. But before she could squeeze closer, Jim had led Sarah out onto the small dance floor. Sarah felt so grateful to have this familiar figure near her. The dinner had brought back memories of the dinner in another ship, with another captain — her captain.

# Chapter twenty-one

The harbour was crowded with ships from all the corners of the Earth. The *Dove* made her way to her allotted mooring, mainsails lowered and lashed to the mast. Portsmouth was cold, and black clouds gathered over the city. A fine mist, not the warm type that James Junior was used to, but a soaking cold bone-shaking mist, whirled around him and his mother, as they walked hand in hand down the gangway and on to the dock.

Sarah was full of apprehension. She had doubted her own common sense in bringing her child to England. *Too late now*, she thought to herself, as they said their goodbyes to the passengers and crew.

'Sarah, I'll contact you, perhaps we might meet for dinner. That's if you have the time.'

Jim, who had formed a deep friendship over the months at sea with Sarah, placed her travel bag on the wooden walkway near a coach that was waiting for her.

'You just remember, you are as good as any of them and far better than most.'

With that he bent over and kissed her gently on the cheek. A spritely gentleman walked towards her. 'Sarah, it is so good to see you, and look, who have we here?'

Sir Charles had received word of her impending arrival only two weeks earlier. Tom had written to him, asking him to assist her, and the letter had arrived on a fast clipper just in time. There was a feeling of security as the older man threw his arms around her.

'How did you know I'd be on the *Dove*?' asked Sarah.

He stood back and took a long look at this girl, who had

blossomed into a beautiful self-assured woman.

'Sir Charles, may I introduce my son?' Sarah looked down at her son, motioning to the older man.

'James, this is Sir Charles.'

The boy shook hands, and then stood up straight as he looked directly into the eyes of Sir Charles Fitzroy and asked him, 'Sir, do you fight dragons?'

Trying to hide his amusement he replied, 'No, son, only two-legged ones.'

James looked at his mother, he didn't think that was the right answer, but this was a strange country.

'James, Sir Charles was only joking.' She smiled at her friend. 'How is your wife and little Lucy? I'm so looking forward to seeing them again.'

'They are well, and Lucy is a delightful child.'

A look of sadness passed over his face as he recalled his own daughter and the shame that she had brought to his family. Sarah blushed and quickly looked away.

'Sarah, I've booked you into the Doncaster Hotel for two nights. I thought that you might like to shop and show James some of London, then my wife and I were hoping that the two of you would stay with us, at least until you get your land legs back.'

'Thank you, you are very kind.' Sarah's eyes filled with tears. 'I know that this is silly, but standing here brings all the memories back.'

'Well, we can fix that.' He winked at the boy, who was clinging to his mother's hand. 'Into the coach with you both and I think sweets and jelly might sort out that problem.'

'Thank you, sir, my mother would love that.' James spoke up and patted his mother's hand.

Looking at the boy, Sir Charles Fitzroy mused, *you are your father's son.*


James loved London. They inspected the palace where he spoke to the mounted horse guard, enquiring if they swam their horses in the river. They were amused at his questions but answered him in a most sincere way.

A sergeant asked James how he looked after his pony in Australia.

The boy thought for a minute, then informed the sergeant that in Australia, men rode large horses, and that he could also use a stockwhip.

Sarah took him for a ride on the open top deck of a horse-drawn bus. The child waved down to the cabbies as they trotted by. London was a world full of wonder for a young man from the bush.

'Madam, there is a gentleman asking after you, a Mr Cobb. Do you wish to speak with him?' The doorman at the Doncaster had held his position for over forty years. He had seen all types come and go, from the want-to-be to royalty and he had a fair nose for sniffing out a gentleman or a cad. He stood as straight now in his heavily trimmed uniform as he had as a lad of fourteen.

'Yes, thank you, I'll meet him in the lounge room.'

Sir Charles had collected James Junior and they were heading downtown to Hyde Park, to attend a performance of a circus. Sarah wondered who was the most excited, James or the knight of the realm.

She had chosen to wear a deep red serge dress, and a coat that had been trimmed with a black piping. A dressmaker in Sydney had picked the style, insisting that it would be in fashion. Sarah didn't care much for the whims of the élite, as long as she was warm.

'How are you managing, Sarah?' said Jim in his thick American accent.

He had felt so sorry for her, when he had been told of James's death. But now his heart was full of admiration for what she had achieved on the banks of the Murray River. Sarah reminded him of his sister in the New Mexico Territory, who had lost her husband to an attacking band of renegades and had gone on to rear her children alone.

'It's strange to be back here, Jim; I really don't know how I feel. I'm looking forward to seeing my mother, of course, scared of seeing James's parents but most of all, I'm missing the property and my people there.'

'When are you leaving London, Sarah? I'll try to catch up with you before I leave for the old US of A.'

'We are to leave after breakfast tomorrow, Jim. It will take about three days to reach Sir Charles's estate up north.'

Jim Cobb raised his glass in a salute to this most remarkable woman.

'More champagne, sir?' asked the waiter as he topped up the bucket with more ice.

The city was covered in thick fog as the coach wound its way through the streets. Cab drivers stood by their horses, waiting in line for the next paying passenger. The stench in the air brought back memories that Sarah had tried to suppress for the last ten years.

As they pulled into the main city street and passed near Trafalgar Square, Sarah looked out the window and back towards the narrow alley and the small house that had claimed her innocence.

'Mummy, look, there is the Queen's palace. Do you think that the knights will be fighting any dragons today?'

James Junior didn't know where to look first, it was all so wonderful and for him, the magic was everywhere.

'No, darling, not today, it's Sunday.'

Sir Charles chuckled to himself as the child stared with wonder at everything that went by.

The inn was clean, and a plain but wholesome meal was served to the three guests that evening. The dining room was packed with travellers; many were travelling to the yearling sales, where the best studs sold their young stock. Warm bloods and racing stock were in demand by the gentry to fill the hunting clubs and the gambling stables.

James Junior was fascinated by all the talk about horses, his knowledge of breeding and selection astounded the buyers, and they questioned his mother as to where the boy had gained his knowledge. Sarah took pride in telling the men about her property and how Tom and she were contributing to the army's cause, in producing the finest types of military mounts.

Sarah admired the landscape as they made their way along the country lanes. She had forgotten how lovely the English countryside was, even in winter. They climbed higher, leaving the rolling hills and winding their way up to the village where Sir Charles had purchased a manor house surrounded by an acreage. It was nightfall as they pulled into the iron gates that marked the beginning of the rural estate.

All the lights were on in the main house and a warm friendly greeting met Sarah as she stepped down from the coach. Lady Fitzroy encased Sarah in her arms.

'How I have wished for this, Sarah, to have you both here with me, thank God for this mercy.' The older woman choked back a sob as she held the girl. 'Who have we here?' she said as the lad stepped up beside his mother.

James Junior smiled and shook the matron's hand. 'I'm James, your ladyship, and I'm here to slay the dragons that might attack my mother.'

'James, I have a little princess who lives with us, I think you two will be the best of friends.'

James wasn't sure about that. He didn't really like girls that much, except his mother. They always seemed to cry a lot. He liked the Aboriginal girls. They swam with him in the river, sometimes with no clothes on. He had asked his mother about the different body parts that they had, but all she said was that Uncle Tom would tell him all about them when he was older. *Very curious*, he thought.


Little Lucy was a sweetheart and even James seemed to like her. She had a little pony and could ride, which impressed James.

'Mummy, I think I might teach her how to use a stock whip, just in case a dragon turns up and I'm not here.'

'Perhaps you should ask Sir Charles, dear?'

'No, Mummy, he is very busy running this country for the Queen. Besides, he has told me to call him Uncle Fitzroy now that we are to live here.'

Later that day, Sarah had a chance to speak to the older couple. 'I'd like to arrange transport to visit my mother. I know that my sea trip will have worried her a great deal.'

Sarah didn't have the heart to tell them that she would be moving on as soon as possible. Sarah realised that her ladyship still wanted her to fill the void that had been caused by her daughter's death at sea, after she had murdered James, in her insane greed for wealth.

After three days they started out again. This time the trip only took two days. Sarah's mother was now living in her new home on the west coast of northern England. Her father had died in an accident on the estate, where he had been a game warden for thirty-five years. With the house that Sarah had provided, and a pension paid annually to her, Sarah's mother was enjoying her new life. Sarah understood her mother. She had grown up watching the way her domineering father treated his wife. Her mother was an intelligent woman, who had not been allowed to voice her own opinion. Now at least she could live a life without tyranny.

'Miss, we will be pulling into your village in about thirty minutes.'

Sir Charles had asked Sarah if she would mind if a passenger travelled with them. The passenger turned out to be a retired schoolteacher. A lady in her mid-sixties and quite different from what Sarah had imagined.

'Single, you said?'

She turned to speak directly into Sarah's face, so that the lad couldn't hear. Sarah hadn't mentioned anything about her married status to her fellow traveller.

'Good, dear, I don't like men, I never did. You can't trust any of the blighters, far better off on one's own.'

With those pearls of wisdom spat out, the schoolteacher sat back and smiled at Sarah. Sarah discreetly took out a hanky and wiped away the spit that had landed on her bodice.

'Are you staying long with your mother? Perhaps we might have tea together.'

'Thank you, but I believe all my time has been accounted for.'

Sarah didn't like nosey people and knew that her mother liked them even less.

The village of Manning was small, consisting of a group of houses built around the village green. A church with a residence and a grocery shop stood to one side of the street while on the other side a blacksmith and feed merchant lined the road. The small lane swung out near the cliffs and turned down into a small valley. Lining the road were large old oak trees and behind them the land had been divided off by stone walls into small paddocks.

The coach pulled up in front of a large two-storey house that was set well back from the road. A gabled roof overhung the old Tudor beams and the thatch roof had been trimmed with finely tied bracken. A rose trellis covered the front walls, and a wooden picket fence divided the road from the front garden, keeping the cows out. This was a constant battle as they broke through the fences and tried to attack the vegetable garden. At the side of the house a large farm building stood, separated by a taller stone wall.

'Miss, you are here. I'll see if the occupants are at home.'

The coachman knocked on the door but before he could knock again, the door was flung open.

'Sarah, my darling, is it really you?'

Mrs Noonan ran down the path, past the coachman, and into the arms of her daughter. After letting Sarah go, she hugged James and kissed him on both cheeks.

'I'm your grandmother, James, and I just know that you really don't like kisses, but I had to.'

James took a shine to Sarah's mother immediately. She had a way with children, she always did, especially the boys.

'Can I call you Granny? And did you know, I am going to kill dragons with my stock whip?'

# Chapter
## twenty-two

Sarah was thrilled with the property that Sir Charles Fitzroy had bought with her money for her mother. It was comfortable and large enough for her as well, should she want to stay in England. The large building to the side of the house was being used as a brewery and her mother received an annual rent for it.

As the weeks went by, the ladies and James explored the country lanes and spent hours walking along the cliff top. The inlets were lined with caves and shell beaches. James threw his fishing line into the sea and wondered what Munu would think of this huge billabong.

'Sarah girl, when are you going to take James to meet his other grandparents?'

Mrs Noonan hated the thought of her grandson being taken away from her but realised that the longer Sarah put it off, the more difficult it would be for her daughter to have to face James Lowe's parents and relive the story of his death.

'Yes, Mother, I know that I can't put off the inevitable. We will leave on Thursday.' Sarah sat down on a grassy ledge to watch her son as he explored the landscape.

'Mummy, can we go down into those caves?'

James could see the tide rushing into the bays and wanted to explore the caves he had heard stories about. The housekeeper had told James about the pirates that had sailed along the coastline and of sunken treasure. Sarah laughed as she listened to the tales again. It was so good to be back.

'James, we had better not, the tide comes in very quickly here, and many people have died in those caves over the years.'

Sarah's mother took James's hand and led him up the steep path to the top of the cliffs.

'Look out there, James.' She pointed to a large sailing boat that was rounding the head water and was making out to sea. 'That ship is going to Ireland with some of our spirits, the type that is made in our barn.'

'Granny, I would have been a captain like my father, but I'm going to breed horses and cattle like Uncle Tom on our river.'

The older woman glanced over to her daughter and with a questioning look asked, 'Who is Uncle Tom?'

Sarah had hired a gig and driver to take her to Mulberry Estate. It was nearly dark when they pulled in through the iron gates. The gatekeeper swung the large gates open, and doffing his cap, let the gig through. The avenue of elms stretched upward, giving a ghostly appearance to those who were trespassing along its way. James's grandmother was waiting in the large entrance hall as the gig came to a halt on the crushed gravel at the bottom of the magnificent carved sandstone stairway that led up to the carved front doors.

Sarah was taken aback by the sheer grandeur of the manor house. The sweeping driveway opened out onto a magnificent lawn entrance. The building consisted of three wings, each being built at different stages. To the west stood a row of stables, the likes of which Sarah had never seen before. On the southern side, a small lake shimmered in the setting sunlight.

A footman opened the door and helped her out. Taking a deep breath, she took James's hand, and they walked up the steps. As fear surged through her, she wanted to take her son and run. She was just being silly. Or was she?

There before her stood a refined lady dressed in a lavish gown of crushed velvet, around her neck hung a matching velvet ribbon and attached to it swung a lovely cameo. She oozed elegance and walked towards Sarah.

'Welcome, Sarah.' Then bending down, she hugged young James. Sarah could see a resemblance between her son and his grandmother. They both had her James's eyes: large and brown.

'Come this way. My husband is eagerly waiting to see you both.'

With that, the matriarch swept along the hall, her velvet dress rustling as it touched the door frame when she entered the room.

Above the mantle, a family crest had been carved into the stone. Sarah looked at the engraving of two eagles; it reminded her of something she'd seen before, but she couldn't remember where. The roaring fire crackled, warming the room to an almost unpleasant heat. A man lay on a daybed near a huge fireplace. This had been a handsome man in his youth. Sarah could see from his wide shoulders and large hands that he must have been a large, strong man. His hair was grey and thinning; the strong colouring had left his face, leaving a shadow of grey around his mouth and sunken eyes. Sarah knew immediately that this man didn't have much more time left on Earth. He raised his hands in a welcoming gesture. The fear left her, and she knew that this was where she was supposed to be.

'It is our pleasure to meet you both. Come a little closer to me, James, so that I can take a better look at you.' Lord Howard Lowe could see that his grandson was the image of his father. 'Did you have a good trip, James?'

'Yes, sir, we did.'

'Your mother has written that you can ride. I have a special pony for you, James.'

'Thank you, Grandfather, but I ride horses.'

'Then a horse it will be, my boy.'

Looking into the eyes of Sarah, he said, 'Sarah, you have done a wonderful job rearing this child, he is so much like his father at that age.'

Sarah often wondered if her child resembled his father. He was not at all like her, except for the eyes; he had her shaped eyes but with his father's colouring.

'Howard, let them be now. Sarah will want to settle in.' Beckoning to the younger woman and smiling gently, she said, 'Sarah dear, a maid will take you up to your rooms. We will dine at eight.'

'Thank you, your ladyship.'

Sarah left James in the care of a groom who had taken him to inspect the stables. The rooms were lovely, newly decorated in pastel creams. On the dressing table sat a crystal vase containing roses. Sarah wondered to herself, where they could have possibly got roses from in the middle of winter?

Over the next weeks, Sarah got to know and understand these people. She watched the pleasure that young James was bringing to his grandparents. They welcomed her as a daughter and reminisced about their dead son.

Young James loved to ride around the grounds, with a troubled groom not far behind him.

'Hold up, Master James, I'm not supposed to let you out of my sight.'

James could jump his horse over the logs and was about to try for the wooden gate when the groom grabbed his reins and pulled the horse up. Speaking angrily to the boy, he said, 'Please, lad, do you want me to lose my job? The master has given me strict orders that I'm to keep you safe.'

James thanked the groom after his ride and hurried in to speak with his grandfather.

'Sir, why can't I jump the gate? I'm quite good at jumping. Uncle Tom taught me to jump and how to use the stockwhip.' He thought for a minute and asked a very important question. 'Grandfather, do you have dragons here?'

Howard Lowe had come to love this little rascal; he saw the innocence in the child and didn't want to spoil James's fantasies.

'James, when my father was very small, the Knights of the Realm killed all the dragons. But I feel safer now knowing that you are here, with your stockwhip to protect the women in the castle. But, James, I would like you not to jump the gates and fences.'

Later that night, after dinner, and after James was taken up to bed, Sarah was asked where the boy got all his knowledge about horses and why was he allowed to use a stockwhip.

'Father,' as she had been asked to call him, 'James has been riding since before he could walk, and he swims too. Tom, our manager and friend, taught James how to use the whip as a protection against snakes and also it is necessary when herding cattle on our property.'

'But surely, dear, you don't mean to take the child back to the colonies? There's his education to think about. And he'll inherit part of this estate. In fact, Sarah, I want you to think about what I'm about to ask you, very carefully.'

Sarah wasn't sure if she really wanted to hear this.

'Sarah, without a marriage to our son it will be difficult for the boy to be accepted into society. We can offer him land and money only. If you were to allow me to adopt him as my son, he would inherit the title should anything happen to his uncle, and he would be accepted everywhere. I realise I'm asking a lot, but I would like you to think about it. And of course you would live here and want for nothing.'

Sarah sat back and let the words sink in. Yes, she would have to think about it but for now the answer would be a definite *no*. Sarah wanted to ask about James's elder brother but as the parents hadn't mentioned John, she thought it inappropriate to mention him.

The old, retired gamekeeper Ted and his wife Nan had taken a shine to young James and had invited Sarah to the cottage for tea. They talked about their deceased James and the nasty brat of a brother he had.

'So what happened to him?' asked Sarah.

'Miss, the master had him sent to Europe to manage an estate that they own. I think he is in one of the Italian states. Good riddance to bad rubbish, I say. He will be there just waiting for the master to die, then look out for all of us.'

'Surely, he wouldn't interfere with you?' asked Sarah.

'Miss, he'll have us out on the street, quick smart, if he has his way,'

'But the mistress wouldn't let him.'

Although Sarah hadn't known her for very long, she could see that her ladyship was a kind and fair woman.

'Ah, Master John is growing stronger, and our sweet mistress is getting older. Only God can help us now.'

Sarah sat down to write to Tom. In her letter she told him of the lovely time that she was having with her mother and of the warm acceptance she had experienced from James's parents. And of all the people that she was being introduced to, but mostly she wrote about the old gamekeeper and the stories of James's family. She mentioned briefly about the adoption.

It took months for Sarah to receive a reply to her letter.

*Dearest Sarah,*

*What in the hell are you thinking of? James is Australian bred and as true as my horses. Don't turn him into one of those toffee-nosed brats that chase foxes and women.*

*Are you well? Are you considering coming home? You have a large property here, just in case you might have forgotten. Charley and Munu send their love to you. By the way, I've deposited money into your bank. The sale went extremely well for us.*

*Please don't do anything until you hear from me again.*

*With all my love to you both*

*Tom.*

Sarah reread the letter. It was short but she could read the words that weren't written. When she considered the life that she was denying James, the guilt ate into her. She knew that his father would have wanted this for his child. A stream of visitors called to meet James's child. Sarah was astounded at the wealth and influence that these people had. Could her boy fit into such a life? Money seemed to be of no consequence. They lived in a world never knowing poverty or hunger. Did her James deserve better than this? Was Tom right?

'Miss, you have a caller. Do you wish to see him?'

The footmen and indeed all of the servants liked Sarah. She brought a whiff of fresh air into their stuffy existence. Sarah turned to see a man in naval uniform walking towards her. For a moment her heart was in her mouth. Then a handsome captain reached out his arms to her.

Brian Lewis, James's second-in-command, had matured into a strikingly debonair man. He stood over six feet tall; his face had a rugged appearance; his eyes were set well apart and coloured a deep blue, as blue as the sea itself.

'Sarah, I heard that you both had returned. God, it's good to see you again.'

'Brian, who told you I was here? Never mind, this is such a lovely surprise.'

She hung on to him, a friend from the past. No, more than a friend, the man who wanted to marry her; to protect her, in her hour of need.

'Sarah, I often call on James's parents when I have shore leave. They told me that you were coming. It's so wonderful to see you; you look a picture of colonial beauty.'

Colonial beauty was something that Tom would have said. Her mind flashed back to the present.

***The Australian Bush, 1864***

The summer was hot, stinking hot. The yearly drive had started. Flies swarmed around the cattle like bees to a honey pot as the herd was being driven to the sale yards. This was the second drive that Sarah had missed.

Tom had grown increasingly moody. The stockmen had threatened to leave if his attitude didn't improve. Paul Adams, the army horse buyer, was on his annual trip when he called in on Tom. The two had remained good friends and Paul was probably the only person that Tom listened to.

'You can't go on like this, Tom. You're driving yourself and the men mad. I think Harold made a lot of sense in his last letter to you.'

'What, up stakes and leave these properties, travel around the world and to find out what, that I would never have a chance against the English gentry? Who in the bloody hell is going to run these farms, Paul, while I go gallivanting around the English countryside?'

Tom had polished off a jug of beer, and settled back into his seat at the pub, staring down on to the letter he had just received.

'I will take leave, the army owes me plenty. Or don't you trust me with your bloody cows?' Paul watched his friend struggle with the idea of leaving. 'Harold has asked you to stay with him, he'll see you right. He is nobody's fool, least of all with that bloody upper class.'

'I'll have to think on it.'

'For Christ's sake, Tom, that's all you have done for the last ten years.' Paul shook his head and walked away, leaving his friend stewing over his beer.

The rain pattered softly down onto the canvas tent. Tom held his head between his hands, the noise sounded like a herd of cattle stampeding through his brain. He sat up and looked over to where Paul was seated.

'A cup of coffee wouldn't go astray.'

While still nursing a hangover, Tom spoke to his friend. 'All right, I'll go, but only if you can run these properties.'

Tom sailed three weeks later. This was a different trip from the one that had brought him to Australia. He thought back to his childhood. The youngest of seven children, he was bright and quick to learn. At the age of fourteen, his father had apprenticed him to a local blacksmith. Tom learnt quickly and was good at his trade, but he soon realised that opportunities were far and few between in England.

Gold! The word had been everywhere. In Australia, the streets were paved with it. Australia, the land of hope and prosperity, that's where his opportunities lay.

He had paid his own way out, by taking care of horses that were destined for work in Sydney. Heavy Warm Bloods, Clydesdales and Percherons were used on the work gangs, in clearing the timbers and pulling the heavy loaded drays full of sandstone, for the new government buildings.

On landing, he had headed straight for the goldfields of Bathurst, finally ending up in Sofala. Tons of dirt later, and not much gold to show for a throbbing back and calloused hands, Tom decided to take up blacksmithing in Gulgong.

Tom entered his cabin; it was on the first deck and quite near to the dining room. The cabin was relatively large with a porthole. Hanging in his locker were two suits and a few pairs of work pants. In a hessian bag laid his stockwhip, riding boots, and on the top, a well-worn hat had been lovingly placed.

Feeling a sense of excitement, Tom looked back as the clipper sailed forward, leaving Australia in her wake. There was a balmy breeze blowing, the clouds were very high, no sign of rain. Tom watched the rest of the passengers go below. The crew had all the mainsails up and as the wind increased, the ship glided across the rising waves.

The passengers mainly consisted of families returning to England. They were military and government employees, all having served their time in the colony. Young ladies returning to finish their education and to have their 'coming out' in society, which was one sure way to guarantee a good marriage.

At the far end of the deck, a lone figure stood by the rail, staring down into the water. He neither smiled, nor took any notice of the other passengers as they shuffled past. Tom studied the man; he started to walk over to him but decided against it.

'Sir, the captain would like a word with you at your convenience.'

The cabin boy didn't look any older than thirteen. Tom smiled down at the lad and thought how he looked more like a four-penny rabbit than a working boy. He then remembered that young James Junior was only two years younger.

'Where do I find the captain, son?'

The lad smiled and started towards the main deck. Tom followed the lad up onto the bridge.

'Thank you, Mr Brian. I know you must be wondering why I've asked to speak with you.'

The captain was well into his sixties. He had a fine naval history, before taking command of a trading clipper. Short in stature, he barely reached over the large steering wheel. Tom could see by the strength in his forearms that they were in safe hands.

'Yes, I was a bit curious, Captain.' Leaning back against the rail, Tom waited for the next sentence.

'Mr Brian, I have aboard a few horses, a gift to the Queen. I've been told that you are an expert in animal husbandry. Could I ask you to take a look at them from time to time? They have their own grooms, but I would feel a whole lot happier knowing that someone with knowledge was keeping an eye out.'

'It would be my pleasure, Captain. Don't give it another thought.'

The voyage was pleasant enough; the passengers were hospitable and the crew friendly. The weather stayed calm, well into the Indian Ocean. Then on the 24th April, the weather broke. The Gods in their heavens beat on the drums and lightning lit up the sky. Tom went below to speak to the grooms.

'Men, keep their leads short; if they jump around they could break their necks.' The grooms liked Tom and took his advice. He had explained to them what the voyage out had been like and of the pitfalls that they were to look out for.

After a few days, the wind dropped and for a week they made little headway. Tom had only occasionally seen the lone stranger; he chose to eat in his cabin and ventured out on deck in the solitude of night. The nights were too hot to sleep, the children cried listlessly, and tempers were frayed.

Tom strolled along the deck trying to catch any slight breeze. On a pile of coiled-up rope, which had been neatly stowed on the quarter deck, sat the stranger. He would have been hard to see but for the glow from his cigarette.

'It's very hot tonight, sir.'

Tom walked over to the man, reaching out his hand to introduce himself. It was then that Tom noticed the pinned-up sleeve and the stump that had once been an arm. On closer inspection, Tom realised that the stranger was no older than in his early twenties.

'My name is Tom Brian and I'm a farmer.'

It took a few moments before the stranger spoke. 'Mr Brian, I'm, or I use to be, a horseman with the cavalry. After my accident, they pensioned me off, *"no use to them now"* they said. My name is Jimmy Hill.'

'Well, Jim, what are you going to do in England, is your family there?'

'No, sir, I don't have anyone left, my parents died of the fever in fifty-eight.'

Tom nodded back to the young man and stubbed out his smoke, 'Well, Jim, I'm off to bed, I'll see you around.'

Tom lay in his bunk thinking about Jim. *That could have been me,* he thought. It was a few days before Tom saw the lad again. He was reading in the saloon when he noticed Jim.

'Jim, I would like to talk to you, if you have time. I had an idea but of course you would have to be agreeable.' The lad sat down at Tom's table.

Tom told him about the Murray River, their properties and how he was engaged in breeding horses for the army. The man listened with interest as Tom asked him outright if he would consider returning to New South Wales and working for him.

'Don't look at me like that, this is not pity. I need a good horseman to oversee the breeding program. And with your military training, you are just the man. Think about it, you don't need to give me an answer straight away.'

As Tom stood to walk away, a hand grabbed his arm. 'Thank you.'

The rest of the trip was uneventful. Tom finalised arrangements with Jim to meet him in London and he would arrange passage back to Australia. Tom thought it would be wise for the young man to take a break for a couple of months to rest. This would give him time to write to Paul and explain the situation. An advance on his wages would take care of any money worries that the lad might have.

'Land ahoy!' They were the words that they all wanted to hear. It took one more day before the ship berthed. After saying goodbye, Tom caught a coach to London. The weather was warm as they trotted into the coach rest on the outskirts of the city.

'Here we are, sir.' The driver tossed down Tom's bag and waved the tall stockman goodbye.

The street was alive with carriages, horse-drawn trams, and cabs. Piles of manure lay uncollected on the cobbled streets with flies swarmed around them.

The smell of all that forgotten humanity was the thing that Tom tried to forget.

'Looking for a good time, mister? Only a bob or I can do better, two bob for the night?'

Tom looked over at the woman who had spoken and to his dismay he found not a woman but a child no older than thirteen. He tossed her two bob and walked on. He booked into a clean tavern and sent a message to Harold.

After ordering dinner and a bottle of beer, he asked the waitress if he could have it sent to his room. The food was plain but tasty, and after he had finished it he lay on the bed thinking, *Why in the hell am I here?*

It only took three days before Harold arrived to rescue him. In this time, he had dined with Jim and the lad then left London, excited about his new position back in Australia.

'Master Tom, this is such a pleasure. I never thought that I would ever see you again. Oh, sir, this is just wonderful.'

The older man grabbed his hand and shook it until Tom gently prised the older fingers open.

After a few beers, Tom opened up to the man. 'Harold, look at me. Oh yes, I can buy the best clothes, a fine carriage, but I'm still a rough bushman.'

He looked squarely into Harold's face. 'She has been living with the gentry, and you know that I will stick out, in fact I will never be allowed into their hallowed halls.'

'Sir —' Harold started to speak, but was interrupted.

'For God's sake, Harold, please call me Tom.'

'Well, sir, I mean Tom; we can do something about that, can't we.'


Two months had passed. Two months of army-style training. Walking, dancing, learning about society and engaging a man's man. Harold had made Tom invest in a whole new wardrobe of clothes and boots. By the time Harold was finished, Tom not only looked a new man but felt one also.

Harold still had enough pull with some of James's friends to be able to introduce him to the people who could expand on Tom's knowledge and invite him to their estates. As Harold had told him, the invitations started to arrive. The first came from an old school friend of James's, the Hon. Alfred Smith.

> *The Hon. Alfred Smith, requests the pleasure of your company at*
> *13 Cambridge Ave,*
> *Tuesday evening.*

'Harold, what will I wear?'

'Semi-formal wear, and stop worrying and remember to enjoy the evening'

The cab pulled up at the address. 'Two and six, thank you, sir.'

The cabby took his money and drove off. Tom looked up at the town house. It was painted white and was one of ten that formed a semi-circle around a park. Three steps led up to the front door and three steps led down under the street to the servants' entrance.

Tom knocked at the front door. A footman answered and showed him into an elegant drawing room, where other people were mingling and deep in conversation.

'Tom, let me introduce you.'

Alfred Henry 3rd or Alfie, as he liked to be called, had invited Tom to the annual get-together of James's naval captains. They were all friendly and interested in Australia. The whole evening went well with Tom receiving an invitation to a country estate for the annual shoot.

'Harold, do you think I should go? This is really out of my class.'

'Rubbish, Tom. I'll tell you what we shall do; I will go with you as your second-at-arms. You will have to take your manservant also. Stop worrying, my boy, this is all going to plan.'

'Hurry up, lad, Master Tom can't be late. Have you packed all the clothes that I listed for you?'

Harold had made sure that all was in readiness for the week away. He had picked out the shotguns and had packed the hunting clothes himself.

'The coach is here, Tom. Stop hanging back! Best foot forward. I'll be there every step of the way.'

Harold understood the younger man's reluctance to go. He didn't like the gentry much either.

The manor house was large; ten guests had been invited along with their spouses. They were settled into their rooms and the servants were busy pressing their employers' clothes and engaging in much enjoyed gossip. Harold checked in on Tom's man, who was more interested in eyeing off a maid than attending to his jobs.

'Look lively, man. I want Master Tom to shine. Do you understand me?'

The lad jumped and muttered 'Sorry' as he started pressing an evening suit. The evening went off without any hitches. Tom was aware of the females' eyes that followed him. He still had an English accent and with Harold's help had polished it up to perfection. This left the ladies wondering.

'Mr Brian, my husband tells me that you own a very large holding in the colonies. Your parents must be very proud. Exactly where do they come from?'

The older matron was well known for her malicious tongue and took great delight in the spreading of gossip, much of which she made up.

Tom summed her up. 'Madam, alas, my parents passed away years ago. Please excuse me, I'm being summoned.'

Tom bowed and escaped the old biddy before she could get her claws into him.

'Tom, be careful, that woman is trouble. The night games here are well known.'

'Thanks, Harold, but I'm not interested in other men's wives.'

'Good man, we don't need any trouble before you begin. Remember, we need to be up by six, early start. By the way, I've checked and cleaned the guns.'

'Thanks, Harold, but I checked them also.'

As Harold had always known, it was not inheritance that made a gentleman.

It was quite misty next morning as the men drank their brandy and started out. The beaters had already left, and the men-at-arms stood waiting at the back entrance for their gentlemen. They walked ten yards apart in a straight line, each taking their turn at the birds. Tom never missed, much to the annoyance of a few of the men. Tom couldn't believe they thought this was sport, but he had learnt how to play the game.

'Tom, where did you learn to shoot like that?'

Alfie was so impressed with this man from the colonies. So was an elderly retired admiral, who in turn invited him to a shoot at his brother's place, Mulberry Park.

'You have cracked it, Tom. They will all be there; this is the closing shoot of the season, and it is followed by a ball. Have you planned what you will do when you see Sarah?'

'No, Harold, but I've got a month to figure it out.'

# Chapter
## twenty-four

Tom had caused quite a stir in London's society. He had attended two balls, and now pushy mothers were leaving their calling cards and invitations to dine. All of this was driving Harold to a state of frenzy. At night, they would sit and discuss the day's occurrences.

'We must be so selective, Tom.'

Before Harold could continue, Tom spoke up. 'Damn you, Harold; I'm not some little prima donna. I don't care for all of this blarney. I just want to see Sarah,'

'You'll have to be patient. We have gone too far for you to slip back. Besides, what's wrong with dining with the mamas who want to unload their daughters onto a rich man?'

Tom saw the irony in it and started to laugh. Who would have believed that two months ago he was an unpolished farmer from the colony, that the gentry wouldn't have given a second look at?

'Tom, you told me yourself that some of your new acquaintances were most interesting.' Harold felt the man's anxiety. 'By the way, I've made arrangements for you to travel to Mulberry Park, and I will accompany you personally. We will leave on Saturday.'

'Harold, you're right.' A feeling of gratitude for the man, who had worked so tirelessly with him, made Tom feel a little ashamed at what he had said. 'I do like some of the lads from the admiralty, in fact I've invited a few of them to my property, when I return.'

'Good man.' Harold saw a similarity between his James and this rough diamond standing in front of him.

'All right, Harold. I'll attend one of these bloody fancy dos.'

Tom sat correctly, his coat tails hanging in just the right way. He knew exactly which glasses to use and how to hold his smile when the conversation was most boring. He spoke graciously when young girls of marriageable age were directed to him and watched the clock tick away slowly.

He was starting to wonder if the young ladies had an ounce of sense between them. Had Sarah been like this? He very much doubted it. But then again, she had never had the chance to be young.

Sarah was enjoying the company that attended the social events at Mulberry Park. Since she had arrived there, her ladyship had invited a constant stream of people to meet her and young James.

James had settled into life there. Lady Lowe was horrified when Sarah refused to engage a tutor for the boy.

'Sarah dear, it is quite unheard of that you tutor the boy yourself. I'm sure that I can find a likable man who would be most suitable.'

The older lady cringed at the thought of her grandchild not having a tutor.

'Thank you, Mama, but I would prefer to teach James myself, or I could send him to the village school.'

Sarah watched the older lady as her eyebrows rose, but no word was spoken again on the subject.

'Brian Lewis is coming up for the shoot. He is really a very nice gentleman and comes from excellent stock.' Lady Lowe looked over to catch Sarah's expression. 'I think he is smitten with you, Sarah.'

'Yes, I'm very fond of Brian; he has been a good friend to me, especially after James's death.'

Sarah didn't often speak about those tragic events. She knew the pain that it brought to the older couple.

In a villa north of Florence, John Lowe casually opened a letter from his father. *What does he want now?* thought John, as he started to pour himself a glass of red wine. He had been sent out here over two years ago, in some preconceived idea of his father's. Some slut of a maid had got herself pregnant and had refused to take his money and leave. No, she went running to his father, who in turn had threatened to disinherit him.

Life out here wasn't so bad; it had its own pleasures. Plenty of women, wine, a generous allowance and no bloody interfering father. After James had been killed — the happiest day in his life — he knew that all he had to do was to wait and the title would be his, along with all of the money.

After using a letter knife to open the letter from his father, John sat down to read it. His temper exploded and his anger centred on a glass he was holding. The Venetian glass goblet hit the far wall, red wine dripped down the beautiful tapestry, and John's knuckles turned white as he finished reading the letter.

'How could they?' he screamed. 'How could they accept James's bastard and want to adopt him?'

The servants kept their distance. They had seen their master in his temper before.

'Get in here, you mongrel,' he yelled to his manservant. 'Pack my things, we are returning to England.'

With that he turned and walked towards the door. Raising his hand, he struck the young footman across the face.

'That's for the impertinent way you looked at me.'

The room was pleasantly warm as Sarah sat in the library reading Homer's *Odyssey*.

*'Twenty years later back in the arms of her lover.'* Sarah put down the book and murmured aloud, 'Oh well, for me it's only a dream.'

Sarah had decided to have a new gown made for the Hunt Ball. As always, she had been very thrifty with her money, making sure the bulk of it was reinvested into her property. There was also an opportunity to buy into a printing firm that was setting up a daily paper in Melbourne. And by all accounts it would be a great investment for her son.

Tom and she had, in the previous year, bought a steam paddleboat between them. It was working on the Darling River, carrying down wool clips and taking up fresh supplies. As long as the water held, they would make money, a lot of money.

'Come, dear, the dressmaker has arrived.' Lady Lowe had insisted that only the best seamstress work on Sarah's gown. 'Sarah, do you really think that style will be right for you?'

The older woman liked the modern cut, but Sarah knew what suited her and had designed the garment herself.

News that John Lowe was returning had reached the estate.

'When will John arrive?' She was feeling apprehensive about their meeting. Maybe time had mellowed the older brother and James could certainly do with an uncle.

'He'll be here by the end of the month, Sarah.'

'I was thinking of returning to see my mother. We will be back in plenty of time for the ball.'

Sarah felt that the older woman was going to say something, but she remained quiet.


The sea air was exhilarating. Sarah held on to James's hand as they climbed down the steep steps that led to a small cave above the waterline.

'Mummy, why can't we go any further down?' asked James.

'No, James, you can see that large boulders have blocked our way. Besides, your grandmother will have tea on the table.'

'Mummy, it's nice how Grandma cooks for us and what I like is how we eat in the kitchen.'

James always felt a little strange eating with servants standing behind him, watching. 'Can't Grandmother Lowe cook?'

For a lad born in Australia, without servants and with only Charley and Munu to set him right, it was all a bit confusing. Later that evening after James was put to bed, the two women sat, relaxing in front of the fire.

'Sarah, are you serious about Captain Lewis? He's been paying you a lot of attention over the past months, and he would make a fine father for James.'

'I care a great deal for him, Mother, but as to marriage, that I'm not sure of.'

'Sarah, you will be thirty soon. How long do you want to remain without a man in your bed? Don't look at me like that, I know a woman's needs as well as you do.'


The last two weeks had been a pleasant relief from the formality of his lordship's manor. But tomorrow they would have to return to Mulberry Park. Sarah had walked around her mother's village making friends and leaving a large contribution to the local parish. She had sat for hours pondering over the question that kept raising its head: the future of her son.

'James, this is your last night with Grandma. Would you like to take a walk back down to the beach after supper?'

Mrs Noonan hadn't been told about the adoption plans of the

Lowes. Sarah knew better than to open that Pandora's Box. Her mother would never agree to such a decision. Sarah's mother had worked in a large manor house for too long not to know how the upper class acted. And she had little respect for any of them.

The sun was still up as they walked along the cliff top. Down below, the sea was rushing in on the tide, smashing into the coves and sending up great mountains of white foam that gave way to a fine mist of many colours as the sun's rays shone through.

'Please, Mummy, can't we look at the cave over there?' The boy pointed to an opening in the cliff face behind the sandbar. 'We could walk through the water, it isn't deep.'

'James, your grandmother has already told you that many people have been killed down there. So, son, the answer is no.'

'But, Mummy, that's the exact place that a dragon would live.'

'No, James.'


John rode into the stable yard on his bay hunter, ahead of the coach carrying his possessions.

'Boy, come here and attend to my horse.'

John stepped down and after removing his riding gloves took in a deep breath and looked around.

*Nothing ever changes here, except maybe the stupid servants.*

He walked over the cobbled stones, stepping around the piles of horse manure and through the side door to his home.

'Mother, I'm back.'

John placed his hat on the oak hallstand and after throwing his gloves into his hat, marched over to the study. Lady Lowe was sitting near her husband and reading to him, as their son entered the room. John was shocked by the deterioration of his father.

*Perhaps things will work out.* He smiled.


Mulberry Park was a hive of activity as Sarah's coach turned into the drive. The sheep were being driven from the front paddocks and large roped bunting hung across the drive. Men, who were cleaning the upper windows, looked down and watched as Sarah walked up the stone steps and into the arms of Lady Lowe.

'Sarah, it's lovely to have you back. Where is James?' The matriarch looked around, her eyes searching for the little boy.

Sarah laughed. 'He saw his horse in the gamekeeper's paddock behind their cottage and asked if he could ride him back. The men will accompany him here.'

Sarah smiled as she recalled the way James jumped down from the carriage and bolted over to the fence and into the arms of the retired gamekeeper.

'Ah, Sarah, that brings back memories for me. That is exactly what his father did. Come in, dear, we have missed both of you. Your dress has arrived too. It's lovely, quite lovely.'

Servants were putting the final touches to a well-cleaned and much-prepared house. The kitchen's larder was full. Venison, geese, hares, and hams all hung from the rafters, along with trestles laden with a large selection of cakes, puddings, and freshly baked bread. *This is enough food to feed a hundred families in the slums of White Chapel,* thought Sarah.

Sarah washed and changed out of her travelling clothes then made her way along the landing towards the marble staircase, which led down to the entrance. She didn't see the man leaving a room further along the hall and was surprised to hear him speak.

'So, who do we have here? A house guest, no doubt.'

John took a look at the woman who had produced James's bastard. *My, she is lovely, no wonder James couldn't keep his hands off her,* he thought, watching her turn. There was something familiar about her, but he couldn't remember where he had seen her.

'Sorry, sir, I didn't see you there.'

Sarah turned fully and stared up into eyes she would never forget. Fear crept over her, punching at her chest, taking away her breath. Her skin crawled; she spun away, back through her bedroom doors.

Standing with her back against the door, her hands clutched at her breasts. One hand crept down to her thigh, and she ran her fingers along the scar that had been ripped into her on that night in the back streets of London. Was this real? Was it James's brother who had taken away her innocence?

'Oh, come on, Sarah, I'm not as bad as they all say. I won't eat you.'

John stood outside Sarah's room, waiting for this little morsel to reappear. 'Please go down without me, sir. I'll be down directly.'

Sarah stumbled onto her bed. She clutched at the cream brocade bedspread in an attempt to make some sense out of it all. Minutes seemed like hours but finally a knock on the door brought her back to the present.

'Miss, the mistress is enquiring after you. Are you ill?'

The young maid had taken a shine to Sarah and had asked to be her personal maid. She had seen the exchange between the man and woman on the landing and was worried about Sarah. The young lass knew all about Master John; all the servants did.

'No, I'll be fine, just a small headache. I will be down for dinner. Please tell your mistress not to concern herself.'

Sarah hoped that John would not remember her; after all, it was eleven years ago, and she wasn't the woman then that she was now.

They all sat around a large dining table that night, just the family. John played the perfect host, gracious and very endearing to young James.

'I hear that you are a fine rider, James. Maybe, with your mother's permission'—he winked at Sarah—'I might take you out riding with me.'

The child's eyes shone as he waited for his mother to reply.

'James, for now I think you had better stay with your groom in the paddock. Your horse is still getting to know you, it would be safer. Don't you agree, John?' Lady Lowe asked.

'Of course, Mother.'

John hid his true feelings towards the brat who was to share his inheritance.

The shooting guests were all dining at a neighbour's estate after a most successful day, each bagging many pairs of birds.

Tom had arrived at the manor the day before. He had made discreet enquiries about Sarah and learned that she was expected back for the ball. Harold introduced him to anyone of importance. Lord Lowe made him very welcome and enquired about his property in Australia. No mention was made of their deceased son, James, and for now no connection had been made to Sarah.

## twenty-five

The morning was fine and quite warm for that time of the year. The coaches had started to arrive, and the ladies were shown up to their rooms to rest before they dressed in all their finery for the gala ball that evening. Sarah had slept in and lunched alone in her suite while James had disappeared out to the stables to see his horse.

There was a knock on the door and footmen carried in buckets of hot water for her bath.

'Miss, the hot water ran out, so I had the men carry more water up for you.'

The maid thought of everything, she wanted her charge to shine in front of all the other fine ladies.

'Miss, try to eat a little more, it will be quite late before supper is served.'

Sarah bit into another sandwich. She had lost her appetite when she had seen John. She had to play the game for a few days more. She knew that another disappointment would kill the old couple, but how she would have loved to get her hands on the arrogant man, if only she had been male. It was eight o'clock when she stepped into her dress. The length of silk draped over her right shoulder and fell into deep folds to form the front panel. To the back of the skirt, the panels formed a small train. The deep plunging bodice emphasised Sarah's bust line to perfection. Her maid had taken her time, making sure that every part of Sarah's hair was curled. Around her neck she wore her single pearl drop.

'Miss, you look a picture of elegance, and there's no denying it.'

There was a knock on the door, and a friendly voice spoke up. 'Sarah, it's Brian, are you ready, dear?' There he stood in his ceremonial whites, offering her his arm. 'You are so lovely tonight, dear, it is truly my pleasure to escort you.'

They lined up to be announced as they entered the ballroom.

'Captain Lewis and Miss Noonan.'

Lady Lowe walked forward and placed her arm on Sarah's and kissed her on the cheek. She knew that most of her guests would find it hard to accept Sarah but with this show of affection they would be forced into some pretence of acceptance.

The couple mingled and the music started to play. Brian led Sarah out onto the dance floor. The crowd watched as the couple spun around the room, and gradually more couples joined them.

To the back of the room, leaning against a marble column, Tom watched. He overheard the conversation of the matrons sitting in front of him.

'They make a lovely couple; they say that his lordship is playing matchmaker. Probably place a dowry on her. Personally, I think he wants to get rid of his responsibility regarding her, don't you know…'

Yes, Tom had to agree that they did make a fine couple. Suddenly he wasn't sure. What gave him the right to interfere in her life?

The beat of the music picked up. Brian swung her around with ever-increasing speed. The lights of a hundred candles reflected on the rows of mirrors that hung around the room. Sarah's head swung back, and as if in slow motion her eyes glanced over the people around the room.

There, standing alone, dressed in formal evening attire, stood Tom. Her Tom. He looked splendid in his well-cut coat. His hair was glossy in the candlelight, and his warm brown eyes glowed with an emotion which was a mixture of satisfaction, hope, excitement, and something else known only to himself. Everything seemed to slow down. She watched him turn and start to walk out. Suddenly, people were talking, and she was moving through the crowd towards him. Brian watched as she ran up to the tall stranger.

Sarah froze. Tom was making his way back to the door. A voice came from somewhere.

'Don't leave me, Tom.'

He turned and pushed through the crowded ballroom and scooped her up into his arms. The room went silent, and it was like time stood still.

'I think we had better dance, Sarah.' Not another word was spoken.

The chandeliers threw the soft light across the room, reflecting rays of shimmering light off the polished floor. Sarah could feel a hand being laid on her arm; gently guiding her onto the ballroom floor. Before her was the love of her life, her hero, but most of all he was her best friend. As his arms slowly entwined around her, the music increased in strength. The master of the waltz lifted his violin and Sarah started to feel her feet moving to the beat.

They twirled around ever faster; she couldn't take her eyes off him as they passed other dancers in a blur of fantasy. The hypnotic lull enlightened her senses. The smell of the daphne floating on the air stirred the mind and pulled at her heartstrings. Faster and faster they pivoted around the floor, then the music stopped, and Tom led her to a seat on the far wall.

Leaning over her, he whispered, 'I love you, Sarah, I always have.'

Sarah was so taken back that her first words were, 'When did you arrive, Tom? And what made you come?'

Before he could answer, Brian walked over to Sarah and spoke. 'Would you like to introduce us, Sarah?'

'Captain Brian Lewis, this is my neighbour and very good friend, Tom Brian.'

'Mr Brian, I've heard so much about you from Sarah and young James. It's a great pleasure to meet you at last.'

Tom's first impressions were usually true, and he liked this man. He wished he didn't.

'Before you start, Sarah, the farms are in good hands. Paul is overseeing them while I'm away.'

'Sarah, Tom, I know that you must have a lot to talk over, so I will say goodnight.'

Captain Lewis bent down and kissed Sarah tenderly on the lips, shook Tom's hand and left. The gesture hadn't been missed by Tom. *Staking his claim*, he thought to himself.

They talked well into the early hours of the morning. The subject of James's adoption was not spoken about. Sarah was anxious to hear all about the farm and his trip to England. There was something different about him; he was more assured in what he said, more polished.

'We'll talk more in the morning, Sarah. It is very late, and I wish to pay my respects to our hosts.'

Tom smiled and moved away, leaving Sarah astounded at the ease with which her friend fitted into the gentry. Sarah stood there, watching Tom walk over to the gentlemen, who were standing by the entrance hall shaking hands with the men as they left. They had been deputised by Lord Lowe, who had taken to his bed earlier in the evening.

The night's proceedings had been observed by John. He sat watching; one hand strummed the table while the other hand came up to his face. His eyes followed the man, but quickly returned to the woman. His fingers plucked over his moustache, and he leaned back, considering this new development that had occurred.

'Hurry up, Mummy! Uncle Tom will be waiting for us.'

James jumped from his bed like a jack-in-a-box when Sarah told him of Tom's arrival. The men had left very early for the last day of the shoot, but Tom had told Sarah that he would come back later to take them out riding. She had been awake and had heard the men leaving at dawn for the shoot. The seconds who carried the guns, had already set out, the beater close behind.

'I've had breakfast, and I'm going down to the stables, Mummy.'

Sarah was nearly dressed as the little scamp shot through the door and down the staircase. Across at the stables, John was checking the girth on a horse and looked up as James Junior came running over to him.

'Uncle John.'

John looked up. How he hated being called that name by the little bastard.

'Is that my horse you are saddling?'

'Yes, boy. Do you want to try him out? We could go for a quick ride before your mother comes out. It can be our secret.'

John smiled; the boy could be moulded like putty in his hands. John rode high up into the hills. James kept up with him, jumping the lower hedges. John was astounded that the boy could jump so well.

*The little bastard isn't going to break his neck*, he thought to himself.

'We had better go home, sir. Mummy will get worried.'

'Of course, boy, we'll go back by a short cut I know.'

John circled up behind the hills.

'Sir, aren't we too close to the shooters? I can see some of the men.' James bent forward to pat his horse, which had become nervous at the sound of the shots.

'No, boy, but I'll go on ahead to make sure. You follow at your own pace.'

And without further ado, John whipped his horse into a gallop, leaving the child far behind. The horse trembled and pawed the ground, white foam dripped from its steaming nostrils as John reined it in behind a clump of saplings. He dismounted and lifted a shotgun down from its leather cover behind the saddle. Loading the gun, he checked the sights and glanced back towards the path. All he had to do now was to wait. The dew slowly fell from the tips of the leaves. John couldn't help smiling as he rested back against the tree.

Back at the stables, Sarah was becoming worried about James. It wasn't like him to disobey her.

'Tom, I can't find James anywhere. The groom saw John lead him out behind the back forest; I don't trust John with him.'

One look from Sarah told Tom that his own thoughts about the missing uncle were correct. He tried to speak calmly. 'I'll go and get him but please, Sarah, stay here.'

Tom grabbed a saddled mount that was tied to the stable rails and after a second thought, grabbed his gun and stockwhip from the inside locker. He headed up the old trail, following the horse tracks. He could see that a horse had galloped away, leaving one following at a slower pace.

Higher and higher he climbed. It was sunny up there on the slopes; he could see the men shooting below. The mist hadn't cleared but now and again a movement would alert his senses. He knew better than to rush in like a bull in a china shop. Where in the hell were they?

Over by a group of trees, Tom caught sight of a horse tethered to a tree. As he looked closer, he saw a man standing there and by his side a gun stood up against the tree. Tom edged his mount closer. To the left and about fifty yards away, Tom saw James trotting his horse towards the man.

The man lifted the shotgun and waited. The air became alive. Suddenly the gun flew up and across the ground. A second crack of the whip brought a scream from the man as it wound around his body. By the time John Lowe realised what had happened, Tom's fist had landed on his jaw.

'You bloody bastard, I'll kill you with my own hands.'

Tom was about to strike him again when a group of men broke into the clearing.

'I saw what he tried to do, sir, I'll witness for you, Mr Brian.'

Alfie hated a cur; he and all of James's friends felt particularly protective towards the wee lad.

John stood up and moved closer towards the horse and while all the men spoke to Tom about getting a constable, he jumped into the saddle and belted the animal into a gallop. Alfie raised his gun and took aim.

'No! Let the bastard go. We'll find him, or better still the law will.'

John's uncle's face looked like stone. 'Why did the decent brother have to die and leave a cur like that behind?'

The pain was easily detected in his voice.

Lord Lowe was told of what nearly occurred earlier that day. He insisted that the law be notified, but didn't want his wife told until it became necessary.

'Tom, why would he do such a dreadful thing, especially to an innocent child?'

Sarah was horror struck when told of the day's events.

A kindly old groom took James to see a new foal: her lad was quite unaware of the plot to kill him.

Nan Lyn, the gatekeeper's wife, had also seen John take the lad out riding and had sent a groom to follow them. With all the commotion that was happening, the old groom took the initiative to lead James back to the house before he could see his uncle receive a thrashing from Tom.

The evening meal was sombre. After they had finished, Tom suggested that the three of them go for a walk and maybe James could show him the horses.

Sarah's look of gratitude lightened Tom's heart. They strolled around the stables and James showed off his latest stockwhip trick.

'Do you know that they used to have dragons here, Uncle Tom?'

As Tom lifted the boy up to give him a hug, he noticed smoke billowing from the top floor of the manor house. Flames shot out the windows in the right wing.

'You two stay here,' he shouted as he started running towards the house. The servants were bucketing water onto the flames on the staircase.

'It's Master John, he's drunk and has knocked over the lamps in his parents' suite. He has barricaded the entrance.'

The butler was badly burned as he tried to break in. The maids were screaming something about her ladyship being in one of the rooms.

Tom wrapped a blanket around his head and upturned a vase of water over his face. With large steps, he made it up to the landing, but the whole top floor was ablaze. Deep in his heart, he knew it was too late for whoever was in there. The place was now an inferno. He could hear the beams hitting the floor as the roof caved in. There was nothing he could do. The heat and smoke drove him back out, through the doors and into the fresh air.

Sarah watched in terror from the safety of the stables. Around her, the servants stood in silence. The men had carried out Lord Lowe on his daybed from the lounge below and placed him near Sarah. James cuddled into the old man as they all looked on in horror.

There in the bedroom window stood John. His arms outstretched, he didn't waver as the flames latched on to his clothes. Sarah turned James's face into her skirt, as the human fireball plunged out through the window to his death.

# Chapter
## twenty-six

Sarah had taken over the household, which had been set up in the gatekeeper's house while the right wing of the manor was rebuilt. Some local builders bought the old stone and had it taken away to build houses in nearby villages. Sarah sent some of the blocks to her mother's house too so that a wall could be built.

'Sarah, do you really want to go ahead with the paperwork for James's adoption?' asked Tom when he returned from the northern pastures of the estate.

'Yes, Tom. It is only a formality to ensure that the estate goes to James. You know that there are no younger living relatives. Admiral Lowe wants James to inherit it when his brother dies. It is the least I can do for a dying man. It is the only thing that kept him going.'

The following Saturday, the family lawyer arrived, and young James was legally made the next lord in waiting.


The church was packed as the villagers and gentry alike came to pay their respects to the frail old man, who had survived his wife and his two sons.

On the 1st of July, six weeks after the death of his wife and son, Lord Lowe, tenth in line to the throne, died, and was laid to rest beside his beloved wife.

'What now, Sarah?'

Brian Lewis had come to pay his respects and to try to finalise his life with Sarah.

'Brian, we are going home.'

'Is it that tall neighbour of yours? He also deserves an answer, Sarah.' Captain Lewis was well aware of Tom Brian's intentions towards Sarah.

'Brian, if Tom asks me again to marry him, I will say yes.'

'I've asked Sir Charles's advice on this estate. He is on his way here.' Tom realised the enormity of the responsibility that Sarah had taken on for James. It was good to see Sir Charles Fitzroy. He brought with him a sense of stability that Sarah needed.

'Sarah, I can manage this place for you. You have very good staff. Most of them can manage without any help. Stop worrying, go back home and see to your affairs. This place has been here for four hundred years; it can manage for a couple more.'

'Are you sure? What about James, should he start school here?'

'That decision is yours, my dear. You can leave him in our care. He would be a great friend for Lucy and your mother is here also. Why don't you talk it over with James?'

'I've been told that unless he goes to boarding school, the university can't accept him, should he want to go.'

'Sarah, James now has enough money to build his own place of learning, besides, who is going to refuse the tenth in line to the throne?'

The peer smiled at her and bent forward to kiss her on the forehead.

Later that evening after the guests had retired, Tom and Sarah sat looking out over the rolling hills as the last of the sunset disappeared. At last silence filled the air. Tom got up to pour himself another brandy; he had been thinking about home, it was winter there now. He wondered how the cows were standing up to the cold conditions. Had they stored enough hay?

'Are you sure you don't want a drink, Sarah?'

'Speak up, love, I didn't hear you.' He looked up as she started to speak. 'Tom, I've been thinking, will you marry me?'

For the first time in his life Tom was speechless.


The wedding was small. Only Sir Charles and Lady Fitzroy, Brian, and all the staff attended. It was held in the small chapel near Mrs Noonan's home. A tea was held in the grounds of the home, which ended up as a great knees-up by all the staff. Never in their living memory, had there been a reception like it. The gentry never acted like that. The married couple drank beer and danced the jig along with the rest of the servants. All this merriment went on until the wee hours of the morning. The finale was Tom demonstrating his ability with his stockwhip.

That night, their lovemaking was intense. Tom, who had adored her from a distance, was finally her husband. She slept, her hands above her head as her soft curls, now streaked with fine strands of grey tumbled down over her breasts. He wanted to wake her, to resume their passion, but knew how exhausted she was. The last few months had taken their toll.

'Mother, come back with us to Australia.'

Sarah indeed did her best to persuade her mother to leave with them.

'Nay, love, this is my home now. Besides, young James will be returning in a few years, and he will need me. I have Sir Charles looking out for me and I enjoy the visits with young Lucy when he brings her. No, I will be fine.'

The day was warm as one of the *Dove*'s sailors yelled down from the crow's nest, the words that they all wanted to hear.

'Land ahoy!'

The coastline of Victoria was quite dangerous. Many ships had been lost along this stretch of the coast, whalers and traders alike. The ship stayed well out to sea, passing the port of Portland and not sighting land again until they sailed into the bay.

Tom held James's hand with the other arm looped around his wife's waist.

'We are nearly home, love, just the three of us.'

Tom bent over and kissed her cheek.

'No. Actually, Tom,' she whispered in his ear, 'there will be four of us.'

Sarah had known for a month that she was pregnant but waited until now to tell him. Their lovemaking was so perfect that she didn't want him to stop and start worrying. She knew that would have happened. But he was ecstatic about them having their own child.

'All ashore, first-class passengers only.'

The crew threw down the gangway and Sarah was the first to step onto the Australian shore. How different this homecoming was. Sarah looked out through the people swarming along the wharf. There to the back, she caught sight of Charley and the dray. She had brought back with them items to fill up their home, fine linens and some furniture along with crates full of books. She took great pleasure in buying presents for all her people.

Sarah broke away from Tom and ran to the Chinaman standing near the team of horses. 'Charley, I've missed you so much.'

She threw her arms around him. Through the crowds she noticed a Chinese woman standing to the rear of the dray.

'Who do we have here, Charley?'

'Please, Missy, this is Sue Lee, she is me new wife.' His face broke into a large smile.

Sarah walked over to the girl and placed her hand on hers. 'It is lovely to meet you, Sue Lee.'

It was then that she noticed the little bump protruding through the girl's smock. Before she could say anymore, a whirlwind on young legs ran around her and grabbed hold of Charley.

'You been good boy for Missy, James?'

A cheeky grin looked up at him.

Tom took Charley's hand and shook it, the way that only a friend can do.

'Come on, Charley; let's get all our gear and start back.' He turned to Sarah. 'I'll put you and James on a coach, love, and it'll be more comfortable.'

'No bloody fear. We are not in England now, the dray didn't do any harm to James, and it won't do any harm to this baby either.'

*Oh my God,* thought Tom, *Sarah is home.*


The sun hadn't yet appeared over the tree line as Tom stoked the kitchen range ready for the day ahead. Bread making day, he knew Sarah would want to bake early to try to beat the heat. He was trying to be quiet. He slipped out of their bed hoping she might get a little more sleep. Her pregnancy was advancing and as he remembered back to young James's birth, Sarah became anything but calm.

Charley burst through the back door, his old face alight with happiness. 'Boss very good. Me, daddy, very fine son.' Before Tom had a chance to reply, he was gone.

'Tom, what was all the noise?'

Sarah was entering the kitchen tying her pinny around her as she walked towards the stove.

'Love, it was Charley, something about him being a daddy.'

It took only ten minutes for Sarah to reach Charley's cabin. There, lying in the large carved bed, a present from Tom, Sue Lee slept, a small baby with jet black hair cradled in her arms. He looked around, his large dark eyes full of wonder.

Sue Lee woke up to see Sarah brushing the tears from her eyes.

'Why didn't you send Charley to get me?'

'Missy, you need your sleep too, I have Charley.'

Sarah remembered back to her son's birth and to the wonderful little Chinese man that had cared for her too.

'We want to call him Tommy, if the Boss is pleased.'

Sarah felt Tom's arms press into her side.

'Sue Lee, I would be very honoured.'


Munu leaned on her walking stick as she walked up to the homestead. The old lady had slowed down but was still a force to be reckoned with. Sarah was sitting on the verandah nursing her baby daughter and watching out for Tom and James, who had left at dawn to check the northern paddocks, when she caught sight of Munu.

'Missy, give old Munu that child. She needs to meet her people and know woman's way.'

The old lady had not trusted the doctor when he arrived to deliver the baby and insisted on being there, encouraging Sarah and yelling at the young man. Munu understood the necessity to take this child and introduce her to the spirits of Munu's tribe.

Sarah handed the child to Munu who was still trying to get Sue Lee to bring down her son to the tribe to meet him.


The dust rose in clouds as the men pulled up their horses. And as James led them over to the stables, Tom hurried up to see Sarah and hold his little daughter.

'Love, the stock is fine, and the grass is as lush as I've had ever seen here.' He took out a letter and handed it to Sarah.


*My dear Sarah, Tom, James and little Kate*

*I will be calling in to see you all. I have a buying trip to Ballarat; tell Tom I'll look out for another fifty cows for him. Give my regards to James and a kiss for my god daughter.*

*See you soon. Your friend,*

*Joe Henely.*

'Tom, we are starting to act like the older folk, sitting here, rocking on our verandah.' Sarah was at peace with the world. She sometimes thought about James and the life that he would lead in England in a few years, but for now all was at peace with the world.

Kate didn't thrive as James had. They took her to Melbourne to a doctor who specialised in children's conditions.

'I'm so sorry, Mr and Mrs Brian. I've seen this before. The white blood cells are enlarged. The best thing you can do is to leave Kate here in the hospital and we will take care of her until the end.'

Sarah bundled up her baby, thanked the doctor and the staff at the hospital and took Kate back to the farm. The end came quickly. Little Katherine died in Sarah's arms, and they buried her high up on the hill overlooking the river.

The properties prospered and on Sarah's thirty-seventh birthday, the whole area was invited to celebrate with the family. Sarah's only sorrow was that James wouldn't be there with her. He was enrolled at Eton in England.

'Sarah, please take it easy, you look very white, dear. Maybe you should lie down?' Tom left before he heard her reply.

*Men,* Sarah thought to herself, how do they think the work gets done? As she rose from the chair a wave of nausea came over her. Sarah quickly recovered and the party was a great success.

The nausea continued every day; until Sarah convinced herself that it must be her time in life.

'Love, I want you to see the doctor next time you go into Echuca.' Tom had never seen Sarah unwell and became worried at her decline.

Melanie, their neighbour, was taking her youngest in to see the doctor about a croup cough that had plagued the child and asked Sarah if she would like to accompany them.

Sarah left the surgery in a state of shock. Pregnant.

'Tom, I can't be expecting, not after all this time. How could it have happened?'

'Well, darling, I seem to remember a late-night swim.'

Even after all these years, Tom could make her blush.

On the 6th August, 1873, Josephine was welcomed into the world.

She became the apple of Tom's eye.

Josephine was a spoilt child. In her daddy's eyes, she could do no wrong. Sarah was the one to hand out any discipline needed. Jo, as she was called, would then run to her older brother, when he was at home from boarding school, or to her dad for sympathy.

'I'm telling you, Tom, our child is growing up more a working lad than a refined young lady.'

'Well, dear, she is your daughter.'

With that, Tom smiled to himself and made a hurried retreat from the kitchen, grabbing a thick slice of damper spread thickly with butter and honey.

The morning was already hot; for ten days the heat had remained above the century. The bush was dry and parched, the heat taking its toll on man and beast alike. Sarah had started making bread at dawn and not wanting to waste the remaining heat in the fuelled oven, she quickly made a damper for morning tea.

Sarah knew deep down that Tom was right. She had encouraged her daughter to ride horses and had not stopped Tom from teaching her to shoot. Jo swam in the river with the boys, forming a friendship with the local Aborigines who had remained with Sarah, living on the riverbank below the jetty.

'Tom, I think that your daughter needs a year in finishing school.'

The sky might as well have fallen in for Jo, who continued to argue her case for not leaving, right up until boarding the ship with a lady companion.

'Well, can I stay in Nan's house?'

'Definitely not. The house has been closed since Nan died.' Sarah tried to diffuse the situation.

'Josephine, my dear, twelve months at school will do wonders for you and in the holidays, James will pick you up so that you can stay with him. Don't look at your father like that. This time we both agree. Darling, you will meet lots of people, so please embrace this opportunity. Behave yourself, and please don't cause James or Lucy any concern.'

Tom listened in silence. *Concern,* he thought, *more like trouble.* On her twentieth birthday, Josephine sailed for England to join her brother and his wife.

After the birth of James and Lucy's daughter, Prudence, Lucy didn't regain her strength, and she died of pneumonia when the child was three years old.

Josephine couldn't twist her older brother around her finger as she had done with her father. So, after years of disagreements, Jo moved to Paris.

# Chapter
## twenty-seven

Josephine had been gone for five months, and as Sarah sat at her desk looking over the bank statements, a shudder made her hands shake. Tom had bought another steamer to work the Darling. This had been against her better judgement, but she had always followed Tom's savvy advice when it came to investments. Hadn't the purchase of the army horses proved to be a gold mine for them?

The rains had been good that year and he thought there would be plenty of water in the river catchments, so why not take advantage of the high price wool was bringing. Thinking back, she recalled their conversation.

'Sarah, instead of just carting the bales, we could buy them direct and make a much larger profit. I realise that we will have to borrow some capital, so I've taken a loan against my holdings.'

Although many investments were bound together, Tom had ensured that Sarah's land holdings would be safe in case anything happened to him until they could be transferred over to James when he reached twenty-one. So the new ship, the *Sarah Lee*, with Tom aboard, sailed up the Darling, calling in at most landings, where Tom bought up as much wool as possible. The farmers couldn't believe their luck: cash, something they rarely saw.

The captain felt the steering wheel shudder, the paddle wheel grinding to a halt. Tom raced over to the rail where he could see a large, submerged log rammed into the paddles. Invigorated by the last two months, Tom, forgetting his years of hard work, stripped to the waist and dived overboard into the murky water.

By nature, he hadn't been a man to take unnecessary chances. So how could they explain his drowning to Sarah? The stockman had ridden nonstop to bring the terrible news. As he wheeled the horse into the last paddock before the homestead, Harry stopped, pulling the mount to a standstill. He had been with Tom for twenty years, through the bush fires, droughts, and family tragedies. *Let the girl have a few more minutes of peace before I have to break her heart,* he thought.

Sarah was reading on the verandah in the cool as the dust cloud came towards her. As she watched the rider stop at the gate, she wondered who it could be, not recognising the horse.

'Millie, boil the kettle, we have a visitor.'

The tall native girl walked back into the kitchen and set the tea tray. She arranged slices of cake on the plate and waited for her mistress to call her. Millie was the granddaughter of Lillie, an aunty, who had made the trek south with Sarah and had come to Sarah's classes. Sarah had a special place in her heart for the girl. She was a quick learner and walked tall, showing the pride of her race.

A scream ripped through the tranquillity of the home. Millie dropped the plate she was carrying and ran out onto the verandah. Harry was holding Sarah close to his chest; she was struggling, trying to push him away. Men were running towards her from the bunk house.

Sue-Lee had been hanging out the washing at the back of the homestead and in a split second she turned, sending the basket flying and, as if in slow motion, she also started to run.

It took only a short time for the tragic news to reach all the people who had known Tom. Sarah hadn't eaten or even cried since she was given the news. The pain and anguish engulfed her completely, her face resembling a death mask. They all tried to get her to eat, but in the end, it was Charley who spoke the words she needed to hear.

'Missy, we in big trouble now, bank man come nosing around. No more time to be upset, like when Captain James died, you must fight.'

'What are you talking about? What man?' In her grief, Sarah had forgotten about the *Sarah Lee* and the overdraft owing.

It was three months since Tom had died. The stock was not ready to sell, and they still hadn't found the bloody boat. Sarah sat in front of the bank manager watching him sort through the papers.

'Mrs Brian, we can sell up the newspaper and boats or maybe it might be simpler for you if you just sign over Mr Brian's holdings.'

This bank manager was new to the area and saw Sarah as the grief-stricken widow. He didn't know her history and saw a lovely piece of real estate there for the taking.

'No, sir, I still have five weeks until the loan falls due.' And with that, she rose to her full height, smiled, and left his office.

Walking down to the pier in Echuca, she leaned against a pylon, her whole body trembling, and raised her gloved hands to her face as she sobbed. A voice within her said, '*This is not the time, girlie, go and find that bloody boat.*'

'Sarah, you can't go alone. I'll go. You stay here and take care of the properties.' Harry was also worried; the boat should have been back weeks ago.

'Thanks, Harry, but I must go, though I would like you to come too.'

Harry supervised the loading of their horses and supplies onto the paddle steamer, and they left Echuca three days later. The captain told Sarah that the water was falling in the Darling, and he was concerned about his own boat.

'Lass, I'll take thee up as far as the river flows.'

He had known Sarah and Tom ever since he had picked up young James and took him for a ride up the river. He was ready to leave with a heavy load but when he was told of Sarah's plight, he had them unload the cargo so that they could make better time.

The *Cameron* made good time down to the mouth of the Darling River, where they stopped to bring aboard more of the red gum logs. Percy Longbottom, a long-time friend of the captain, signed on as navigator and second mate.

'Captain, the river is dropping. We might be able to make forty miles up if we are lucky.' Percy knew the river like the back of his hand and had not long arrived back at the landing. 'If we go careful like, we might make Griffith's Landing.'

So, with the plumb drops ready to gauge the river depth and a keen eye watching out for sandbars, they set off. Sarah had spent most of her time in her cabin but now she sat at the bow of the *Cameron* watching every movement of the trees and surveying the bends as they glided along.

'Come in, missus, I've got a brew on.'

Percy, like most of the river people, knew and liked Tom and knew of Sarah's plight.

'Thanks, I'll be there directly.'

The wind had picked up and the mist was slowly rising from the murky water. Sarah pulled her shawl down around her shoulders. *How easy would it be to simply step off the deck and join Tom.*

'Boat ahead.' Percy pointed to the boat on the northern side of the river. 'Cut the steam, now,' the captain yelled down the tube to the boiler room. The two lads down below noted the panic in his voice as they jammed the throttle into reverse. A sandbar had completely blocked the river.

'Come on, lads, tie the boat fast and get ashore.'

Sarah watched as the boat slid into the bank. 'Wait for me.' She ran down the gangway to the bank and immediately started walking upstream to where the *Sarah Lee* was held fast, embedded in the sand.

'God, it's good to see someone. Oh, Mrs Brian.'

The captain of the *Sarah Lee* took her hand, tears welling up in the old man's eyes as he started to commiserate with Sarah about Tom's death. 'The water fell so suddenly I couldn't get her through. We tried pulling her with a team of horses the property owner lent us, and I even unloaded the wool bales, but the sandbar was too high.'

Sarah spent that afternoon talking it over with the two captains. 'If we can load the wool clip on to your boat and you leave immediately for Echuca with Percy, he knows the wool buyers that will certainly help.'

Harry unloaded the horses and he and Sarah rode to the homestead set high up on a ridge. The house had been built of gum slabs, with a corrugated iron roof and a lean-to attached to the back. A small garden off the front verandah showed a feminine touch. It reminded Sarah of her first house built before the floods washed it away.

The lady of the house was overjoyed to have a visitor as they were few and far between. Sarah was invited into the sitting room with its handmade curtains nailed to the shuttered windows. Nancy Briggs had come out west as a bride full of hope and romantic notions. After ten years of hardship, all she had to show was a pretty tea set and the small graves of four children who had died before their second birthday. She made tea and set out fresh scones and butter for them while Harry rode out to find her husband.

The landowner, Jim Briggs, was fencing in the top paddock when Harry waved and reined his horse in, to where the men were sitting having their morning break.

'Come on over, sit a bit, have a cup of tea.'

Harry introduced himself and explained that Sarah was the owner of the stranded boat—and the widow of the dead man buried up on the rise.

Nancy told Sarah of the burial service and what words were said over the grave for Tom. Nancy lowered her head when she explained that neither she nor her husband could read but he had held the holy book as he said the words. Sarah wiped away a tear from her cheek and looked over to the woman.

'Nancy, I could not have wished for better people to take care of my husband. I will always be grateful to you both. But I would like to take him back to his own land.'

That night, sitting around the table, they talked over her problems.

'Do you have any explosives, Jim?'

Sarah had seen Tom blast small sandbars but never one this big.

'Mrs Brian, I have a box full.'

Jim thought that the plan wouldn't work, but Sarah had only one thought in mind: to save Tom's property. They worked all night reloading the wool and getting the *Cameron* on her way.

'Please, Sarah, come back with me.' The captain argued that it would be better if she sold her own wool, anything to get the lass back to Echuca. 'Leave the boat until the rains come and then she'll float free.'

'No, Captain, the boat is my responsibility, besides, Percy can sell the clip as well as I could.'

By midday the following day, the steamer with the wool bales safely loaded pulled away. Sarah watched and as the boat steamed out of sight around the bend, she heard the horn and wished them God speed.

All afternoon the men set the explosives and it was just on dark as Sarah heard 'Stand clear!' Four blasts that shook the very ground they stood on sent flocks of birds screeching to the heavens above, turned the sky black, and all the men aboard with Sarah waited to see if the channel they had created was going to allow enough water through to re-float the boat. Slowly the craft shifted — inch by inch it moved forward but then stopped.

'Tie on the teams, one each side of the river.'

Sarah remembered how Tom had used this method when they first came down from Gulgong. So, with the horses pulling, they finally cleared the sandbar.

'Throw off the lines and open the throttle, more steam, men!' yelled the captain down to the boiler house.

The men pushed more logs into the furnace and wiped the sweat from their brows, waiting for the words 'All clear.' Slowly, the boat moved into the open river, the paddle wheel scraping away at the sand beneath. Tom had been exhumed and the rough-sawn coffin was resting in the hold below.

It was raining at last as Sarah walked into the bank. Her eyes were as cold as steel as she handed the total amount in cash to the bank manager. The manager sat very still in his seat as he looked at the woman before him.

'Now, sir, please close my late husband's accounts and have all deeds transferred to this bank account.'

He jumped up, stammering in his attempt to make Sarah understand that he had never had any intention of touching Tom's holdings. Sarah started to walk out but turned quickly to face him.

'By the way, I'm closing all my accounts here as well.'

With Tom now buried on the land adjacent to their property, Sarah set about sending a load of goods and chattels up to the Briggs in appreciation for all their help.

In the following years, men came courting, but she sent them all away. Her life was full managing her vast holdings in keeping for her children.

The years of hard work had taken their toll. It was time to loosen the reins a little. Maybe she should even retire altogether, return to England, and settle down in her house in the village, the one that she had purchased for her mother years ago?

After years of running her ever-growing empire that now consisted of ships, newspapers, and properties, Sarah was finally persuaded to return to England to help rear her rebellious granddaughter. Although James wanted his mother to live at

Mulberry Park, she was adamant that her mother's cottage, which she had bought for her years before, was, as she said, 'Good enough for me.' Sarah had never forgotten where she came from.

# Part Two
# Prudence

# Chapter twenty-eight

**1912**

Prudence was a typical young woman, full of the excitement that the feminist movement was instilling into women of the 1900's. Her father, Lord James Lowe, wasn't a bad sport, even if he had absolutely forbidden her from joining the Women's Rights Movement. James loved his daughter to bits. Prudence was so much like his mother, Sarah. She was self-reliant and at times quite wilful.

He had been forty when she was born, and she was the apple of his eye. Prue had been given the best education possible and had spent many years in Australia on her grandparent's property. Now it was time for her to be presented to society in London. Without a mother for Prudence and as a lone parent, James relied heavily on Sarah's advice.

'James, are you sure she needs all the pomp that goes with your social circle of friends?' Sarah put down her accounts book; it was getting harder to see the printed numbers on the ledger sheets. 'She's more Australian than English. Why don't you forget all about this nonsense? Leave her here with me and you return to London. She could follow you in a year or two.'

'Good try, Mother, but this time Prue is going to return with me. And by the way, where are your spectacles? You know that you must wear them. In fact, Mother, I think it's time for you to return with us also.'

Sarah didn't like to be bossed around and after Tom died, James thought he had the right to do that. She wondered why children always thought elderly parents should be treated like their own children. But the reality of it was, he was right. For the last fifty years, she had run her property, invested wisely, and become a very rich woman.

The years of hard work had taken their toll, and it was time to loosen the reins a little. Maybe she should even retire altogether, return to England and settle down in the village, in the house that she had purchased for her mother years before.

'Gran, please make him leave me here with you.' Prue looked away from her father and down at her grandmother, her lovely brown almond-shaped eyes pleading for Sarah to intervene. Sarah kept silent.

'Prudence, you are sixteen and we have had this conversation before, so for once you will do what you are told.'

James didn't smile as he looked up at his daughter. She was becoming quite beautiful, but she much preferred to be out riding with the stockmen rather than acting like a young lady. He wondered if he'd given his mother too much rein in the rearing of this child. In hindsight and in all fairness, he knew that he had given Sarah the same anguish that Prue was giving him now.

'No amount of pleading to your gran will change a thing. On the third of the month, we are leaving.' And looking over to Sarah, he continued, 'With or without you, Mother.'

James tapped out his pipe on the lounge hearth and left to enjoy the peace and solitude of the riverbank, away from female distractions.

'Are all the crates aboard, James?' Sarah watched as the last of her possessions were loaded onto the steam train heading for Melbourne. She recalled standing on the banks of the Murray at Albury in 1883, watching as the first train steamed over the bridge into Victoria. Children dressed in their Sunday best stood waving their flags as the steam engine blew its whistle and horses trembled in their traces as the locomotive steamed by.

Sadness flooded through her at the realisation that she would never return to this place that she loved, where she had buried Tom years before. Her mind floated back to the sandbar where James had been born on the banks of the Murray River. They were all gone now: Charley, Tom, Joe, and her Aboriginal friends. All she had left was James, Prue, and a wayward daughter Josephine who was living in France. The land was important, but not as important as blood.

James handed her up into the carriage next to Prue. What a difference the railway had meant to the community of Echuca. Long gone were the weeks of pushing horses and drays and sleeping rough by the side of the track. Sarah looked around the carriage. It was very comfortable, with velvet-covered seats and brightly polished brass luggage racks. Yes, prosperity was everywhere. She settled back and stared out the window as people rushed to complete their chores. Sarah took a deep breath in and wondered to herself, *Where have all the years gone?*

'Oh, Gran, I feel so sad leaving, let's jump off the train. Father couldn't stop us, you're the boss here, aren't you?'

Sarah smiled at her granddaughter. *That's just what I would have said,* she thought.

'Behave yourself, Prue, we don't need your father upset with us.' Prue looked lovely in her modern travelling outfit. It consisted of a deep red serge dress and a coat with a pintucked white voile blouse. Her bonnet was covered in the same material and under the brim was a ruche of small rosebuds. The ensemble was stylish, straight from a Paris magazine to the dressmaker.

It started to rain, black clouds gathered, and the wind rattled the glass in the carriages. The train pulled slowly out from the station. Gone were all the market gardens that used to line the sides of the roads, now that industry had started up in the town, supported by the railway. The sound of children's voices in the paddocks had been replaced with the clanging of metal girders. The last of the steamboats lay derelict, lining the side of the Murray River. This had been Sarah's home for more than fifty years. The train gathered speed, trees flashed by, spurting colours of green and gold. The door slid open, and James entered and sat down beside Prue.

At fifty-six, James was still a good-looking man, as tall and straight as a gun barrel. He had the stance of his father and the endurance of Tom. Sarah wondered if he resembled his father, the dashing captain who had died before he was born, or had he grown more like Tom, the man who reared him.

Sarah questioned why he had never remarried. He was certainly one of the most eligible bachelors in England. Superbly dressed, every garment detailed to show off his masculine form.

'Mother, you have made the right decision, you know that I must return to London. The House of Lords will be sitting in the spring, and I need to be there. God only knows what bills they will try to push through.'

It had been a running battle with his daughter to keep her in check. She was so impressionable and stubborn to boot.

'Father, you should have let me join the Victorian Women's Suffrage Society. I am nearly old enough, I could help rally the cause.'

'Prue, please be quiet. Sit still and read your Ladies' Journal and give me a little peace. You will have enough time to drive me mad on the sea voyage.'

Prue wrinkled up her nose and pouted. James ignored the childish behaviour and handed a cup of tea to his mother.

'Mother, I wish you would reconsider about staying in your old cottage and stay with Prue and me at the manor house, Lord knows it's big enough.'

'Father,' piped up Prue, 'I want to live with Grandmother...'

'Prudence, I won't have another word on the subject, you will live at the manor and take instruction on how to become a lady. Not climbing over the cliffs, looking for trouble with your grandmother.'

Sarah was about to answer her son but decided that it would be far more prudent to speak to him alone.

After finalising her business in Melbourne and taking Prue on a shopping spree, they boarded their ship for the homeward voyage.

The voyage was pleasant enough. Prue kept disappearing to talk to the young gentleman passengers.

'This is exactly what I've been talking about, Mother. Prue needs a firm hand; I've neglected that part of her upbringing long enough.'

Sarah observed her son; he had become tense and irritable, a trait that was new to him.

'James, the girl is Australian, not British. You're trying to make her into a person that she isn't. Darling, you float between two worlds, you are a lord of the realm in England and a farmer in Australia and at times you are miserable. Why are you putting her through the same anguish?'

'Oh, Mum.' Suddenly all the pomp was dropped and her larrikin from the Murray stood in front of her. 'Like it or not, she is Lady Prue Lowe, and she needs to act accordingly.'

'James, she means no harm, but I'll have a word with her.'

The voyage passed without any incidents. It was a sunny day, quite warm for England on the morning they stepped ashore. A rail line now ran down to the dock, making the next part of their journey into London much more comfortable. Prue loved the train travel but for Sarah it was dirty modernisation at its worst and the pollution from the coal-driven steam locomotives made everything she touched filthy.

They were booked into the Prince of Wales, an elaborate hotel, modern in its interior design but steeped in tradition. The doorman had been there forever. He knew all the patrons, even some ladies that he needed to turn a blind eye to. As the coach pulled up and James, Sarah, and Prue stepped out of it, he nodded, and spoke up. 'Welcome back, my lord. Your suite is ready.' Turning, he beckoned to a porter standing near the door. 'Look lively, lad, get the luggage and be quick about it.' The boy had lost concentration as he took a sneaky look at the lovely Miss Prue.

'James, will I take Prue up to the house with me, while you attend the opening of parliament next week?'

Concerned about leaving the girl alone at James's estate, Sarah hoped her son would see reason. She waited patiently. After a few minutes, James turned to face his mother.

'Mother, why won't you stay at the manor with her?' James was becoming increasingly irritated with all the women in his life. Didn't he have enough worrying to do about his sister Josephine and her bohemian lifestyle in Paris? He had received a letter from a friend in the diplomatic service living there. In it was a brief description of a soiree given by her. The friend had been careful not to say too much, but James read between the lines. Other sources had informed him about the café crowd that she mixed with. They were the loafers, bludgers, and misfits of Paris's society.

Josephine was still beautiful and a rebel. She had been engaged to a nice chap but on the eve of her wedding proclaimed to the world that she wanted to be an artist. So, without the good wishes of her family, she escaped the dull life, or so she called it, to reside in France. Josephine knew that James would support her, if only to appease their mother.

'James, didn't you hear me?' Sarah's voice was a little short.

His mind snapped back to the present. 'Sorry, Mother. What were you saying?'

'What I was talking about was your daughter, and her safe keeping. I think she should come with me, just until you return to Mulberry Manor.'

James decided to meet her halfway. 'All right, Prue, you can stay with Gran until I return in six weeks. And then you will return with me, without a word of complaint. Agreed?'

Prue gleamed with delight. She would worry about her father later on, but for now she had six weeks of freedom.


James saw the women onto the train and returned to the House of Lords. He listened to all the gossip and remained silent. At two o'clock the king arrived, and with all the pomp and ceremony, Parliament was opened.

'James, it's good to see you back.' Lord MacLauchlan waved to attract James's attention. He was well past his eightieth year, as deaf as a post, and boasted that he had never missed this occasion since he was invested as a young man.

It was very hard to remain focused. James did his best to serve the king, country, and most of all, the people of his county. He had remained a widower, not that he didn't enjoy the company of the fairer sex. There had been affairs throughout the years, but he still remained one of the most eligible men in Britain.

'James, my boy, will you come up for the shoot?' The old man had grown up with James's father and treated James like a son. 'Bring that little girl of yours. It's about time she was shown around.'

Lord MacLauchlan had invested a lot of time teaching James about the finer points of becoming a lord. He watched him develop from a lad with spunk to a gentleman, who could hold his own in any company. With the death of his wife, Lucy, James had retreated within himself. It was this old lord who told him that his responsibilities had to come before his own grief and for this he would always be grateful to the old man.


The robes were heavy and hot. But at last it was over, and James returned to his suite to enjoy a light supper. The cold lamb and potato salad was delicious. He opened a bottle of red wine but decided to have a beer instead. James lit his pipe and sat back, thinking of what he would do with the holdings in Australia. With Sarah back in England and storm clouds gathering over Europe, James realised that it might be some time before he could return. Even if he didn't return for a while, James knew the property was in good hands.

Billy Mathew's grandson, Mark, was now the property manager. Billy had been one of Sarah's original drovers. Sarah had educated Mark and sent him to university to become a lawyer. But on completion of the course, he had decided to return to the land and was a very trustworthy employee. At the age of twenty-six, he had become a force to be reckoned with. Mark had set up a small practice in Echuca, but all could see that the land was his first love; the second was Sarah, as she was his mentor and trusted friend. Satisfied that his land would be looked after well, James wondered how his mother and Prue were holding up to the long train trip and finally settled down to read the London Times.

It was after eleven that evening before the train shuddered to a stop in a cloud of steam as it came into Manchester. Sarah had rooms waiting for them at the Royal Hotel. James had thought it wise for his mother to rest there a day or so, before continuing on to Manning.

Prue was asleep almost as soon as her head hit the pillow. Sarah had gone in to kiss her goodnight and found her granddaughter already asleep. Sarah felt old as she looked down at the young woman. She had been not much older than her when she left her home for Australia. Sarah lowered her hand and gently pushed back the mass of auburn curls that covered the girl's cheeks. As she watched Prue, she wondered what sort of life was ahead for her. Only good things, if she had anything to do with it.

'Are you up yet, Gran? I have a cup of tea for you.' Sarah smiled to herself. She was always up at dawn. There had been too many years worrying about the stock, floods, or fire to stop now.

'Come in, love. Prue, are you packed? An automobile is taking us the rest of the way. Your father insists that they are safe.' Personally, Sarah had her doubts.

The car chugged along, at one time reaching the high speed of twenty miles an hour. The country sped by. Sarah noticed that not much had changed as they turned into the main street of the village. The blacksmith's shop had had an extension added to the right side of the building and the word Foundry was now up in bold letters over the front door. The car stopped at a general store. Sarah wanted to enquire if all her supplies had been delivered. The girl behind the counter curtseyed and in a broad northern accent welcomed her and confirmed that the house had been opened up and all was ready. The lass looked about Prue's age, dressed in a sturdy work dress with heavy boots and a hair style much too severe for her tender years.

'Madam, if you're to be wanting any extra help I'm surely available.'

'Thank you. I'll keep that in mind. What is your name, dear?' Sarah looked at the two girls, one fair as the English rose, the other a golden brown, similar to the summer grasses back home.

'Me name is Betsy, ma'am. Me dad owns this shop.'

Sarah started to tell the girl her name, but as she began, the girl interrupted her.

'Oh, ma'am, I'd be knowing all about you. Me gran worked for your mother, God bless her soul, and before that she worked in the great house before the fire.' As though she had said too much, she threw in 'And I know all about Australia too.'

# Chapter twenty-nine

The bulk of the luggage wasn't to arrive for a month. The house was well furnished, the larder stocked, and a fire burned brightly in the grate. Sarah walked into the sitting room and looked around; little had changed over the years. The dresser still showed off the fine china that she had sent to her mother forty years before, a gift from a rich Chinese man in Sydney. Sarah was grateful that the fire had been lit days before, as the walls were very warm and any dampness in the cottage had dried out.

A stout woman with rosy cheeks opened the door and bobbed a quick curtsey to Sarah. 'I'm May Brampton, ma'am. Everything is in order; there's a pie in the oven and fresh bread on the hearth.' May spoke with a Welsh lilt and, taking Sarah's small travel bag, led her to a comfortable chair beside the lounge fire.

'Hello, Mrs Brampton, I'm Prue.' A swirl of youthful enthusiasm entered the room.

'Yes, Miss Prue, I was expecting you also. Do you require a lady's maid, miss?'

Prue was about to answer in the affirmative when she caught sight of her grandmother's eyes and rethought her reply.

'Thank you, but I'll be fine.' The thought of being waited on appealed to the young girl, but Prue took it all in good grace and was thankful she was there at all.

When May left the room, Sarah spoke to her granddaughter. 'I should think so, Prue! With Mrs Brampton housekeeping, a lady to clean and wash, and a gardener, I rightly think that you can dress yourself.' Sarah was pleased to retire that night, her arthritis was troubling her, and the long trip had finally taken its toll. The bedroom was familiar, the colour scheme was the same as in her mother's time, even though it was freshly painted and wallpapered.

'Would you like hot milk before I leave, ma'am?' May wanted to make sure that her charge was comfortable before she left that night.

'No thank you, May. I think I'll just sit here for a while.' The garden was lovely this time of year, and from her window the fragrant roses and jasmine were enough to soothe the soul. Out across the valley, Sarah could see down to the cliffs. Suddenly, she remembered the woman standing beside her. 'I'll see you tomorrow. Goodnight.'

The night was a mixture of dreams and nightmares for Sarah. She relived the fire at the manor house and the threat to her son's life. Then she was floating on a cloud of silk, looking down on her river. She saw Tom, her young handsome husband, full of life and vigour. Then it was gone. Startled by the sun's rays hitting her face, Sarah pulled herself up onto one elbow and watched Prue open the curtains to let in the day.

'Gran, let's go for a walk to the beach, it's such a lovely day. Please, let's go early.' Prue looked fresh and pretty in a petal-pink polka dot voile cotton day dress. A straw Dolly Varden bonnet hung to the back of her head, tied up with a matching ribbon. Sarah noticed the ease in which her granddaughter bent over.

'Prue, where are your stays? Your father would have a fit if he saw you dressed like that.' Secretly, Sarah agreed with the lass. Surely such restrictions were unhealthy for the growing figure.

'Please don't tell him. Why should I wear them anyway? I want to have a swim.'

'My girl, if you think you are showing your drawers with that skirt tucked up, you have another think coming.'

'But, Grandmother, I used to swim in the river.'

'Yes, Prue, and that's what got you here; the lack of propriety.'


Sarah donned a pair of walking boots. They were black leather and sturdy, made by a tanner in Albury. Mr Schilg was German and had learned his trade from his father. The family had come from the Black Forest area, and he had started his business in wood carving but quickly realised that leatherwork was what the colonists needed and extended his trade to include boot making, a sign of a true master tradesman.

She looked up and noticed that the clouds were starting to bank up across the Irish Sea. Grabbing a cape, Sarah started down the stairs. She reached the landing, then on an impulse she headed back upstairs to the linen cupboard. On the shelf at the back of the towels lay a long swimming cover robe. She pulled it down and after folding it and placing it in a cane basket, she started down the stairs again.

'Ma'am, Miss Prue informed me that you are going on a picnic. I've packed a few sweeties and a buttered loaf of currant bread. There is a bottle of lemonade also.' May was a little concerned when the lass informed her of their route. It was difficult enough for a younger person, let alone a woman in her seventies. 'You'll be careful, won't you?'

'Thanks, May. We'll be fine.'

Sarah had a spring in her step as they walked up the main street, stopping to speak to the rector, who was clearing leaves that had blown up against the church doors.

'Mrs Brian, it's good to see you back. And who is this lovely lady with you?'

Prue blushed with delight. 'Sir, you know me, I'm Prue.'

'Well, Miss Prudence, it is great to see you here with your grandmother. I will look forward to seeing you both at church on Sunday.'

When they had walked out of earshot, Prue leaned over to speak to Sarah.

'Gran, he is only interested in your donation, crafty old bugger.'

'Prudence, don't let me ever hear you speak so disrespectfully again.' Sarah could see that she was going to have her hands full with the girl, even if she was right.

The cottage gardens were full of colour; roses, lavenders, lilacs, and summer daisies filled the streets with a rainbow of shades and their perfume twigged the senses with the pure pleasure of summer. Prue wondered at Sarah's ability to walk at such a fast pace and purposely slowed down so that Sarah wouldn't overtax herself.

'Hurry along, Prudence, the day is not getting any younger. We need to walk at a fast pace to get God's air into our lungs.'

Prue smiled and moved up beside Sarah. They turned left at the junction and continued down the road past a dairy farm. The cows had already been milked and were grazing back in the paddock.

Sarah stopped to look at them; how easy it was to keep the cows in good condition with all the grass here in England. Rain was in such abundance here and in such short supply in her beloved Australia. Even the hedges in these months of summer seemed to glow with the sweetness of the never-ending showers. Hawthorn flowered in a white mist. The beech trees gave off a soft green haze with their leaves, inviting passers-by to stop and take shade under their sweeping boughs.

As they were standing there, a man walked over to speak to them. He was dressed in labourer's clothes and carried a shotgun.

'Good morning, madam, lovely day. Stopped for a spell?' He was short and his face resembled a moon.

Sarah smiled at him and as she was about to introduce herself, a loud sound roared across the paddock towards the fence. A large jersey bull pounded the ground, sending clods of grass high into the air.

'Get clear of the fence! Charlie boy's on the war path,' screamed a lad from the top of the hill.

In a burst of speed, the little man had jumped the fence and was now standing near the two startled women. The lad was still shaking; sweat was running down his face as he stopped running to catch his breath.

'By gum, ladies, that was close. By the way, I'm Stan Berry. I know who you are, Mrs Brian, I worked for your son's manager, over at the manor.'

They all stared at the bull as he turned and trotted over to a herd of young heifers.

'Better come on over home for a cup of tea.' And obviously thinking on the subject for a moment, he added, 'Or a drink.'

'Thank you, Mr Berry. That will be delightful.'

'Madam, please call me Stan.'

'Well, Stan, I would rather deal with a dozen Angus bulls than one Jersey. Nasty blighters, aren't they?'


Stan Berry was now a manager on the Oakdale Estate, a large two-thousand-acre property owned by a retired general. He lived with his wife and three children in a neat stone cottage near the entrance gates. Martha, his wife, opened the door when she heard the squeak of the gate in their front yard.

'Been meanin' to oil them hinges.'

'You've been saying that for years, Stan Berry. Don't just stand there, show the ladies in.' Martha was as round as her husband, with a pleasant smile and the rosiest cheeks Sarah had ever seen.

'Sit right down, madam, and you too, miss. I'll just put the kettle on.' Martha filled the kettle and set it to boil on the stove. 'As his nibs hasn't introduced us, I'm Martha Berry.'

Sarah looked around the cosy room. Over the door, a side-by-side shotgun took pride of place. Stan watched Sarah as she eyed off the gun.

'I was given this after twenty-five years of service, it's a beauty.' Stan's chest swelled with pride.

'Martha love, she needs a stiff drink, had a nasty fright.' Stan purposely didn't look at his wife. He would have seen the frown that she was giving him. He poured out two drinks and handed one to Sarah.

'You had a nasty fright too?' Martha said as she shot another look over into the direction of her husband. Sarah understood exactly how she felt. Tom had manipulated many a situation containing alcohol to his own benefit.

'A cup of tea would be lovely, Martha. Please call me Sarah, and this is my granddaughter, Prudence.'

After an hour of talking, Prue was taken out to see the horses in the large stable complex, and they continued on their way.

For two months, Prue remained with Sarah. They often walked along the cliff top where a rough wooden fence marked the edge of the cliff, protecting them from a precipitous drop to the jagged rocks below. They would circle around and walk back through the wooded valley to the Oakdale Estate. Prue had been given permission to ride on the estate. The groom chose a quiet mare for her, much to Prue's disgust.

'Gran, can't you please speak to Stan? He won't let me take out a hunter. You know that I can handle any horse they have over there.' Prue was determined to have her way and Sarah had started to become irritated at the girl's lack of respect for Stan and the responsibility that she was placing on him.

'Prue, if you don't curb your ways, I will forbid you to venture over there at all.' Two more weeks and James would arrive to claim his daughter. Sarah never thought that she would be glad to see Prue reunited with her father. *It must be my age.*

It was a fine Saturday morning when Prue collected her mare and started out along the riding trail. After a short time, she became bored with the scenery and headed out along the coast road. The wind started to blow and as Prudence looked up, she noticed that the clouds were banking up across the Irish Sea. The mare was becoming restless as the salt spray hit them both at gale force. Prue had started to make her way back as the first heavy drops fell. It was becoming hard to see, and the rain was now falling in sheets. Over the next rise, Prue could see the outline of a barn against the grey hills.

As she dismounted and was trying to lead the spooked horse into the dark barn, a rat ran between her legs. The horse shied and pulled backwards, prizing the reins out of her hands. As she slipped backwards in the mud, a pair of arms appeared from nowhere, wrapping themselves around her.

'Who in the bloody hell are you?' Prue yelled as she turned around to face her companion.

'Well, how about thanks, for a start.' He looked about twenty; tall and as strong as a brick shithouse, as the drovers back home would say. He was dressed in well-cut riding clothes, and in his left hand he still had hold of a whip. Behind him in the end of the barn, a black hunter was tethered to a rail.

'I'm Patrick McPherson, my father owns this place.' He watched as she tied back the mass of curls that had escaped from the velvet-trimmed hair net and straightened her riding skirt that had twisted, before she finally spoke.

'I'm Prue Lowe. Thank you for your help, but I could have managed.'

'Miss Lowe or should I say Lady Lowe. I was told that you ride every day from our stables.' He smiled; a slight sarcastic grin covered his face. 'It is a pleasure to meet you.'

'I don't like being called Lady Lowe. Miss Lowe will do nicely.'

Patrick laughed as he watched the drenched figure in front of him doing a mighty fine job of being a spoilt brat. Patrick tied the mare to another rail and returned to where Prue was sitting on a bale of hay.

'Be careful you don't scratch yourself on that bale, miss.'

'Scratch myself? I've handled more bales than you have seen.' *What arrogance,* she thought. Prue started to untie the reins of the mare.

'Where do you think you're going?' Patrick grabbed the reins away from her.

'Home. I'll be fine, sir.' Prue tried to summon up a degree of dignity.

'It's the mare that I'm worried about.' He glared at her and wondered what the girl was thinking, riding out along the coast with a storm brewing.

Finally, after an hour of intense thunder and rain that seemed to have been bucketed down by the gods, the storm passed, the wind stopped, and blue sky appeared. The rays of sunbeams danced down through the broken roof, attracting particles of dust that floated up and out into the blue sky.

'Goodbye.' Without a second look, Prue cantered away from the barn, leaving a rather amused young man behind. A groom was waiting to take the mare as Prue entered the stables.

'Please give her a good feed, Ben.' Reaching up, Prue started to rub down the horse as the black hunter walked into the cobbled yard. Patrick noticed the girl and was somewhat taken aback to see her attending to the animal.

'Miss Lowe, a groom will take care of my mare.'

'Your mare, sir?' Prue looked a little confused; she hadn't let the previous conversation sink in.

'Yes, I learned to ride on her. A sweeter nature you'll never find. That's why she was given to you to ride.'

'Well, thank you, but I won't need her again.' Prue picked up her coat, stuck her head in the air and walked out, towards her home.

'Wait up. Would you like a lift home? It is too late to walk alone.'

'No thanks.'

'Miss Lowe! Don't be so stubborn. I have my automobile outside. Surely it would be better than walking? We can leave now, if that's what you would like?'

Prue was starting to feel cold, so swallowing her pride, she thanked him and climbed into the car.

Sarah was reading in the back garden when a shadow above her stooped down and kissed her on the cheek.

'James, you're a few days early.' Sarah was delighted to have him there. Prue and the servants were good company, but she was starved to hear about the war news in Europe. She was becoming anxious about Josephine in Paris and wanted to know the latest news.

'James, I was thinking…'

James shuddered. What was his mother up to now? 'Maybe I should go to Paris and bring Jo back. You know how impulsive she is.' Sarah had that look of determination; the look James knew only too well.

Over the years, James had protected his mother by shouldering the responsibility of bailing Josephine out of trouble and supplying her with an annual allowance. It had been only twelve months since he had paid off a German count. The gigolo was intending to bleed the family dry. James knew how Tom would have dealt with him but for the sake of propriety, he didn't kill the count; instead, he offered him a bribe to disappear.

'Mother, it's not the time to visit Paris…'

Sarah interrupted him. 'James, stop treating me like a fool. Don't you think that I've known all these years how you looked after the family? I know the trouble Jo has been, but I'm now concerned. She needs to be here in England.'

'Mother, if you had let me finish…' He spoke in a soft voice, not wanting to upset her even more than she was. 'I have to travel there next week, that's why I'm here, to see if Prue can stay a little longer. The Home Office has given me a little job to do; it should take only a few days. While I'm there, I'll call in on your wayward daughter.'

Sarah knew better than to ask questions, though she trembled when she thought of James's father and the secret business that had cost him his life.

# Chapter thirty

Josephine
**Paris 1914**

James booked into a suite overlooking the river. His manservant was busy unpacking for him in the bedroom. William had been with James for over twenty years and was more of a friend than a servant. Opening up the French windows, James strolled out onto the terrace. He had been careful not to tell anyone that he was coming to Paris.

This was not the first time that the Home Office had called on him to undertake secret missions for them. He had been asked to contact a British patriot working undercover as an art dealer, who lived on the west bank, not far from Jo's address. James changed into a dark pin-striped suit, donned a hat and gloves, and with cane in hand, set out to walk to the street corner, where he could pick up a cab.

He directed the driver to Jo's address, having him stop a few houses away so that he could survey the surrounds. The street seemed quiet, a few children playing on the footpath. Dogs could be heard howling from their backyards. A nanny, dressed in a starched white apron, pushed a perambulator along towards the park. James observed it all.

The residence at 13 Rue De Cardinal was situated in the more affluent part of the city. The street was lined with trees and brick three-storey residences that had been built in a semicircle around a park. Carriages that had once been pulled by matching teams of horses were being replaced by motor cars, which were parked in the mews behind the houses. Yes, this was an affluent area.

His instruction had been final. Investigate the occupant and all the people involved there. The Home Office was fully aware of James's involvement with the resident. Walking up the steps, James let himself in. He'd had a key cut just in case of an emergency. James hesitated; his hand trembled as he entered his sister's apartment. Across from the hall, double doors opened into a sitting room. French baroque furniture filled the room, and the smell of cigar smoke hung low in the air.

There, sprawled across a settee, lay the body of a woman draped in a pink silk negligee, a long-stemmed glass dangling precariously from her hand. Was she dead? James dropped to his knee beside her. He rolled her face towards him. Yes, she was dead; dead drunk.

How many times had he witnessed this scene before? Gently he lifted his sister up and carried her into the bedroom, where he placed her on her bed and adjusted her garment before pulling a sheet up over her. James settled back to wait and looked around the rooms. Empty glasses and tobacco covered the floor. A man's coat hung on the back of a chair. *Ah, Jo… Jo, why do you still let men use you? How long do you need to punish me and yourself?* He walked into the kitchen and, finding the percolator, made a pot of coffee. It wasn't long before he heard Jo moving.

'Here, sis, drink this, it might help.'

'Get away from me, you bastard. I hate you all.' That was the truth of it, Josephine did hate all men. And now, it seemed to James, she filled the void in her heart with alcohol.

'Jo, it's me, James, you're safe.'

Like a frightened child she reached out for her brother, and in a slurred voice mumbled, 'James, I didn't want you to see me like this. Why are you here anyway?'

'We'll talk about it later. Here, drink this coffee.'

Later that evening after Jo recovered enough to wash and dress, James told her about her mother's return to England and how lucky that he had come over to Paris instead of her. Josephine lit a cigarette and started a speech on how her life was hers and hers alone.

'For God's sake, Jo, I've heard this a hundred times. And I'm telling you, pick up your game and come back with me. You are involved with some very nasty types, and there will be no more money while ever you stay here.'

Her face went blank, and she started to scream, 'Well you can shove your bloody money, you…' She stopped short, bursting into tears. 'James, I'm pregnant!'

James sat with her that night. They discussed their return to London before he returned to his hotel. He would put her on the boat and stay on to complete his mission. At midday, he arrived with a coach to collect her.

Opening the door, he sang out to her, 'Ready, love? The men are here to collect your luggage.' The only reply was silence. He ran from room to room expecting the worst; but she had simply disappeared.

James stayed on in Paris to search for her. The police enquiries all led to a dead end. Josephine appeared to have vanished into fresh air.

A large reward was posted, but in the end, James had to return to England to tell Sarah that her daughter had disappeared. On Saturday after he returned to London, James was summoned to the Defence Department. There, a brigadier ushered him into a large conference room. Lord Samuel Bridge was known to James, they sat together in the House of Lords.

'James, this is a terrible time for your family. I have been able to ascertain that a known German agent was seen visiting your sister's address on several occasions. He has gone undercover too.'

'Sam, what are you saying? How could Jo be involved in spying?'

'James, while you were in Australia, she has been under surveillance. I'm sorry to tell you, but she has been entertaining quite a few military men, far too many for it to be a coincidence. We know that she has been hitting the bottle, so I guess we have to wonder why.'


Josephine had confided in her maid; the maid had made enquiries and had been given the name of a woman, who, for a sum of money *righted* girls' lives. Jo booked into a small hotel that backed onto a small lane that ran down to the river. A week later, she walked the grotty back alleys on the east bank in Paris, looking for the woman who performed abortions. *Please, God, make this happen,* she thought, *let this woman take away my problem and restore my life.*

She was about to knock on the front door of a small shop front, when the door opened, and a pale-looking woman staggered out clutching her stomach. Josephine put out her hand to steady the girl, who pulled back and pushed past her. It was then that she saw the blood seeping through the back of the woman's dress.

'Come in, mademoiselle, have you got cash?' There before her stood an older woman dressed in a blood-stained apron.

'Sorry, I think I've changed my mind.'

'No matter, you must pay anyway. My time is money.'

Josephine dropped the cash onto a small table, near a bench containing a row of instruments and a bowl full of bloody water. Walking back, Josephine heard the bells of a church tolling, 'salvation'.

It took all her courage to enter the church and ask the blessed Mother for help. A young priest overheard her and answered her prayers.

Two days later, she entered a new world. Josephine looked around the small room. It contained a bed, open hanging space, a small chest of drawers and above her bed a crucifix hung on the wall. The Sisters of Mercy had agreed to hide her until the child was born. She had agonised over the decision she had made.

How could she go home knowing that the father of her child was a German agent? Josephine had met Hans at one of the parties she attended. He was handsome and loving. She must have been blind not to have realised she was only a pawn in his game. He wanted to marry her and when she refused him, he became violent, telling her he would take the baby, and she would never see it again.

But there was a much darker secret. Josephine had made friends with a young Jewish painter during this time. Josephine checked her dates over and over; no, the child must be Hans's.

Josephine hadn't been as drunk as he had thought the night she lay there listening to him on the phone. He discussed his failure to marry her and thus be able to enter the inner sanctum of her brother's world and others in the British Defence Department. Josephine understood enough German to know that her life was in danger and if she went back to England her family would be under threat also.

No, this was the best decision she could have made. Josephine sat on her bed looking around the room, when a young novice knocked on her cell door.

'Mademoiselle, Mother would like to speak to you. Please come this way.'

Josephine followed the girl down through the cloister, along the back walled garden and into the side entrance of the Mother House.

There she knocked on the door to a study.

'Enter, my child,' came a voice from within. The novice backed away, leaving Jo to enter the holy of holies. The mother superior looked serene as she watched the girl sit down before her.

'Miss Brian, are you comfortable here?'

Jo noticed that the woman sitting before her had a flawless complexion with large brown oval eyes, made even larger by the flowing habit that covered her body. On her left hand, she wore a plain gold wedding ring.

'Yes, thank you.'

'The reason I've asked to speak to you is in regard to your safety and in fact the safety of all my sisters. You have been very forthright in coming to tell me of your fear for your child and your family, and for that, I thank you. But, Josephine, I have decided to move you to a safer convent away from here. You will be transferred as one of our sisters. This must not arouse any suspicion.' She asked the young woman again, 'Are you sure, dear, you would not be better off in England?'

'No, Mother, my family would be in danger. I've made a terrible mistake. I slept with the devil and now I must pay.'

The older woman smiled to herself. Yes, this girl was in terrible trouble but sleeping with the devil, well, that was a bit dramatic, even for her. 'So I will arrange it all, you will go to Orléans to stay.'

Josephine racked her brain. What was it she was supposed to know? What threat was she to anyone? She knew she should regret the way she had woven the threads of her life, but in all honesty, she would not have changed a day of it, well, up until she met Hans. Hans was everything a woman would fall for. He was good looking, well-educated and he had a title—a duke of some Austrian municipality, high up in the Alps. What's more, he was very generous, showing her a good time and splurging money wherever they went.

She knew what the good people of Paris thought of her and why she had not been invited into their homes. What was it they had called her? A tramp, a woman from a pit void of morals. What did she care if they couldn't control their men? The only pang of guilt she felt came when she thought of the shame she had brought on James and her mother. James's generosity had afforded her a very comfortable life in Paris. She dined with dukes and generals. She didn't care for their talk about war. They brought her expensive gifts and in turn used her house for their silly little meetings.

In the week that followed, Josephine kept to her room, only coming out at mealtimes. The young novice kept a close eye on her guest, keeping her company whenever time allowed. Josephine's mind kept racing back to the apartment at 13 Rue De Cardinal and to the events that had taken place there.

# Chapter thirty-one

This all seemed a lifetime ago, as Josephine was bundled into the carriage of a train, along with twelve other nuns. Soldiers mingled on the platform and all around her there was talk of war.

'Come, Sister, remain in the carriage, we will be leaving soon.' A tall soldier doffed his cap to her as he closed the door. She could only smile at him. Mother Superior had warned her not to speak, to keep her head down and her eyes focused on the ground.

It took a day before they arrived in the small industrial city of Orléans. The Mother House was set well back from the street, protected by a stone wall. A bell was set into the stone pillars that stood each side of a gate. The door was solid, with a sliding hatch only large enough to speak into. Josephine entered and was ushered into the office, where a kindly older woman took her hands in a gesture of welcome.

'My child, you will be safe here. Go now and rest. We will speak later.' The mother superior of the convent watched as the exhausted younger woman turned and left her study. She had thought long and hard before agreeing to accept the responsibility of the younger woman and her child. The safety of her nuns was her first priority. She had been told of the girl's decision not to have an abortion and this decision placed the burden of responsibility back onto her.

Josephine adjusted to the orderly life in the convent. At first she stayed in her room, mixing only at mealtimes. Slowly she started to focus on the daily routine and became interested in the lovely intricate lace work that the younger novices did. They sat together at night, talking about the worldly possessions that they were to leave behind as they walked farther down the spiritual road they had chosen.

'Josephine, would you like to learn?' A rosy cheeked novice handed her a length of the most exquisite lace Josephine had ever seen.

'Sister, I could never do that.' Josephine smiled and handed it back. 'But I would like to sew some baby gowns, if you could help me. The needle and I have never been friends.'

All the sisters looked up at her. An older nun walked over to Josephine and rested her hand on the girl's shoulder. She spoke in soft broken English. 'We will all help you.'

It took a few stiff whiskeys before James could face his mother and tell Sarah of Josephine's disappearance.

'What do you mean disappeared, how in the hell could she disappear, James?' The look on Sarah's face drove James to despair. What should he tell his mother, the truth or a lie? Was she well enough to be told that her daughter was a suspected spy, and pregnant to boot?

'Mother, the best detectives are looking for her now and after Parliament breaks, I'll return to Paris. But I need you to promise me you won't go there. Please, Mother, stay and look after my daughter. God knows what trouble she would get into without you.'

Sarah knew that James was right; Prue was a handful and when James was in London that left only her.

'Daddy, I didn't hear you pull up. Where is Aunt Jo?' Prue breezed into the room and threw her arms around her father. James looked at his daughter. She looked the same, but there was something different about her, or was it his imagination?

'Prue'—he leaned back against the door—'let me take a good look at you.' He turned to his daughter; she was radiant. Her dress fitted her body to perfection. Sarah made a mental note, that at least the lass was wearing her stays.

'It's your hair, Prue, you look much more grown up, very becoming.'

'Thank you, Father.' Blushing, she gave a small curtsey and kissed him on the cheek. 'But where is Aunt Jo?'

There was no putting the girl off. 'Jo has decided to stay longer in

Paris, Prue. But tell me, what had you been up to?'

'I, Father?' Prue smiled sheepishly, a look that would melt butter. 'Why, Grandmother and I live a very quiet life here. Except for that rude Patrick McPherson, life here would be wonderful.'

'Prue, are you speaking of the son of our neighbour, who graciously lent you a horse to ride?'

'Oh, Daddy, you don't know him…'

James interrupted her. 'But apparently you do, Prue.'

'Well, Daddy, I had the most unpleasant meeting with him, and I do not wish to see him again.'

Sarah had listened to the conversation for long enough. 'James, we have been invited to a dinner, and I will expect Prue to accompany me and act as a lady. Mr McPherson Senior has been very generous, and we will not show him our lack of manners by not attending.'

James also knew better than to argue with his mother but on this occasion, he did agree.

The days leading up to the dinner, Prue did nothing but find excuses why she should not attend on the following Saturday night. The day had started out drizzling with rain, the storm clouds banking up over the Irish Sea. But on dusk, the rays of sunlight broke through, delighting everyone except Prue.

Prue's new evening gown arrived. Not the typical gathered skirt but a more fitting, softer style; cream silk with a net overlay, encrusted with small glass beads. Her shawl was made of the same overlay. This had cost James a pretty penny. Later that evening, Sarah and James waited downstairs. Thirty minutes later, Prue floated down the staircase. She was a picture of elegance; her hair had been swept up high, only allowing a few curls to escape and frame her face.

For a moment, Sarah saw a long-ago memory of herself, looking down at a dashing sea captain, the years between not existing. But as suddenly as the vision appeared, it vanished, and it was Prue standing there.

The McPherson mansion was a blaze of lights as their car pulled up in front of the formal entrance.

'I'll let you two ladies out here and I'll park the car.' James wouldn't let any young servant touch the Bentley, his pride and joy.

Sarah and Prue walked up the steps and were met by a butler. A maid took Sarah's fur stole and announced the two women. The dining room was decorated in modern tones of white and aqua, with a large dining table and a floral display that spread from one end to the other. A maid offered them a drink from the silver server she was carrying. Sarah took a glass of white wine and as Prue leaned over to pick up a glass also, Sarah placed a hand on her granddaughter's arm.

'I don't think so, dear,' she whispered into Prue's ear. 'Why not take an orange drink for now.'

Begrudgingly, the girl obliged. Prue was still feeling out of sorts when an arm brushed against her own, causing her to spill her drink on the person standing next to her.

'Oh, I'm so sorry,' she stammered.

'I think you should be, Miss, or should I say Lady' — the young man looked into Prue's eyes — 'Prue, although you seemed to have ruined my suit, I must say you look lovely tonight.'

Prue was lost for words. She started to talk, but he interrupted her again.

'This must be your father. Sir, please let me introduce myself. I'm Patrick McPherson.' He shook her father's outstretched hand. 'I met your lovely daughter when she was out riding.'

James observed the whole carryings on between these two young people. *So, this is the man Prue objected to*, he thought to himself. 'Thank you for the invitation, I'm sorry my acceptance was at such late notice, Mr McPherson.'

'Please call me Patrick. Mrs Brian told us that you were in Paris. I hear that things are very bad in Europe, sir, and that war is imminent.'

'You have heard correctly, Patrick. With the death of the Archduke Franz Ferdinand, I expect that England will enter the war at any moment now. It is a tragic situation for everyone. But enough of this, we are here to enjoy ourselves. Will you excuse me? I would like to have a word with your father.'

James made his way to a group of men standing at the back of the room. With James gone, Prue tried to move away. 'Done the damage and now you are leaving?' Patrick smirked as he waited for the girl to reply.

'Sir, I would have thought that your bad manners have been well observed. Now excuse me, I need to find my grandmother.' So with her nose in the air, Prue gently pushed through the crowd, reaching Sarah just in time to hear 'Dinner is served.'

James escorted Sarah to her seat and turned to find Prue being escorted towards him by a smiling Patrick. Later after the formal dinner, and before the dancing started, Prue spoke to her father.

'Daddy, he is intolerable. Surely, you can now see it for yourself.'

'Prue, this is not the place to discuss this. Later at home will do.'

The older matriarchs sat, while the younger women mingled to the far side of the room as the music started up.

'Miss, may I have the pleasure of this dance?'

Prue looked Patrick squarely in the eye and answered, 'No.'

'People are looking at us. Come on, don't make a scene, your ladyship.' Before she could answer back, she was swept onto the dance floor. She couldn't stand him, but she had to admit he was a great dancer. Prue swayed to the rhythm and was pulled gently back into Patrick's arms. The couple were aware that all eyes were on them.

'They'll probably have us engaged before the season is out.' Patrick gave her a tight squeeze just as the music ended.

'Not while ever there's another man living.' Prue pulled away and left him standing on the floor, laughing.

Life returned to normal when James left for London. Prue returned to riding every day and Sarah joined in the activities in the village. After the third week, James returned to speak with his mother.

'War was declared last night, Mother, and as I'm involved with the war department, I think it might be better to leave Prue here with you. I'm off to Paris again, so don't expect to hear from me for a while.' James felt his mother's anguish. 'Oh, Mum, I'll do everything I can to find Josephine, but now I have another agenda also.'

Sarah had suspected that James was involved in intelligence but knew better than to ask him.

'James, the lass will be fine, it's you I'm worried about. Stay safe, dear.' And as an afterthought, said, 'Keep a pistol close.'

He nodded in agreement but said nothing more about it. 'I'll go and have a talk to that daughter of mine. Where is she?'

Prue was reining in her horse when she saw her father standing near the stable. 'Daddy, this is a lovely surprise. What's up?'

'Sweetheart, we need to have a talk. Stable your mare and let's have coffee.'

James told Prue what was to happen, or at least what he could reveal to her. 'Prue, please remember that your grandmother is not getting any younger, so don't give her a hard time, and remember that your actions are a reflection of your upbringing.'

Prudence promised solemnly that she would help Sarah and not cause her any grief. *It will be a miracle*, James thought as he backed his car out of the drive and started on his way back to London and the Foreign Office.

# Chapter thirty-two

**Convent in Orléans**

Josephine's routine was established. In the mornings, she sat in the garden watching the sisters working, and in the evening they all sat in the dining room working on the baby's layette. It was becoming harder for her to walk. Her feet were swollen from the pressure of the growing pregnancy. She was a grown woman who now needed her mother. Josephine had been informed by Mother Superior that a man in Paris had enquired as to her whereabouts and that no information regarding her had been given out.

A nurse came to the convent monthly to treat any sick nuns and now to look after her also. Josephine liked the French woman, and they struck up a firm friendship. On her visits, she fed Josephine snippets of information as to what was happening on the war front. This news was a welcome relief and something that she had to keep secret from the nuns who were kept in ignorance of worldly events.

'Josephine, England has joined the war. Remember what I have told you, you will not be safe if the Germans raid this place.' Tearing a page out of her notebook, she scribbled a few lines on it and handed it to Josephine. 'Just in case I can't come here, this is my address; keep it in a private place.'

'Why mightn't you be able to come here?' Panic gripped her.

'Josephine, there are things I can't tell you, but remember what I *have* told you and only use this address if you are in danger.' The nurse kissed her and left, leaving Josephine in a state of anxiety. The baby kicked and moved all the time now, not allowing Josephine to rest. *Did I do this to Mum too?* she wondered as she rubbed the cramps in her calves. Her back was paining and the cramps in her stomach were not going away, even though she had taken all the medication prescribed.

Sister Thérèse, one of the younger nuns, watched Josephine carefully that day. She was the eldest of ten children and had helped the midwife out on many occasions before deciding that the life of celibacy was for her.

'Josephine, I think your time is here. We had better send word to the nurse, before curfew.' The novice helped Josephine into the room that had been prepared for the birth.

'Bloody Germans, who do they think they are, locking us all up at nightfall.'

Sister Thérèse did her best to calm Josephine, but as the hours went by and the nurse hadn't arrived, she started to panic herself.

'Josephine, I've delivered many babies.' She added some lavender water to the sponge and wiped the sweat from Josephine's face. The nun didn't dare tell the woman that she had only helped in the deliveries. 'You will soon have a beautiful baby, don't worry.'

As the labour lengthened, Josephine became more vocal. 'Where's the bloody nurse?'

'It is all right, my dear; we are all here for you. Scream if you want to, no one will hear.'

And scream Josephine did; until even the good sisters prayed for her quick delivery. In the early hours of the morning in a gush of water, a slippery little girl emerged into the world. Sister Thérèse thanked the blessed saints that it was all over and now mother and child slept. One by one the sisters tiptoed in and left little presents for the child on the bedside table.

Anne thrived and very rarely cried, probable due to the fact that every nun there became her aunty. The fair baby down was replaced by black curls. Josephine's worst fears were now a reality. Her child was half Jewish. Josephine thought back to the brief affair she had with the young art student… yes, it was about the time the baby was conceived. The baby grew and at six months old she was weaned.

'Josephine, can't you hear your child crying?' Mother Superior had listened to Anne's cry and had waited for the child's mother to go to her. At last, she couldn't stand the noise any longer and, shuffling past her desk, reached over for her walking stick. The rheumatics was worse this winter, the cold ate into her bones. 'Josephine, your child needs you.' The old nun stooped to lift the baby. Where was that young woman?

'Mother Superior, we have looked everywhere; Josephine's gone. She has taken her clothes but has left you a letter.' The young nun wiped the tears from her cheek as she took the baby from the older woman. Slowly, she handed over a letter with Mother Superior's name on it.

*Mother Superior*
*Please forgive me. I have to leave, and I can't take the baby. I will not be back to reclaim her. Please keep her safe and later on find a family who will love her as I do. I have enclosed a separate sheet for your eyes only. When you have read it, please destroy it.*

The nun turned to the next sheet and read on.

*Mother, I now know that my daughter is of mixed race. I have enclosed all the information that I know about her father.*

She could see that the pages were written in haste, not the usual neat handwriting for which Josephine was noted.

Josephine wandered through the alleys of Orléans. A small suitcase in one hand and a piece of paper in the other, she stopped to study the house number on the front door and glanced back down at the piece of paper crumpled between her fingers. Yes, this was the right one. Josephine knocked and waited. The door opened partly, and a low-pitched voice asked her what it was she wanted.

'Will you let me in? I can explain.' Fear crept into Josephine's voice. 'Please, I have this name.' She pushed the paper into the hand of a stout Parisian matron. 'I was told that if I needed help, I could come here.'

'Come in child, hurry.' The older woman looked up and down the street before closing the door. 'How do you know Pippa?' she enquired.

It took a few minutes to explain Josephine's connection with the nurse before the woman relaxed.

'So, miss, what will we do with you?' The woman walked around Josephine, examining every feather of her. 'Can you drive a small truck?'

Josephine nodded. 'I can drive a car, so a truck can't be too different.'

'Good, we will have work for you. But first you must change your appearance.'

Josephine re-entered the world a day later, on the arm of a tall man, who she was introduced to as Paul. She was a metamorphosis in the making. Josephine was blonde now, gone were the brown curls and tight skirt. She was dressed in a Red Cross uniform and sewn onto her coat was her new name, Mademoiselle Blare. Together they boarded a bus and walked to the back seat where the man leaned over and spoke quietly to her.

'We are to pick up a truck and drive it to the city of Alençon. There we will be met and given further orders.'

Paul was born in America but had been brought up in France and spoke the language as well as any Frenchman. 'Tell me, Jo, can I call you that? Why in the hell didn't you get out when you could leave?'

Josephine studied this younger man sitting beside her: tall, good looking, intelligent, and a smart arse. 'Paul, let's get one thing straight from the beginning. We may be in this together, but you mind your business, and I'll mind mine.'

The bus seemed to take forever to reach their destination. Women held their children close as crates of chooks were crammed into the aisles. Leaving the bus, they took a cab to a deserted factory in the industrial part of the city. Behind the heavy doors, a truck, painted with the familiar Red Cross was parked and waiting for them, the keys in the ignition.

The city was still sleeping as they drove out of Orléans toward the north. The sun's rays painted a glorious picture as they rose from behind the mountains ahead. It would be so easy to forget that they were in the deadly jaws of war.

Lines of people pushing carts and carrying all their possessions streamed along on the opposite side of the road, all heading away from Paris. They stopped at a roadblock manned by a garrison of German soldiers. Seconds seemed like hours as they waited while their papers were examined. A man on a push bike failed to stop; a bullet lodged in his skull, the blood spraying along the side of the truck. Their papers were stamped and handed back, and they were on their way. Alençon lay only two hours farther north.

Alençon was a small rural city with towering churches and a busy market. They pulled the truck up in the side street opposite a military headquarters. A small man pushing a hand cart wandered over and produced a bag of apples.

'I think these apples are just right for you. Are you ready for them?' He pulled off his cap and wiped the sweat from his brow. Josephine noticed a nervous twitch on the man's face as Paul handed over some coins and a letter.

'These are fine apples. I could take two more now.' Paul glanced in the rear vision mirror.

'Come to the address on the paper bag tomorrow night. All will be ready.' The vendor lifted the handles of the cart and started down the road.

'Apples for sale, get your apples here,' he cried.

The night was dark; the moon was low and reflected across the bonnet of the truck as they stopped on the side of the road to eat. Paul watched his partner as she chattered away.

'Josephine, I think it would be better if you don't talk to anyone, let me do it all.'

'Why? My French is as good as yours is.'

'Jo, I have been at this far longer than you.'

She was about to argue, when out of the blue he leaned forward, and with the knife that he had been cutting up the apple, nicked her throat with the blade. Blood trickled down her front, pooling in the crevice between her breasts.

'You bastard! You tried to kill me.' With all the strength she could gather, she punched out at him.

'No, it's only a scratch. Here, put a bandage on it. If we are pulled up, I will tell them that you have been wounded and that you can't talk.' He felt guilty for having to frighten her, but it could possibly save her life and the lives of others. Some of the French resistance that he knew would have killed her themselves if they had thought she might be a loose link in their chain.

They drove on through the country lanes until they reached the crest of a small hill. There Paul stopped and dimmed the headlights and waited. It wasn't long before a flash of light could be seen from the valley below. With the truck in complete darkness, they drove along at a snail's pace. A man stood by the gate to a farm and flashed his torch as they drove the truck towards him.

'Quickly, drive into the barn. We've been waiting for you for two days.'

The man jumped into the back of the truck, and they proceeded forward. The doors swung open, and they disappeared behind a stack of hay.

Josephine was introduced to the group of people there. They were dressed as peasants, young and old alike. They stared at the English girl, but the story Paul told about her being attacked by a German guard put them at ease and she became an instant heroine. They ate their first hot meal in days and waited as the boards on the tray of the truck were removed and a crate was built into the lower floor. New boards were fitted a little higher up, the space being just large enough to hide two people.

A thin mattress was thrown on to the floor and all was ready. Just before dawn, two men entered the old barn and quickly climbed into the crate, the trapdoor was closed, and the truck started off for the Belgium border.


Josephine hadn't said one word to Paul, just stared out the window watching the country roll by.

'Jo, for God's sake; don't you think I know how you feel? This is war and some of us get killed.' His voice was drenched in pity, not only for her but for them all. 'This is not for you. We might be able to get you onto a fishing boat. There are some who are still loyal to the cause and who could get you across the channel.'

Josephine relented and spoke in a whisper to him, 'Do you think they can hear me?' She pointed to the back of the truck.

'No, not a chance, the engine is too noisy. Poor buggers, they must be so cramped. I can't take a chance to let them stretch though, not here.'

A few miles farther on, they came to their first roadblock. Two guards stopped them. Josephine could feel the cold sweat trickle down her back. A rifle was pushed through the open window into the cabin, and she remained quiet. They sat there, the minutes ticking by, until the paperwork was handed back, and they were waved on. Jo gasped the air, relieved that she hadn't wet herself.

The clouds had banked up and thunder rolled across the valley before it started to rain. A few heavy drops to start with. Josephine's mind travelled back to when she was a kid growing up in Australia. Tom, her dad, had always said, *'Large drops means a drought.'* How he would have loved the rain here; it never stopped. Funny the things you think about when you're scared shitless. She knew he would have said that too.

The truck hit a bump in the road and the jolt brought her back to reality.

'I hate to tell you, but I don't know where in the hell we are.' Paul studied the map that lay open across the steering wheel. 'The bloody road has been closed.'

They stopped and their passengers got out and relieved themselves. After a cold meal, the men were crammed back under the floorboards, the medical supplies arranged on the floor, and they were off again. It was nearly dawn when a shadow of a man waved the truck to a stop. They couldn't see the uniform in the dark and waited until he stepped up onto the running boards of the truck and poked his head in.

'Good day, mate; got a lift for my sergeant? He's been hit in the bum and needs medical attention.' The face of this larrikin brought Josephine to tears. 'No need to cry, miss, he'll be okay.'

The young trooper had no idea why she was crying. This could have been her father. Paul looked at her and threw up his hands in dismay. He knew they couldn't leave the Australian soldiers there to die.

'We'll put you two in the back, keep low and for God's sake, be quiet.'

The two of them had now become six. The trooper knocked on the back window and yelled out to Paul. 'The bridge's gone, we'll have to turn inland and cross near the river landing. There could be an Aussie command still in the region.'

Josephine drove while Paul slept. Through the mist she could see trucks and a brigade of men marching towards them. Reaching over, she shook his arm violently. Paul woke with a start.

'Turn out the bloody lights.' He pushed her aside to reach the switch. Jumping out, Paul ran to the back of the truck and, ripping the flap aside, yelled to the Aussies in the back, 'Get out, quickly. I'll give you a hand with the sergeant. Get into the ditch over there.' Paul half dragged the man from the truck and over the gravel towards a bush-lined depression on the high side of the road. In a few minutes, the truck had moved off. 'God help us.' Jo shook as Paul took over the driving again. The German soldiers marched by, taking little notice of the Red Cross vehicle. A quick look in the back and they were ordered to move along.

Later that evening, they turned back to where the men were still hidden in the long grass. The roadblock had moved on. The evening was still, the air had cleared, and the guns were silent. Burnt out trucks and human remains lay strewn along the roadside, the air was sickly sweet with the smell of death. Josephine tried to forget what she had seen and concentrate on the human cargo hidden beneath their tray boards.

The rest of the trip was uneventful. The Australians were handed over to the underground. For the first time in days, Josephine relaxed. Their passengers were then given to the underground where they disappeared as quietly as they had arrived.

'It's been a pleasure knowing you, Miss Josephine.' Paul smiled as he opened the side door of the cabin. 'You'll be safe with these people here. Just don't say too much. I'll try to arrange a boat for you.'

'Paul, I think I want to stay here.' She put her hand up as if to stop him speaking. 'Don't say anything, I know that I need my head read.'

Paul sat and listened before he made a comment. 'Josephine, if there is one thing I've learned here, it's that people act in strange ways. If this is really something you want to do, I'll introduce you to the right people. They need all the help they can get. But for God's sake, be sure.' He handed her a cigarette and sat back. It took a while before she answered him.

'Paul, up till now my life hasn't been productive, as Mum would say. I've now got a reason to help. If the only thing I can do in my life to help is drive a truck, so be it.'

'Well, love, what can I say? Welcome to Hell.'

# Chapter thirty-three

**England**

The summer passed and Prue became more involved in the Women's League war effort. Gone was the girl, and a young woman had taken her place. She attended the village sewing groups and helped with the packing of food for the troops. She seldom rode the mare now; the snow covering the roads had made them impassable.

Sarah and Prue had been out visiting the sick, when the parson's wife had informed them of the young men in the village who had joined up. On top of the list was Patrick McPherson. It was a bleak November morning as the whole village turned out to see the train off.

'Please move.' Prue pushed past the groups of families until she saw him standing with his father at the end of the platform. He looked very handsome in his captain's uniform, quite dashing, with an air of confidence about him. He stared over the heads of the families and suddenly his eyes locked onto hers.

Prue spoke first; her voice was loud as to cover the fear she felt in her heart.

'Patrick, I just wanted you to know that I will look after your old mare…' He swept her into his arms and kissed her with a depth that took her breath away.

'Prue, I will be back for you, even if I'm the only man left alive.'

Sarah watched the scene unfold. *At last, girlie, you have met your match.*

Sarah longed for the times James would visit. They sat in the sunroom talking about the war.

'I'm telling you, James, they're using the Australian lads as pawns. Look what they did at Gallipoli. Any fool knew that trying to land on that part of the peninsula would be suicide.'

James couldn't argue with her; he felt the same and had tried to change the landing site. Winston Churchill had just been made Lord of the Admiralty and wouldn't budge. Looking down at her, a thought crossed his mind, *If only the men of means had half Mother's sense, the war would have been won by now.*


**France 1918**

The black clouds of war lay low over the French countryside; the sickly smell of blood tainted the once beautiful landscape.

Josephine had to harden her heart to all the things she saw. She learned how to shoot a pistol, which wasn't difficult as Tom had taught her to shoot a rifle at a tender age, and to drive her truck through the back roads of France. Sometimes she would play a game trying to forget the senseless deaths she witnessed every day. She would imagine that she owned her truck, and she was transporting people from one marketplace to another. She watched the cows in the meadows, and she would breathe in the aroma of the freshly cut hay.

Through all the devastation of war, sparks of daily life remained. Josephine felt a great sense of satisfaction; she had transported over forty people now. *Forty people the bastards didn't get* she thought as she reached for another hanky.

The summer had now given way to the cold, bleak days of winter.

She had picked up a cold, *Bloody thing. I just don't seem to be able to shift it.* With a bottle of aspirin on the seat beside her, she started off again, conscious of the two women nestled into the crate beneath the floor. The older woman was an American teacher suspected of spying for the English, the younger being her niece. Josephine alternated the farms in which they spent the night. German spies were everywhere. Only a week ago, she had witnessed a family being shot outside their farmhouse.

'Miss, you are sick. Let me drive them on, you stay and rest.' The lad was no older than a teenager. He dressed in a tweed coat and cap, and around his waist a cartridge belt held up his pants; he carried his rifle slung low over his shoulder.

'I'll be fine; I just need a hot drink.' As Josephine stepped down from the running boards of her truck, she felt faint, and if not for the boy standing there, she would have hit the ground. She woke up in the main bedroom of the farmhouse. A tall thin woman was wiping her face with lavender water and adjusting the bed sheets. Try as she might, she couldn't lift her head from the pillow.

'My truck…?' The rest of the words wouldn't come out. Saliva dripped from the corner of her mouth.

'Don't try to speak, madam. Your truck left two days ago, and you are safe here, for the time being.' Madam Layler knew how sick this woman was. The doctor had warned them that this flu was in epidemic proportions and thousands had already died. But what could she do? Turn this woman out, this woman who had saved many people? No, it was her Christian and patriotic duty to care for her. Josephine requested a letter to be written for her brother. The old lady sat beside the bed with pen in hand as Josephine began.

*I know that I'm dying, James, but I have to let you know that I had a daughter. I asked the sisters to find a family for her. James, I realise that I made the wrong decision. Please find her. Love you, Jo.*

The doctor brought what little drugs he had, but her condition worsened. On the tenth day of her confinement to bed, Josephine Brian, sister of Lord James Lowe, died in the arms of a woman she didn't know, in a strange land but with the people she had learned to care for.

It was late evening; the sun was hidden behind a storm cloud when they buried Josephine in the orchard with not so much as a bunch of flowers to mark the spot, just in case the Germans became nosey. As the coffin was lowered into the ground, a letter fluttered down, settling onto its owner. A woman spoke softly from the grave surround.

'Madam, forgive me, but I cannot keep this letter.'

# thirty-four

**Anne**
**The morning Josephine disappeared from the convent.**

Mother Superior folded the letter and replaced it into the envelope. *My dear Lord, what will I do with the child?* It was more of a thought process than an actual prayer. The young novice watched the older woman; she saw the distress and pain that this news had given her. Mother Superior sighed.

'Sister, will you take care of the baby until I can arrange a placement for her?'

The young novice said hesitantly, 'Mother, where is Josephine?'

'My dear, only God knows that.'

Sister Thérèse knew better than to ask further questions. She watched the Mother replace the letter into the locked drawer and with a wave of a hand dismissed her.

No longer did the German soldiers remain at the gate of the convent, they now searched the building looking for anyone who resisted them. It would be impossible to move the child at that moment. They told the German captain that one of the sisters had fallen by the way and the child belonged to her. This amused the man no end.

The baby thrived with fourteen aunties to care for her. It was impossible to obtain cotton fabric, so the sisters cut up an old habit to make little smocks for her. Mother smiled when she saw her youngest member of the fold. After the bombing of the surrounding buildings, all the sisters, including the toddler, were to be sent back to Paris to the Mother House. The entire records of the convent except the letters given by Josephine had been destroyed. Only these letters travelled with Anne and the sisters on the long slow train ride back to Paris.

As much as the sisters pleaded with the Mother House's community, Anne was placed into care.

Fredrick Hayes, an Australian soldier, had been recuperating in a French hospital after the Germans were defeated. Attached to the hospital was a small orphanage where Anne had been placed. Fred came from a large family and missed the sound of family life. He had written to his fiancé telling her of his wounds and letting her know of the possibility that he would never father a child.

He gravitated towards the sound of the children. His sense of humour and genuine affection for the kids made him become a part of their daily routine. It took a week or so before Annie, as she was called now, overcame her shyness and climbed onto Fred's knee. But once there, a deep bond was formed.

'Sister, I want to take her back with me to Australia. I'm engaged to a girl back home and I've told her all about Annie.'

'Mr Hayes, as honourable as your intentions are, the French Government will not allow its children to be exported.'

The young novice entered with a tea tray just in time to overhear the end of the conversation.

'But, Mother, Anne is English, not French.' Smiling at Fred, she backed out of the room, not wanting to be reprimanded for speaking when not spoken to.

'Then, Mr Hayes, it would be entirely up to the English ambassador.'

Five months after Fred landed back in Sydney, Anne, along with ten other children, arrived under the umbrella of the Red Cross. It was drizzling as the new parents waited on the dock for the children.

Fred looked up at the ship that had just docked and leaned against a rail on the quay. He could see the white uniform of a nurse and in her arms, he watched a squirming little girl: Annie. With all formalities completed, a policeman watched as the children were given over to their new parents.

'She's a lucky little girl to have found a family.'

'No, sir, we are the lucky ones.'

Annie recognised Fred at once and locked her little arms around his neck. He kissed her and handed her to Jane, his wife. 'This is your mummy, love.'

Over the course of that terrible war, Prue corresponded with Patrick McPherson. She continued to ride his horses and in due course became very friendly with Patrick's family. On Patrick's leaves, they both continued to play their childish games. Somehow, she was able to make his departure a game, blocking out the senseless waste that was war. She knew that she loved him.

The long Indian summer wound to an end. James returned to his estate when Parliament went into recess. Sarah sat on her verandah and watched the last of the apples fall from the tree. Hating waste, Sarah noted that she would have to ask Mrs Murphy, her housekeeper, to make a little more sauce with the fallen apples. Longer shadows cast a gloomy haze over the nearby hills and a cool breeze blew across the Irish Sea. The housekeeper noticed Sarah shudder and ran to get a rug from the sitting room to tuck tightly around her mistress's knees.

'Would you be wanting a cuppa before supper, Mrs Brian?' Sarah waved the woman away.

Things seemed to get a little muddled now. Her elderly body sat still, while her mind floated back to a large land where the flocks of cockatoos sailed like ships, caught in the clouds.

Where was Tom? Why wasn't he here? *I know, he is out droving.* 'Munu where are you?' she called out. 'Gone walkabout again? And why isn't James doing his homework?'

Walking out of the tall timbers, a tall young man waved to her. His stockwhip curled around his shoulder and on his head he wore an old felt stock hat.

'Come, my love, it's time,' he whispered into her ear. Taking her hand, he led her down to the riverbank. They stood there watching the water run, watching her river.

Sarah didn't live long enough to see Prue and Patrick marry and produce two children. After the war ended and peace was restored, England started to repair the damage done to the lives of its people. Prue felt a need to take Patrick and the children back to Australia, back to the Riverina, back to her second home.

# Part Three
## Maggie

*If life could only be as we wished,* thought Prue, as she gave her maid orders to unpack. Patrick had remained on the land helping his father to improve their estate. Six years had gone by, which seemed to Prue to have been lost in the blink of an eye. She had still not been back to Australia.

'We'll definitely go in the spring, love.'

But there was always a crisis to fix. Finally, when the estate was running smoothly and a new manager had been hired to replace Sam, who was well past retiring age, Patrick started to think about his own career. He often spoke to Prue about France, leaving out the vivid details that often plagued his dreams about the war. The large vineyards and lavender farms in France had made his own farming interests expand in many ways not attempted in Britain.

'Prue, where are you? I've got some great news.'

Prudence watched her husband bound through the French doors. How many times had she asked her boys not to use that entrance? But her 'third child', Patrick, rushed in, forgetting that she had placed a table holding a pretty porcelain vase in front of the doors.

'Pat, watch out!' She darted forward, scooping up the vase in the nick of time.

'Sorry, love,' he said, giving her a sheepish grin. He was carrying a large envelope in one hand and with the other he gently pulled her down onto the lounge beside him.

'Prue, my official orders have finally arrived, we can leave for Paris in a month's time.'

Patrick had remained involved in some capacity with the War Office and later on, he entered the diplomatic corps.

'I can't believe our good luck to get my first posting to Paris. Prue, you will love living there and it will be great for the boys to experience another culture.'

Neither Prue nor her husband believed in sending their children to boarding school at seven, which was the expected thing to do. So there was no suggestion that the boys wouldn't travel with their parents until they entered their teens. Prue smiled to herself as she watched Patrick read through his paperwork. He looked like all his Christmases had come at once.

## Paris 1934

It was late spring when the transport arrived in Paris, depositing Mr and Mrs McPherson and two rather tired and mischievous teenagers at the British Embassy. Patrick settled into his job and after the boys started at school, Prudence had plenty of time to absorb the Parisian way of life.

They entertained the other embassy staff as well as the business community. Prue loved to search Paris for the small boutiques. Although a rich woman in her own right, she was very thrifty in what she spent, a legacy taught to her by Sarah. She became a client of a small dressmaker, who had immigrated to Paris from Germany. The family were Jewish and quickly became firm friends with the chic British lady with her strange Australian accent.

For three years they entertained; fully enjoying the night life. Simone Fleurire, the darling of the cabaret set, would often attend their parties. Pat often took Prue to the Casino de Paris and Folies Bergère; they attended the after parties and mixed with the socialites that followed the cabaret stars. Life was good for the young couple. Nobody could have guessed what the future was to bring.

'Prue, have you seen my tie, the one with the emblem?'

'Pat, it's hanging with your uniform.' Prue wondered why her husband had pulled out his army uniform and was about to ask him when the phone rang.

'Love, can you get it? I'm still in here.'

After replacing the receiver, Prudence walked slowly into their bedroom to face her husband.

'Patrick,' she said in a slow, rounded voice. He knew what was coming.

'Yes, love, I'm still in here.'

'That was the Defence Department in London, they have arranged for you to fly out tonight. What's going on, why didn't you tell me?'

'Nothing to worry about. I'll be back in a few days.'

He bent over and kissed her. She suddenly felt cold as he held her close.


Patrick sighed after attending the briefing in London. It was time to send Prue back home. He knew that she would put up some resistance about leaving him; he just didn't know how much.

'Patrick, if you think I'm about to leave you just because Hitler is mouthing off, you are wrong.' Prue poured both of them a drink and waited for the next round.

'Love, this time I have to insist. I'm sending all the unnecessary staff and their families home. How would it look if I let you remain here with me?'

'The boys are already away at university and safe.'

'I know, love, but you must go too.'

It was a sunny day as the plane took off for London. Pat walked back to his car wondering when he would see his family again. The War Office was now coding all transcripts. He had been told that war was inevitable and to destroy all correspondence and prepare to close the embassy.

'Don't be silly, Patrick,' said the Polish representative at the meeting they were all attending. 'The bastards won't be able to cross the Maginot Line.'

Three months later, on May 10th, the German army marched through Poland and on May 12th, they crossed the Somme River. Patrick was putting the last of his coded messages into his attaché case when his driver pulled in through the gates and sounded the car's horn. He pulled down the picture of the king and replaced it with a hand-written note saying, *we will be back.*


It was six months since he had returned to England. The Germans were occupying France and he was on active duty again.

'Patrick, we can't take the chance of you being caught. You are too well known. The Nazis would have a field day with you.' The general understood his captain's need to contribute.

'Patrick' — he handed Pat a cigarette — 'you can help more with your intelligence operation.'

'General Loam, I know more about the terrain than anyone. I only need one trip, and I could meet with the French underground.' He sighed and waited.

'Pat, let me talk it over and we'll get back to you. In the meantime, go home, and enjoy your family.'

One week later, Captain McPherson boarded a transport flight to be parachuted back into France. That was the last Prue heard from her husband. The War Office had marked him down as Missing in Action.

'Please help me to get to Paris. I know that I might be able to find out more.' Prue begged the War Office to help her. They were adamant; no. She had kept in touch with some of the Polish Air Force men who were now flying with the R.A.F. and wondered if they could help her.

It was a very cold day; the snow was banked up in front of the gates as the car entered the Lowe estate. Prue brushed the snow from her shoulders as she entered the main house.

'Dad, where are you?'

'I believe Lord Lowe is in the study, madam.' The old butler smiled as he recognised Prue. She was his favourite, his little girl.

'Thanks, Gregory, I'll find him.' Handing her coat over to him, she pushed open the study doors and entered. 'Dad, I need your help.'

'Absolutely not, Prudence, you must be mad. You would leave your boys when they need you the most?' James Lowe knew his daughter only too well. He expected her to argue back, and he was not expecting her to sit still and just gaze out the large picture window that looked out onto the grounds. Slowly she turned, and walked towards her father.

'Dad, he is my life. Please help me or I'll go anyway.'

'My God, Prue. I lost Jo and then we lost Pat, how can you ask me to lose you also?'

'Please help me, Dad, I have to know.'

The crossing was rough. The small fishing boat under the cover of a pitch-black night pulled into a lonely beach. There wasn't a star showing; the clouds covered the moon, and a brisk wind brought a chill to the slim figure as she climbed into the rowboat. The sailor's intention was to deliver her to an outcrop that was protected by the overhanging rock face.

Prue watched the boat disappear, then reached for her revolver and removed the safety. A flash of light caught her attention, two quick, one slow. She followed the path upwards until she was approached by a man with a rifle slung over his shoulder.

'Madam, we've been waiting for you, do you speak French?'

'Yes, I do, my name is —'

Before she could go any further, the man interrupted her. 'No name, madam, your name here is Madam Goux, you come from a small village of Sault, your husband is dead, and you now work on your lavender farm. We chose this as we know that you and your husband spent a lot of time in that region.' He bent over to offer her a cigarette. She noticed that even as he talked to her, his eyes still darted around, always watching.

'We have located a prisoner who is being held not far from here in the Chateau de Sault. He could be your husband.'

It took three months to confirm their suspicion. A double agent working for the Germans was able to see Patrick, or what remained of the once upright captain.

'Madam, your husband can barely walk.' The time to spare feelings had long passed. 'They are keeping him alive just in case he can be traded.'

'Traded! Whenever have the Germans left their prisoners alive long enough to trade?'

An older woman who had been sitting quietly in the corner of the room placed a gentle hand on the younger woman's shoulder. 'This is *guerre bidon*, my dear, the phony war.' She looked back down, continuing to read the underground newspaper *Gare de Lyon*. Looking up from the paper and in a slow determined voice, she said, 'We need a plan to get this man out and back to England.'

Madam Ouverney, with all her pretty, gentle ways, was one of the most ruthless killers in the French underground and was responsible for the escape of many people.

Ten days later, a travelling cabaret troop performed in Sault. Prue watched from the wings of the old theatre as the performers sang and danced. Madam Ouverney had gone over every detail to safely pluck the British captive from the Gestapo. He was to be drugged and his body exchanged with a dead corpse.

It was a crisp, cold night; most people were indoors enjoying what warmth there was from their sparsely fuelled fires. Nobody took much notice of the small cart being pulled by a donkey along the back streets of Sault. Later that evening, a bundle was gently dropped off near the back door to the theatre. A large prop basket had been placed opposite the door waiting for its precious contents.

Prue had been dressed as a clown, a costume that hid all her features. The hours dragged by and every car that pulled up put the fear of God into the waiting woman. They were packing up the set, the show was over. Prue's fear grew with every moment that passed. The Germans had started to check their papers. An officer stopped in front of Prue, she smiled at him, keeping her eyes focused on the floor. He closely checked her papers and was about to speak to her when Madam Ouverney spoke up.

'She is simple, sir, she doesn't comprehend.' The German officer sniggered as he walked away, remarking on the stupidity of the French. A sudden crash behind them made him turn to see what the noise was.

'Sorry, sir, my boys are oafs. Be quieter with the crates, you are upsetting the captain,' she yelled to the performers. No one saw the rolled-up carpet being dropped gently into a crate or the soft pillows placed carefully on top.

The plan was to reach the coast where a boat would return them to England. But as is well known, the best plans are never a sure thing. On the second night, the troop performed thirty miles from the coast. All the arrangements had been made, when a lad burst into their dressing room, breathless and bent over with exhaustion.

'Madam, Pierre has been shot. The rest have been rounded up by the Boche, we can't go any further. They are waiting for you.'

'Settle, Andre. Catch your breath.' A look of anxiety crossed the faces of the cast. Madam Ouverney glanced across to an older man standing inside the doorway. 'We will have to cross the Pyrenees and get them into Spain. The resistance have set up a route out by air.'

Prue clung on to her husband. His mind was wandering, and he acted more like a child, a gift from the Gestapo. Terror filled Prue as she digested the conversation.

'Madam, I will take him away, we will leave you at once.'

'Don't be stupid, you wouldn't last one hour alone.'

Looking at the British woman and how she was trying to comfort her husband, Madame felt a stabbing pain of compassion. Why the British Government had let a foreign minister work in their underground was plainly stupid.

'All right, dress him in warm clothing. We are walking over the mountains.'

They drove as far as they could before leaving the cars, proceeding on foot through the snow-covered Pyrenees. Patrick hung on to Prue while a man held him on the other side. It took seven hours before they walked into a small village in Spain.

'We will leave you now, madam. The Spanish have arranged transport for you both.'

Prue turned to thank them, but they were gone. Looking up to the skyline she saw the silhouette of a woman waving before she disappeared into the night.

It took many months for Pat to recover. Little by little, he returned to his former self. Physically he seemed the same, but the night terrors remained with him throughout his life, a legacy of a senseless war. Lord Lowe realised that his daughter could not manage the property in Australia and sold it.

'Dad, what will we do about the furniture? Gran's table and settings are still there.'

'Prue, I believe that she would want it to stay with the homestead. Tom was Australian through and through and I've given first offer to our manager. It seems only fair, since his grandfather made the trek down with Mum and Tom.'

She felt her father's arms close around her and sadness engulfed them both. This was another closure in the story of Sarah's life.

# Chapter thirty-six

Maggie

**Sydney, autumn, 1966**

After reading the journal Mr Barnaby had given me, I started reminiscing about the stories my mother had told of her family. To the best of my memory, they went like this…

Annie was twenty when she married Ray Jamieson, a butcher from Gundagai. War had broken out in Europe and the men were all enlisting. Ray stayed on his dairy property north of Penrith and was exempt from the compulsory enlistment. Essential services were all exempt.

'What are you? A man or a mouse?' Fred was a good father-in-law but on this subject he made no attempt to keep his opinion to himself. These arguments over the years caused a rift between the two men that lasted until Fred died.

In 1962, Annie died, leaving Ray with a rebellious teenage daughter: me, Maggie. Life wasn't hard for the two of us, but it wasn't that easy either. Ray was a good, sober dad who only wanted the best for his only child. I, like most girls of the 1960s, loved the good life or what she perceived it to be. A boyfriend, a drag of marijuana, and makeup made up the necessities. Little could I have guessed how my life was about to change.

It took two months to arrange my passport and living expenses. Mr Barnaby arranged everything. He even threw in his own advice. On my second visit to his office, a travel cheque and an itinerary was handed to me by his secretary.

'I wish I was going too,' she said as she slowly handed me the ticket. 'Mr Barnaby wants a quick word with you, dear.'

I was shown into the office, and given more advice.

'Margaret, you have been advanced this money to see you through, please don't waste it, as it will be difficult for me to supply you with more.'

Dad joked all the way to the airport. I think he was more nervous than me. The loudspeaker called for passengers on my flight, and I walked towards the sliding door that would take me from my world into the abyss.

It was raining and cold when I landed in Heathrow. The plane's wheels screeched as they hugged the runway. Sheets of water covered my window as we slowed down and finally came to a halt.

Two weeks before, I'd had a 'blue' with my best friend, and she decided not to come with me. She thought I'd been trying to make out with her boyfriend, *as if*, and then she became angry when I called him a loser. At the time I had thought, *Her loss*, but now I really wished she was here. I had apologised, telling her she was welcome to the fool. The customs man checked my luggage, as if I would try anything dodgy, and I was free to leave. I walked out of the terminal, pulling my case behind me and stopped by the taxi rank to read over my travel itinerary again.

- Get Tube to London—don't take a taxi
- Don't take slow train
- Walk to Trafalgar Square
- Do not talk to any strangers unless lost

The fast train belted along, houses shot past, then the daylight was snuffed out as the train entered the Underground. I struggled up the moving stairs and burst forth into the mad crowd they call Londoners. I found my hotel; it was in York Street just off the Square. I had been booked into a room on the second floor. This floor was not serviced by the lift, as it was on the older side of the building. Dad would have loved it; all the rooms and doorways were out of square. This was his style of building.

The maid was a pleasant lady, dressed in a black uniform

complete with a white apron, very *Upstairs Downstairs* type: nosey, but nice. After she had extracted from me the reason I had come to London, which I might say, was like pulling teeth, she too started with the advice. Why did they all think I needed advice? I had turned eighteen one week before, I was now almost an adult, or so I thought.

The following day was a Saturday. I awoke to banging on the door and tried to focus on opening my eyes. I felt so tired; this must be the jetlag people talk about. The door vibrated with another knock.

'I won't be a minute.'

*Where did I throw my wrap?* Pushing the hair out of my eyes and holding my wrap shut, I answered the door.

'We were told another Aussie booked in, just wanted to check. I'm Hilda, and this is Sam. We are in the rooms opposite.'

How could anyone be so cheery at this hour? 'You're right. I'm from Sydney. Sorry, do you want to come in?' Before me stood the tallest girl I'd ever seen. She was dressed in trackies and boots, not my look, but who was I to talk. The bloke was quite good looking, about the same height as the girl.

'No thanks,' he replied. 'If you are alone and want some company, we are close by.'

They smiled and returned to their rooms. Just as they were about to enter, Sam turned and said, 'By the way, I'm going up to Covent Gardens, there's a group of Aussies playing. I think they are called The Seekers or something like that. It's a freebie if you would like to come. I'm leaving about two, be ready.'

'Thanks, I'll get some more sleep and see how I go.'

At twelve, the alarm went off. I quickly dressed, made toast, and looked for my Vegemite, which I found in one of my good shoes. Around 1:30 p.m., Sam knocked on the door, calling through the wood,

'Are you ready?

'I'm almost finished, Sam. Where's Hilda?'

'She has basketball practice; she's captain of the Australian side.'

We took the red bus to Covent Gardens. There were people everywhere. Most of the girls wore miniskirts, with thick woollen stockings and belted coats. I liked this fashion, but most of all, I liked their small, peaked hats. The concert was a blast, there were Aussies everywhere. Afterwards, we went to a local pub. The building was very old and there was only one bar; it was all in together, not like in

Sydney where we had ladies' parlours. I didn't like warm beer with no head, so I had a Pimms. Sam told me this part of London was known as Kangaroo Valley. Most of the kids were on working holidays and the majority very friendly. Later that night in the lobby, we met Hilda who was sporting a beaut bruise.

'God, that must hurt,' I said as I watched her rubbing her arm.

She smiled back at me, saying, 'Practise hard, and play harder.'

After ordering more drinks, we settled down on the comfy lounge, and I told them why I was in London. They too couldn't believe my good luck.

'So, when do you find out?' asked Hilda.

'My appointment is on Tuesday, but I just can't wait.'

'God, that's heaps better than working in pubs, like I'm doing,' laughed Sam.

Tuesday morning, dressed in my best coat, and newly acquired cute hat, I sat in the back of a black cab as it circled the streets, pulling up at the door of Jones, Jones, and Blackburn. I was shown into a large office. Behind the largest desk I had ever seen, sat a middle-aged man with large rimless glasses perched on his nose. Two strands of hair had been combed over the large bald spot on his head. As I entered, he stood up and walked around the side of his desk to shake my hand.

'Good morning, Miss Jamieson. I'm Barry Jones and I'm handling your claim, please sit down.'

I really felt like saying, 'This is not my claim,' but I smiled and sat down on a leather chair that had been placed in front of the desk.

'As you know, you are the sole heir to the estate of the late Sarah Brian. Usually we can transfer monies, but this is a most unusual bequest.'

*Please, just get to the money.*

'Miss Jamieson, the sum of one thousand pounds will be deposited into your Australian Commonwealth Bank account. There is also a small dwelling on the north-western coast, which you now own. The terms of the will are explicit. You are to live in the cottage for six months, all expenses found. After that time, the property is yours.'

One thousand pounds and a house, my God, I'm rich. I wish Dad was here, not stuck in our commission house in Liverpool.

'If you accept these terms, I'm to hand over the keys to you.'

After I had signed all the legal papers, and placed the envelope containing the keys inside my handbag, I shook Mr James's hand again and left.

Once back in the hotel, I rang Dad. 'You will never guess what? I've got a house and cash, but the solicitor explained that I've got to stay there for six months, all found.'

'That fantastic, but, Marg, please try to save your money. Didn't you say that they would fund your living expenses?'

As I lay on my bed, thinking over what had happened that day, I wondered what type of lady Sarah had been? And what great luck, that I was her relative. London was a blast; I loved the people but hated the weather.

It took a week for me to make all the arrangements to travel north. The shop lady in Marks and Spencer, my new most favourite shop, advised me what clothes I would need to take up north.

'Yes, dear, sturdy boots, and a thick woollen coat, something to cover up your bottom, not like the ones the girls wear down here.'

I didn't know what to feel, excitement or annoyance. Why did I have to waste my time in a village, when London had everything I needed? I caught the early train from Paddington, seen off by Sam and Hilda, with waves and kisses and all of that. Although I had only known them for a short time, we had become good friends. As the train was pulling out, I yelled, 'I'll write as soon as I'm settled.'

Staring out the door and along the platform, I watched Sam waving to me. Dressed in brown slacks and a cable knit jumper, he stood out from the crowd. Yes, he really was a dish.

The first few hours on the train were great. I chatted to the other people in my compartment. Six of us fitted in the small space: two teachers, a bloke that worked in a mine, an elderly lady returning home from visiting her grandchildren, and last of all, a young copper, who wasn't bad looking for an English bobby. Of course, he wouldn't say what he was up to. Mrs Bee, the elder of the ladies, introduced herself to me and spoke about her children, and as I looked at the pictures she was carrying, I felt a stab of pain in my heart. I missed my dad.

Everyone settled down to read or sleep. I cleared away the condensation from the glass and looked out the window. The villages gave way to fields of green. The cattle in the paddocks and hedges sped by. I listened to the sound of the rail, and it seemed to be talking to me. 'Go back, go back.'

At seven that evening, I was standing on the station watching the train disappear into the distance. The wind whistled along the deserted platform and as I gathered up my bag, a ticket collector helped me into a taxi. Panic grabbed me; what in the hell was I doing here alone?

Sliding through the snow, we stopped outside a neat brick house on the outskirts of a small village. There were rows of quaint houses lining a central green. I had noticed a small pub and a general store as the taxi veered to the left of a large stone church.

'Here you are, miss, 12 Orchard Lane.'

I stared out the window from the back seat towards the house.

'Are you sure this is the right address?' The house was much better than I had expected. What had I expected? A small fibro cottage similar to what my neighbours had in western Sydney?

'Yes, this is the address on the letter you gave me.'

I opened the front gate and stared up at the large brick building, my new home. A few minutes later, I was standing on the porch. Across the street, from behind a window, a pair of eyes watched me fumble the key in the lock. The door wouldn't budge. I pushed, kicked, and swore.

'Give me a go, girlie.'

Swinging around, I came face to face with an elderly man, dressed in one of those tweed coats older people wear. I handed him the keys, and he stepped forward. The key turned in the lock and the door opened. He didn't look dangerous, kind of grandfatherly but then, what did I know about old men?

'It's a bit temperamental to folk it doesn't know. I'm the vicar, but don't let that frighten you, and also the unofficial caretaker of Rose Cottage. Jim Swisp, at your service.'

Mr Swisp carried my bag into the parlour. The place was in darkness.

'Stay where you are, and I will go outside and turn on the electricity. I'll only be a jiff.'

The light flickered for a moment then burst into brightness. I looked around. The room was clean. A large Welsh dresser lined the far wall, displaying a set of china cups and saucers. Fresh flowers decorated the chiffonier. Soon, a fire crackled in the hearth and the aroma of a stew filled the air. My god, I was hungry.

'Don't look so surprised, Miss Jamieson, a solicitor from London phoned me. He thought you might be glad of a little help to settle in.'

I walked over to this man, and as I started to thank him I did the most embarrassing thing — I bawled like a baby.

'There, there, I think that they expected far too much from you, travelling around the world and staying up here. Why, it is more than a body could stand.' He patted my arm and somehow the fear I was feeling vanished. I liked this man.

After seeing him out and finishing all the stew, I started to explore my new domain. I found a bed with the cover turned down and fell into it. I lay there, looking around my room, content and full. I felt at peace, like the days when I had stayed with Nan. It reminded me of Nana's meals full of love and vegies.

'Come on, Robbie, out with you, I think the owner will be here early today.'

No sound came back from the downstairs bedroom.

'I think she is here now,' I yelled back. Scrambling to find a wrap, I peered into the kitchen, where the sound had come from.

'Gee, I'm sorry! I thought it was Robbie sleeping it off. I'm the vicar's cleaning lady, Mrs Been. He will be back later, dear, to see if you are settled in. Oh, don't worry about Robbie, sometimes the vicar allows him to stay here overnight when the weather is bad.'

*I don't think so!*

With a flourish, a small plump woman, dressed in a clean pinny, pushed a plate of pikelets onto the table. She reminded me of the fairy godmother in Cinderella; here one minute, gone the next.

'We will unpack a bit later, oh yes, that we will,' she muttered to herself.

Then she was gone. Maybe I was still in bed, dreaming. My toe hit the corner of the table, confirming that no, I was definitely awake. *Shit, that hurt.* I dressed, made a coffee, and ate the pikelets. The sun shone into the breakfast nook, making sunbeams dance over the brightly papered walls. On the wall closest to the foyer, a large grandfather clock chimed the hours as I stared out through the picture window into the back garden.

A high stone wall surrounded the yard and to the right of the house, a large building stood alone. The trees were bare, and the snow piled up in drifts. Looking past the windows into the back yard, I noticed a path had been cleared to the fence. Why a path would lead to a blank wall was something that I would have to investigate.

I looked all through the house into every nook and cranny. Upstairs there were three bedrooms; the master had a large iron bed and a bay window overlooking the street at the front. Under the window, a covered seat fitted neatly into the space. The ground floor consisted of a lounge, sitting room, kitchen, and a laundry. I even had a below stairs, nothing like I imagined larger manors to have. It had two rooms, one of which contained bags of coal, the other was piled up with old boxes.

Through the back door, the friendly round face of the vicar peered in at me.

'Morning, are you ready for a spot of exploring, Miss Jamieson?'

'Sure, grab a coffee or should I say a tea, I'll only be a minute.'

'Make sure you put on heavy boots, it's cold out here.'

The snow crunched and sank under my feet as we started to walk around the house. Dark timbers lined the upstairs windows and climbers invaded the small dormer turrets. Even to my inexperienced eye, I could tell that the building materials were very old. We had walked the perimeter of the house chatting, and sliding through the snow, when the vicar stopped and said, 'Please call me Jim; we don't stand on formalities here.'

'Well, Jim, I'm Margaret but if you would like, call me Maggie, everyone does.'

We stopped and stood by the chimney; it was out of the wind and quite warm and as I pressed up against the brickwork, I could feel the heat penetrating through the bricks.

'Where are you taking me?' I blurted as I grabbed onto the vicar's arm to stop myself from sliding backwards on the ice.

We walked down the path towards the back wall. With my nose almost touching a flat stone that jutted out to the side, I stumbled forward as Jim pushed on the wall and a small panel slid open.

'Many of the older cottages were built with escape walls. This part of the coast was notorious for smuggling. In fact, your stable was once a distillery.'

'How old is this property?'

'The first part was built in 1775, when it was part of an estate. It should all be in the deeds. I know that over the years further extensions were added. I believe the barn could be much older.'

'I still can't believe I own it. Mum never spoke of any relatives in England. So it was a total surprise to Dad and me.'

'Come on, let's look in the village.'


The main street was quite small. It consisted of a bakery, post office, general store, and a pub. Not like the ones in Sydney, but like the ones out of a story book. I pushed the door of the tavern open to have a look. The bar was small. The ceiling was low with dark beams crossing it. A large fireplace stood along the far wall, with a coat of arms above it.

'Come on, Maggie, my wife wants to meet you. The vicarage is in the lane behind here. Al, the publican, won't mind us cutting through his yard.'

May Swisp was not what I expected of a minister's wife, although I really didn't know any. She could have been the local beautician for all I knew. She was tall and dressed in a modern pantsuit. Her makeup was faultless, and as she took my hands in hers, I noticed that her nails were well-manicured and painted red. The song, 'Jezebel', sprang to my mind. I thought twice about humming it, as it might not be appreciated! After a yummy lunch of beef dumplings and a wine trifle, I thanked them both, and started off to walk home.

After turning at the end of the street to wave, I decided to walk off some of the calories that had taken up residence around my waistline since moving to England. Looking at a map Jim had drawn up for me, I decided to walk around the scenic drive along the cliff top and back through the golf course. Walking along the road, I heard the sound of horses' hoofs clipping on the road. I turned and waved but nothing was there. Perhaps I imagined it. Feeling like a goose, I dropped my hand down to my side. Oh well, Dad always said I had a vivid imagination.

Crunching over the fairway of the golf course and up through the drifts of snow, I felt a bit strange, and I wished Dad were here now. I started to run, but I couldn't escape the feeling of impending doom. As my house came into sight, I slowed down to catch a breath. The hairs on the back of my neck were standing on end.

As I burst in through the front door, the cleaning lady whom I had met that morning was adding coal to the fire. I really didn't like the way everyone let themselves in. People back home in Liverpool would never have done that. I made a mental note to have the locks changed. Dad would do that.

I went to each door, clipping shut the locks and checking the windows. Sitting by the fire, I peeled off my shoes and wet socks and wondered if the English really liked all this bloody snow. My legs were aching as I trudged up the stairs to my room with a hot water bag pushed under my jumper. Now, I was really cranky; all my suitcases were unpacked. My toiletries and alarm clock were sitting on the table beside the bed.

'See you tomorrow, miss,' called out Mrs Been as she closed the door behind herself.

*Yes, and we will have to have a little talk!*


At 7:00 a.m. the alarm went off, which had to be a first; who gets up on a Sunday this early to attend church? Swallowing a cup of coffee, I headed off. The small church was full, so I sat at the back behind the locals. The pew was cold. As I started to straighten my gloves, I could feel Nan sitting beside me telling me to sit still. Stop fidgeting. By the time the service was finished, I was fully awake.

'Lovely service, Reverend,' said the large man sitting beside me, who turned out to be my butcher. He was round with a small moustache, and very large hands. Jim introduced me to the entire congregation, who all seemed to know more about me than I did. On the way back from church, I stopped in at the bakery.

'You're the lass from Rose Cottage, I've been meaning to call by. I live across the road and down a bit.' A gorgeous red-headed girl about my own age came around from the back of the counter. 'I'm Susan. My dad owns this shop. I help out on the weekends.'

'Hello, Susan, I'm Margaret, but call me Maggie. Please come over any time. I was starting to think that I was the only young person here.'

'There's a few of us, but most work in the larger towns, and some are away at college. Have a coffee sand a bun on me.'

The bun was great, much better than Safeway's at home. Beside the coffee, on a saucer, Susan had placed a small chocolate. It was all delicious. After leaving the bakery, I strolled through the town centre and headed back home. Later that night after stoking the fire, I settled back to write to Dad and Sam. I really envied Susan. I was starting to get a bit bored, and concluded that what I needed was a job.

Bright and early the following morning, I walked to the general store to enquire about work.

'Sorry, miss, I don't have any vacancies,' said the manager. 'But have you tried the library? Mrs Parton was talking about needing a break, might be worth a gander.'

I thanked him and hurried up the hill, past the vicarage, to a small stone building with a sign in large capital letters that read Library. The smaller sign said Closed until Thursday. I scraped the snow off the wooden seat and flopped down. As I was sitting there, a lady appeared from a back room. She looked like the sixty's version of Mary Poppins, with round cheeks, a round figure, and deep blue eyes. She was dressed in a bright red woollen hat and scarf that didn't match her pink dressing gown and brown slippers.

'Looking for someone?' As she tried to say more, a coughing attack made her stop and she beckoned to me to follow her inside. I trailed behind her into a warm friendly kitchen, where she pointed to a chair.

'I'm sorry, I thought this was the library.' As I continued to apologise, she raised her hand.

'You're right. I'm Mrs Parton and I live here at the back of the library. Won't you have a cup of tea with me? I'm as parched as a pheasant in a dust storm.'

We talked for a while, mostly about me. I then got the guts to ask her about any jobs that might be coming up.

'I can use a filing system, and I love reading books.' I threw that in between the story of my life.

'Well, dear, as you can see, I'm no spring chicken. What say you come in on Tuesday, and we will see how you like the work.' I knew that this was a polite way to ask if I could manage. The library was very old. Dark cedar shelves lined the walls. The bottom shelves were clean, and everything was in order.

Tuesday came at last, and I met Mrs Parton, eager to start.

'Maybe you could straighten up the top shelves, dear?' said Mrs Parton.

I found a ladder in the back room that led off the kitchen. Armed with a duster, I climbed the steps like a knight mounting his charger.

Dust was my enemy, and I charged. Mrs Parton gasped for air.

'You have the job,' she said. 'I'm away home to bed, come in for lunch.'

After I finished dusting, I sat at the desk waiting for people to arrive. A small boy blew in with the wind and snow, and handed me a pile of books.

'Me mum wants the next ones, miss, she's held up in bed. She said Mrs Parton always knows what she likes.' The kid had a cheeky grin. I watched as his hand crept into a jar of lollies that was sitting on the desk. 'Can I have two, miss?'

'No, one will be enough.' Thinks he is smarter than me, cheeky bugger. All things considering, the first day went quite well. My next customer picked out the books for Billy's mum and by the end of the day I had met twenty more people, who all knew my story.

'Come down to the tavern after work and meet the rest of us. I'll buy you a pint.' The invitation came from a younger man, who had introduced himself as Leo, a local farmer. Leo told me he had three brothers and a sister. Being the eldest, he stayed on the farm to work.

'Is that what happens in your country, Maggie? Do the youngest get to go and the older stays on?'

'I don't really know, Leo. I live in a large town. The parents there kick us all out to work as soon as they can.'

The weather turned bitterly cold. Storms were battering the coast and 'Stay Put' notices had been circulated around the area. I piled on more clothes, two pairs of gloves and two jumpers. I was starting to feel like a snowman when I finally reached the tavern.

The parlour in the tavern was warm and friendly. Every time the door opened, a cloud of smoke swirled around the room. 'Close the door!' became our war cry. Leo introduced me to his family and neighbours. I received a Sunday lunch invite, and I joined the pub's Friday night dart club. It was nice to mix with people again.

*Dad,*

*I wish you would come over here. I'll send you the ticket. I know you would like it here, the people are so friendly, and the pub is great. You could teach them how to pour a beer. I have asked Sam to come up. Don't be worried, NO hanky-panky.*

*Write soon, love, Maggie.*

# Chapter thirty-seven



I had been working at the library for three months. The summer days were warm, not like the stinking heat of back home. The locals wandered down to the library just to chat and drink gallons of tea at the table and chairs that I provided for reading. Mrs Parton had taken an extended holiday; from the library room to her little flat in the back. I seemed to have been accepted by the villagers and most people called me by my first name.

Leo and his family invited me over to lunch most Sundays. A family nosh up, his mother called it. I must say, the food was great; everything was cooked in butter with lashings of cream on the puddings. Leo picked me up from church in his truck, a large grey Dodge he called 'The Beast'. As we rumbled down the road, a hand crept along the back of the seat and around my shoulders, trying to find an opening to my blouse. The truck came to a screaming halt, with Leo vigorously rubbing his foot, where my stiletto heel had rammed into it.

After Leo's attempt to feel me up, the only place I saw him was every Friday night when I played darts at the local pub. That was always followed by pies and a pint or two.

It was Tuesday and I was locking up the library, when the postie called out to me. 'Here, take your letter, I was just leaving to deliver it. Could be from Sam.' All of the village seemed more interested in my friend Sam than I did.

'Thanks, Burnie.' Taking the letter, I shoved it into my backpack and started to think about tea. Yes, fish and chips would be the go. Everyone in England seemed to have fish and chips on a Friday; what's more, I liked them.

'Hi, Susan.' I waved to the girl in the bakery. 'Want to have tea with me?'

'Good stuff, thanks. I'll be over in thirty minutes. I'll bring a bottle with me.'

Susan and I had become good friends. Her older brother had tried to hit on me, but I put him in his place. She told him he was nothing more than a weasel, and that pleased me no end. I had cut some of the roses from the front yard the day before and placed them in the front foyer. As I turned the key and pushed open the front door, the beautiful perfume made me linger there. I could feel Mum's presence, and I looked up the stairs, half expecting to see her waiting for me on the landing. Mum loved her roses; it was hard to believe she had been dead five years. I hoped Dad was still looking after the garden.

I'd finished setting the table and checking on the fish, when I remembered Sam's letter. Settling in a lounge chair, I tore the letter open and started to read.

*My Dear Maggie,*

*Thank God my finals are finished. I have applied over here for work, and I've an appointment this week, so here's hoping. I know the oldies want me to go back to Australia now uni is finished, but I need the experience in a London firm first. The real reason I'm writing for is to ask you if I can doss down with you? I would like to see your house and you, of course. If all is okay, I will see you Sunday night.*

*Cheers, Sam*

I had told Sam all about my house, its age and the history surrounding it. As an architect, he was very interested in the 1800s and sent me interesting bits of information about the properties in my area. I was folding up the letter when Susan came in the back door, sporting a bottle of red.

'Want to share what's in the letter, is it from your dad or Sam?'

'Well, sticky, it's from Sam. He'll be here on Sunday.'

'Good, I want to meet this man of yours.'

'I've told you, he is not my bloke. Come on, let's get stuck in, I'm starving.'

Fish and chips, and a glass of wine, what could be better! We talked and Susan produced the latest records of a local pop group. Singing, dancing, and drinking was good fun. Susan slept over, and we helped each other up the stairs; all in all, it was a great night.

'Thanks a lot, Maggie, but I had better scamper now. See you in church on Sunday.'

Susan returned home before church was to start. I really was finding it a battle to get up early every Sunday morning. But when in Rome do what the Romans do, I guess, and besides, all the villagers went, including the lads.

It was getting dark as Susan and I sat in her father's Morris Minor at the station on Sunday night. The express from London was late. We waited until people started to move onto the platform before putting away our bar of chocolate and climbing out of the car.

I could see Sam even before the train stopped. His head and shoulders were partly pushed out of the narrow windows, his arms waving to me. Gee, he looked good, not a hair was out of place. Sam must have left straight from work; the dark blue suit he was wearing made him stand out from the crowd. He looked debonair and sexy.

The train had barely stopped when the door shot open and out he jumped. His legs were running as they hit the platform. I could smell his aftershave as he swooped me up into a bear hug, his arms tightening around me, pressing my breasts into his chest, and I felt myself melting into his arms.

'Gee, it's good to see you again,' he said, and then looking over to Susan, he smiled and murmured, 'Who is this gorgeous girl beside you, Maggie?'

Susan, as Dad would say, was in like Flynn. She introduced herself, and slinked up to him, acting like a little tart. The trip back to my place was full of talk and laughter. Once there, we had a coffee, and as the hour was late, I suggested that Susan go home so that we could go to bed.

'Would you like another cup, Sam?'

'No thanks, but sit down for a minute, I really want to talk to you.'

I sat down on the sofa opposite Sam. He looked relaxed. His eyes were studying the room.

'This is a great place you have here, Maggie. I just can't wait until the morning to see all of it.'

'Would you like a glass of wine?'

'Yes, thanks. Are you having one, Maggie?'

I went to the kitchen to get our glasses. When I returned, Sam was leaning up against the door jamb.

'So tell me about the job offer. Are you to be placed in London?'

'No, I'm to work not too far from here actually. Up the coast on a large office complex with a marina attached. The Arabs have commissioned this project; it will be a great stepping stone for me if I get it right.'

'You'll be great. It will probably be the eighth wonder of the world. Here, let's drink to it.' I raised my glass. 'To the Aussie who will design a masterpiece.'

Sam's bed was already made up. I had given him the back room that overlooked the stone wall and out towards the coast. I kissed him goodnight and I retired to my own room. For a fleeting moment, or maybe longer, I wondered what he would be like in bed.

The sun shone through the blinds, and the smell of bacon floated up the stairs as I pushed back the duvet, ready to start the new day. Sam had the table set, coffee percolating, and the toast ready to go.

'Sorry I couldn't get the week off, but I really don't want Mrs Parton popping in. It has taken all this time to wean her away. But all isn't lost… I'm closing earlier this week.'

'I can fit around your work. I want to stop by later to look into what records might be stored in the library's archive.'

'Well, we could have lunch together.'

I took extra time dressing, as I knew the gossipers would be out in full today. I selected a modest skirt, only three inches above the knee and a cotton blouse, all teamed up with my favourite boots, and to top it off, my Carnegie hat. Right on lunchtime, Sam strolled into the library.

'Nice place, Maggie. I'm looking forward to doing a spot of research here later. But first, let's eat.'

'Come on; let's go to the garden out the back.'

We unpacked the hamper that he had picked up from the bakery, thanks to Susan. Cold pork pies, crusty bread rolls, and an apple pie that was to die for. After we finished, and I started back to work, Sam poked around the old records in the back room. After a while, I asked him, 'What are you looking for anyway?'

'A lot of buildings have disappeared over time. I want to get a feel for the whole area. Tell me when you want to leave, Maggie. I'll keep snooping in here until you are ready.'

This became our routine, me working, Sam snooping, then off to the pub to meet the locals and share a pint or two. Wednesday was sunny and I decided to give myself a little holiday and close earlier. We walked along the foreshore and back over the golf course. I had not told Sam about my ghostly experience or the fact that I never walked around the bluff at night. Gravel rubbed my foot. I grabbed at Sam's arm to steady myself.

'Steady up, what will the good people say, Maggie; you throwing yourself at me like this?'

I hit him with my other hand, and we spiralled out of control. Sam toppled back, landing on his bum with me on top of him. He lay there laughing. I quickly looked around; good, no one was in sight. Sam pulled me to my feet and tried to dust the gravel from my pullover. We started wandering across the golf course until a ball landed in front of us.

'That's our cue, let's go into the club and have a drink.'

Three drinks and a meal later, we went home. Later that evening, Sam unfolded his latest find from the back room at the library. He had discovered a large, detailed map of the whole area dating back to the mid-18th century.

'Maggie, look at this.'

I followed his finger along the streets, until it stopped at a large, imprinted drawing of a manor house and what looked to be a series of canals.

'Where is it, Sam?' I tried to follow the imprint, but it was completely different to the area I now knew.

'This is about where your place is. See, follow the headland and cut across to the main road, continue up the road until it divides.'

'But where is the main house now? And why are there waterways marked?'

'Well, according to this, your house is built onto a canal of some sort. It must have been filled in a long time ago. Have you got a copy of your deeds here?'

'Yes, they're in the box seat in my bedroom.'

After retrieving them, Sam continued to study the map, while I cleaned away the supper dishes.

'Maggie, didn't you wonder why the brickwork of your house was all the same, when the first part was built in the 1800s and the rest a hundred years later?'

Sam once again became the architectural snoop. Lines appeared on his forehead as his mind became lost in deep thought.

'You must be joking, Sam. What do I know about that stuff?'

'I'm spending tomorrow here; this has really got me intrigued. Houses that disappear, a house that just grew from nowhere, next you'll start with the ghost stories.'

'Shut up, Sam.'

'Sorry, I didn't mean to annoy you.'

There was a pause before I spoke. 'Don't mind me, it's just a headache. I think some aspro and an early night will do the trick.'

After I went to bed, I lay there feeling guilty about the way I'd spoken to him. Perhaps I should tell him about what I had seen that winter's night. Why did it all seem so real to me? As if I was a part of it.

Sitting at the table in the morning, we both started to speak at once.

'You go first, Sam.'

'No, Maggie, spit it out.'

'You know when you made a comment about ghosts, well, I had an experience, in fact it frightened the begeezus out of me. You are the first person I've mentioned it to.'

'Go on, unload it.'

He sat there listening as I told him the events of that terrifying night.

'I'm not a sceptic, and I've heard my uni pals talk about what they or their family have witnessed here in jolly old England. Has anything else occurred?'

'No.'

'Well, let's get back to your house, I think it is much more interesting. I'm driving over to where the old manor is marked on these papers. Do you want to come? Susan has offered to show me around, I know she would love you to come along.'

'No thanks, I had better do some catching up, but you have a good time.'

After they had left, I threw myself into the housework. The more

I thought about that little tart with Sam, the faster I worked. She hadn't mentioned their little jaunt to me when she slinked in the night before, inviting herself to tea.

# Chapter thirty-eight

I was sitting under a large tree reading when the car pulled up. I listened for doors to shut, but only one slammed, then nothing. I waited. Sam came strolling along the back path, with a smug smile on his face.

'Where's Susan?'

'I dropped her at her dad's place.' Sam seemed somewhat amused as he watched my face. 'I thought you might enjoy a night out, just the two of us, no distractions.'

My bum left the seat in record time. The backrest flew backwards as I scrambled to my feet.

'Where will we go? What do you think I should wear, casual or not?'

'Whatever you want, love.'

What was all this about? Love? Oh well, at least Susan wasn't coming. Throwing all my clothes on the bed, I finally decided on a mini, silver in colour, with black leggings. Sam had hired a car, which was a great surprise, and we dined at a pub in the next village.

The building was very old—mid-18th century. The waiter showed us to a small dining room where a booth had been prepared. The lights had been dimmed and you could feel the romance in the air. Two other couples were seated across from us, but they didn't seem to notice our arrival. We dined on steak Diane, followed by strawberries and cream. After our Irish coffee, Sam told me what he had discovered.

'You know the old manor house; well, it burnt down in 1875. The old earl and his wife, along with a lot of other people died in the fire. The remaining buildings were taken down, their bricks used to build a lot of this village. But this is where it gets interesting; your barn was left intact. Your house was the original gatekeeper's and must have been extended from the rubble.'

'I don't understand, you told me all the bricks were the same age.'

'Ah, that's the mystery, but there is more. The barn seems to have been built over one of the main water supplies. I think that is where we should start looking.'

At the crack of dawn and after a much-needed coffee, Sam produced a large measuring tape that he must have bought the day before, and with a sense of excitement we headed to the barn. First, we measured the inside walls and then the outside perimeter.

'It looks okay.'

We entered the building; the air had a strange smell, more like old seaweed that had been washed up at low tide. The temperature seemed to drop, like when you open a fridge door. I watched as Sam went forward into the barn.

He yelled back to me, more like an excited school kid than an architect. He pulled out old straw bales and packing crates; a whirlwind couldn't have worked faster. I choked as a cloud of dust covered me in its attempt to escape him.

'Here it is.'

We seemed to have found something that I didn't realise was missing. Set into the stone floor laid a metal ring.

'Give me a hand, Maggie.'

Sam's hands closed over the ring. As he pulled, a large flagstone began to move.

'Get something to jam under it. Over there.' He pointed with his elbow towards a length a wood lying against the wall.

I wedged the beam down under the stone. Sam was turning a shade of crimson as he pulled on the ring. Suddenly the stone moved, and little by little an opening appeared. We both peered down into the black void. The obvious then struck me.

'I won't be a tick,' I yelled to Sam as I headed back to the house to find my torch. Where was it? Only after emptying out my undies onto the bed and replacing the drawer did it occur to me that I had left it on the top dresser. After returning to the barn and handing the torch to him, I watched as he lay down and moved closer to the edge and peered into the darkness.

'There is some sort of stairway, but the first two yards have been broken off. I might be able to reach the top step if we use that ladder hanging up over the door.'

I retrieved the ladder then lowered it until I heard the metal rung hit stone.

'Here, hold the torch until I get down, then you can throw it to me.'

Sam disappeared over the edge. Leaning in, I shone the beam down to where he was standing.

'Can I come down now?'

As I leaned over to look, a small rock fell in. We both heard the splash, and then there was silence.

'Are you all right, Sam?'

'Of course, but I'm going down to investigate. The stairs seem to be solid enough. Maggie, I want you to tie a rope onto yourself and then to a thick beam, just in case.'

I could barely see Sam as he descended into the black hole.

'Maggie, come on down now. You will never guess what's down here.'

I climbed down. The air was musty and damp. Clinging to the wall with one hand and the other on the rope, I finally stood beside Sam. The stairway had broadened out on to a sort of a landing. A wide, bricked canal at least ten feet across stretched out in either direction. A strong current of water flowed into the darkness. We both gaped at each other in disbelief.

After climbing back up into the barn, I sat staring at Sam, as flashes of secret pirates' caves filled with treasure crossed my mind, and in my place too! We covered up the hole in the floor of the barn, in case any nosy parker fell in, and Sam bolted the wooden doors before turning our backs on our newly found treasure.

Back in the cottage, Sam bent over the maps of the waterways.

'There's no mention of your canal, old girl. This'—he pointed to the map—'shows that the canals all meet up further north, but I think your one is much older.'

I sat back with a glass of red, watching Sam. He was really good looking; I wondered why I had not noticed it before. I thought of Barry, my ex-boyfriend, and then of Sam; yes, it had been a long time between drinks. Sam was looking better all the time.

That night I lay awake, listening to the rain striking the

windowpanes. Shadows bounced off the walls as the lightning lit up the room. A grey mist filtered into my room. Slowly, I reached for the doona, and feeling it between my fingers, I reefed it up over my head, and lay in the darkness until a sense of calm overtook me, then nothing. The night passed quickly and as I pulled down my duvet, the sun reflected on my mirror, and the smell of toast induced me to get up.

*Did that mist really happen last night, or did I dream it?* Sam was dressed in cream slacks and a brown knit jumper, when I joined him in the kitchen for breakfast.

'Morning, Maggie. I'm aiming to catch the 1:00 p.m. train. But before I go I would like to poke around again in the archives, see if I can turn up anything more about this property.'

I suddenly felt overwhelmed with loneliness when he spoke about leaving.

'When will you come back, Sam?'

'As soon as I possibly can; you can't get rid of me now. Not with all this to sort out.'

I helped him pack and tried not to show how miserable I felt.

'I have thought this through, so don't argue. I'm going to buy a car and leave it up here with you to use. Besides which, I've got no parking space in Manchester, and it will be here for me to use when I come up.'

I didn't want him to go, and I held back the tears until he was on the train; then the floodgates opened as I watched until the train disappeared under the overpass. I would miss Sam; within minutes of him leaving, I felt a cloud of loneliness surround me. I was alone again. I needed to call my dad, to hear his voice. Crossing the road, I spotted a red phone box and, emptying the whole contents of my handbag on the ledge, I found two quid in coins and rang.

'What's up, Maggie, coming home soon?'

'No, Dad, I like it here, really I do. It's, uh…' I didn't want to tell him about my dreams, or whatever they were. 'Couldn't you come over now?'

'Sorry, love, but we have been through this before. You know how I feel about you accepting this money and house. The lot of them, your mum's adopted family, were all bastards. The way they treated her, up until the day she died.'

'Dad, the villagers here have nothing to do with Mum's relatives in Australia…. The money is about to run out, love you, Dad. I —'

I stood there looking absently out of the booth when a lady asked me if I had finished with the phone. I smiled at her and walked from the post office over to the taxi rank and climbed into the back seat of an old London cab. The driver folded his newspaper and asked me for an address.

'Home, James.' The cabby must have thought I was mad, but I'd always wanted to say that.

# thirty-nine

**Christmas Tidings**

It was hard to believe that ten months had gone by. I now knew every volume of works on the small library's shelves. The complete works of Shakespeare no longer sat beside a Mills and Boon. There wasn't a speck of dust anywhere. And in place of the lolly jar, a little bribe to all the kids who frequented the library stood a bowl full of apples.

Christmas was almost upon us. The weather had turned cold and snow drifts were backing up along the fences. The fog didn't lift until noon, keeping the mothers with prams indoors. I had the library's heater on full belt, and the condensation made weird patterns on the windowpanes as it slowly dripped down onto the linoleum, but at least we were as warm as toast.

I was perched on a ladder one Friday afternoon, stretching up to place another decoration on the Christmas tree I was decorating, when I heard a small voice. 'Be careful!'

Looking down, I saw Tommy, a small boy dressed in his older brother's topcoat, clutching a bundle of books he was returning.

'Me mum sent you a pudding, miss. Says to come over after work to the tavern, we are going to have a party.'

'Thanks, tell your mum I'll see her later.' Climbing down the ladder, I bent over and scooped an apple up, and threw it to the lad.

'I'm goin' to play cricket for England. Goin' to give you lot a thrashing, one day.'

I smiled. Cricket was a big deal here, and it was the Aussies — namely me — against all the villagers. I thought about tonight; I really didn't want to go. Sam was coming up tomorrow to spend the holidays with me, and the house needed a clean. Besides, it had been a big week, with carols in the streets and endless invites.

The locals had taken me into their hearts. Invitations had come from everyone. I was now a member of the choir, darts club, and cycling fraternity. Leo, the farmer with the wandering hands, broad shoulders, and cute butt, lent me a bike. Once a fortnight, a group of locals peddled around the countryside, ending up at the tavern for drinks. I was about to climb further up the ladder to place the angel on top of the tree, when the doorbell sounded. There at the bottom step, with one foot on the rung and brushing snow from his hat, stood my dad.

'Surprise, love, I just couldn't let you be alone at Christmas.'

I flew down and flung myself into his arms. I laughed and I cried, but most of all, I just hung on. I pulled Dad through the village, showing him everything on the way up to my house. I noticed some of the women giving him the eye. I suppose you could say he was a bit dishy, if you were old.

'Steady up, love, this bloody snow takes some getting used to.'

Dad pulled his case through the gate and stood behind me as I turned the front door key.

'Welcome, Dad, come on in.'

Dad had come from a working-class family. He had worked hard all his life to give me a home and the best education he could. He had dreamed of me being a lawyer or a doctor and was bitterly disappointed when I left school to enter secretarial college. After the death of my mother, I had become his world, not that he didn't go out on an occasional date.

'Gee, love, this is a mansion!'

Suddenly, I felt ashamed. This had been given to me, and I blushed with embarrassment.

'Don't look like that, Maggie. I love this place of yours.'

'No, Dad, of ours,' I said, bursting with pride as I pushed him through the entrance.

After giving him the royal tour, I settled Dad into the spare bedroom. He lit the fire, and we settled back to talk. The big S. Claus had come down my chimney two days early this year.

'Dad, let's go to the tavern, that's what they call the pub here, you'll love it, and we won't stay long.'

'Are you sure? I'm really tired, love. It was a long trip for your old man, all those lovely girlies on the plane waiting on me.'

'You are only forty-two, come on, grab your coat. Besides, I want to show my dad off.'

We had a great time. All the locals made a fuss of him, and at 1:00 a.m. we landed home.

'Why didn't you tell me this was such a great place? I would have come over earlier.'

I just laughed; there was no use trying to explain to Dad, he just wouldn't get it.


Sam's train arrived in the afternoon. He got a taxi over to my home. Dad opened the door and looked squarely into Sam's face. Shaking his hand, Dad pulled him in.

'I've heard all about you, but Maggie didn't tell me you were built like a brick shithouse.'

'Oh my God,' I sighed. 'Sam, this is my dad.'

I dumped Sam's things in the small room behind the kitchen. The room was in the oldest part of the house. Three of the walls had been replastered, leaving a small brick panel that seemed to form part of the back structure. By the time I returned to the lounge, Dad had poured a drink each for the three of us, beer for the boys, and a Pimms and lemonade for me. I smiled as I looked over to where Dad and Sam were engaged in deep conversation, bonding the way men do.

'I'm telling you, Ray, I've been searching the records, but there is not a trace of any of it.'

'Any of what?' I asked, as I had only caught part of what was said.

'Ah, Maggie, that canal under here, must be older than the 1800s.'

They chatted on all evening through dinner, and as I cleaned up, Sam produced more paperwork about the area. By this time, he had Dad, hook, line, and sinker. I said goodnight to Sam, and Dad and I walked up the stairs together. At the top, Dad kissed me goodnight and as a last-minute thought said, 'I like this boy of yours, Maggie, good down-to-earth type.'

'He is not my boy, Dad.'

'Fine, but I find that hard to believe, love.'

'Goodnight, Dad.' He had that cheeky smile on his face, that face I had missed so much.

I let Dad sleep in. The jet lag had caught up with him. Sam and I were having coffee and trying to warm up. We had been down to the village to top up on the last-minute shopping, you know, the bits and pieces we all forget. The snow was still falling, and black ice had made the road slippery. Families were making snowmen, and the kids pelted all passers-by with snowballs.

'Morning all.' Dad entered the room rugged up to the eyeballs in a thick cable jumper.

'Morning, Dad, do you want some breakfast?'

'Had it already while you two were out. Your old dad can still cook, you know. Sam, I can't wait to see this canal of yours.'

After a final cup of coffee, we set out through the yard to the barn.

'Ray, ram that beam under there and watch out it doesn't slide forward.'

Sam, like the Pharaohs of old, had us working unearthing our vast treasure. The boys reached the landing below and I was left above, their reasoning being, 'This is men's business.' It wasn't men's business when Sam had only me to help him. They weren't down there long before emerging with smiles on their faces. Sitting back in the kitchen, we all discussed our next move.

'We need to trace the water course and see where it leads to, Sam.'

'As we don't know where it starts, I don't see how we can, Ray.'

'Leave it to me. By the way, where is the closest camping store?'

I left them to their discussion to nick out and pick a present up for Dad. The one I sent him wouldn't help me now as it was sitting back home. I was happy that Dad liked Sam. To have them both with me was just great.

Susan waved to me from the bakery; obviously she had seen Sam, the little tart. 'Want a coffee, Maggie?'

*Oh well, why not,* I thought. She would come over anyway. Sam attracted her like a mosquito to a bare bum.

'Thanks, Susan.'

'Bring your dad and Sam over tonight, me dad's throwing a knees-up, come about eight, okay?'

I walked back slowly, knowing the boys would be a while yet. The village looked like a fairy wonderland. Icicles hung from the high-pitched roofs and the snow sat like millions of diamonds on the windowpanes that crossed the windows. To a girl who had grown up in Liverpool, Sydney, this was like a scene out of a Charles Dickens story. I walked down the middle of the street, so as not to be dumped with snow that fell from the roofs.

A seat in the old rectory was still visible when I looked into the churchyard. I really don't know why I opened the gate and walked over to it. After wiping the snow from the seat, I tried to read the inscription on the little plaque on the backrest. All I could make out was a faded surname — Noonan. I don't know why I hadn't noticed it before. Was this a relative of mine? I couldn't think about it too much now as it was time to go home and get ready to go out.

We all had a great time at the shindig. Dad and Sam were in demand. And I must admit Leo paid me a lot of attention too. The barmaid took a fancy to Dad and at the stroke of midnight landed a sloppy one on him. Dad was, by this time, two thirds under the weather, so with Sam on one side of him and me on the other, we retired to the duck house, as Dad would say.


'Help me carry it over there. Be careful, don't drop the bastard, it was the only one left.' Dad puffed as he balanced the crate.

'What is it?' My curiosity was killing me.

Dad and Sam were being very secretive about the whole thing. They had arrived home from God knows where, by taxi, carrying a very large container.

'Is it a present for me?'

'No,' their voices spoke in unison.

They left the container in the back room. It was a wooden crate bound together with a metal strap. I kept looking at it. I could see by the expression on Dad's face that he had no intention of telling us what it was, well, not yet anyway. So dressed in all our finery, we settled down to Christmas.

The day itself was great. We all opened our presents. Sam gave me a beautiful kid handbag and matching gloves, I gave him a jumper that I had knitted. It was my first attempt; the fact that I even finished it was a present in itself. Dad received a scarf and hat set, and in return he had brought me a painting of Sydney Harbour. It took him an hour to find the exact right position to hang it and by this time we had settled back to eat, drink, and play kids' games. Susan did her bit, arriving late and smelling like a perfumery then sleeking around in her show-all leather mini, tarting up to Sam. But in all, it was a great day.

# Chapter forty

Early the next day I was woken by the sound of Dad's voice bellowing through my usually quiet house.

'For Christ's sake, be careful.'

My head was pounding, after having one too many drinks the night before. I pulled my warm gown around me and slipped into my huggies, the sheep skin slippers I had brought with me from home. It was dark outside, and the moon was still up. They must be mad!

'Oh, Dad, it's too early. Why are you both up at this time anyway?'

'Go to bed, love, this is men's work.'

Well, let me tell you, I was dressed in ten minutes and raring to go. After finishing breaky — bacon, eggs, and muffins — we all lugged the container through the back yard, along the path that led to the panel in the stone fence, and up to the barn. The sun was just peeking up over the eastern hills, the sunbeams dancing over the snow as we crunched onwards. Sam opened the large bay doors and with the help of a few poles, we slid the container in. Dad produced a hammer and started to open it up. The panels of wood came apart quite easily. I picked them up and placed them on the far wall.

'Bloody good wood there, Sam, it would be a pity to waste it.'

My dad didn't waste a thing; we recycled everything.

*'Never know when it might be needed'* were the words I grew up with. Dad kept on chattering as he unboxed whatever it was he had.

'I could knock up a bookshelf for Maggie with it; what do you think, Sam?'

'Careful now, don't tear it.'

By this time, I couldn't stand the suspense a minute longer. 'What in the hell is it, Dad?'

Dad turned to me, and with a big cheesy grin, said, 'It is a two-man blow-up fishing raft.'

The boys secured the raft with rope and with a lot of heaving, it was lowered onto the landing below. Sam went down first, and Dad followed. I watched from above as they unfolded the raft. They started pumping with the hand pump, so after a lot a grunting, the craft sprang to life.

'Maggie, hand down the paddles, you might have to come down the ladder a way. Be careful, love, the ladder is slippery.'

'Wait a bit, Dad.' I handed the paddles to him. 'I want to come too. Don't you dare try to say no! That raft is as big as the one that you, Joe, and me used to go fishing in up at Lakes Entrance in Australia.'

I knew I had Dad stumped. They lowered the raft over the edge of the landing and into the water. Sam held on to the rope as Dad and I climbed in, and with a belly flop, he landed beside me. The current pushed us forward, ever forward into the unknown. Dad sat in front with the torch. The light shone for about twelve feet in front of us, casting shadows against the dappled-grey walls.

The canal was at least ten-foot wide, some parts were stone, but the majority of it was brick. Sam noted the time we started and then he produced a small compass. The voyage was becoming very eerie; the silence was only broken by an occasional word or cough. I felt the side walls. A trickle of slime stuck onto my hand, and the air was becoming rank the further we went along. Even the sound of Dad farting was a relief from the total silence. Thank God for Dad. The canal changed directions from time to time. The boys only used the paddles to keep us off the walls.

'How far do you think we have come, Sam?'

'Well, by the time and according to the compass, I think about two miles, but the speed is picking up a bit so let's give it thirty minutes more. If we don't come out by then, I think we should turn back and attempt it tomorrow, maybe packing more supplies.' Sam's face was becoming grimmer the further we proceeded. Suddenly, the raft surged forward, we were now skimming along, and Sam was desperately trying to push us away from the jagged walls.

Dad shouted to me. 'Hold on, Maggie, duck down.'

The water surged and we shot under a ledge. I screamed as the front of the raft went under the swell of the incoming tide. Around we spun, like undies in a washing machine. I lurched backwards against Sam. Just as I thought we had all had it, the water became still, and we floated out into a huge cave. I could see that the water was very deep and to the right a large flat outcrop of rock, with large iron rings attached to it, seemed to lead nowhere. Above it a shaft, and a light beamed down, illuminating the cave. The reflection of the water against the walls reminded me of drawings out of a book I was read as a kid, *The Little Mermaid*.

The cave opened out into the ocean. I could smell the salt as the spray hit our faces. Sam and Dad paddled towards a rocky beach. Thank God the wind was blowing us ashore, or we might have ended up in Ireland. I was wet through but felt exhilarated. I could see the small rocks through the waves. I stepped into the water and helped the boys pull the raft up and onto the shingled beach. We all sat there looking at each other, and Sam was the first to speak.

'Where in the hell are we?'

'I think we are south of the bluff. You know, around from the stony beach. I think that the road is up there, Sam.' I nodded with my head. God, my arms were sore from hanging onto the raft.

'Ray, why don't you stay with Maggie, and I will climb up and look?'

'I can't see the point, Sam, we might as well all go; we've got to climb it sometime.'

'What about the boat? Will we leave it, Dad?'

'It will be okay. Give us a hand, Sam. We can deflate it and pull it up into the grass. Look, there is no watermark up here.' He pointed to a level ridge several yards above the water. With both heaving and swearing, we got the raft up there, and continued to scramble up and over the ridge.

'I'm fucked, Maggie.' Dad bent over to try to catch his breath. Sam wiped the sweat from his face. 'Sam, how can you feel so hot, when that wind comes straight from a stepmother's breath?'

This was one of only a few times I had ever heard that word come out of Dad's mouth. Sam helped us both up, and pointed across to the road.

'Stay here, you two, and I'll see if I can find us a lift.'

I looked out over the coast; it had a rugged beauty all its own. The shades of grey blended from the clouds to the sea. It was so wild and frightening; the shivers running up my back were not from the cold.

True to his word, Sam returned, sitting in the front seat of Leo's lorry. With a bit of effort, the raft was hauled onto the back of the truck, and the four of us squeezed into the cabin.

'Mum will be as mad as a hatter if I don't take you all home to dry out and have a feed.'

I smiled to myself and thought how my Aussie slang was catching on. Leo's mum took charge, and within minutes we were in her warm kitchen. It was a typical farmhouse kitchen: large, with a combustion stove that supplied the hot water and on the hot plate a large pot simmered away producing a delicious smell that made my mouth water.

'Get all that wet clothing off, or you'll catch your death.' Leo's mum rounded up a change of clothes for us all and with a hot meal under our belt, we settled back to tell Leo what had happened.

'Aye, I knew that there was a cave under the bluff, but it is very hard to get into, you have got to know when the low moon tide is, and even then it is very dangerous. But I have never heard of a canal running into it. Must be hundreds of years old.'

Leo's mum had finished in the kitchen. She was a proud woman and would not allow any help in her domain. Sally was quite good looking, small in build, but since the death of her husband, ruled her kids with an iron rod.

'I've been listening to you all and I might be able to shed a little light on the story of yours.' Sally lifted a tray of coffee onto the table and settled down beside us.

'There was a story that my gran used to tell us, it was told by her gran to her and so on. As I seem to remember, it went like this...'

Sam caught his breath and looked over to me.

'In the seventeenth century, the western coast was alive with piracy. The ships from the new world sailed along our coastline, close in to avoid being boarded, but the people who lived 'round here weren't fools; they saw all the gold floating past and realised it was lining the halls of the very unpopular barons. So they decided to take a little for themselves. The trouble wasn't getting it, as often ships were wrecked in the northern storms, but because the military patrolled the bluffs, the folk couldn't hide it in time. So the cave was used for a while. Getting it in was easy, but our tides made it almost impossible to get the loads out. I believe it took many generations to complete a canal that was to run inland. Eventually the entrance was found and blocked in, although legend says there was more than one exit. The story has changed many times over the years, but gossip has it that the local lord was involved in some way.'

'There might be something in the library archives about it.' Sam literally shook with excitement.

'Well, we had better start with your deeds. I will ring the Deeds Office in London. Maybe they can trace them back further?'

Sam helped me up and as we walked towards the door, Dad sang out, 'I'll catch up to you kids later; Sally has invited me to stay on a bit, chew over the fat. She has promised to show me over her farm.'

'The old fox, he doesn't even like farms.' I giggled as I moved closer to Sam.

Sam smiled at me. 'Let him have his fun, spoilsport."

Dad wandered in the next day, whistling as he climbed the stairs. 'Had a nice time, Dad?'

He smiled down at me and said, 'It was very instructive.'

I kept thinking of the churchyard and the seat that sat under the large elm by the western wall. Later that day, I went to visit Mr Swisp, the vicar, to ask him what he knew about the Noonan history. I found him gardening near the back wall of the old church which had been built in the sixteenth century from large blocks of granite and had one of the only Knights Templar windows in England. I liked Mr and Mrs Swisp; they often called on me to check if I was okay. The reverend was a typical English gentleman: he was very refined and quiet, whereas Mrs Swisp reminded me of an ex-model. Her nails and makeup were always perfect, whatever the time of day.

'Well, my dear, I remember Vera, I believe she was your benefactor. She was a spinster, almost a recluse, she always dressed in black, old Edwardian styles like my granny wore. She attended the Sunday service. I was only a deacon here then. I remember she always sat in the front row and spoke to nobody. My mother did for her in her later years.' He patted me on the back and continued to talk, 'But in the meanwhile, why don't you start by checking the church records. All deaths and births had to be recorded in their local parish. And afterwards call in for tea, Peg is always asking after you.'

I spent the afternoon looking through the church records. All I could make out was Noonan, __ Brian, daughter of Sarah Noonan. Father __ Mother born 18-something, could have been 55 or 65. I could see that the numbers had faded, and it looked like someone had written over them.

'Can you make this out, Mr Swisp?'

We both looked, and even took the ledger out into the sun, but time and a helping hand had made the letters illegible.

'I can pull up the other ledgers for you, but it will take a few days.'

Life settled down. Sam returned to Manchester, where he was working on his grand building plans, and Dad seemed to have taken to village life like a duck to water. Sally kept inviting him to supper and that gave Leo grand ideas about me also.

'Maggie, are you and Sam an item?' Leo asked, for the tenth time.

'No, Leo; and besides, that's none of your beeswax.'

'It's my business, because I'm in love with you!' Leo looked at me the way kids looked at a lollipop: big cow eyes and drooling at the mouth.

I tried not to smile. I was sure that I was the first girl Leo had ever had a crush on.

'Thank you, Leo, but I only want to be friendly with you both. You are my friends and that's how I want it to stay.'

Leo mumbled something and left, closing the gate behind him. I could see the curtains moving across the street. The Johnsons were nice enough, the wife was always trying to get an invite over and the old man was always pissed, but happy. Dad had them baffled; they could not understand his Aussie slang. But Dad liked the husband and reckoned that anyone would have to drink to live with Mrs Johnson. Later that day, when we were sitting enjoying a hot chocolate with a dash of rum in it, I decided to bring up the subject of me staying in England.

'Dad, I'm thinking of applying for a permanent residency and I want you to apply too.'

Six months before, I couldn't see Dad moving out of the western suburbs of Sydney. So I waited for him to speak.

'You go ahead, love; I can see that your life is here now. But I'll have to think about it. At my age it's hard to start over again.'

I bent over and kissed him. Not until now, had I ever

contemplated him getting old.

'Dad, we both have nothing to go back to. Mum will be with us wherever we go.' It had been a while since I'd noticed the depth of sadness in his eyes. Dad stretched and he continued to stare at the clock that he had straightened and reset an hour before. He stood and walked over to me, patting me on the shoulder.

'Give me some time, love, give me some time.'

# Chapter forty-one

**England, summer, 1968.**

The long summer days were full of busy commitments. I started a storytelling morning in the library. I made my costume; a red dress with a long black flowing cape, and a tall hat, with a bright purple striped silk scarf tied to the top. I opened the doors at ten every Saturday morning. The local kids came in droves, eager to hear the stories I would read them, followed by a morning tea that Susan provided. At first I decided to lay the table with all sorts of lollies and small cream cakes. These yummy goodies were placed at the back of the room, but I soon moved them all outside, after a cake found itself on the polished floor.

'You little buggers! Maggie is good enough to do this for you and look how you pay her back. If I was her, I'd send you all packing.' Susan grabbed a mop and started to clean up. 'And I'd tell your mums, too.'

'Ah, don't do that, miss. Me mum and dad is havin' a sleep in. They sent me here. Charky' — he pointed to a skinny lad with flaming red hair and a cheeky grin on his face — 'made me do it.' David started to pick up the jelly that had mysteriously travelled through the air and landed on little Kelly's pink pleated neatly ironed dress.

'I didn't do nothin', miss.' With his fists closed, he threw a punch at the kid standing near him.

'That's it; you are banned for two weeks.' I waved my finger at the lad.

'What you mean banned, miss?'

'What I mean is that you can go home and not come back for two weeks.'

The cheeky smile changed to a glum frown. Later in the morning, after I had locked the doors of the library, Sue and I settled into a booth at the tavern.

'I don't know why you do all this for those little buggers, Maggie,' said Susan, sipping on her Pimms and lemonade.

'Sure, the rest of the kids are really very good, and they love the stories. Did you see Kelly laughing and clapping her hands when the witch got boiled in the pot?'

'You have more patience than I've got.'

I had started this program to improve their literacy and enjoy books, and it had paid off. The kids were now all anxious to join up and the reading program the school had initiated was well on its way. Dad had returned to Australia and life had settled down again. Sam's holidays were due in two weeks' time, and I had decided to join him in London for a week. I settled down to write to Dad to bring him up to date with my plans and the goings-on in the village.

*Dear Dad,*

*Let me tell you what happened to me last week. As I was sitting in front of the tavern with Sue, a blur of psychedelic colour pushed his bike into town. The guy had long hair, and Dad, he was wearing a jerkin in brightly coloured stripes. On the back of his bike he had strapped a couple of saddle bags and a dog. I liked him, every second word he said was 'groovy' but he was always off his face, you know, the big M. Anyway, Constable Bert Smith moved him on with a warning.*

*Sam has found out more about our mystery waterway. There seems to be more that we need to investigate. I will write as soon as I know more. Look after yourself.*

*Love, Maggie.*

The train was crowded, with kids everywhere. An historical exhibition, Life after the Roman Conquest, was opening in London during the school holidays. Personally, I would have thought that there was enough old stuff there without showing more, but each to their own. I made my way to the dining car, trying to find a spare seat; dodging people who were being thrown around as the train rattled through the passes. It looked hopeless. Then, over towards the end of the carriage, a man stood up and beckoned to me.

'There's a spare seat here, miss. Move over, Jack, give the lass a seat.'

Looking around, to find exactly where the voice was coming from, I spotted a couple of elderly blokes waving to me from halfway up the carriage. The taller of the two stood up to let me push in and sit by the window.

'It's a wee bit crowded. Always is on school holidays. I'm Bruce Werthby and this is Jack Middleton.'

'Thank you, I'm Margaret Jamieson. I didn't think I would be able to have lunch, it's so crowded.'

The two men went back to eating, and after the waiter delivered my lunch — a fish dish and potatoes followed by a chocolate pudding. God it smelled good. The men offered me a glass of wine and we settled back in the club car to talk. Mr Werthby told me that they were teachers of Antiquity at the University of Manchester, and they were going to attend the exhibition also.

'Do you have tickets to the opening, Miss Jamieson?' enquired the neatly dressed professor.

As I looked at the two men, they reminded me of Tweedle Dum and Tweedle Dee. They were kind of cute, in a grandfatherly way. Both wore tweed jackets and the university tie.

'Well, actually no. I wasn't going,' I said, starting to feel guilty as I saw the expression on their faces. 'But I will try to get some, now that you have told me all about it.'

'Look no further, dear girl. We have a few spare ones given to the university. We would like you to accept two. I know you will find it very interesting. Can you bring someone with you?'

I told them all about Sam and our waterway. By the time the train was pulling into London, they had given me their address and an invitation to join them at the Hotel Trafalgar for a high afternoon tea.

I had forgotten how busy London was, the crowds of people all jostling for position on the footpaths. The weather was quite warm, and the humidity was high. In fact, it was bloody steamy. The teahouses were overflowing with tourists, and I'm sure every tourist asked me to take their photo. Later that afternoon, I found the right platform and boarded the train to South End. The seaside town and its inhabitants walked at a slower pace. The whole town seemed to me to be living in the past. The main street came alive with coloured awnings and clusters of small tables facing the seafront.

I hailed a taxi, and it was not long before it turned into a small lane and made its way to 14 Sea Drive, pulling up in front of a wooden two-storey boarding house. The cabby carried my case up the steps, something they didn't do in Sydney, and I entered the foyer and rang the bell on a desk that was set under the stairwell.

'Room 17, miss, and have a nice stay. Mr Butler is waiting for you in the lounge.'

The receptionist was a woman of about forty, stout, and had her hair pulled back in a bun. She smelled of lavender, which reminded me of Nana, and Ponds face cream. As I entered the lounge room, I noticed Sam sitting at a table by a picture window overlooking the harbour.

Sam kissed me on both cheeks, and his enticing scent reached my nose. 'That's how the Frenchies do it, Maggie.' I hugged the big galoot before sitting down and pouring our tea. 'I'm so glad you could get away. We need to do some more exploring in the records office.'

The next day we met the two professors for high tea.

'Are you interested in the exhibition, Sam?' asked Jack, who had caught his breath and plopped down beside me.

'Yes, sir, this is right up my alley. We don't have much of this back home,' said Sam, smiling at the older men. 'How about tea, my treat?'

The men seemed to be very impressed with him as they chattered about their work.

'Maybe you can help Maggie with her canal. We seem to be running out of ideas and curiosity is killing her.'

I overheard what he said. 'Killing whom, Sam Butler? You have not stopped talking about it since I told you.'

Sam had pricked the older men's imaginations. Suddenly we were all going to the Library of Records. I didn't know there was such a place. The boys decided to investigate further while I returned to the boarding house to change my shoes. Later that night as we sat on the patio, Sam couldn't help laughing as he told me about the two men's antics in persuading the librarian to allow them into the restricted section.

'But, Maggie, it worked! They were able to obtain a lot of information that will help us determine what did happen to your house. I wish you had seen the library. We were ushered into a large room lined with shelves covered with glass and doors that were locked. I forgot to tell you we had to walk through an air lock, to stabilise the temperature. The stuff they have there is incredible, old documents of the Norman Conquest and a very interesting section on the Druids.'

The sound of the waiter brought me back to reality. Sam was still telling me about what he had seen. What an interesting guy he was. I felt a surge of pride as I listened to him. The time we had together was great, we shopped, or rather I did, and Sam carried the packages for me. The week went by quickly. We were given an old canal map that was supposed to be my canal but even I could see that this one ran in a different direction. Back at the Records Office, the clerk was very helpful but that may have been due more to the attention Sam was giving her than good customer relations.

'Well, Mr Butler, I think this will help you. I photocopied the last two pages of the deeds and caveats. You can see from this.' She hummed and moved closer to him, rubbing her shoulder against his. I looked at her; she was not pretty, and in the words of my dad: '*She had fallen out of the ugly tree and hit all the branches on the way down.*' I leaned forward and quickly removed the papers from her hand. She stiffened, but I was onto her; hadn't I learned from the best? That was Susan, of course.

'Thank you, miss, you have been very helpful, but my boyfriend and I must leave now.' Smiling, I turned, avoiding Sam's eyes. God, why did I say that? Why did I act so childish when I was around him? Weren't we both adults?

Back at the boarding house we studied the deeds. I glanced at Sam and wondering if he would comment on my revelation back there in the library. We traced the whole estate from James 1st through to Lord Lowe. The last owner was a Prudence nee Lowe.

'Look, Maggie! In 1861 the land was sold and there is no mention of the main manor.' Turning the document over, Sam read out to me a clause at the bottom of the page. 'The remains of the buildings are to be sold, and the balance of the money to be placed into the account of a Master Noonan. These monies are not to be released, until he reaches the age of twenty-one. The custodial signature looks like a Lowe. Maggie, I have never seen such documentation ever recorded on a deed. This is really unusual.' Sam sat back and studied the papers before him. 'Well, guess this proves that the old buildings were pulled down, but who this distant relative is, God only knows.

Anyway, enough of this tonight. I want to show you an invitation I have to the Architectural Ball in Manchester next month. I'm hoping you will come with me.'

I looked at him and as I started to speak, he interrupted me. 'I know it will be a bit posh, so if you would rather not…'

'Sam, I would love to come.'

I watched as his eyes lit up like a child getting a lollipop. We left for London the next day. I sadly waved goodbye as he boarded the Flying Scotsman for Edinburgh, where he was to work on a new project.

I had one more day here by myself to soak up the atmosphere of the street stalls and pick up a few small gifts. After stepping off the 121 bus to the East End, I walked through the open street markets with their stall owners of mixed nationalities. The West Indians wore brightly coloured clothes and were very pushy in trying to sell their wares. The air was pungent with the smell of curries that wafted from the Indian stalls. I grabbed a coffee and settled back to listen to the street bands and watch the buskers as they twirled their firesticks and chanted tunes of freedom and pure love for all.

Later that night, I rang the two old professors to thank them for all their help and invite them to stay with me if they had time. Truly, Bruce Werthby and Jack Middleton were two of the nicest old men I had met here.

The journey back home was uneventful. I stepped down onto the platform with its hanging baskets of red-and-white geraniums, and looked around, half expecting Susan to be there. George, the station master, a nice bloke who lived at the back of the station with his wife and four kids, ordered me a taxi. I didn't realise how happy I would be to step through the gate and look into my own front door. I swear the front windows smiled at me as I entered the house.

After placing my parcels in the back bedroom, I sat on the bed thinking of Sam when suddenly the door slammed, and a cold feeling crept over me. I felt someone watching me from the corner; my legs became heavy, and try as I might, I couldn't stand to run. I breathed in slowly and in what seemed an excruciating length of time, I quickly exhaled; my heart raced, and I tried taking long deep breaths, in and out. It didn't conquer my fear but calmed me just enough to reach slowly over to the dressing table. I lifted a heavy vase and with an almighty scream, I threw it into the back corner of the room. It smashed against the wall. I reached the lounge room, gasping for air as I ran. The temperature seemed warmer as I slammed the door closed, or was it?

I was still sitting in the lounge room when the back door slowly opened, and a head looked in.

'Good, you're back. I missed you.' Susan's face changed from a warming smile to deep concern. In her hand, she carried a bottle of red. 'Christ, what's up, kid, you look dreadful! Looks like you saw a ghost.' She sat beside me as I told her about the bedroom.

'Stay here,' she said as she armed herself with a shovel that I kept near the back door. Bursting into the room like a banshee on the war path, she screamed that she would crown any person in there; it ended in nothing, a big zero.

'Maggie, you're safe. There's no bastard in here,' she said with a note of disappointment in her voice. We both looked at each other in disbelief.

'I must be overtired, Susan, or completely potty, but I could swear someone was in there. Oh, hang it all, Susan, how about we crack that bottle. Will you stay the night?' I said with all the Dutch courage I could muster.

The early morning was clear of clouds; only a soft breeze disturbed the trees whose branches scraped against my bedroom window. The sun streamed into the bottom floor windows warming me as I drank my coffee. I grabbed the broom, half convincing myself I needed it to clean the back bedroom. Susan was still asleep but before I came downstairs, I opened her door just a little, in case I needed her in a hurry. I didn't know what to expect as I opened the door. But there it was, one broken piece of pottery and a scratch on the wallpaper. As I attempted to repair the wallpaper, a large sheet tore away and fell to the floor. There seemed to be a crack in the brickwork. I grabbed a butter knife from the kitchen and returned to suss out the crack. The more I traced it with a butter knife, the more it resembled part of a building structure. I lifted the handpiece of my phone, but it was dead. There was probably water in the line again. I quickly threw on a coat and headed down to the post office.

'Sam, I'm telling you, it really scared me this time.' The line went quiet for a few seconds. 'So you want me to stop fiddling with that wall?' I mulled over his reply before I uttered a non-committal, 'Um … okay, I'll leave it until you come back, take care.' I hung up the receiver and walked out of the phone booth.

Kelly, a local uni student on holidays, some relative to my butcher, had been opening the library for me while I was in London. I liked Kelly. She always smiled and smelled of cabanossi. As we sat and chatted about the kids' program I had been running this summer, she told me of a group of bikies that had ridden through. The Bodgies and Widgies were known even in Australia. These people were a hippy lot of bikies who wore bright colours and practised lots of free love. And I'd missed it all. A misty rain hit the front door of the library and floated onto my polished floor as the door swung open.

'Want lunch, Maggie?' Susan came in with a small basket full of goodies she had packed for us from the display case in her father's shop.

'Thanks, I'm starving, pull up a pew.' I smiled at her. I know I bag her a lot, but she really is a good sort when she's not chasing Sam. I told her about the invite to a ball in Manchester and immediately she was away, suggesting places where I could buy a dress. It was good to be back. The kids seemed pleased also and I have to admit I missed the little buggers too.

Joe Collicio, our local fruiterer, considered himself a bit of an artist and had decided to start classes; 'An Italian Experience' he called it. A short, fat, happy man with a Calabrian accent, who thought himself another Michelangelo, twirled an overgrown moustache between his fingers as he presented his grand plan to me. 'Margo,' that's what he called me, 'we are going to paint your house, and it will be *magnifico!*'

It was early Saturday morning. Opening one eye, I glanced at the clock near my bed—fifteen minutes more before the alarm would go off. Turning over and pulling the blanket up over my head, I settled back to snooze. I was slipping into a dreamy state, only to be woken when I heard people chattering and my front gate opening.

'Margo, we not disturb you?' The words came bouncing through the bedroom window.

Screwing up my eyes, I looked down to the garden below. My God, there on my lawn were at least ten people, all adjusting easels and canvases.

'Top of the morning to ya,' yelled up Jack, a neighbour from down the street.

He was a nice old gent, came over from Ireland. Very sad story though; he came over here to keep his wife safe from the bombings in Belfast, only to have her die of cancer a year later.

'Would you guys like tea or coffee?' I yelled down to the crowd below.

'We wouldn't want to be putting you out. But if you insist, it would be tea all round.'

*Putting me out? Well no, not now that I'm awake!* Suddenly, the alarm went off and my day had begun.

On the following Tuesday, Susan and I drove over to Manchester. After finding a car park and with an enthusiastic bounce in our step, we started dress shopping. After three hours, I was starting to give up the idea of finding a dress. I was sick of hearing 'that dress is you' from salesgirls who just wanted to make a sale.

Suddenly, there it was in the window of a small boutique: a glittering masterpiece, my perfect creation. Ten rows of red tulle that ended just above the knee. I could see myself in the dress; so, fifty quid later, complete with black lace stockings and a pair of black patent leather high heels, I left Manchester broke. Sam arrived back in Manchester, and I was to meet him at his flat. Turning out my handbag to find his spare key that he had entrusted to me, I came across the slip of paper with Jack's number on it. Making a mental note to ring him when I got home, I searched frantically for the key. There it was, caught up in the bag lining. As I turned the key, I noticed the curtains move on the flat next door. God, these Brits have long noses! Nobody sticky beaked back home in the housing commission suburb of Liverpool; they all minded their own p's and q's.

It took me an hour to dress. The person who was looking back at me from the mirror had little resemblance to Maggie. An older, more sophisticated woman smiled back. Sam had dressed at work as he was running a bit late. Earlier in the evening, he had rung me, apologising and asking me to order a taxi to the venue where he would be waiting for me. Staring over the cabby's shoulder, I watched as a large, brightly lit building loomed up ahead.

'You're here, miss, two pounds, thanks.' *The cab drivers in England sure know how to charge like wounded bulls*, I thought as I handed him a fiver. Stepping out from the taxi, I looked around and saw Sam. He looked elegant in a black dress suit. On spotting me, he waved and walked towards me. God, he looked handsome.

'Maggie, you look gorgeous!'

'You scrub up pretty well yourself,' I replied as he took my arm and led me into a massive room. On the stage, a band was playing soft music while we were shown to our seats.

'Margaret, I would like to introduce you to my work colleagues.'

Sam became very formal as I was introduced to his boss and his wife. Sally McFane wasn't what I had expected. She was very down-to-earth, a mother of four kids and a historian. Sally had a gorgeous figure, large boobs, and oh, how I envied her.

'Sam is very talented,' she told me. 'He has a great future with the firm. You know, my husband thinks the world of him.'

Sam kept up his stiff-necked attitude until his boss, who was three-quarters under the weather, told him to loosen up. Then the party rocked. We danced until I couldn't feel my feet at all. Jiving to the Mersey beat was fun but not as much as clinging tightly to Sam. The music slowed and we slinked around the room.

After all the goodnights were said, we bundled into the cab. I felt like Cinderella, I didn't want the night to end. We tried to be quiet as we climbed the stairs, not wanting to wake the neighbours. I carried my shoes and Sam carried me; I couldn't stop giggling as we stood on the landing. Sam fumbled with the keys but finally we were inside his lounge room.

'Come on, sexy, I'll help you into the spare room.' Sam bent over to assist me and landed on the floor with me on top of him. He lay there laughing. I stood up and made for the kitchen.

'I'm making coffee for us both, don't go far.'

I think we must have drunk a gallon of black coffee. Between laughing, peeing, and being generally stupid, we must have sobered up a lot. I sat down beside Sam, and suddenly I didn't feel like a kid anymore. All the silly things seemed irrelevant. Sam smelled good. He looked good and I wanted him.

The air became electric; I could feel Sam's arms closing around my body. It seemed the feelings were mutual. We walked towards the bedroom. Suddenly, we were scrambling to remove each other's clothes. First the dress, then the bra flew across the room, finally a pair of lace undies landed on top of the pile.

The golden glow of the bedside light illuminated every move we made. I felt myself succumbing to a nervous hesitancy as I felt Sam nuzzling against my nipples. It was pure ecstasy. It had been a while since my last lover; would I measure up? I pushed in close, kissing the base of his throat. My heart pumped the blood faster through my veins as I bent over to nibble his ear. Looking down I saw his manhood, and before me stood a hero from Greek mythology. When my back hit the mattress, I knew I wasn't in Manchester, I was soaring above Mount Olympus. Sam was a great lover; he took me to heights I had never reached before. As he gently reached for me again, I pushed him back onto the bed. Straddling his hips, I felt him enter me. This time it was my turn to love him. And I did. Sweat poured from both of us, and I wished this night would never end.

This was different from the fun I had enjoyed with my ex-boyfriend. I looked the same but the child in me was leaving.

Next morning we lay there, Sam started to talk. 'Maggie, I've been trying to tell you for months how I feel towards you.' He put his hand over my mouth as I started to speak. 'Please, for once shut up, and let me finish.'

I looked into his face; it oozed with god-like appeal. I knew then that I loved this man.

# Chapter forty-three

**English countryside — midsummer.**
The cycling club, of which I was a reluctant member, met on a Saturday afternoon. We had peddled over to the Swan's Inn in the next county. I knew my face was the colour of beetroot. The whole gang had crowded into the small bar, eagerly awaiting their pint and catching up on any gossip that may have raised its juicy head. Pushing through the crowd with a beer in his hand, Cyril sat down and, speaking up above the crowd, said, 'Maggie, are you staying home for the holidays?'

'No, Cyril, I'm going to stay with a friend in Edinburgh.'

I had decided to accept Bruce and Jack's invitation to stay with them. After much deliberation, I decided to take Sam's car for a spin. He was staying in Manchester, for a conference or something, so I was totally free for the next two weeks. This turned the conversation around to me again.

'Want to be careful on those roads up there, the Scots are mad.' Mrs Jones loved to have the final word on any subject, especially the Scots. Seemed that her sister ran away with one and the whole family blamed all the Scottish clans.

'Is Sam going?' asked Susan.

Her mouth dropped when I informed her that he wasn't coming up. And she was not invited to holiday with me either.

June 1st was the first day of my adventure. It took me six hours to find Edinburgh. You wouldn't think it would be so difficult to find a city. I swear the town kept moving but as the lights were starting to glow in the streets (or was that the headlights of the approaching cars?) I pulled into a motel for the night. After a night of little comfort (but what do you expect from a two-star motel?) I decided to explore the local sights. I really wanted to see Edinburgh Castle.

Leaving my car at the motel, I decided to walk. A marked map led me up the old, cobbled streets, through the grey stone buildings and along the narrow alleys that led to the castle's entrance, where I paid to enter one of Scotland's most historical castles. A tour group was about to leave, so I tagged along. We wandered through the banquet rooms, the living quarters, and at the top of the buildings we entered a small chapel called Margaret's Chapel. It was tiny in comparison with the rest of the buildings. The crowd left and I remained in there, held spellbound by the majesty and beauty of its carved altar and the simplicity of the white-washed walls. Later I saw the crown jewels and was given a history lesson as to why the Scots don't like the Poms.

I had done it all arse about face, by walking to the top of the mountain where the castle was located and getting a taxi down. My next port of call was a whisky distillery, which proved very interesting, especially the free tasting. That night I slept like a babe. Edinburgh was a cold, grey city. To the people who call it home it must be pleasant enough, but to me it was lifeless, and that's saying a lot from a girl from the western suburbs of Sydney. Next morning, I ordered a cooked breakfast which included a black pudding. Having just about finished it, I made the grave mistake of asking what was in it. After two cups of tea, I could still taste the blood. I realise it was all in my mind but there it was stuck.

Jack Middleton had given me a map to his house. It was located twenty miles due north, two miles west and through the village of Middleton. The same name as his, which I figured must be a distant relative of some kind. The day was pleasant enough although the sky was overcast. The village was small, similar to the one I now lived in. It had the usual tourist trappings: a pub, cake shop, gift shop, and post office. Pulling up in front of the shop, I nicked in to pick up some fresh milk. If these men were like my dad, they would be out of milk for sure. I decided I might as well get a cake also.

Heading out of the village along the main drag, I drove very slowly, looking for a small older period house. The road was narrowing, and I passed a large stone wall set back from the road along with a terrace of cottages, but none seemed to fit my professor.

After twenty minutes, I turned around and started back. Stopping to make some inquiries at the local police station, where the constable on duty gave me further instructions, I ended up again in front of the stone wall. In the middle of the iron gates, the word Middleton had been written in old script.

I drove up the tree-lined driveway, and there it was in all its glory, one of the biggest, most regal kingly types of houses you could imagine. Jack must have some cool friends, to allow him to lease a house in here somewhere. The gravel crunched under the tyres as I pulled up near the entrance to the house or should I say, palace. I sat in the car, not sure if I was to enquire at the front door or at a tradesman's entrance. But as my nana would say, 'Suck it up.' I tried to put on an air of importance and after placing one foot after another, I reached the front door and rang the bell. All of a sudden, my leg felt itchy, and as I bent over to scratch the irritating spot, the door opened.

'How may I help you, miss?' There before me stood a butler right out of the series *Upstairs, Downstairs*. He was dressed in a black suit, with not a hair out of place. I was suddenly conscious of my faded blue jeans and a blouse that could have visited the iron.

In my posh voice, I asked, 'Could you please direct me to Mr Middleton's house, thank you?' I was never sure if you thank before you got a reply or after.

'Whom may I say is calling?'

I raised my voice. 'You have it wrong, I only want directions.' I thought he might be a little deaf, being older.

The round and not-so-tall man smiled and stood back a little from the door. 'His lordship is at home. I didn't hear your name, miss.'

I didn't hear any more. I stumbled through some ridiculous spiel about visiting a professor.

'Please, miss, step this way.' In a daze, I followed until I stepped or maybe stumbled into a large, beautifully decorated room. I now knew what Alice felt like when she fell down the bunny hole. The walls were lined with books, and at the far end of the room a stone fireplace graced the entire wall, with a coat of arms that had been carved into the stone above it. A smiling professor greeted me.

'Maggie, how good of you to come.' And with that he threw his arms around me, squeezing me in a bear hug.

'You didn't tell me that you were royalty.' Oh my God, I shouldn't have said that.

'Well, not exactly royalty, I'm only twentieth in line,' he said with a twinkle in his eyes.

'Please, what should I call you? Your lordship?' I took a step back and tried to sum up the situation. Jack had on an old pair of gardening pants teamed with a woollen jumper that had seen many good years of wear. Around his body there was a distinct odour of potting mix.

'This is why I didn't tell you or Sam. I wanted you to call me Jack.'

'Well, Jack, Dad won't believe this.'

He pressed a button near his desk and the butler reappeared. 'Tea, thank you, and I know Miss Jamieson loves coffee. We will be on the south terrace, Burns. Come on, Maggie, I'll give you a look-see at all this old stuff of mine.'

We toured the first floor of the east wing, ending on a covered patio. Burns was setting up our tea and little sandwiches. It was all very posh.

'I want to hear all about your house and canal. Have you any more information?' He sat back chewing on a pipe and waiting for my reply.

'Jack, why don't you light your pipe? I love the smell, my pop used to have a pipe.'

'Does he still smoke?'

'Oh no, he's dead now.'

'Well, if you don't mind.' Striking a match, he sucked back on the pipe as the flame grabbed on to the tobacco. I had seen Pop do this a thousand times and the feelings of joy and love rushed out to this older man sitting beside me.

'By the way, I've asked Bruce to come down, he's always good value. I went to the Edinburgh Institute to search their archives. I think your canal was built to accommodate the illegal smuggling trade. It's where it ends that we need to find out. Bruce has had an idea, but I'd better let him tell you himself. I don't want to steal his thunder. When we are finished, Burns will show you up to your suite.'

'This way, miss, if you are ready?' Burns led the way up a

staircase, past portraits of family members both past and present, and along a wide corridor until we reached my room.

'A maid will be in to help you, and may I say, miss, I hope you have a lovely stay.'

Burns placed my bag on the bed and left me to explore this large room. A four-poster bed, complete with lace hangings, took centre stage. The door opened and a small-framed woman entered. She introduced herself as Elfie and asked if she could unpack. Elfie was an encyclopaedia of knowledge; she seemed to know all the family history but far more importantly, she knew how to fix my hair.

'Miss, dinner will be served at seven in the dining room.' My two dresses were hanging in the wardrobe, and I watched as my jeans left the room on Elfie's arm to be pressed. I didn't ever iron jeans. Later, she returned with the jeans pressed and looking like new.

'Elfie, what will I wear tonight? I wish Jack had told me about this living as a princess stuff.'

'Don't worry, miss, we'll fix you up a treat. Will I run you a bath?'

'Where is the bathroom?'

'It's through those doors, miss.' Elfie opened the smaller door to a lovely, tiled bathroom. 'I had better put on the wall heater for you. These older rooms are very draughty.'

Scrubbed, hair done, and makeup applied, I descended the stairs and made my way into the study. This room was smaller than the adjoining room. Jack stood as I entered the room and put down his novel before he walked towards me.

'You do look quite lovely. If I were thirty years younger, I'd give that Sam a run for his money.' Jack smiled and poured me a drink. 'White wine wasn't it, Maggie?'

'Yes, thanks, Jack.' I took the drink and settled back to wait and see what happened next.

'Jack, what made you decide to study and teach?'

He laughed. 'You mean instead of lording around and living the life of Reilly.'

Just as I was wondering how to get out of this conversation with a small degree of dignity, Burns entered the room and announced the arrival of a Mr Bruce Werthby.

'For God's sake, man, I've been coming here for thirty years, Bruce will do, please, no more formalities.' Bruce marched in; I could almost hear the Colonel Bogey March being played. He was dressed in a grey suit, very professional. There before me stood my saviour, as round as ever and beaming from ear-to-ear. Bruce noticed me and his face broke into a smile.

'Great! I'm so pleased you could come; I've got a bit of news for you.' Looking over to Jack, he said, 'You didn't tell her, did you, Jack?'

'After we eat, I will go into…'

'Dinner is served.'

With a cool gent on each arm, we entered the dining room. After a great feed and a glass of port, I settled onto a very comfy lounge to wait for the next instalment of my life. I was becoming accustomed to everyone knowing more about it than I did.

'Maggie dear, I sent all the information that you gave to a fellow who specialises in this part of your county and in the history surrounding it. Gregory Bingle is his name and after exploring all avenues, he has come up with a clue and, blimey Charlie, the fellow thinks you may be a distant relative.'

*Another relative? Oh well, what's new, I always wanted a brother.*

'The canal that runs under your house could lead up to the old manor. Parts of it were destroyed in the 1860s. It has been recorded that large deposits of treasure found their way up into the manor but after the fire there was no record of any precious finds being made. Bingle has been searching the family history for years. Jack, I took the liberty of inviting him up for lunch tomorrow. I hope that is fine with you.'

'Excellent, old boy.' Throwing his arms up in delight at the news, Jack set about pouring more drinks.

I loved to watch the bantering between these older men, their brilliant minds exploding with enthusiasm and knowledge.

I really don't know why I woke up so early the next morning. It wasn't the bed—that was great—but I had a feeling that I wasn't alone. I walked over to the drapes and pulled them aside; the moonlight was still dancing over the well-laid-out gardens. Lights were on in the rooms above the stables, and I could hear a motor running from a building south of the main house.

I quickly donned my pressed jeans and blue cotton top then wandered down the stairs and through the back rooms that led to the kitchen. People there seemed surprised when I entered, and a kindly faced cook offered to have a maid fetch me a morning tray in my room. I think I was making them feel uncomfortable; I asked directions to the garden and left them wondering why a guest would go below stairs. The gardens were lovely, so I wandered over to the dairy, to check out the cows. Looking up to where my room was situated, I caught a glimpse of a woman standing in the window and as I waved she disappeared. Something was different, but I couldn't put my finger on it. I re-entered the house and made my way to the dining room.

'Come on out onto the terrace; I thought we would have breakfast out here. What do you say, Maggie? I know you Australians like to eat outside.' Jack and Bruce had already started when I sat down.

'Who is that pretty woman I saw in my window? Is she a maid I haven't met yet?'

'Don't worry about her.' Jack choked on his toast then he continued, 'You could have seen our resident ghost. Women over the years have often seen her. She doesn't seem to like men. Sorry if she has scared you. I'll have you moved to another room.' The men watched me; I guess to see if I was going to faint or something.

'Jack, I'm not scared, but I'm now intrigued. What do you know about her?'

'Not very much; she was a nanny who came out from your country and died in a mysterious way. The first record we have of her is when she travelled up here with her charge, a grandchild of a former governor from Australia, the child's mother died at sea.'

'Maggie, she has never interfered with anyone.' Jack sounded quite apologetic.

God, what would Dad say when I phoned him? I wish he was here.


Gregory Bingle arrived at eleven. Huge in build; mid-thirties, not bad looking, and he drove an Italian sports car. Were they all rich here?

'Maggie, I would like to introduce you to Gregory.'

Bruce looked like the cat that had just swallowed the canary. As he shook Bruce's hand, Gregory winked at me and I heard Bruce say, 'Maggie is from Australia, some sort of relative, you said?'

Gregory's large, powerful arms lifted me up. He had the strength of a bear and smelled of Apollo aftershave. I sniffed the air. God, he smelled good. I couldn't help giggling as his moustache tickled the edge of my nose, causing me to sneeze. That sensation brought back memories of my pop. He loved to do that when I was a small child and to watch me squirm away.

'Good morning, cousin. Welcome to Merry Old England, or should I say Scotland.'

I tried not to snigger, but he even looked like Little John of Robin Hood fame. This distant cousin or whatever he was of mine, oozed sex appeal. After he released me from his arms, Gregory stepped back and took a long look at me. I felt myself blush. Gee, I hated how men had the ability to do that to women.

'Seems we are related through the Noonan side. I've been looking forward to meeting you. I have only recently discovered the Australian branch. Bruce tells me you have a mystery of your own.'

'Well yes, but I didn't realise it was such an interesting topic until the boys became involved and now it seems as big as Ben Hur.'

'Come on, chaps, let's get Gregory inside.' Jack ushered us all into the large living room and proceeded to speak to the butler about the evening meal.

'Maggie, Bruce has filled me in on your property. I've been studying the family history for some time now and I'd like to be involved in helping you uncover what secrets are buried on your side of the family. For some reason, the main property was burnt down, and a lot of the history was lost.'

'Give Maggie time to absorb all this, Gregory. You are inclined to act a bit like a bull in a china shop.'

'Come on, Maggie, up and at them. We've a lot to do today.'

For a moment I thought it was Sam but as my mind cleared, I remembered Gregory. I opened one eye and looked around; the sound was coming from the other side of the door. My God, where had the night gone to?

'Are you up, Maggie?' asked Gregory. 'I'm going down now.'

'I'll be down directly, go ahead and start without me.' I quickly slipped into the shower, dressed in my neatly pressed jeans and was about to leave when Elfie entered the room.

'Oh no, miss, let me fix your hair, and may I suggest a warm coat. It's a bit nippy out still.'

After breakfast, I entered the study, the smell of the pine logs made me shiver with excitement. I still couldn't believe that this was real. I looked around the room, with its lovely paintings and a medieval tapestry that must have been worth a fortune. Over on the far wall stood a large period desk and there, covering the desk and lying on the floor, were pages of a family tree. On top of the pages, circled in a highlighter was the name Noonan. I started to study the family tree, when Gregory turned from the window where he had been watching the cows being herded into a new paddock.

'Maggie, this is our common denominator, our common family tie. A Sarah Noonan purchased a property on the west coast of England. In fact, part of the estate was a smaller cottage that you now own. I'm finding it difficult to trace before or immediately after 1860, as there was a fire that destroyed most of the records.'

'Gregory, I don't understand why you are so interested in my little house.'

'Well, my dear, it's not so much the house as the canal that runs under it. There's been a lot of Chinese whispers about gold being smuggled into this country during the gold rush days in Australia. But now that your boyfriend has dated the first half of the canal to pre-18th century, we can only speculate to its purpose.'

I listened to what he was saying. It all started to feel like a plot out of an Errol Flynn swashbuckling film. I could see myself as the damsel in distress, hands to the face, leaning out of a window as flames roared in the background, and then through the air with sword in hand, he swung to my rescue. Of course, it went without saying it was Sam.

'As I was saying…'

Oh God, what was he saying? I jerked my mind back to the present.

'With your permission, we would like to undertake an historical exploration of your canal. Of course, Bruce, Jack, and your Sam would be included.'

I looked at him, suddenly my smile curved into a smirk. 'What about me?'

He coughed softly. 'Of course you are included.'

*Kiss my arse!* 'So tell me, Gregory, you don't really expect to find buried treasure, do you?'

'No, Maggie, I believe any bullion is long gone but there are many parts of this story untold and with the new twist of your canal, it has become a juicy riddle to solve. Your part of the coast was used by smugglers for centuries but due to the Great Fire, a lot of records were lost there also.'

It all seemed a game to these men. I wondered if any of them ever considered that real people were involved, that women might have lost their lives in all these fires that were now only words escaping from male lips. Later that night, I phoned Sam to let him have the latest gossip.

'Love, this is super. Has a date been set?' Sam's voice quivered with excitement as I spilled the beans about the last two days.

*Gee, I love you too!* I thought as I hung up. *Boys with their toys.*

The second weekend in January seemed to suit everyone. At least seven people were to come, excluding me of course, or that's what they thought.

Jack was a perfect host. He was entertaining, not at all like royalty. On the following Saturday night, he had invited a gathering of people over. Elfie warned me that it would be formal. That gave me only three days to buy yet another dress. Early on Wednesday, Elfie and I set off for Edinburgh. It was Elfie's day off and she asked for a lift in with me. Actually, I was very pleased to have her company, since two minds were better than one when it came to buying dresses.

We toured the back streets where the boutiques were housed. I used to love the mod designs but lately I was leaning towards a more sophisticated look. I ended up with a black crepe creation and a silver shawl and more shoes. His lordship was costing me money, but I didn't want to let him down. I didn't have any idea who his mates were, probably lords and ladies and the gentry. Thank God for Elfie. She helped me dress and do my hair, and by the time she had finished, I felt like a million dollars.

The ballroom was lovely, cut flowers filled the tables and the light reflected off the mirrors that lined the walls. The crystals in the chandeliers sparkled like diamonds. I looked up to the ceiling, where wall panels of cherubs looked down on us, their eyes seeming to follow the mottled mob that made up our human race.

'You look enchanting, Margaret, and it's my great pleasure to introduce you to my friends.'

Jack smiled as he led me through to a crowd of people sipping champagne. As we entered the room, heads turned, and I felt unsure if this was all real or a scene out of Cinderella. Here I was, Maggie from Liverpool in Sydney, hobnobbing with the best of them. Gee, I was pleased that I had splurged on another dress; the women were all dressed to the nines, wearing jewels like you wouldn't believe, and not made from paste.

The night flowed, filled with eating and dancing and being introduced to them all. These people were very friendly and accepted me as one of them. I forgot that their lineage went back hundreds of years; they were so entertaining, and they all seemed interested in me and my story, which Jack told at every opportunity. But like Cinderella, the night ended, except I now had a lot of invitations to people's places. I supposed that meant more clothes.

And like all fairy stories, my coach was leaving. Next morning, a driver brought around my car and the butler, for whom I had a soft spot and I thought was definitely worth more money, lifted my case into the boot. Those two old men, my heroes, kissed me goodbye. I couldn't help the tears from running down my face. They were a mixture of my dad, my grandfather, and my good friends. I turned to wave goodbye. I could barely see them, two specks still standing on the steps waving their hankies. I'm sure this was not what a lord and his friends are supposed to do, but then again, my lord was different. Then it suddenly hit me… they were gay.

**Christmas**

It was hard to believe Christmas was just around the corner again. I loved this time of the year and as a child, I would open a picture book and look into the snowy scenes, imagining myself being one of the little characters. I'd be eating all the Christmas goodies and sliding on the snow with the wind in my hair but now, by a chance of fate, I was living within my own story book village. As I read to the kids in the library on Saturday morning, I glanced out the window half expecting to see little magical figures in their long cloaks walking past.

Feeling a bit down, Christmas alone, I rang Dad and received his good news. He was coming here in January; he had resigned from the council and with his superannuation, hoped to start a small handyman business. Dad was very impressed with my tale of Lord Middleton and had told all and sundry that my Lord M was his friend by association. Sam had been in touch and was coming up for the holidays, much to the delight of Susan.

'Susan, I've told you things are serious between Sam and me.'

'Well, are you going to marry him?' Susan knew the answer but waited for a reply.

'Of course I'm not right now, but who knows, maybe later on? In the meantime, you just keep your mitts off him. Anyway, you have that new schoolteacher on the string, haven't you?'

'Oh, Maggie, he is okay, but not like your Sam.'

We both jumped as the front door knocker banged. I pushed past Susan to open it. As I opened the door, snow blew into the hall, floating up onto the picture rail.

'Quickly, let me in, it's bloody cold out here.' Gregory Bingle, distant relative, stood huddled on the top step.

'Gregory, this is lovely surprise, but why didn't you let me know you were coming. Don't just stand there, come in.'

'I knew that I should have given you a bell, but Sam said he was coming up, so I thought it would be a great time to meet him and go on with his project.'

His project? What's this *his* project? Why do they think that my house, my canal, and more importantly my life all belongs to Sam?

Still brushing the snow from his shoulders, Gregory followed me into the lounge room. Susan stood up and going all coy, muttered something about being in the way.

'Sorry, have I interrupted something?' Gregory looked at me, waiting for an introduction. 'And who is this lovely lady?'

*She's no lady!* I thought to myself. 'This is my friend Susan…'

Before I could finish, Susan was shaking hands with him. Poor sucker, he's had it, or has he?

'Maggie has told me all about you. I feel as though we are good friends already.' Susan smiled sweetly at him.

I thought I would throw up.

'Maybe it is time for you to go, Susan, don't you have a meeting or something to attend tonight.'

She was still saying goodnight as I bundled her out into the cold, cold night. Serves her right.


I took Gregory with me to meet Sam's train. He drove since the roads were barely visible. High drifts of snow had blocked many of the side exits and only the main branch roads were open. Even the train was thirty minutes late. Sam was the last passenger to leave. Bending over, he fought against a gale to reach the car. Opening the backdoor, he pushed in, pulling his bag behind him. After introducing them, I sat back, listening to their conversation, as I couldn't squeeze a word in edgeways. When we arrived home, Sam turned to speak.

'Gregory, do you think this confounded weather will stop us looking further into the canal?' asked Sam.

'No, the canal is cold and wet whatever the day is like. By the way, Maggie, the rest of the team will arrive in the New Year.'

Gregory looked over to me and smiled. 'It's all right, they are staying at the tavern, and it's already been taken care of. The uni is footing the bill.'

'Maggie, where will I put my gear?' Sam looked over at Gregory, not knowing if I was going to say, 'In my room,' and looked disappointed when I pointed to his usual room opposite mine.

Gregory was firmly planted in the back room behind the kitchen. After dinner, I sat back on the lounge, my legs folded under me, leaving Sam to fix us a drink.

'Maggie, I like your new hairdo, very mod.'

'Thanks, Gregory,' I murmured, just loud enough for Sam to hear me. He looked over at me. I sensed that he was seeing me for the first time. I was a bit disappointed that the comment hadn't come from him. There seemed to be something different about him, more vague, more spaced out. Maybe he was just tired?

Christmas was fun. I insisted Gregory stay with us since he and Sam got on like a house on fire. They had gone over the old site plans many times trying to work out the most logical explanation for my canal, and then decided to investigate the covered-up arch in the back room. The two boys tapped the wall and started to prise off the plaster.

'You keep on going and I'll nick out and get a bag of cement and plaster. Do we need some beams or will that wood in the barn do?' asked Gregory.

Sam thought a minute and replied, 'No, get three four-by-twos. I wouldn't like to be responsible for using Maggie's dad's lengths of timber that he dressed for a cabinet he is planning to make her.'

'Is he a bit of a tyrant?' Gregory put down his hammer to hear the reply.

'No, he is a pussy cat, a really big one.'

They had opened up the arch and behind the plaster a sealed door appeared.

'Sam, do you think it is wise to break through the brick? It will probably lead to the outside of the cottage.'

'Not according to the measurements Maggie and I did last summer.'

'What do you think, Maggie, are you game?'

I considered the statement for about two seconds. 'Let's go for it.' I stood back and covered my eyes as the boys started pulling down my home.

'What's that stink?' yelled Gregory.

'It seems to be coming from the wall, stand back.'

Sam lifted the sledgehammer to make one last swing at the wall, and with a crash the bricks gave way. After the dust settled, we could see a room or tunnel and peered in. I was overcome with a sense of sadness and then gripping fear. Stumbling back, I tripped over the rubble and fell into Sam.

'Maggie, for God's sake what's wrong?'

'I don't know, but I've got to get out of here, I'm choking.' I pushed past him, and as I reached the kitchen, the air in my lungs cleared and the panic stopped. I stood at the sink, looking out the window when Sam came over to me.

'What happened to you, Maggie, you look dreadful. Here, have a drink of water.' Sam stood by as I gulped the water down.

'Sam, it was the same feeling I had in my bedroom that first winter. I told you, don't you remember?'

'It might have been the stale air, or a panic attack.'

'Pig's arse it was stale air, and I've never had a panic attack in my life.'

Just then Gregory walked in. 'Such language from a young lady.' Gregory looked quite amused.

'Gregory, there is something very odd here. Last winter…' I finished the story with a glare of condemnation towards Sam, who just stood there looking at me.

'What in the hell is wrong with you anyway, Sam?'

Gregory tried to buffer the situation by saying that we all needed a hot drink.

'I've taped plastic sheeting over the entrance. I think we have done enough for today, better to get an early start in the morning.'

'Thanks, Gregory, I'll start dinner.' I left them in the lounge, wondering what in the hell was wrong with me.


The sky was clear as I looked out from my bay window. Much to my surprise, I had slept like a log, and I was starting to feel a bit childish with the way I had acted towards Sam. I could hear the noise in the kitchen and a lovely smell of bacon and eggs floated up the stairs and lingered around my room. As I opened my door, Sam was waiting for me. He grabbed me and pushed me against the wall, his mouth covering mine. He held me tightly, but I started to feel uncomfortable and struggled to get free. He let me go and stood back. I lifted my hands to touch his face, to stroke his cheek.

'I have met another girl,' he blurted. 'Not like you, but I have some feelings for her…'

I couldn't hear what else he was saying. I wasn't angry; I don't exactly know what I felt.

'…and she works for me.'

He was talking about our great friendship, wanting to still help me, wanting nothing to change. Who was he kidding?

'Please tell Gregory I've got a headache, I'll be down later.'

Sam tried to hold me, but I pushed past him away, and slammed the door shut behind me. Flinging myself onto my bed, I lay there crying into my goose down pillow.

The door opened and Gregory came in. He sat on the bed beside me, stroking my hair. 'Maggie, Sam told me what happened. He is packing to leave; he mumbled something about you having the car.'

'Oh, Greg, I feel such a fool. I should have seen this happening. Please ask him to stay until I've calmed down, and I'll just wash up in a bit.' I felt numb as I walked into the lounge room. Sam stood there, all his bags lined up by the door.

'My God, Maggie, I'm so sorry. I didn't even sleep with her.'

He was as white as a sheet as he stood there snivelling and watching me. *As if that is supposed to help the situation,* I thought as I looked over towards Gregory for support.

'Maggie, where is he supposed to go? The roads are blocked and there are no trains. I guess he could go to the tavern?' Gregory looked at me and then Sam. Suddenly, I felt ashamed that he had to be involved. I could only imagine the gossip that would circulate if Sam went to the pub.

'Stay here, Sam, and you can tell me all about your lady,' I said with a mouth full of acid, spitting the words out towards him.

'Please, Maggie. I only took her out a few times when you were up north.'

'Yes, Sam, I remember, that was when you were too busy to come with me. Anyway, stay put for a few days, I think Gregory could do with your help.'

We all sat at the table, with Greg now sitting beside me and trying to keep the conversation civil. His archaeologists were to arrive in three days, and I knew that they needed Sam's expertise in building.

'Sam, I realise that you are a very important part of the team, and you're needed here. I'll keep out of the way, and we can be civil to each other while people are here.' I grabbed my coat and scarf and left the security of my home, slamming the door behind me.

The waves were pushing copious amounts of white foam up against the rocks as I headed to the waterline. The snow had stopped, and the wind had changed direction, bringing large amounts of driftwood onto the pebbled beach. I walked down the path and along the foreshore, feeling the salt spray covering my face as I plodded through the small rock outcrops trying to avoid the rock pools.

*Why did he do this to us, to me? I love this man, I must be stupid.* The words kept echoing in my mind. I could drown myself but no, it was too cold. As I came to the end of the beach, I heard a voice yelling from above.

'While you are down there, love, can you check me line?'

'Okay, Bill.'

The line was empty, so I threw it back out into the breakers. Bill Bunty was a pensioner, a one-legged returned soldier, who caught fish to sell to help supplement his pension. He called into the library every Friday with his catch for me.

'Thanks, Maggie, it's getting hard to climb down when the wind's up.'

I just waved to him, not wanting to engage in any conversation. At the end of the beach, I looked up at the cliffs. Funny how I never really saw them before. Yes, I knew they were there, but I had never taken the time to study them, their sheer drop that ended in the rocks below. I pulled my woollen coat tighter around me. Until now, I hadn't even felt the cold or the salt on the mist that was spraying onto my face.

Looking up, I saw the outline of a man silhouetted against the grey storm clouds that were covering the sky. I was out of breath by the time I reached the road and started to feel a little uneasy as I looked in both directions for the stranger. Why had I come this way? I started to feel my skin crawl as I thought of the night when horses passed me and then vanished.

A fog was rolling in and within ten minutes it had turned into a pea souper. I grabbed for the fence that ran beside the golf course and led back into town. Everywhere was still. The silence was creepy, but I assured myself that as long as I kept the fence gripped tightly, I would be all right.

As I watched, the eerie light had turned from a pale grey to a deeper shade of dark blue with iridescent pearl lights shimmering through it. It was hypnotic. I stood there, staring into the void. Suddenly, I was being pushed backwards towards the cliff. A weight heaved on my chest as I tried to scream. I clawed at the wooden posts, trying to hold my ground. I was being pushed closer and closer to the edge of the cliff. Then out of the fog a hand appeared, and pulled me forward. Suddenly, the lights were gone. Lying on my stomach, I felt as though terror alone was holding me in a trance.

A hand gently rubbed my back, and I sprang to life, hitting and kicking out until a voice, soft and reassuring, rang true in my ears. 'Hold on, girlie, you're safe now.'

After rolling on to my back, I opened my eyes, to see Bill balanced on his crutch bending over me.

'Please don't let it get me.'

'Nay, girlie, nothing is here, you just walked too close to the cliff. I've got me car close by, I'll take you home.'

# Chapter
## forty-six

I woke the next morning safe in my own room. The previous night seemed surreal. As I rolled the covers down from my face, I noticed that blankets and a pillow had been placed on my chair. As I started to get out of bed, the door gently opened and Sam, the one I was trying to hate, looked in.

'Stay there, Maggie, I've got a tray here.' Sam pushed the door open and walked in. He looked tired and started to fumble his words.

'Did you sleep here, Sam?' I waited and wondered what pearls of wisdom were going to spring from his mouth.

'Yes, of course I did. You were petrified when Bill brought you in. Maggie, what really happened out there? I know you, love! There is no way you would walk that close to the cliff.'

The words just rushed from my mouth. I needed to have someone believe in me and for now Sam was that person.

'Sam, it was the same feeling that I felt before, it terrified me, and time seemed to stand still. I could actually feel myself being pushed back to the cliff's edge.'

I couldn't hold back the tears. Sam reached out to me, and I clung to him; I needed his strength but more than that, I needed his love.

'Hush, love, you are safe now.'

I felt the warmth of his heart through his jumper, on my cheek. *Oh, Sam, why did you let someone come between us?* I composed myself and that awkward tension returned. Later that day, as I was about to open a door, I heard Sam say to Gregory, 'Gregory, what do you make of all this? The way people spoke, anyone would think she was losing her marbles. Maggie is a very sensible woman, she doesn't scare easily. This type of thing keeps happening to her — there has to be a plausible answer.'

Sam sat with Gregory as he retold all the things that had happened to me over the last two years.

'Sam, I don't want to frighten her further, but I'm starting to think that a demonic spirit may be attacking her.'

'You've got to be joking, Greg. Those things don't really exist, do they? And how in the hell could she get mixed up with any of those things? She's from Sydney.' I almost snorted in disbelief. Demonic spirits? What next? The Brits must be nuts.

'I've heard of these things before, there are reams of papers written about them. You know, Sam, there are more recorded paranormal activities in England than anywhere else on earth.' I must have made a noise as I shifted on my feet. Their conversation ended abruptly as Greg said, 'Here she comes, shut up about it for now, the kid's scared enough.'

'Maggie, I've just made coffee, want a cup?' Gregory had already started to remove the plastic sheeting that covered the hole in the back room.

I started to move towards the opening, noticing that the smell had gone, and I was breathing okay. Sam was rigging up a light before he stepped through the black opening into the unknown.

'Greg, stop making this sound all spooky, we've only knocked down a bloody wall into another room.'

Pulling the plastic sheeting behind him, Sam walked along into the dark room. 'Maggie, come in here, it's like walking back in time. Wait till you see all these things. Gregory, let out more light cable and come on in.'

We all stood there staring at the past. Chests and wooden furniture had been piled up against the wall, and at the far end was another bricked-up doorway. The air had warmed, and the dust had settled.

'Well, what are we doing now? Carrying on, or going through this stuff here?'

Greg could hardly contain himself; his hands were everywhere, his eyes absorbing all he surveyed.

'Maggie, I can't believe it, this has been lying here and nobody bothered to explore this area.'

'What do you think we should do, Sam?'

Although he was a bastard, I trusted his judgement.

'While the weather is holding, I think we should open the next door.'

'I'll bring in extra timbers and we'll start.' A look of pure joy shone from Gregory's face. 'Thanks again, Maggie, I wouldn't have wanted to miss any of this.'

It was a lot harder to break through the panels this time.

'There must be something holding it closed from behind. Look out of the way, I'm going to pull it forward not back.'

Sam pushed the edge of the pick into the doorjamb and started to heave it forward. I was glad that I'd asked him to stay. After all, he did say that he hadn't slept with her. Gregory was a mountain of knowledge but as to being able to demolish, he was lost. Slowly, board by board, the opening appeared. I listened to the old oak beams groan; not wanting to give up their secrets.

'Jesus Christ,' Sam groaned, as he peered out through the small opening.

'There is something blocking the way. Greg, will you go and get the wheelbarrow and shovels? They're in the barn. And, Maggie, I could do with a Coke.'

It was good to be working together again; I had to put my feelings at bay until this project was finished. I poked my head in and took a look. The air was stale but breathable; slowly my eyes became accustomed to the dim light, and I saw the problem ahead. There in front of us was a heap of rubble; it looked as if part of the roof had collapsed.

'How old do you think it is, Greg?' asked Sam as he bent over the beams to examine the fallen brickwork.

'Maybe it is as old as the late 17th century, but Lord only knows how it was attached to this cottage? Are you sure the walls are safe, Sam?'

'I guess we'll soon find out. Let's start digging.'

We were now into our third day clearing the fallen roof; the boys worked like Trojans, and I tried to keep up, to do my bit. They had decided it had been a tunnel but where it would lead was anyone's guess. The men from Edinburgh were expected tomorrow to investigate the canal and hopefully throw some light on our mystery. I had long given up thinking it was mine alone. I had to return to work, and in some ways it would be easier to spend the days away from Sam, although I also wanted to be here.

The library was quiet at this time of year, kids were away on holidays and the rest of the folk were still getting over Christmas. I unlocked the doors and started the heater before replacing the books onto the shelves. I didn't hear the door open; it was the smell of his aftershave that alerted me to his presence.

'Sam, what are you doing here? I don't want to argue, but I can't take much more.'

'Maggie, I have to ask you, will you ever forgive me?'

I looked up to face him; he had been my life. 'Truthfully, Sam, I don't know, maybe in time but what I don't understand is why you didn't tell me? In fact, Sam, why did you come at all? Was she going away for the holidays?' I watched his eyes mist over and waited.

'Everything I say hurts you, but I'll say it anyway. I was lonely. She is a lovely lady, and I took her to the pictures and out for a few meals. Yes, I found her attractive, I'm only human, but I didn't step over the line. I can't make you believe me, can I?'

He looked into my face, waiting for me to reply. My gut was telling me to be very cautious, but my heart wanted to forgive.

'Sam, leave it for now, please, we have the blokes arriving and I need to concentrate on that.' People were now filtering in, so I spoke more softly to him. 'I'll see you at home; we can talk more later on tonight when Greg goes to the pub.'

Sam looked at me but decided not to reply. Shortly after he left, Susan popped in, to drop off afternoon tea for me.

'Maggie, Bill told the grocer, who told Dad, that you nearly fell over the edge out by the bluff. What in the hell were you doing out there in that weather?' She sat on my desk, eating one of her dad's cakes, waiting for the goss.

'Susan, someone or something tried to push me over the edge.'

'Are you serious?'

She stopped chewing and gulped the rest down.

'Yes, Susan, it was like the night in my bedroom, when you charged in. Do you think I'm going mad?'

She didn't hesitate for a moment. 'Don't be stupid, Maggie, I was there that night, I saw what happened to your bedroom.' She thought for a while and then made a suggestion. 'I think we had better see the vicar, this place is bloody haunted.'

I sat in the study of the vicarage, sipping tea and waiting for the vicar to arrive. The room was homely, with bookcases full to overflowing covering three walls and a small desk that was overcrowded with this Sunday's sermon, sitting against the fourth wall.

'Maggie, more tea?' Mrs Swisp popped her head around the door to check up on me. 'My husband won't be long; he's just shovelling the snow away from the church doors. We can't have any falls.'

'No thanks, I'll be fine. I've found a book to squiz at.' The large leather-bound book – *The History of Manning Village* – caught my attention. As I turned the pages and skimmed through the titles, the vicar opened the door and smiled at me where I sat in a well-worn but comfy armchair.

'Hello, Maggie, won't be a minute. I just want to change my boots.' Reverend Swisp brushed his wet hair out of his eyes as he walked barefooted across to the fire where a pair of well-worn but loved slippers had been placed.

'To what do I owe this pleasure?'

'Mr Swisp, I think, or at least Susan thinks, that my house is haunted by a ghost, and he seems to want to do me in.'

'I doubt if your place is haunted, and I know that nobody wants to "do you in" as you most eloquently put it. Susan has an over-ripe imagination and was quite a precocious child.'

He watched me as I wondered how to explain to him all the events that had led up to me sitting here before him.

'All right, Maggie, I think you had better start at the beginning.'

A pile of sandwiches later and I think he had the drift. He didn't laugh but sat there thinking over what I had told him.

'Let's start with what we actually know about your property. On the deeds you showed me, it was purchased by a woman named Sarah Noonan. Then there was a gap of time when it was left vacant. I think the best thing is to try to find out why those parts of your deeds are blank. Perhaps that might lead us to know why any soul would want to linger around your home. And, Maggie, I'm reserving my judgement on all of this for now.'

I thought I caught a twinkle in his eye, as he climbed up on a chair and lifted down a ledger from the top shelf of the bookcase. The pages were old and had faded to cream with a tinge of brown around the outside. The writing was very difficult to read, but after searching through the pages, we found a reference dated 1866 made to three people who had been buried in our little churchyard.

'Look at the name on the bottom of the page, see, near the bottom date. It looks like Lowe overprinted with Noonan.'

Mr Swisp studied the page under a large magnifying glass, then replaced it on the table and closed the book.

'We will never know why the name was changed by these records. The Shire Office might have more up-to-date records of this period. In the meantime, a prayer might help.'

I think he was only saying this to try to pacify me. 'Mr Swisp, don't you do exorcisms like the Catholics?'

'I've never done one, nor have I seen one being performed. But any help from our Lord would be acceptable, so let's go over and I'll see what we can do.'

'Are you going out, Jim? Make sure you wrap up warmly, the weather is turning nasty.'

Mrs Swisp's concern for her husband reminded me of my own mother and of how much my father had missed her over the years.

'I won't be long, love, I'm just taking Maggie home.' After pulling his boots on again, we left to walk across the open paddock, stepping around the steaming presents left by the cows.

We crunched our way through the snow drifts and Mr Swisp — I don't like to call him Jim, as it doesn't seem appropriate — pushed open my front gate. The wind picked up and we were nearly blown into the porch. I glanced at myself in the hall mirror as we walked by. Gor blimey, my hair was enough to terrify any ghost. Susan pushed a drink into our hands even before our bums hit the lounge chairs.

'Oh, Reverend, Maggie is in perilous danger, you have to help her!' Susan swept her hand up to her face and with an academy award-winning performance, draped her body over the chair and looked up into the older man's face.

'Susan, please stop being so melodramatic. You are not trying out for the village theatrical company.' Mr Swisp looked over his glasses at Susan, who was now sitting up with an angelic Sunday-school look on her face.

'This is not to be taken lightly, girls, so let us pray.'

# Chapter forty-seven

Two days after the boys had started to excavate the walkway between the older rooms, they discovered that the floor started to descend.

'There seems to be at least ten steps. Greg, throw me down that shovel, I'll have to clear away this rubble.'

'What did you say? I can't hear you!'

Just as Greg was about to ask again, the floor suddenly gave way and Sam toppled down into the darkness.

'What's down there, more steps?' I heard the thud as Sam crashed through the rubble and boards that had been hidden underneath. I rushed into a cloud of dust and saw a blackened face looking up at me.

'Are you all right?' yelled Gregory from beside me.

'Never better, what do you think?' Sam replied sarcastically. 'I nearly broke my bloody neck!'

'I was trying to tell you that the floor didn't look too sound.'

'Well thanks a lot, mate.' Sam pulled the boards away and climbed back up.

'Maggie, I'll have to take the torch down, but I think we have hit a tunnel of some sort.'

'That's enough for tonight. The others will be here tomorrow, and they can help us. Besides, you've a few scratches to be cleaned up.' Gregory helped Sam up into the small back room.

'Sam, I want to start sorting through the boxes.' I had been patient, but curiosity had now got the better of me. 'Do I have to record what I uncover?'

'Yes, thanks, that would be helpful.' Sam tried to keep a straight face, but I saw the smirk. Smart arse.

I was lying in bed thinking over the previous day's work when the doorbell rang. I quickly grabbed my dressing gown and headed to the door. As I opened it, five cheeky faces met me.

'God, it's cold out here. Step aside, Maggie.' Jack and Bruce, followed by three strangers pushed into the warmth of my sitting room.

'A spot of tea would go down a treat. You get dressed, Maggie, I will make it for the boys,' said Gregory, who had been close on my heels to answer the door.

Bruce looked around the room as he walked over to me and, in a fatherly gesture, planted a kiss on my cheek.

'Nice room, very homely.'

'Where's Sam? Is he here yet? Nice place you've got, cosy like.'

Jack removed his hat and coat and bundled the rest of the men in.

'Oh, Jack, my whole place would fit into one of your rooms.'

'Girl, it's not the quantity but the quality,' he answered. This was one of the things that made Jack a lord and stand out as being a great human being.

'Gregory, where is Sam anyway?' I watched as Greg thought before he spoke. And I considered him to be a little too cautious for this time of the morning.

'He went into the village He shouldn't be long. I'll go and start breakfast while you meet the boys.'

Sam didn't give any explanation for his early trip to the village when he returned. Maybe he was ringing that girl? No, I wasn't going there.

The three lads turned out to be graduates from the uni where Jack taught, a bit geeky but nice. One look at them told me that Sam had better get used to that shovel. The house became Head Quarters. Jack was left organising the troop as I slipped into the room to start filtering through all the boxes. Pulling up a stool to sit on and with a screwdriver in hand, I set about demolishing the first crate. I found crockery, old and pretty well all broken but as I examined it and looked over the newspaper it had been wrapped in, headlines caught my eye.

*Gold Strike Ballarat*

*Strikers again barricade themselves to protest their rights. Eureka flag flies again. Joe Heneley, beef baron, was accidently killed as he tried to mediate between the prospectors and the law, trying to stop bloodshed similar to 1854. Joe was attending a stockmen's meeting when the local magistrate asked for his help. He was killed by a ricocheting bullet. He will be sorely missed.*

So, some of this stuff must have been sent here from Australia. Now my curiosity was up. I prized open the next box. The interior had been lined with oil cloth and under a covering a straw, I pulled out two journals. The first was marked 1852. The pages were in very good condition, the print easy to read.

'Sam, have you got a minute before you disappear again? I think I've found more journals of the Noonans'.'

Gregory pushed in first.

'That's marvellous, Maggie! This will help to explain the missing parts of our family jigsaw.'

Sam poked his head up through the hole in the floor and added his bit. 'Good stuff! Keep on opening them up.'

As if I needed him to take charge of me.

Dad's inflatable raft was commissioned back into service. The students, led by Sam who had given up being a mole for the time being, had re-entered the daylight and along with my two professors, headed towards the barn to start their descent into the canal. This time they had packed provisions, torches, and a thing that could send up a signal if they became lost.

I had decided not to go with them, not that they had asked me to. I wanted to find out more, and to open the last three crates. I'd placed the pieces of unbroken crockery on the dresser along with the journals, and cleared out the empty crates to make some room; then I attacked the remaining boxes. There wasn't much of monetary value but a lot of older medals and a shawl that had been wrapped in an old bedspread. It was a wonder that the moths hadn't attacked them but maybe the person who placed them there had never had the opportunity to unpack them.

I heard the backdoor close. 'Is that you, Susan? Come in here and see what I've uncovered.'

Susan looked over the finds and sat down on the overturned crate. 'Maggie, this could be something to do with your ghost.'

Susan's eyes stood out like light globes.

'Don't get carried away.'

'Have you started to look into the books yet?' Susan asked, as she turned over the journals, half expecting to absorb the contents without doing the reading. Susan was good at that. 'Maggie, give the books to me and I'll read them tonight.'

'Sorry, Susan, but these are family records.'

She got the shits and mumbled something about being needed in the shop and left. After carrying the books, quilt, and shawl upstairs and placing them in the window box in my bedroom, I stared out the window. What to do? Stay and read or check on the men? Stay and read. I figured that the blokes would be still preparing, so I might as well get started. I pulled out the journal; the cover was worn, and a water mark covered the leather bindings. Although the room was quite cool, the book felt warm and inviting to my touch. Odd. I sat on my bed and tucked a blanket over me and started reading.

The entries read like a novel, the story of Sarah Noonan. It started aboard the ship *Harcourt* in 1852, and I read on through Sarah's highs and lows; the death of the man she loved, the birth of her son and of the heart-wrenching decisions that no woman should be called upon to make. I put down the journal and looked back out my window. This woman had been my age when she was forced to escape to a foreign land without even being able to own her own farm. How easy my life was in comparison with hers. God, men were bastards, not only now but throughout history.

I thought of Sam and wondered what Sarah would have done. Probably kicked him in the balls and dumped him! The door slammed, announcing that the two boys were back. I carefully placed the book into the window box, along with my deeds and other treasures, and started down the stairs.

'Maggie, we're back, what's for tea?'

Gregory looked a little embarrassed at Sam's outburst. *What's for tea?* I had completely forgotten about tea, and I must have looked guilty because Greg came to my rescue.

'I fancy a steak at the tavern, my shout.'

I smiled; even Greg was picking up Sam's Aussie slang.

I loved the ambience of the local tavern. The dining room was warm and friendly. A large log crackled in the fireplace and the smell of pine lingered in the air. It was the custom of the publican to throw on the pinecones, which added to the whole Christmas atmosphere. After we had eaten and were sitting back enjoying a coffee, Gregory asked me about the journals.

'Gregory, I would like to finish reading them before we talk about that stuff, if that's okay with you.' I suddenly didn't know if I wanted any man to read them. She was my great-something; I wasn't really sure what she was to me. But she was mine and I felt a need to protect her.

'Enough about the books; what happened with the raft?' I leaned closer to Sam to hear his reply as the noise level increased. Susan's dad, along with the two professors and the students were pushing into the booth behind us.

'We will start off tomorrow, but we had to buy another craft. There are too many people for the one boat.'

'If there's enough room, then I'm going with you.'

'What did you say, Maggie?'

Sam knew what I said. He just pretended he didn't hear. So I yelled it again. 'I'm coming too.'

'By the way, old girl, we aren't deaf.' Jack smiled across to Bruce. I guess he had watched the whole comic scene unfold.

'Anyone for another round of beer?' Sam asked as he smirked at the scowl I shot him across the table.

The light on the wall opposite my bed was flickering. I reached over to look at the clock. Damn, I was late, that bloody alarm hadn't gone off. I looked out my window and witnessed a line of little gnomes carrying torches, all marching towards my barn. *Those bastards, they think they can sneak off without me.* Flinging the window open, I stuck out my head into the icy dawn and after taking in a deep, lung-piercing breath, I screamed out to them. 'You lot down there, wait for me.'

We all crowded into the barn. The boards over the entrance to the steps had been prized off and the ladder lifted off the wall and placed down into the hole to reach the first step.

'I'll go first, Gregory. You can lift down the rafts and the pump. Only one at a time though, there's not much room down there.'

Sam pulled on his waterproof jacket and with his torch balanced in his pocket, stepped over the edge and into the void. The rafts were lowered, Dad's first. After a lot of swearing, the blow-up craft slid into the water and was tied to the iron ring that protruded from the stone wall.

'Come down, Greg, I'll need you with the second raft and to pass down the provisions.'

Love him, or loathe him, Sam knew how to take control and get things moving. With a well-organised descent, we all entered the hole and clambered down the steps, trying not to touch the wet, moss-covered walls. You could almost taste the staleness in the air. The ambience of this place was enough to make my hair stand on end.

'I'll take the first raft along with Maggie, Bruce, and one student. The rest of you climb into the larger one with the provisions. Jack, is that all right with you? By the way, Maggie, do you need to go to the toilet?'

I could have killed him.

Sam handed the second walkie-talkie to Jack, who was so excited he nearly dropped his jacket into the canal.

'Steady up, Jack, or you'll burst a puffer valve.' Bruce lent a hand to help his friend into the second craft.

All we needed was a bottle to send us off into the deep blue yonder. This trip was going to be much more difficult than our first one with Dad. We were travelling against the water flow this time. Gregory had purchased two small outboard motors for the rafts. I guess the thought of paddling, as we did in our first attempt, sounded far too strenuous for him; boy, was I glad. Sam pushed off from the wall and we started upstream. Close behind us, Gregory guided his craft into the centre of the underground canal, and our adventure began.

The impervious walls, steeped in history, watched as we went by. The passage was becoming increasingly narrow as we glided along. Long tentacles of slime reached down, just missing our heads. The direction of the canal started to change, and the roof became lower.

'Maggie, get down lower in the raft.' Sam sat in the bow, using the paddles to help keep the raft from scraping along the walls. Gregory was not managing quite as well. We could hear the second craft as it bounced from side to side.

'Gregory, catch.' Sam tossed a rope over the stern of the raft. Jack reached over to grab it and suddenly water started to rush over the side of the raft.

'Jesus, Jack, be careful, or we will all be in the drink.' Gregory pulled the older man back and, taking the rope from him, tied it to his raft.

Slowly we pushed on. The second outboard had to be turned off for safety reasons, leaving our craft pulling a tandem behind. The air was stale but every now and then a whiff of fresh air came in from the broken bricks that had crumbled from the roof. We had been travelling for about an hour and the walls had changed to a brick upper and stone lower. On the left side of the wall, a flat platform of stone jutted out. Sam guided the raft over towards the platform. Sam jumped over the side of the raft and slid onto the large slime-covered stone.

'Hang on, I'm going to try to attach us to that stone. Maggie, I need more light.'

'Throw up the rope, Bruce.'

It took some fine balancing before Sam was able to secure the rafts.

'What can you see, Sam?' I tried to shine all our torches on to the wall near him.

'There seems to be a cut away here in the brick.'

He started to climb up. Sam had climbed out of sight when suddenly we heard a roar. Down he came, hitting the rock and tumbling into the water. We could hear his fingernails as they clawed on the moss-covered walls. Stench was everywhere. I screamed as he sank under the boat. Two of the students jumped into the freezing water and Gregory swung the torches to shine into the black depths.

'I can't see him,' screamed Bill. 'Further down, towards the back.' Gregory was struggling to remove his heavy coat. The last thing I saw, as I dived in, was Bruce trying to climb over into the water. The water was as black as ink. It swirled around in no particular order. Luckily, I was a strong swimmer, and the current wasn't that strong, but I couldn't find him. Where could he be? I re-surfaced, only to suck in a breath of fresh air and then dive back into the murky depths again.

All of a sudden, I was being pulled along by an unexpected undercurrent. Kicking to the side, I pulled my hands along the rough stone. It cut into me deeply. *Oh my God, where is he?* My legs were being sucked into the wall; I forced myself to relax and slid through an opening and along another passage. I gulped for air; the stream slowed, and I found myself floating in a larger, brighter chamber. A rainbow of colours reflected on the walls and a shaft of sunlight hit the pool of water, bursting through the surface and exploding into ripples of shimmering lights.

# Chapter forty-eight

On the other side, crumpled up against a landing, I caught sight of Sam's coat. I swam closer to it. The walls were rough, but the stagnant slime had gone, and the stone appeared to be clean and in surprisingly good order. The coat moved and a leg appeared.

'Sam, please answer me, please.'

'I'm up here, above you.'

'I see that. Are you all right? How on earth did you get up there?' I tried treading water as I looked up.

'I climbed up, how would you think I got here? More to the point, why are you here?' He tossed his head to the side; you know the way men do when they are feeling guilty about something. How could he be so arrogant? Then all of a sudden, the bubble burst.

'You stupid creature!' I was feeling so angry, how dare he worry me like that. 'I should have left you to drown! Do you realise that the boys are in the water looking for you, probably for me too.'

Sam gave me his hand and with a quick jerk I was sitting beside him. We both stared around the cavern. To the far side I could see a stairway that led upwards. The light streamed in and coloured the walls with a pearly lustre. The water that had been black and murky was now an iridescent green. I could see down to the bottom where a rock ledge formed part of the floor.

'Sam, where are we? This doesn't seem to be built similarly to the canal; it looks more like a cavern.' Sam's eyes followed my arm as I pointed to a platform to the left of the stairs. 'What's that up there?'

'I'm not sure but let's think about this for a moment. Perhaps we could swim back down and through the opening we came through. The only trouble being that the rafts might have moved on. So, my dear, I really think our best option is to swim over to that ledge and try to reach the stairway. It has to lead somewhere.'

Sam was holding me tightly and I slowly started to warm up. The thought of having to re-enter the water again didn't thrill me, but besides my grazed hands I knew that I would survive, and Sam was healthy enough to make it. Being able to see around the cavern was comforting and I thanked God they didn't have sharks or snakes or other nasties, like in the scary movies here or at home.

'You'll be fine, Maggie, hold on to me. I'll get you there.'

'Sam, I can swim you under the table any old time.'

And with that I pushed off. It only took a few minutes to reach the other side. Sam was right behind me.

'Maggie, you'll have to try and get up onto me, and then I can push you up there.'

We struggled as Sam dived under my legs, coming up with me astride his shoulders. This was not the best look, as somewhere in the canal my track pants had slid off. Only a scant pair of undies stood between Sam and my modesty. *Oh well, he has seen the lot anyway.*

We climbed the rough stone stairway. As we got closer to the side platform, a carved statue of a beautiful woman looked down on us.

'My God, Maggie, this must be a part of a Roman temple, or maybe a spa.' Sam ran his hands over the Roman numerals and Latin script.

'How old do you think it is?' I asked as Sam looked again at the carved letters. 'I know the CXII is one hundred and fifty-two but what else does it say?'

Sam studied the carving without answering.

'Well come on, what does it say?' I hadn't paid attention in my Latin classes in high school, mainly because I always needed to go to the toilet, usually for a fag.

'For God's sake, Maggie, can't you see I'm freezing my balls off here.'

'Keep your bad language to yourself, Sam Butler.' I sniffed as a tear rolled down my very cold face.

'Come on, stop blubbering, let's see where it leads us.'

'What about Gregory and the boys? Do you think they'll be safe without us?'

'Without *us*?' he stammered.

I saw that smirk on Sam's dial. How dare he? He landed us in this mess. Sam threw his hands up and with a determined look, sang out, 'Let them find their own temple.'

The stairway opened into a small cave. As we walked out into the sunshine, a voice boomed.

'Thank God you're alive, we've been worried sick.'

Across the rocky outcrop and slightly above us beamed a mixture of happy and relieved faces.

'Sam, give me your shirt.'

I suddenly became aware of my appearance, having my knickers up my butt wasn't a pretty sight. I had just finished tying the shirt around my waist when the first of the boys reached us.

'Where are the rafts?'

Gregory piped up. 'They are tied to the wall where you left us. We found another outcrop of rocks and continued up to the entrance to go for help. We searched as far down into the water as possible for you, Sam.'

Just then two arms grabbed me, and Jack pulled me into his chest in a bear hug.

'We thought that you were both goners. How did you get out here anyway?'

'Questions later, these kids need something hot inside them. The closest place around is that farmhouse over there.'

Jack pointed to a rambling old house that was set almost on top of the cliff. The students reached the house before us and had returned to give us the good news. The kettle was on.

There is one thing these farmers are great at: thinking that the newcomers to their village are completely mad. But being good folk, they drove us back to my place to recover and regroup. Gregory wasn't very interested in the Roman statue, but my two professors were bursting with excitement.

'Maggie, there's no known record of any temple complex in this area. Do you think we could go back there today, Sam?' Jack had already rung the university to report what we had found.

'Jack, the rafts are more important, don't you think? That Roman thingy won't go anywhere.'

Sam had warmed up his car, and we were off again. It took two trips to get us all there, so I changed my clothes while Sam dropped off the first carload of explorers. The steps down to the rafts were quite dangerous. It was a relief to see the rafts still tied there, bobbing up and down on the murky water. So like the Three Stooges plus four, we set out again. I had the feeling that we weren't alone. Nobody else seemed to notice the drop in temperature. Sweat started pouring from me, and I couldn't catch my breath; I made a grab at Sam.

'What's wrong, are you sick?'

'What happened?' I opened my eyes. The men were lifting my head up off the bottom of the raft.

'You seemed to have fainted. Take a deep breath.' Gregory looked very concerned as he pushed the hair out of my eyes. 'Do you want us to turn back?'

'No.' I pushed myself up onto one elbow. 'No thanks, I feel lots better now. It must be the stale air.' I ignored what had happened and the chill of the air around us and peered into the black hole ahead that we were being pushed through. Our little motor was doing a great job of pulling both rafts. Dad loved his Yamahas. We used them on our fishing boat back home. 'Bloody good motors' he always said.

We were on the water for about thirty minutes; it was becoming shallower, and I could now see the bottom. The canal made a right-hand turn, and we burst into a man-made cavern. Light streamed in from the opening in the roof. A small waterfall overflowed from the sheer rock face, filling the tunnel and throwing up a fine mist in all the colours of the rainbow.

'Look over there.' Gregory pointed to the far side of our cavern. 'What do you think it is?'

The light was now strong enough so that our torches could be turned off. There, in the natural rock ledge that formed part of the waterfall, was a row of small statues, carved in the form of stairs.

'This is the most mysterious thing that I've ever seen.' Jack turned to Bruce. 'Can you make out those markings?'

'Can we get the raft closer, Sam? Those markings look very old, maybe pre-Christian.'

Bruce sat back to study the wall as Sam steadied the rafts which were trying to drift back with the current.

'Sam, see over there—' Bruce pointed to the loose boulders protruding up out of the water. '—the rocks have collapsed, opening up this cavern. It was probably caused by the stream up there.'

'I'm going to climb up. I might be able to see what's behind that stairway. It looks safe enough.'

'Sam, remember last time you went exploring. You nearly bloody drowned me.' By the time I had finished, he had swung himself up onto the steps and was heading out of sight around the curved stairway.

'Come on, all of you, it is quite safe up here. There's something you need to see.' Sam's voice sounded strange, excited.

'My God!' The words escaped from my lips and then there was silence. We all stood and stared at what lay before us.

The whole area looked like a temple of some sort that had been chiselled out of the rock mass. It didn't look to have been disturbed.

'It doesn't look to be the same period as the statue back there. That was definitely Roman.' Jack turned to the students, who were standing with their mouths open, catching flies. 'Well, boys, what do you think?'

Jim, the older of the two, walked further into the room and ran his hand over the carved figures that stood guard over their secrets. 'Professor, I believe this predates the Romans. Look, the markings are not nearly as finely worked. And by the look of those boulders, this whole area has only been exposed for a short time, maybe only fifty years or so.'

Gregory sat down on a slab of stone in the middle of the area to roll a cigarette.

'So, the stairway had been carved separately, probably with a doorway into the temple. I don't think the people who used the canal would have cared a damn about the past. They had their own agenda here.'

Gregory lit his smoke and inhaled deeply. The temple had two rows of carved sentries that led up to the altar. Above it a female form, with very large breasts, looked down on us. I stared at the stone altar; it looked like a place where someone may have had their throat cut.

'Gregory, do you really think that you ought to be sitting on that? Someone's blood and guts might have been on it.'

Gregory shot up and brushed his pants down as if to erase the past. The rest of the crew roared with laughter.

'The university will make a proper and thorough examination of this site, and the publicity won't hurt in the fund-raising department either.'

Jack couldn't get that look from his face, the proud father's look. This was his baby. Sam sang out to us, and we gathered around him again

'Let's see where this canal finally ends.'

Like the dwarves of Snow White fame, we trouped upwards. Exactly thirty-four steps later, we walked out into a cold, grey, English day.

But where were we? The sea crashed onto the menacing rocks below and to the right-hand side, a stone path led upwards. Thick bracken covered the path, making it very difficult to push past. Small grooves had been worn in the path, allowing the water to run off.

To the left the path stopped, probably caused by a landslide in bygone times. We all looked to Sam for advice; he was our leader and chief. What a shame that he was such a low-down rat.

'I think we will be better off with the scrub, rather than trying to climb up there.'

When we started off, I took the last position. I didn't want any of them looking at my bum, as we climbed along almost on our knees. The wind started to howl, and the sleet turned into snow. I kept licking the snowflakes off my nose — annoying little things.

The men were waiting for me as Gregory gave me a hand up for the last four yards or so. In front of us stood a deserted building that must have been used by shepherds to protect them in case of bad weather. I was cold and wanted to go home, but not the boys.

'Jack, let's go down and check out our temple.' Sam was carrying on like a child.

'Sam, Maggie's had enough excitement today, and frankly so have I,' replied Gregory. He continued straight on, before anyone else could add their two pence worth. 'I want to examine all this and I'm sure Jack will want to telephone the university as soon as possible, before the press get hold of it.' Gregory looked over to the students, who had their heads together and yelled out to them. 'Don't you dare ring the press, at least not until your professors have notified the authorities.'

Thank God for Gregory.

We walked along a nearby road that headed back down into the village. A tractor pulling an empty hay trailer offered us a lift. We dropped the boys off and then thanked our driver, who was stopping off at the tavern to have a pint with Sam. Gregory and I walked down the main drag towards home. As we went past the church, I thought of my distant family and pointed out the bench under the large elm tree with the name Noonan on it.

*Sarah, how do you fit into all of this?* The thoughts kept churning through my mind. *What clues are hidden in your journals?* The one thing I knew for certain was that she was trying to tell me something. 'Oh Sarah,' I sighed, 'what is it?'

I fumbled with the key in the front door but as we entered the hall, the phone rang. I reached it just in time and made a grab for the receiver, lifting it to my ear as a soft voice said, 'Is that you, Sam?' It hurt. I just stood there holding it until a hand gently took the receiver from me and spoke to the caller.

'No, Sam is at the tavern, have you got the number there? Best you ring there in future. Goodbye.'

'Thanks, Gregory.'

He handed me a drink and lit the fire. It wasn't long before the warmth filled the room, and the effects of the brandy had calmed me down.

'Maggie, I know that this stuff with Sam, well it isn't any of my business, but, love, wouldn't you be better to have it out with him, once and for all?'

We spoke about our find for a while but as Sam hadn't come back, we ate. Later, I excused myself and went to bed. I tossed and turned and in sheer desperation turned to Sarah's journals again.

I read about a flood that took away her house and how she rebuilt again and how a bushfire nearly killed her. I studied a page of financial returns. She had become wealthy over those ten years. She was making mention of her letters but to date I'd not found them. The next years all seemed to be similar then all of a sudden she was up and off with her son to England. But that was enough for tonight; sleep was beckoning me.

I kept away from Sam over the next few days. I had my work, and he and Gregory were struggling with the passageway behind my house.

'Maggie, quickly get up! Look what's in the paper. It's all about this place and your canal.' And there it was in bold print:

**Historical Find All Thanks To Young Australian.**

**A Roman temple has been discovered, almost in Miss Jamieson's back yard. Earlier findings, likely pre-Roman, were also discovered. An official announcement will be given by Professor Middleton tomorrow. All credit is given to Miss Jamieson and her friend, Sam Butler. The outcomes of the finds are still being investigated.**

Sam Butler, my *friend*. The words hit me square in the heart. I didn't have time to reflect before Sam and Gregory came crashing through the back room into my kitchen.

'Maggie, we have broken through into the main shaft that leads down to the canal landing.' I looked blankly at them. 'Can't you see? This is how goods were smuggled. They used your building. I would say the pirates were the first illegal gold trade, followed then by the brandy runners.'

'My God, Maggie, they had balls to bring their whale boats over the sandbars and into the cave. And then they had to row against the tide up to the landings.'

Sam did a bit of a jig, and then grabbed me, the way he used to muck around and pulled me into his arms. 'Let's dance.'

I didn't want him to touch me, let alone dance with me. I must have worn that look of despair; the one that women are so good at. I noticed a figure pushing the table back against the wall, leaving an open space.

Gregory bowed and stepped up. 'May I have this dance, Miss Maggie,' he said in a soft voice as he placed his mouth against my ear. 'This is history in the making.'

As we started to waltz, the room changed. Large mirrors lined the walls, and I caught sight of myself. Was that me? The gown was so lovely. Crystal chandeliers hung from the ceiling and the music grew louder. The chandeliers threw a soft light across the room, reflecting shimmering beams off the glass floor. I could feel a hand being laid on my arm, gently guiding me onto the ballroom floor. Before me was the love of my life, my lover, my hero but most of all, my best friend. As his arms slowly entwined around me, the music increased in volume. The master of the waltz lifted his violin, and I started to feel my feet moving to the beat. We twirled around ever faster; I couldn't take my eyes off my love as we passed other dancers in a blur of fantasy. The hypnotic lull enlightened my senses. The smell of the daphne floating on the air stirred the mind, pulling at my heartstrings. Faster and faster we pivoted around the floor. Just as I reached up to feel his cheek against mine, I was ripped away.

Falling back, I fought desperately to hang on. The scene changed as Gregory came into view, his fingers brushing the hair gently from my face.

'It's all right, Maggie, you fainted again. I'm so sorry; I was such a fool pushing you around the room when I knew you weren't well. Please forgive me.' Gregory looked as though he had killed his best friend.

I took his arm as he helped me up. 'Gregory, I don't know how to tell you what just happened to me.'

Sam was sitting on a chair watching us; he walked over and squatted beside me.

'Maggie, when you were dancing, your whole facial expression changed. It was weird.'

# Chapter forty-nine

The following weeks were a blur of engagements. Newspaper articles were written, and a local TV station even invited me to talk, although this I rejected, as I thought these accolades should go to my professors. The university was doing its thing at the ruins. Why the Romans had built a temple here may never be known. Jack started to research a breakaway cult that he believed may have gone north to this region. I found that quite interesting.

I asked Gregory to stay on so we could look further into our family tree. The truth was I really liked his company, with no complications. The sun shone through the open window as I sat on the lounge with my feet tucked up under me. As I turned the pages of the Sunday News, Sam walked in.

'Maggie, I'll finish closing up the wall. There is still a bit of plastering to go. Two days and I'll be out of your hair.'

What was I supposed to say? 'Go, leave it, never darken my door again.' That would sound a bit melodramatic and childish, and besides, I needed the work finished. Getting tradesmen here was very difficult.

'By the way, Sam, a tart rang you here the other day. She was told to ring the tavern in future.' I know I shouldn't have said anything to him; I know I stopped our affair. So why did I feel so bloody terrible?

'Yes, thanks, Maggie. I spoke with her. Nice girl.'

The bastard, that's all he said to me? *Nice girl*. What does this mean? I watched his face closely, wondering did I want to scratch it, or kiss him?

'Well thanks, Sam, I really appreciate your help.' The words were sickly sweet, but they seemed to please him.

'Is Gregory staying on?' Sam glanced to the side as he waited for my reply.

'Why do you need to know anyway?'

'No reason, I was just wondering. He seems to be getting very close to you.' He now looked me straight in the face.

'Really?'

'I told you before, sarcasm isn't one of your strong points.'

*Crash!* The paper hit the wall behind him. At least my aim was getting better.

'I'll see you later when your disposition improves.'

I watched him walk up the path to his car. God, how I wanted to run after him, to have him say the things to me that I needed to hear.


Dad rang. He had sold the house and was booked on a Qantas flight. He firmly believed that they were the only safe planes in the air. *'None of that foreign lot; they fall out of the sky.'* With a date set for his arrival, I had to start getting Dad's room ready. He had asked for the bedroom downstairs, waffling on about privacy. Well, he didn't have to worry now; it was back to the nunnery for me.

The plastering was finished and on Sam's last night, Gregory took all of us to the tavern. I felt uncomfortable, but he insisted, saying the reservations had been made. What to wear? I looked through the wardrobe, maybe my black velvet mini and white sequined top. I still had a new pair of black net stockings. Yes, that would do nicely.

When I arrived, it was like coming home. The fire was burning in the hearth, gone were the pinecones that spelled out 'Christmas'. Millie the waitress showed us to our table. Sam was waiting at the bar, a brandy in his hand. He looked good; he wore a cable jumper over cream slacks, which showed off his great bum. I noticed that Millie had a second look at him as she seated us. He walked over to us and smiled down at me. It was enough to break my heart.

'What do you two want to drink? White wine for you, Maggie, a beer for you, Gregory?' Sam caught the waiter's eye and placed our order. The manager strolled over to our table. 'Mr Bingle, there's a phone call for you. You can take it in my office.' Gregory excused himself and returned within a few minutes.

'Sorry, Maggie, I'm going to have to cut this short, some sort of crisis at the office. I'll be back in a couple of days, but you and Sam enjoy dinner.' He kissed me on both cheeks, French style, grabbed his coat and left.

I could have killed him, since he was the only reason I was here. There was a deadly silence and Sam spoke, breaking the silence.

'Look, let's enjoy this night. You know I have to return tomorrow. My secretary has been stalling for me as long as she can, but the boss is starting to ask questions. So please, can't we try?'

'Your secretary… is that the tart who kept ringing you?'

'Maggie, that's enough!' Sam suddenly became quite angry. 'She isn't a tart. The bloody woman is sixty years old and very nice.'

I could feel the seat shrink under me. If I could have died there and then, I would have. 'I'm truly sorry, Sam,' I whispered in a soft, embarrassed voice.

'What was that, Maggie? I can't hear you.' He seemed to enjoy my humiliation.

'I said I'm sorry.'

I raised my voice and silence filled the room. You could hear the proverbial pin drop. I guess everyone heard me since they all turned to look.

'Would you like a refill?' Millie asked.

Over on the long table, a group of people chattered away: old Mrs Parson, the last librarian, sat opposite Leo and his mother. There was something about this group… then it struck me; I should have been there too. I walked over to their table to apologise.

'Maggie, no need to worry, we will fill you in tomorrow at work. We all knew it was Sam's last night and you would want to spend it with him. By the way, I received a letter from your dad with his great news. I'm looking forward to seeing him again.'

Sally and Dad had a thing going last Christmas. I liked her, but I was more astounded that Susan had not spilled the beans about my bust up with Sam. We finished our meal. To tell you the truth, I couldn't even remember what I ate. Sam paid the bill while I went to the ladies'. What now? Cut and run? No, I couldn't do that.

'Come on, Maggie, I've got the car out front. I'll give you a lift home.'

'Sam, it's not far, I can walk.'

'Don't be so stupid, get in.'

The house looked sombre as we pulled up. When I looked up at the windows, they seemed to say to me, *Stay out*. I knew I was being silly and besides, what else could I do, stay with Sam?

'Maggie, give me your keys and I'll go and put the lights on. You know how easily you fall in the dark.'

I was so stupid not to remember to leave the light on when I left. I couldn't really get my head around the fact that Sam was leaving me. The house lit up, and I stepped out of the car. The wind was picking up, blowing straight from Iceland. A chill ran through me as I clipped the gate shut and walked up to the front door.

'Do you want a cup of coffee before you leave?' I was feeling uneasy and hoped he would say yes.

'No thanks, Maggie. I had better get back. Early start and all of that.'

He hesitated for a moment then bent down and kissed me gently. I knew I had to say something, but what?

'Thank you seems little enough to say, Sam. You have done so much here for me. You've been a rat as a lover but a great friend. I know Dad would like to see you later on.' I couldn't stop the tears. It seemed senseless even wiping them away. He held me for a while, then turned and let himself out. I don't know how long I stood before I started climbing the stairs.

*Crash!* Down I slipped, pulling a vase of flowers with me. Sam heard the commotion as he started to walk towards the front gate.

'For God's sake, Maggie. I haven't left yet and look what you have done to yourself.' With that, he carried me up to bed.

'Sam, you know I will be all right. Send Susan here in the morning, if you are worried. But before you go, could you hand me those journals in the window seat, please?'

Sam fussed around for another hour before he finally left. The pain tablets that I had taken were now working. I closed my eyes and waited for sleep to overtake me. In what seemed to be an eternity, probably only thirty minutes or so, I opened my now fully awake eyes and started to read Sarah's journal. She no longer seemed like a stranger but more and more like a friend. I thought of her Tom, did he ever go astray? How could she have been so strong? Would I ever have her courage? And what in the hell is trying to frighten me?

The sun was streaming in through the windows when Susan knocked and opened the door. She was balancing a tray and juggling a newspaper when she walked in.

'I've got all the things you like — chocolate croissants, coffee, and a slice of Dad's sponge.' At this moment, I loved Susan. 'By the way, Sam left early, said to say goodbye, and that he would ring. Good riddance to bad rubbish is what I say.'

The phone rang and Susan answered it. 'Maggie, that was Gregory, apparently Sam rang him; he is on his way back.'

I screwed up my face in frustration. 'Didn't you try to stop him, Susan?' Why did they all think I couldn't manage? Yes, I've had some accidents, but doesn't everyone?

'Maggie, don't be cross, but lately you seem to have a lot of accidents.'

I heard the car pull up, then the front door slam, and I sat there waiting for my bedroom door to burst open.

'Maggie, what happened? Don't tell me you tripped, because I don't believe it.' Gregory stood beside my bed, all six foot six inches of worry.

'Take it easy, Gregory, I look worse than I am. How about you make a coffee, and we will talk.' It took three cups before I had finished telling him.

'I don't know what to think. I have never really believed in the supernatural, but on the other hand I do believe you.' He sat there patting my hand and in some way, it brought a sense of relief to me. 'Now that we can leave the canal and all of that to the uni, I think we should concentrate on our family, or at least yours. Have you finished with the two journals yet?'

I looked over to the leather-bound books and suddenly I felt more like a protective parent than a reader. 'You can read the first one.' I couldn't give him the second one. That was too personal for any man to read. She was my Sarah, and I needed to protect her story.


Dad arrived the following week, and he and Gregory got on like a house on fire.

'Nice bloke.' Dad said with that 'I know something is going on' look. 'How's Sam? I spoke to him before I left Sydney. He brought me up to date on everything, well, almost everything.' He was now staring at me. 'See you used the Yamaha on the rafts, good little motors.'

'Dad, number one, Gregory is only a good friend, two, Sam is a friend, who is acting like a low-down pig.'

Dad whistled and grabbed me. I needed those arms around me, to hold me. As like magic, the clouds opened up and I sobbed into his chest.

'I know it hurts, love. I could read between the lines of your letters. Maybe things will work out for you both.' He looked at me and I knew what he was thinking. A leopard never changes his spots.

'Maggie, when a bloke goes to bed with another lady, well that should tell you something.'

'Oh no, Dad, he said they only went out to dinner.'

'Whatever you say, love.'

Sally was a constant visitor; Dad was now walking with a spring in his step and a twinkle in his eye.

I was sitting at my bedroom window looking down at the daffodils and jonquils as they swayed gently in the spring breeze. Dad had gone out to Sally's farm and Gregory had returned to his home, promising to return in the June break. We had become very close. I know he wants to go all the way, and it must have taken some guts to say what he said to me, the night before he left.

'Maggie, I'm not Sam. I saw the way you looked when your dad mentioned him. Love, until you sort yourself out — by either going back to him, or ending it and I mean really end it — we can only be friends.'

*So, Sarah, what would you do?* I thought. To me, she had become a real person, and I found that I often spoke to her, in the privacy of my bedroom. I opened the window seat and took out her journal; it was warm to the touch, and I started to read.

*I really can't believe Tom has come to England. He is so debonair and self-assured. Tomorrow, James and I are going riding with him. John is furious and put up quite a scene in front of his parents. He really shows his true colours, and I had to excuse myself from the table to escape his outburst. James is very wary of him also. We will leave the day after tomorrow. I don't think I can ever return while he is here.*

'Maggie, I'm home.' Dad's voice shocked me back to reality. 'Get dressed, we are meeting Sally at the pub for tea. I put a letter for you on the table, love.'

*Hello, Maggie,*
*How are you? Have you and Gregory cracked that family puzzle yet? I*

*called into the land's office for Greg. Your place passed from a Noonan in 1918. Apparently, the same woman owned it until you inherited it. Hope this helps.*

*Love, Sam*

*P.S. I'm flying home to see my parents next week. I'll say g'day to Sydney for you.*

We sat in the back garden at the tavern. Dad had convinced the owner that beer gardens were all the go in Australia and as he was becoming a great customer, a beer garden was made out the back. Susan joined us with Leo. They were becoming an item, and it was great to see her so happy. It also stopped Leo from chasing me.

'What's happening with Jack and Bruce these days? We don't hear much from them.' Sally liked both of them. 'Good to see such gentlemen, not stuck up at all.'

'They're driving down in a couple of weeks. Jack rang me; he wants to talk over an idea with me and wouldn't give much away on the phone.'

It rained all the next week. So much for the beginning of summer! I missed the summers back home; at least you knew it would be hot. Dad's handyman business was taking off. He was now talking about putting on a lad to help him, probably Sally's youngest. The local council had been given a large grant of money because of the publicity received from the opening of our canal. Some of it was to rebuild the library. Of course, Sam had his finger in that pie too. We had decided to retain the old building as an art and local craft centre.

'Maggie, will you call in to the rectory? I've got something to show you.' The reverend waved to me from his front gate. I could see a piece of paper in his hand.

'Sure, Mr Swisp, I'll call in after work.'

The days were busy packing up the books and recording all the titles. I discovered crates in the cellar that hadn't been opened but they'd have to wait. I had enough work with the blighters in front of me.

Mrs Swisp had a jug of cordial waiting for me when I arrived at the rectory that evening. 'Come on in, Maggie. We have had a reply to your letter about the burial in the church yard.'

I sat there and read it. I thanked Mr Swisp and walked slowly across the cow paddock to my gate. As I looked into my front garden,

I wondered how different my garden looked now, compared to Sarah's mum's time. The house was becoming a residence for me, Dad, and all my ghosts.

'Good to see you again, Ray.' Jack slapped Dad on his back as he came into the lounge.

'Where's Bruce?' asked Dad.

Bruce's voice boomed out like a foghorn. He put the luggage down and grabbed Dad's hand and shook it. 'Good to see you again, Ray.'

That night I couldn't get a word in sideways. Dad had to have a blow-by-blow account of the exploration. But at last things quietened down and Jack sat down beside me.

'Maggie, have you ever given any thought to further study? I know that you do a sterling job in the library, but Bruce and I want to put a proposal to you. Because of your contribution to the uni, they have offered you a free scholarship in my faculty of Ancient History.'

'You must be kidding, me go to university? Could I become an archaeologist?'

'Steady up, dear. You have to fill in the application first.'

# Chapter fifty

'You're sixteen' was playing on the car radio as I drove towards Manchester. Dad was settled into my place, and a replacement was found for the library. The university was large and very old. On the first day after I registered, I was given directions to my accommodation. It was in a newer residential building, only a five-minute walk from the main hall.

Like most first-year students, I was completely lost. The maps that were supplied were hard to read and each corridor looked like the one I had previously tramped down. The day before classes were to commence, we all gathered in the Great Hall, and the drone of human voices filled the air with anticipation as we all waited, not knowing what was expected from us.

It was a huge gothic structure, the only original part of the building to remain. Along the far wall were tables with literature piled high, while the older students tried signing us up to every club imaginable. The university's coat of arms hung above the double doors leading to a grand stairway. There, at the top of the landing, a sign read Chancellor, and scribbled on a piece of paper stuck with sticky tape, was someone's idea of a joke — Enter Who Dares.

As I wandered down the hall looking at the posters, a vision of the perfect hunk waved to me. I walked over and started to talk. It was then that I realised he had been waving to the girl behind me. A very embarrassed me blurted, 'Sorry, my misunderstanding.' Turning, I tried to escape, only to feel a hand grab my arm.

'Don't apologise. I'm David Cole, president of the History Club. Can I talk you into joining?'

At that moment, he could have talked me into anything. I quickly pulled it together and introduced myself.

'Maggie, we've been expecting you. Professor Werthby has told us all about your finds, and I've been looking out for you. We're meeting tonight in the old library at 7 p.m., I hope you can make it.'

At ten minutes to seven, I was navigating myself around the buildings and literally ran into a guy, who introduced himself as Tim Gindley, or Ginger for short. He was tall, thin, and displayed a carrot-top spike. On his nose, he balanced a pair of black-rimmed glasses.

'Ginger, are you looking for the old library and the history club?' I instantly liked him. 'I'm on my way there too. It will be great to already know someone.'

At the far end of this Tudor-inspired room, high up on the wall, a stained-glass window depicted a scene from the Bible — a knight dressed in a white cloak with a red cross on it. The antique fittings and rugs had been changed to endure heavy foot traffic. Along the back walls was shelving marked Archives.

'Over here, you two, near the fire.' David beckoned to us.

'Maggie, Ginger, I want you to meet the rest of us.'

There were ten of them and then David explained that the rest wouldn't start back until the following week.

'What do you do in the club, Cavid?'

I nudged Ginger and said quietly, 'His name is David.'

The rest tried not to smile. I felt a twang of protection towards Ginger, the same way I did when I brought home every stray dog in the district.

'We go on digs and help with deciphering different cultures and languages. It's all great fun.' David must have seen the look of confusion on my face because he walked over to me and said, 'Maggie, you won't be expected to do any more than you are up to.'

The next weeks flew by. I met many people from different countries, and as I had expected, a few toffee noses amongst them. Every Friday night I dined with my two old friends in their rooms. Until now I hadn't realised what a wealth of knowledge they were, and not only were they respected in England but throughout the world. Professor Werthby was a hard task master. He was kind but expected the best from each of his pupils.

Midyear exams were looming. I crammed but finally decided that a few private lessons wouldn't go astray. High up on the Wanted board was the notice I needed. Standing out in bold print it read:

**Private Lessons**
**History and Literature**
**Reasonably priced**
**Apply David: 6754386**

We arranged to meet on Monday nights at the library. The lessons were a great help, the teacher even better. The night was dragging when David put down the text and said, 'That's enough work for tonight. How about a coffee? There's a coffee bar still open on campus.'

He placed my coat over my shoulders, his hands running along my arms. I hadn't felt a man's touch since Sam. Those old feelings were not so easily rekindled. The bar was open, and a uni band was playing; the Mersey beat was in. As soon as we sat down, David attracted girls like bees to honey. I could see that he enjoyed the limelight. I think all blokes were the same. Afterwards we walked home discussing the exams. Although David was two years ahead of me, I enjoyed our discussions.

'Maggie, I was wondering if you would like to go out with me this Saturday night?' It took me exactly two seconds to agree to go. May have been a shade fast in my acceptance, but I didn't care. It had been three months since Sam returned to Sydney and not one letter had come. Oh well. The date with David was nice—dinner, a picture, and a few kisses. Nice and safe; no complications. I didn't trust men in that way again.

That night as I climbed into bed, I thought of Gregory. He called in whenever he was in town. He had started tracing back the family tree. I decided that the next time he called, I would give him Sarah's journals to read; after all he was family, or thereabouts.

A week or so later, I was returning from lectures, and I took a shortcut across the central park. It was getting dark, and I really needed to get home earlier. I required coffee and to answer a letter from Susan. As I balanced against a stone signpost to shake loose a stone from my shoe, I noticed Gregory's sports car parked illegally on the kerb.

'Maggie, I'm over here.' He was waving and hurrying across to me. 'Good, I didn't miss you. Not doing anything now are you?' He bent down and kissed me on the cheek. 'Maggie, I've been able to find out more info. It seems Sarah had a daughter. Took off to Europe, caused a stir. There seems to be a reference about her in Paris, so I thought that we might pop over there. I believe you have a few days off. So what do you say?'

What I said was 'Give me thirty minutes to pack.'

The crossing on the car ferry over the channel was rough. By the time we arrived, I was completely seasick.

'Come on, old girl. Chin up. Enjoy the scenery while I drive. Won't be long and we will be in Paris.'

He must be joking. Would I ever stop throwing up long enough to get my head out of this ice cream container?

Paris was the city of love. How I loved visiting here: the museums, galleries, and the bridges. I was romancing in my own little world, when I heard Gregory speak.

'Maggie! A penny for your thoughts. You seem a bit quiet, is everything all right?'

I could feel Gregory's eyes flickering over towards me. 'I was just thinking about Sarah's daughter and where she fits into the picture. Where are we going to start?' Gregory handed me a map of Paris and pointed to a street circled in red.

'We'll start at the Government Department of Land Titles Ownership. The deed department might show up something. I rang and spoke to the secretary, who has agreed to help us.' Gregory rambled on as I watched the French countryside whizz by.

We pulled up in front of an impressive structure with a brass plaque that Gregory translated as Title Building. Thank God the secretary spoke English. He was a small man, bald with the sexiest accent.

'Sir, I have located some information for you. A title was registered to a Miss Brian in 1913 at 13 Rue de Cardinal. Later it was transferred to a Lady Lowe.'

'My God, there's another kid around somewhere. Gregory, why wasn't this known?' I was starting to unlock the cupboard, and the skeletons kept falling out. Later that night, Greg came knocking at my door.

'Aren't you ready yet? I'm starving, Maggie. I'm so bloody

hungry I could eat one of your skeletons.'

We dined that night at a small eatery on the banks of the Seine. The food was delicious. The wine was chilled, and the company was great.

Early next morning, we pulled up in front of a three-storey semi. The architecture dated it back to the 18th century. Typical of that period, it was brick with a small terrace on the second storey facing the street. The building had four stairs leading up to the front door.

'Well, Maggie, up you go.'

Gregory sat back and watched me. I was about to ask him, 'Who made you boss?' when the front door opened, and a lad bent down to collect the milk bottle that was perched precariously on the top step.

'Excuse me, do you speak English?'

I started up the steps in time to hear the lad answer, 'Of course I speak English. Do you speak French?' I then felt stupid. I was the intruder in his country.

'Could I possibly have a word with the owner please? I'm Australian.'

I thought I would mention it, as I knew the French didn't like English for some reason.

'Ah, mademoiselle, it's my father you need to talk to. Please come in.'

I walked into the living room where a middle-aged man stood. He smiled and offered me a chair. We introduced each other and the son stayed to help out in the language department.

'My son has told me of your request. I will tell you all that I know. But first, coffee, I think. The man in the car, would he like to come in?'

While I waited for Gregory to arrive, I studied the surrounds. The room was beautiful. Antiques lined the walls. Above a mantle, a framed degree showing that the man before me was a Doctor of Medicine.

'My dear, you are on a magnificent journey, let me tell you what I know.'

*My God*, I thought to myself, *are all these men Casanovas?* My host smiled, the way only a French man can, and then carried on.

'My father bought this property from an English lord in 1920. The property was used to hide Englishmen during the war. It was common gossip at that time that an English woman was involved in spying. I'm not sure for what side. I know that there was a child, a girl. Here the story becomes personal. The child was left with my mother who worked in an orphanage. I just remember my mother talking about her. I believe she was sent away, and we never heard any more about her journey.'

He threw up his arms in despair and dropped them to his sides in a way the French express themselves. I tried to sum up this man. He was sincere and friendly and as I drank my coffee, Gregory conversed in French with him. They smiled and laughed. I think I was the centre of their joke. We left our gracious hosts and drove out of the city, along the avenue following the Seine. The city gave way to farmland, large areas set aside to flower growing. The smell of the city was left behind and the heavily perfumed air dulled the senses and lulled us both into a quiet state, as we rethought this journey we were on. As I pondered over these latest findings, it became pretty obvious that this story had been deliberately hidden, but by whom?

'Gregory, where are we going?' I was tired and it was becoming difficult to think.

'I thought we might try the Department of War Antiquities. All papers of that time have been released for public viewing. If she was a spy, there might be some reference to her there.'

'What can we do about the little girl? Someone must have a record of her, surely.'

Gregory sighed before he answered me. 'Love, it was the war years, she could have gone anywhere. They sent kids all over the place.'

'Greg, there's no mention of her in any of the journals. I would have thought that Lord Lowe would have taken the child. After all, she was his niece.'

It took over an hour to reach the city of Orléans. The area was breathtaking: small villages and mountain pastures where cows and goats grazed alongside chateaus and fine wineries. On top of a mountain sat a large monastery and in the valley the city gave way to the river Loire. Gregory stopped the car near the entrance to an estate. Acres of grapevines bordered the long drive up to the buildings. The drive itself was lined with poplars that stopped just before the monastery.

Gregory parked the car on the grass verge, and we were just about to enter the main building, when a rather cross little man waved frantically, pointing to a sign at the other end of the lawn. I gathered that we were parked illegally. So with the misunderstanding corrected and with a great show of humiliation, we entered the building marked Library.

The library was impressive. The glossy parquetry flooring was set in a beautiful pattern and polished until you could see your face in it, and the northern wall was built entirely of glass. All records were now on microfilm, so with little information to work from, I started to trace all records involving a Josephine Lowe. Gregory was becoming bored and smartly came up with, 'Maggie, we both can't look at the film, so why don't I check out the wine list?'

'That's right, Greg, bugger off.' I ignored his apology, then the door closed, and I was alone. I had had no luck finding what I was looking for by the time the librarian came looking for me.

'Mademoiselle, we close in thirty minutes.' The librarian knew her stuff and was a great help. 'Maybe you should look at adoptions. Perhaps there is a reference to the child. Come back tomorrow, we will look further.'

She took my hands and held them; my quest had become hers.

Later that evening, we strolled down the banks of the Loire. A farmer's market was in full swing. Ropes of garlic, bottles of lavender oil, and crates containing geese were strewn under the canvas awnings that covered the produce. An array of home-sewn garments hung from coat hangers attached to the rope stays. I picked out a blouse embroidered with the most delicate pastel rosebuds. If only I had somewhere to wear it.

The accommodation was rustic but clean. My bedroom had a black iron bed covered by a brightly coloured silk duvet, a washstand, and opposite the bed, French windows opened onto a small patio. The evening meal was included so we dined with the family in true French tradition.

Next morning, at five minutes past nine, I sat at the fiche looking at the film. At ten thirty it shone out at me like the proverbial dogs' balls.

| Female | Mother's Given | Mother's Surname | Father's Surname |
|---|---|---|---|
| One year old | Josephine | Lowe | Unknown |

Child adopted by Australian couple: Hayes.

I couldn't breathe. The words danced in front of my eyes. Anne Hayes was my mother. Why hadn't the solicitor told me?

# Chapter fifty-one

Our four days were up. Josephine Brian was my biological grandmother. The web of intrigue was closing in.

'Didn't I tell you we would turn up something?' Gregory ruffled my hair and slapped me on the back. 'Maggie, your side of the family is bloody well more scandalous than mine.'

'Greg, I can't believe that the family knew about the adoption and never told me. Do you think Dad knows?'

'That's something only you can ask him, love. But what I do know is that if you don't get a wriggle on, we'll miss the ferry back.

Ginger was sitting on the bottom step of the library as we pulled up. Ginger started with the questions; he really could be annoying at times. My answers were short: Yes thanks, I had a great time; no, he is not my boyfriend. My head was aching by the time I had registered for the History Club and started on my way back to the dorm.

'Look, Ginger, I'm really tired, I'll tell you all about it tomorrow.'

Immediately, he dropped his head, making me feel like the person who had just smacked the puppy. I had to put family findings aside and concentrate on the task ahead, passing the exams. Both my old professors gave me no quarter. They pushed me harder than the others and I wanted to please them. I wanted this more than I had ever wanted anything, except Sam maybe.

In the blink of an eye, it was Christmas again. I had packed my car, said goodbye to everyone and headed home. I'd gone over the conversation in my head a hundred times, but still I wasn't sure how to approach Dad about my findings without hurting him. It didn't seem half as long on the drive back and soon I saw the familiar street with my home beckoning to me. Unlocking the front door, I stepped into the hall. The place was in darkness. I wondered why Dad wasn't there. Feeling a bit disappointed, I felt for the light switch and flicked it on.

'Surprise!' People appeared from everywhere. 'Merry Christmas, welcome back.' I think the whole village was there. Susan had already started the party. She was sloshed. With a glass in her hand, she hugged me, spilling wine down my back.

'Gee, it's good to see you, love.' Dad made his way towards me. 'I've missed you terribly, kid.' After a hug and a quick rundown on how the car was—a typical Dad question—I mingled with the folk. God, it was good to be back.

It doesn't matter where you might stay, there's nothing to replace your own room and mattress. It was great to be home. I ran my fingers along the top of my desk and chest, and without noticing it I had opened the lid and lifted out Sarah's journals. I turned to a back page and started to write.

*Dear Sarah,*

*Please allow me to add to your story. I found another granddaughter of yours and guess what, she was my mum. So that now makes you my great-grandmother. Granny, I hope that name is all right with you, I'm still trying to find out what happened to your daughter. I'm so excited that we are really a family.*

I patted the cover of the book, much the same way as you pat a baby's bum, and replaced it into the chest.

'Maggie, lunch is ready.' Dad had discovered cooking; he looked comical with an apron tied around his waist. Pity the footy boys back in Liverpool couldn't see him now. 'Enjoy.' He handed me a bowl full to the top of some Italian recipe he was experimenting with.

'Dad, I want to ask you something.'

'Fire away.' He replaced the carafe of red wine onto the dresser and walked back to the table.

'Did you know that Mum was adopted?'

He stopped dishing up and looked straight at me.

'Maggie, your mother only found out herself after we were married, and you were born. It caused so much trouble in the family when she wanted to know the whole story. Your grandmother—her adoptive parents — didn't want her to pursue it at all. We talked it over and she decided to leave it for a bit, then she died. Your grandmother begged me to forget all of it. And after all, it was her decision, love. The next thing was you being told that you had inherited this cottage.'

'Dad, I have so much to tell you, but it can wait until we have eaten.'

He sat back, sipping his brandy. After finishing the dishes, I joined him.

'Dad, we went to Paris, and that's how it all came about. So what do you think?'

I waited for him to swallow and replace his glass on the table.

'Maggie, I think if I were you, I would finish this now but knowing you, love, you will continue. Just don't let it interfere with your studies.'

This was my third Christmas in England. The routine never changed. Church, eat until you drop, and then visit friends. I loved it all. Susan was very involved with her boyfriend, and Dad still had a thing going with Sally. It was sunny but cold as I walked into the village through the golf course's shortcut someone waved to me and a deep voice boomed, 'Hang on a minute, Maggie.'

My God, it was Leo. I hardly recognised him, as he'd put on a heap of weight.

'Leo, it's good to see you, what's up?'

'Mum wants you and your dad to come over tonight, food and drinks, you know, all that stuff. Say about seven. Could you pick up Susan on the way? My truck is off the road.'

It was a gloomy black night when we all squeezed into my little Mini. The road out to the farm was slippery, and we had to be on constant lookout for cows that seemed to wander onto the road whenever I drove by. It was a relief to see the lights of the farmhouse shining through the mist.

'You look lovely tonight, Sally.' Dad gave her a peck on the cheek and arm in arm they entered the dining room. I watched Sally; there was something special about her tonight.

Sally put on a great spread and after we had finished eating, Sally and Dad slipped into the kitchen to clean up. I left them alone. Susan was all over Leo and they decided to look at his broken truck in the barn. So that left me twiddling my thumbs. I walked over to the window and looked out over the dales. There was a loneliness that teetered on the edge of eerie. What was it? The past three years rolled out in front of me. Hadn't I done enough? I was starting to get tired; it was like people from the past wouldn't let go of me.

'One more drink before you leave?' Sally thrust a glass of bubbly into my hand.

'Gather around, you lot, we've something to say.' Dad took Sally's hand and pulled her forward. It was the first time I had ever seen Sally nervous and acting more like a teenager than a mature woman.

'Sally has agreed to become my wife. There, I've said it.'

There was a moment's silence before the house broke into applause, or should I say that all the kids there yelled and hit Dad on the back, a man's way of kissing. I kissed and hugged Dad and Sally. His face glowed with happiness and my heart went out to this man who had reared me. To see him with someone to care for and cherish felt good. Maybe a small spark of jealousy burnt me a little, but I guess two now became a whole bunch more. We had just returned home, when the phone rang.

'Maggie, Merry Christmas. What are you and your father up to?'

'Professor, it's good to hear from you.'

'Call me Jack; you're not at uni now. I was wondering if you and your father would like to spend the New Year with Bruce and me. Nothing grand, only a few people over. Gregory is coming. So what do you say?'

I accepted for myself and told Jack Dad would ring him back. Later that evening while Dad was polishing his boots, I spoke to him about Lord Middleton's offer.

'I don't want to leave Sally, Maggie.'

'So take her along.'

'She won't leave the brood at this time of year. No, you go along and have a good time, love.'


It was a bleak trip up to Scotland, but my little Mini knew the way. Middleton Manor looked grand, decked out in all its Christmas finery. The place sparkled. Even the old armour had been polished. Lord Jack Middleton — I still smiled to myself every time I heard the title — was as welcoming as ever.

As I was shown into the sitting room, an arm appeared from

behind a large bust of some Roman conqueror. It grabbed me and pulled me into a doorway where a branch of mistletoe had been hung. Gregory kissed me on the cheek and, looking around to see if we were alone, he kissed me again on the lips, deep and passionate.

'I've missed you, Maggie.'

'Unhand that young girl.' Jack laughed and slapped Gregory on the back.

'Come on in, you two, there are a few people I want you to meet.'

A little later, I was shown to the same bedroom I had stayed in on my last visit. There were French windows facing south that led out on to a small balcony, and at the far end of the room, a large fire crackled in the grate.

'It's lovely to see you again, miss. I know you will enjoy your stay with us.'

The maid giggled as she retold the story of our last shopping escapade to Edinburgh.

'What do you think of this dress?' I pulled a fine jersey wool dress out from my suitcase. I called it my French madness. The price was exorbitant. I had fallen in love with it the moment I saw it in the window of a boutique in Paris. It was the colour of champagne and fell from under the bust into rows of folds. She stepped back to examine it properly.

'Oh my, miss, it is lovely.'

That night I dressed for dinner. I wore my hair up in a French twist and I pinned Mum's amber brooch to my dress. Gregory escorted me to the dining room where all the guests had assembled. Jack and Bruce sat at opposite ends of the table. Until meeting them, I hadn't realised that love could come in so many forms. The old men showed me off like one of their trophies. I didn't mind, as they were both like grandparents to me.

'Maggie, Gregory has been filling us in on your French trip. You know that the French government might be able to help you. Maybe they have some type of records of your grandmother. I've got a week off, would you like me to accompany you? My treat.'

Until then, I hadn't realised I would be going back quite so soon. Bless them; if there was a mystery to be solved, they were always in the midst of it.

'I'd take them up on it if I were you. They've contacts everywhere.' Gregory had changed; my mate seemed to be more aloof. It was all arranged; I would meet Bruce in London on the 16th January, two days before the boat was to leave. The few days passed and once again I stood waving goodbye to my hosts. I couldn't help but scan the upstairs windows. Was the pretty ghost of Sarah's era looking down at me?

Paris, 18th January

The wind blew with such savagery, tearing the canvas awnings from the coffee shops and driving the customers indoors. I pulled my trench coat tightly around me, thankful that my scarf and gloves were made of Merino wool, a present brought over to England from Dad. Jack sipped his coffee, and I indulged in a double hot chocolate. We had two days to fill before the Government Offices reopened. Our accommodation was four star. Jack never skimped.

'Maggie, I've an idea, let's visit the Louvre. They have opened an Egyptian exhibition. We should see it. I've heard that the Egyptian Government has won the right to have these finds returned to Cairo.' Jack waited for me to reply. 'Besides which, I intend to set a paper on Egypt for your class next semester. So you really do need to take this opportunity.'

I smiled at the crafty old bugger.

'Okay, let's go.'

An officious little man sporting a Hitler-type moustache proceeded to tell Jack that no information could be given to foreigners. Jack summed him up and made a phone call, and then we waited. Thirty minutes later, a black limousine pulled up and a man stepped out. My, what a commotion! The Minister for Education marched in, grabbed Jack by the shoulders, and planted two kisses, one on each cheek.

'My Lord Middleton, you must excuse this man. Of course you can have access to these files.'

Jack introduced him to me. The old devil took my hand and kissed it.

'Please, you both must be my guests for dinner tonight, say eight o'clock? I'll send a car for you.'

During the rest of the afternoon, our French clerk couldn't do enough to help us. He recovered records that stated that an English woman had become involved with the French underground but had disappeared and no record of her death was found.

'I think this is as far as we can go. Without more information to go on, we have hit a dead end.' Jack patted me on the arm. 'Don't be disappointed, dear, look how far you have come.'

'I would have liked to have known how she died. And to let her know that someone cared.'

Jack gave me a fatherly hug. 'Come on, Maggie, get into your glad rags, we are going to have a great time tonight. These French certainly know how to party.'

The channel crossing was calm. I sat on the deck, reflecting over the last three days. It didn't take long before the main car deck was cleared, and we were travelling north. Jack dropped me off and stayed for a day. He and Dad had plenty to gasbag about. Ray invited the two old boys to the forthcoming wedding, and I overheard him asking how I was managing at uni. I stood close to the door to hear Jack's reply.

'I was really surprised, Ray. She has a real aptitude for dead languages. I don't give her special praise, might swell her head, but she is a great student. Bruce and I often talk about her abilities. There will be a job out there for her, you mark my word.'

They say listeners never hear any good of themselves, but I say rubbish. I walked around the rest of the day with a smirk on my dial that couldn't be wiped off.

After Jack left, I walked up to the church, and after brushing the snow from Sarah's seat, I sat down. I don't know why but tears started to run down my cheeks. I ran my hand along the plaque on the backrest. Yes, I had relived a lot of Sarah's story. The murder that had sent her on her epic voyage, the birth of her children and the inheritance that awaited her son, and now the loss of Josephine.

The wind howled through the graveyard at the back of the church. A grey shadow mingled with the snow, and I knew I was not alone. I could smell the eucalyptus around me, so I sat there and waited, tasting my own fear.

'Sarah, I really hope it is you here with me.' There was a pressure on my left shoulder, a soothing hand stroked my back, and I felt at ease. 'Sarah, I have tried to find out about Josephine. Do you know that my mum is your granddaughter? Good, isn't it.' The wind started up again and the shadow disappeared. 'You don't have to go yet.' Deep down, I knew that only the bare trees and I were left.

'Maggie, what are you doing sitting in the snow?' Susan walked over and sat down beside me.

'Susan, she was here. Can't you smell the gum leaves?'

Susan's hands shot up to her ears. 'No more, don't tell me another thing. I didn't sleep for a week after that time in your bedroom. What is it, Maggie, are you a ghost magnet or something?' She stood up and looked around the yard. 'Come on, let's get out of here.'

I didn't tell Dad about Sarah's visit; this was to stay between Sarah and myself.

Later that evening as I sat cross legged on my bed, I held Sarah's journals tightly to my chest. I now knew their words, their hopes, and their loves. Everything seemed to fall into place, all except the gold. Did it ever exist? Maybe there was a lead somewhere. A good snoop might be able to check it out.

I finished reading Sarah's journals. Tears slowly dropped down onto my duvet as I read the last entry dated 3rd January 1918. This woman had led such an extraordinary life. She questioned women's role in society and within her own church. She was a true pioneer of her time, a worker for the equality of women in Victoria, a property owner, mother, and a wife.

I picked up my pen and started to write.

*Dear Sarah,*
*Your granddaughter had a happy life, and her husband loved her very much. I hope you can now rest in peace.*
*Your loving great-granddaughter,*
*Maggie.*

I closed Sarah's journals for the last time and placed them in my window seat along with the quilt. Looking out the window, I could feel the calm and a sense of peace engulf my little cottage. The ghosts seemed to have gone now.

As I started to stand, the box slipped out of my fingers and hit the floor. The side shot open and as I bent down to pick it up, I noticed a small lever poking out. Carefully, I pulled it down. The whole side slid open, and a bundle of letters tied up with a pink ribbon fell out.

I lifted them up and noticed that caught in the middle lay a gold chain with one single pearl hanging from it. I understood a lot more about Sarah's life now. There was heaps more that I needed to research into my distant family's lives. I'd have to get Gregory on the case.

As I packed away Sarah's treasures, the full magnitude of the journals hit me. She had entrusted to me the lineage of the past. A tear rolled down my face and as I wiped it away, I felt that a part of my youth was now carefully folded between those letters. I heard the front door open, and a familiar voice yelled up the stairs to me.

'The car is packed, Maggie, and the uni won't wait, you know.'

Gregory, my steady friend who was always there in the background.

Gregory or Sam? It was all too hard to think about now. The future would have to take care of itself.

The End

# Characters
## Main

**Maggie** — Fourth generation and narrator of the story. She is an Australian teenager who inherits a cottage in England and uncovers the family ghosts that lead to a web of intrigue.

**Sarah** — Educator who fled England after being accused of murder. Took up a land grant in Australia in 1853 and gave birth to James Junior and Josephine.

**James Lowe** — English sea captain sent to Australia to trace missing gold bullion. Father of James Junior.

**Tom Brian** — Stockman and hero who devotes his life to protect Sarah, whom he married. Father of Josephine.

**Munu**                        Aboriginal woman who
                                befriends Sarah; delivered
                                Sarah's child, James Junior.

**Josephine Brian**             Tom and Sarah's daughter who
                                defies convention to take up a
                                bohemian life in Paris before
                                World War One.

**Prudence Lowe**               Daughter of James Junior.

**Charley Wong**                Station cook and protector of
                                his little missy, Sarah.

# *Characters*
# Supporting

| | |
|---|---|
| **Lord and Lady Lowe** | James's parents. |
| **Brian Lewis** | Lieutenant, second-in-command on the ship *Harcourt*, a friend to Captain James Lowe and Sarah. |
| **Reginald Lowe** | British Admiral. |
| **John Lowe** | Eldest brother of James, who plots the death of his family then dies by his own misfortune. |
| **Harold** | Manservant of Captain James Lowe, who remains a friend to Sarah throughout her life. |
| **William Masters** | School friend of Captain James Lowe who holds a high position in Government in 1852. |

| | |
|---|---|
| **James Cobb** | Starts Cobb and Co coach line and meets both James and Sarah. |
| **Bradic Poplavich** | Russian Captain in Sydney. |
| **Mr Lo Lee** | Chinese businessman, friend and adviser to Sarah. He is involved in smuggling gold. |
| **Inu** | Aboriginal aunty. |
| **Sir Charles Fitzroy** | Governor of NSW. |
| **Paul Adams** | Captain in the army, horse buyer, friend of Tom Brian. |
| **Joe Henely** | Rich land baron of the Australian Alps, in love with Sarah. |

ABOUT THE AUTHOR

Lorrae Victoria was born in Sydney, growing up in a housing commission area in the western suburbs. She soon realised that education was the way to a better life.

Her grandmother, a teacher and medium, told stories of the family's history, making the past very real to a young Lorrae.

Lorrae became a nurse before marrying and moving to the Riverina in NSW to a dairy-beef property on the banks of the Murray River. This connection would surface in Sarah's story much later.

In her forties, Lorrae became a ceramics teacher, converting a farm shed into a studio. Following the death of her husband, Lorrae returned to nursing.

Travelling the world, the plotline for "Sarah's Story" emerged in her mind as the characters revealed themselves.

After completing a Doctorate, Lorrae began writing down the stories of the past, and "Sarah's Story" became a blend of fiction and her own family's history.

ACKNOWLEDGEMENTS

I would like to thank the following people who gave me the inspiration to complete these stories.

My friend and mentor, Alex Pederick, who gave me her expertise and the courage to follow my dreams.

It would be remiss of me not to thank my supervisor, Dr Michael Danaher, for all the frustration I caused him.

My friend, Kathie Veitch, who often had to put up with a temperamental writer.

To the good people of Yorkshire who opened their homes and hearts to me when I travelled to the UK to find locations for the story lines.

None of this would have been possible without the editing and publishing skills of Amanda Pederick of Wordalicious Publishing.

Through the last years of her life, Dr Colleen McCullough Robinson's letters lifted me up when the skies turned grey.

Proudly brought to you by:

Wordalicious
PUBLISHING